THE TRIUMPH OF THE SUN

I ... f the
N ... this
e ... most
c ... s of
t i misgov... Egyptian
K edive in Cairo precip... come and bloody
rebellion and Holy War headed by a charismatic
new religious leader, The Madhi or 'Expected
One'. The British are forced to intervene to protect
their national interests and to attempt to rescue the
hundreds of British subjects stranded in the
country. Along with hundreds of others, Ryder
Courtney is trapped in the capital city of
Khartoum. It is here that he meets Captain Penrod
Ballantyne of the 10th Hussars, as well as the
British Consul, David Benbrook, and his three
beautiful daughters. Against the vivid and bloody
backdrop of the siege of Khartoum, in which
British General Charles George Gordon is killed
and the British retreat, these three powerful men
fight to survive.

THE TRIUMPH OF THE SUN

Volume 1

Wilbur Smith

**WINDSOR
PARAGON**

First published 2005
by
Macmillan
This Large Print edition published 2005
by
BBC Audiobooks Ltd by arrangement with
Macmillan

ISBN 1 4056 1147 2   (Windsor Hardcover)
ISBN 1 4056 2134 6   (Paragon Softcover)

British Library Cataloguing in Publication Data available

Printed and bound in Great Britain by
Antony Rowe Ltd., Chippenham, Wiltshire

This book is for my helpmate, playmate, soulmate, wife and best friend, Mokhiniso Rakhimova Smith

The earth burns with the quenchless thirst of ages, and in the steel blue sky scarcely a cloud obstructs the relentless triumph of the sun.

The River War, Winston S. Churchill, 1905

Rebecca leant her elbows on the sill of the wide, unglazed window, and the heat of the desert blew into her face like the exhalation of a blast furnace. Even the river below her seemed to steam like a cauldron. Here it was almost a mile wide, for this was the season of High Nile. The flow was so strong that it created whirlpools and glossy eddies across the surface. The White Nile was green and fetid with the taint of the swamps through which it had so recently flowed, swamps that extended over an area the size of Belgium. The Arabs called this vast slough the Bahr el Ghazal, and the British named it the Sud.

In the cool months of the previous year Rebecca had voyaged upstream with her father to where the flow of the river emerged from the swamps. Beyond that point the channels and lagoons of the Sud were tractless and uncharted, carpeted densely with floating weed that was perpetually shifting, obscuring them from the eyes of all but the most skilled and experienced navigator. This watery, fever-ridden world was the haunt of crocodile and hippopotamus; of myriad strange birds, some beautiful and others grotesque; and of sitatunga, the weird amphibious antelope with corkscrew horns, shaggy coats and elongated hoofs, adapted for life in the water.

Rebecca turned her head and a thick blonde tress of hair fell across one eye. She brushed it aside and looked downstream to where the two great rivers met. It was a sight that always intrigued her, though she had looked upon it every day for two long years. A huge raft of water weed was

1

sailing down the centre of the channel. It had broken free of the swamps and would be carried on by the current until it dispersed far to the north in the turbulence of the cataracts, those rapids that, from time to time, broke the smooth flow of the Nile. She followed its ponderous progress until it reached the confluence of the two Niles.

The other Nile came down from the east. It was fresh and sweet as the mountain stream that was its source. At this season of High Nile its waters were tinted a pale blue grey by the silt it had scoured from the mountainous ranges of Abyssinia. It was named for this colour. The Blue Nile was slightly narrower than its twin, but was still a massive serpent of water. The rivers came together at the apex of the triangle of land on which the City of the Elephant's Trunk stood. That was the meaning of its name, Khartoum. The two Niles did not mingle at once. As far downstream as Rebecca could see they ran side by side in the same bed, each maintaining its own distinct colour and character until they dashed together on to the rocks at the entrance to the Shabluka Gorge twenty miles on and were churned into a tumultuous union.

'You are not listening to me, my darling,' said her father sharply.

Rebecca smiled as she turned to face him. 'Forgive me, Father, I was distracted.'

'I know. I know. These are trying times,' he agreed. 'But you must face up to them. You are no longer a child, Becky.'

'Indeed I am not,' she agreed vehemently. She had not intended to whine—she never whined. 'I was seventeen last week. Mother married you when she was the same age.'

2

'And now you stand in her place as mistress of my household.' His expression was forlorn as he remembered his beloved wife and the terrible nature of her death.

'Father dear, you have just jumped off the cliff of your own argument.' She laughed. 'If I am what you say I am, then how can you prevail on me to abandon you?'

David Benbrook looked confused, then thrust aside his sorrow and laughed with her. She was so quick and pretty that he could seldom resist her. 'You are so like your mother.' This statement was usually his white flag of defeat, but now he struggled on with his arguments. Rebecca turned back to the window, not ignoring him but listening with only half her attention. Now that her father had reminded her of the terrible peril in which they stood she felt the cold claws of dread in the pit of her stomach as she looked across the river.

The sprawling buildings of the native city of Omdurman pressed up to the far riverbank, earth-coloured like the desert around them, tiny as dolls' houses at this distance, and wavering in the mirage. Yet menace emanated from them as fiercely as the heat from the sun. Night and day, the drums never stopped, a constant reminder of the mortal threat that hung over them. She could hear them booming across the waters, like the heartbeat of the monster. She could imagine him sitting at the centre of his web, gazing hungrily across the river at them, a fanatic with a quenchless thirst for human blood. Soon he and his minions would come for them. She shuddered, and concentrated again on her father's voice.

'Of course, I grant that you have your mother's

raw courage and obstinacy, but think of the twins, Becky. Think of the babies. They are your babies now.'

'I am aware of my duty to them every waking moment of my day,' she flared, then as swiftly veiled her anger and smiled again—the smile that always softened his heart. 'But I think of you also.' She crossed to stand beside his chair, and placed her hand on his shoulder. 'If you come with us, Father, the girls and I will go.'

'I cannot, Becky. My duty is here. I am Her Majesty's consul general. I have a sacred trust. My place is here in Khartoum.'

'Then so is mine,' she said simply, and stroked his head. His hair was still thick and springing under her fingers, but shot through with more silver than sable. He was a handsome man, and she often brushed his hair and trimmed and curled his moustache for him, proudly as her mother had once done.

He sighed and gathered himself to protest further, but at that moment a shrill chorus of childish shrieks rang through the open window. They stiffened. They knew those voices, and they struck at both their hearts. Rebecca started across the room, and David sprang up from his desk. Then they relaxed as the cries came again and they recognized the tone as excitement, not terror.

'They are in the watch tower,' said Rebecca.

'They are not allowed up there,' exclaimed David.

'There are many places where they are not allowed,' Rebecca agreed, 'and those are where you can usually find them.' She led the way to the door and out into the stone-flagged passage. At the far end a circular staircase wound up the interior of the turret. Rebecca lifted her petticoats and ran up the steps, nimble and sure-footed, her father following more sedately. She came out into the blazing sunlight on the upper balcony of the turret.

The twins were dancing perilously close to the low parapet. Rebecca seized one in each hand and drew them back. She looked down from the height of the consular palace. The minarets and rooftops of Khartoum were spread below. Both branches of the Nile were in full view for miles in each direction.

Saffron tried to pull her arm out of Rebecca's grip. 'The *Ibis*!' she yelled. 'Look! The *Ibis* is coming.' She was the taller, darker twin. Wild and headstrong as a boy.

'The *Intrepid Ibis*,' Amber piped up. She was dainty and fair, with a melodious timbre to her voice even when she was excited. 'It's Ryder in the *Intrepid Ibis*.'

'Mr Ryder Courtney, to you,' Rebecca corrected her. 'You must never call grown-ups by their Christian names. I don't want to have to tell you that again.' But neither child took the reprimand to heart. All three stared eagerly up the White Nile at the pretty white steamboat coming down on the current.

'It looks like it's made of icing sugar,' said Amber, the beauty of the family, with angelic features, a pert little nose and huge blue eyes.

'You say that every time she comes,' Saffron remarked, without rancour. She was Amber's foil: eyes the colour of smoked honey, tiny freckles highlighting her high cheekbones and a wide, laughing mouth. Saffron looked up at Rebecca with

5

a wicked glint in those honey eyes. 'Ryder is your beau, isn't he?' 'Beau' was the latest addition to her vocabulary, and as she applied it solely to Ryder Courtney, Rebecca found it pretentious and oddly infuriating.

'He is not!' Rebecca responded loftily, to hide her annoyance. 'And don't be saucy, Miss Smarty Breeches.'

'He's bringing tons of food!' Saffron pointed at the string of four capacious flat-bottomed barges that the *Ibis* was towing.

Rebecca released the twins' arms and shaded her eyes with both hands against the glare. She saw that Saffron was right. At least two of the barges were piled high with sacks of dhurra, the staple grain of the Sudan. The other two were filled with an assorted cargo, for Ryder was one of the most prosperous traders on the two rivers. His trading stations were strung out at intervals of a hundred miles or so along the banks of both Niles, from the confluence of the Atbara river in the north to Gondokoro and far Equatoria in the south, then eastwards from Khartoum along the Blue Nile into the highlands of Abyssinia.

Just then David stepped out on to the balcony. 'Thank the good Lord he has come,' he said softly. 'This is the last chance for you to escape. Courtney will be able to take you and hundreds of our refugees downriver, out of the Mahdi's evil clutches.'

As he spoke they heard a single cannon shot from across the White Nile. They all turned quickly and saw gunsmoke spurting from one of the Dervish Krupps guns on the far bank. A moment later a geyser of spray rose from the surface of the river a hundred yards ahead of the approaching steamer. The foam was tinged yellow with the lyddite of the bursting shell.

Rebecca clapped her hand over her mouth to stifle a cry of alarm, and David remarked drily, 'Let's pray their aim is up to the usual standard.'

One after another the other guns of the Dervish batteries burst into a long, rolling volley, and the waters around the little boat leapt and boiled with bursting shells. Shrapnel whipped the river surface like tropical rain.

Then all the great drums of the Mahdi's army thundered out in full-throated challenge and the ombeya trumpets blared. From among the mud buildings, horsemen and camel riders swarmed out and galloped along the bank, keeping pace with the *Ibis*.

Rebecca ran to her father's long brass telescope, which always stood on its tripod at the far end of the parapet, pointing across the river at the enemy citadel. She stood on tiptoe to reach the eyepiece and quickly focused the lens. She swept it over the swarming Dervish cavalry, who were half obscured in the red clouds of dust thrown up by their racing mounts. They appeared so close that she could see the expressions on their fierce dark faces, could almost read the oaths and threats they mouthed, and hear their terrible war cry: 'Allah Akbar! There is no God but God, and Muhammad is his prophet.'

These riders were the Ansar, the Helpers, the Mahdi's élite bodyguard. They all wore the *jibba*, the patched robes which symbolized the rags that had been the only garb available to them at the beginning of this *jihad* against the godless, the

7

unbelievers, the infidels. Armed only with spears and rocks the Ansar had, in the past six months, destroyed three armies of the infidels and slaughtered their soldiers to the man. Now they held Khartoum in siege and gloried in their patched robes, the badge of their indomitable courage and their faith in Allah and His Mahdi, the Expected One. As they rode they brandished their double-handed swords and fired the Martini-Henry carbines they had captured from their defeated enemies.

During the months of the siege Rebecca had seen this warlike display many times, so she swung the lens off them and turned it out across the river, traversing the forest of shell splashes and leaping foam until the open bridge of the steamboat sprang into sharp focus. The familiar figure of Ryder Courtney leant on the rail of his bridge, regarding the antics of the men who were trying to kill him with faint amusement. As she watched him, he straightened and removed the long black cheroot from between his lips. He said something to his helmsman, who obediently spun the wheel and the long wake of the *Ibis* began to curl in towards the Khartoum bank of the river.

Despite Saffron's teasing Rebecca felt no love pang at the sight of him. Then she smiled inwardly: I doubt I would recognize it anyway. She considered herself immune to such mundane emotions. Nevertheless she experienced a twinge of admiration for Ryder's composure in the midst of such danger, followed almost immediately by the warming glow of friendship. 'Well, there is no harm in admitting that we are friends,' she reassured herself, and felt quick concern for his safety.

'Please, God, keep Ryder safe in the eye of the storm,' she whispered, and God seemed to be listening.

As she watched, a steel shard of shrapnel punched a jagged hole in the funnel just above Ryder's head, and black boiler smoke spurted out of it. He did not glance round but returned the cheroot to his lips and exhaled a long stream of grey tobacco smoke that was whipped away on the wind. He wore a rather grubby white shirt, open at the throat, sleeves rolled high. With one thumb he tipped his wide-brimmed hat of plaited palm fronds to the back of his head. At a cursory glance, he gave the impression of being stockily built, but this was an illusion fostered by the breadth and set of his shoulders and the girth of his upper arms, muscled by heavy work. His narrow waist and the manner in which he towered over the Arab helmsman at his side gave it the lie.

David had taken the hands of his younger daughters to restrain them, and leant over the parapet to engage in a shouted conversation with someone in the courtyard of the consular palace below.

'My dear General, do you think you might prevail on your gunners to return fire and take their attention off Mr Courtney's boat?' His tone was deferential.

Rebecca glanced down and saw that her father was speaking to the commanding officer of the Egyptian garrison defending the city. General 'Chinese' Gordon was a hero of the Empire, the victor of wars in every part of the world. In China his legendary 'Ever Victorious Army' had earned him the sobriquet. He had come out of his

9

headquarters in the south wing of the palace with his red flowerpot fez on his head.

'The order has already been sent to the gunners, sir.' Gordon's reply was crisp and assertive, edged with annoyance. He did not need to be reminded of his duty.

His voice carried clearly to where Rebecca stood. It was said that he could make himself heard without effort across a raging battlefield.

A few minutes later the Egyptian artillery, in their emplacements along the city waterfront, opened up a desultory fire. Their pieces were of small calibre and obsolete pattern, six-pounder Krupps mountain guns; their ammunition was ancient and in short supply, much given to misfiring. However, to one accustomed to the ineptitudes of the Egyptian garrison, their accuracy was surprising. A few clouds of black shrapnel smoke appeared in the clear sky directly over the Dervish batteries, for the gunners on both sides had been ranging each other's positions during all the months since the beginning of the siege. The Dervish fire slackened noticeably. Still unscathed, the white steamer reached the confluence of the two rivers and the line of barges followed her as she turned sharply to starboard into the mouth of the Blue Nile and was almost immediately shielded by the buildings of the city from the guns on the west bank. Deprived of their prey the Dervish batteries fell silent.

'Please may we go down to the wharf to welcome him?' Saffron was dragging her father to the head of the staircase. 'Come on, Becky, let's go and meet your beau.'

As the family hurried through the neglected,

10

sun-bleached gardens of the palace, they saw that General Gordon was also heading for the harbour, with a group of his Egyptian officers scampering behind him. Just beyond the gates a dead horse half blocked the alley. It had been lying there for ten days, killed by a stray Dervish shell. Its belly was swollen and its gaping wounds heaved with masses of white maggots. Flies hovered and buzzed over it in a dense blue cloud. Mingled with all the other smells of the besieged city the stench of rotting horseflesh was sulphurous. Each breath Rebecca drew seemed to catch in her throat and her stomach heaved. She fought back the nausea so that she did not disgrace herself and the dignity of her father's office.

The twins vied with each other in a pantomime of disgust. 'Poof!' and 'Stinky-woo!' they cried, then doubled over to make realistic vomiting sounds, howling with delight at each other's histrionics.

'Be off with you, you little savages!' David scowled at them and brandished his silver-mounted cane. They shrieked in mock alarm, then raced away in the direction of the harbour, leaping over piles of debris from shelled and burnt-out houses. Rebecca and David followed at their best pace, but before they had passed the customs house they encountered the city crowds moving in the same direction.

It was a solid river of humanity, of beggars and cripples, slaves and soldiers, rich women attended by their slaves and scantily clad Galla whores, mothers with infants strapped to their backs, dragging wailing brats by each hand, government officials and fat slave traders with diamond and gold rings on their fingers. All had one purpose: to discover what cargo the steamer carried, and whether she offered a faint promise of escape from the little hell that was Khartoum.

The twins were rapidly engulfed in the throng so David lifted Saffron on to his shoulders while Rebecca grasped Amber's hand and they pushed their way forward. The crowds recognized the tall, imposing figure of the British consul and gave way to him. They reached the waterfront only a few minutes after General Gordon, who called to them to join him.

The *Intrepid Ibis* was cutting in across the stream and when she reached the quieter protected water half a cable's length offshore she shed her tow lines and the four barges anchored in line astern, their bows facing into the strong current of the Blue Nile. Ryder Courtney placed armed guards on each barge to protect the cargoes against looting. Then he took the helm of the steamer and manoeuvred her towards the wharf.

As soon as he was within earshot the twins screeched a welcome: 'Ryder! It's us! Did you bring a present?' He heard them above the hubbub of the crowd, and had soon spotted Saffron perched on her father's shoulders. He removed the cheroot from his mouth, flicked it overboard into the river, then reached for the cord of the boat's whistle, sent a singing blast of steam high into the air and blew Saffron a kiss.

She dissolved into giggles and wriggled like a puppy. 'Isn't he the most dashing beau in the world?' She glanced at her elder sister.

Rebecca ignored her, but Ryder's eyes turned to her next and he lifted the hat off his dense dark curls, sleeked with his sweat. His face and arms were tanned to the colour of polished teak by the desert sun, except for the band of creamy skin just below his hairline where his hat had protected it. Rebecca smiled back and bobbed a curtsy. Saffron was right: he really was rather handsome, especially when he smiled, she thought, but there were crinkles at the corners of his eyes. He's so old, she thought. He must be every day of thirty.

'I think he's sweet on you.' Amber gave her serious opinion.

'Don't you dare start that infernal nonsense, Mademoiselle,' Rebecca warned her.

'Infernal nonsense, Mademoiselle,' Amber repeated softly—and rehearsed the words to use against Saffron at the first opportunity.

*   *   *

Out on the river Ryder Courtney was giving his full attention to the steamer as he brought her into her mooring. He swung her nose into the current and held her there with a deft touch on the throttle, then eased the wheel over and let her drift sideways across the stream until her steel side kissed the matting fenders that hung down the side of the wharf. His crew tossed the mooring lines to the men on the jetty, who seized the ends and made her fast. Ryder rang the telegraph to the boiler room, and Jock McCrump stuck his head through the engine-room hatch. His face was streaked with black grease. 'Aye, skipper?'

'Keep a head of steam in the boiler, Jock. Never know when we might need to run for it.'

'Aye, skipper. I want none of them stinking savages as shipmates.' Jock wiped the grease from his huge calloused hands on a wad of cotton waste.

'You have the con,' Ryder told him, and vaulted over the ship's rail to the jetty. He strode towards where General Gordon waited for him with his staff, but he had not gone a dozen paces before the crowd closed round him and he was trapped like a fish in a net.

A struggling knot of Egyptians and other Arabs surrounded him, grabbing at his clothing. 'Effendi, please, Effendi, I have ten children and four wives. Give us safe passage on your fine ship,' they pleaded, in Arabic and broken English. They thrust wads of banknotes into his face. 'A hundred Egyptian pounds. It is all I have. Take it, Effendi, and my prayers for your long life will go up to Allah.'

'Gold sovereigns of your queen!' another bid, and clinked the canvas bag he held like a tambourine.

Women pulled off their jewellery—heavy gold bracelets, rings and necklaces with sparkling stones. 'Me and my baby. Take us with you, great lord.' They thrust their infants at him, tiny squealing wretches, hollow-cheeked with starvation, some covered with the lesions and open sores of scurvy, their loincloths stained tobacco-yellow with the liquid faeces of cholera. They shoved and wrestled with each other to reach him. One woman was knocked to her knees and dropped her infant under the feet of the surging crowd. Its howls became weaker as they trampled it. Finally a nail-shod sandal crushed the eggshell skull and the child was abruptly silent and lay still, an abandoned doll, in the dust.

Ryder Courtney gave a bellow of rage and laid

14

about him with clenched fists. He knocked down a fat Turkish merchant with a single blow to the jaw, then dropped his shoulder and charged into the ruck of struggling humanity. They scattered to let him pass, but some doubled back towards the *Intrepid Ibis*, and tried to scramble across to her deck.

Jock McCrump was at the rail to meet them with a monkey wrench in his fist and five of his crew at his back, armed with boat-hooks and fire axes. Jock cracked the skull of the first man who tried to board and he fell into the narrow strip of water between the ship and the stone wharf, then disappeared beneath the surface. He did not rise again.

Ryder realized the danger and tried to get back to his ship, but even he could not cleave his way through the close pack of bodies.

'Jock, take her off and anchor with the barges!' he shouted.

Jock heard him above the uproar and waved the wrench in acknowledgement. He jumped to the bridge and gave a terse order to his crew. They did not waste time unmooring, but severed the lines to the shore with a few accurate strokes of the axes. The *Intrepid Ibis* swung her bows into the current, but before she had steerage way more of the refugees attempted to jump across the gap. Four fell short and were whipped away downstream by the racing current. One grabbed hold of the ship's rail and dangled down her side, trying to lift himself aboard, imploring the crew above him for mercy.

Bacheet, the Arab boatswain, stepped to the rail above him and, with a single swing of his axe,

15

neatly lopped off the four fingers of the man's right hand. They fell to the steel deck like brown pork sausages. His victim shrieked and dropped into the river. Bacheet kicked the fingers over the side, wiped his blade on the skirt of his robe, then went to break out the bow anchor from its locker forward. Jock turned the steamboat out across the current, and ran out to anchor at the head of the line of barges.

A wail of despair went up from the crowd, but Ryder glowered at them, fists clenched. They had learnt exactly what that gesture presaged, and backed away from him. In the meantime General Gordon had ordered a squad of his soldiers to break up the riot. They advanced in a line with their bayonets fixed and used their rifle butts to club down any who stood in their way. The crowd broke before them, and disappeared into the narrow alleys of the city. They left the dead baby, with its bleeding mother wailing over it, and half a dozen moaning rioters sitting, stunned, in puddles of their own blood. The Turk who Ryder had floored lay quiescent on his back, snoring loudly.

Ryder looked about for David and his daughters, but the consul had shown the good sense to get his family away to the safety of the palace at the first sign of rioting. He felt a lift of relief. Then he saw General Gordon coming towards him, stepping through the litter and bodies. 'Good afternoon, General.'

'How do you do, Mr Courtney? I am pleased to welcome you. I hope you had a pleasant voyage.'

'Very enjoyable, sir. We made good passage through the Sud. The channel is well scoured out at this season. No necessity to kedge our way

16

through.' Neither deigned to remark on the gauntlet that the steamboat had run through the Dervish batteries, or the riot that had welcomed it to the city.

'You are heavily laden, sir?' Gordon, who was fully six inches shorter, looked up at Ryder with those remarkable eyes. They were the steely blue of the noonday sky above the desert. Few men who looked into them could forget them. They were hypnotic, compelling, the outward sign of Gordon's iron faith in himself and his God.

Ryder understood the import of the question instantly. 'I have fifteen hundred sacks of dhurra sorghum in my barges, each bag of ten cantars weight.' A cantar was an Arabic measure, approximating a hundredweight.

Gordon's eyes sparkled like cut sapphires, and he slapped his cane against his thigh. 'Well done indeed, sir. The garrison and the entire population are already on extremely short commons. Your cargo might well see us through until the relief column from Cairo can reach us.'

Ryder Courtney blinked with surprise at such an optimistic estimate. There were close to thirty thousand souls trapped in the city. Even on starvation rations that multitude would devour a hundred sacks a day. The latest news they had received before the Dervish cut the telegraph line to the north was that the relief column was still assembling in the delta and would not be ready to begin the journey southwards for several weeks more. Even then they had more than a thousand miles to travel to Khartoum. On the way they must navigate the cataracts and traverse the Mother of Stones, that terrible wilderness. Then they must

17

fight their way through the Dervish hordes who guarded the long marches along the banks of the Nile before they could reach the city and raise the siege. Fifteen hundred sacks of dhurra was not nearly enough to sustain the inhabitants of Khartoum indefinitely. Then he realized that Gordon's optimism was his best armour. A man such as he could never allow himself to face the hopelessness of their plight and give in to despair.

He nodded his agreement. 'Do I have your permission to begin sales of the grain, General?' The city was under martial law. No distribution of food was allowed without Gordon's personal sanction.

'Sir, I cannot allow you to distribute the provisions. The population of my city is starving.' Ryder noted Gordon's use of the possessive. 'If you were to sell them they would be hoarded by wealthy merchants to the detriment of the poor. There will be equal rations for all. I will oversee the distribution. I have no choice but to commandeer your entire cargo of grain. I will, of course, pay you a fair price for it.'

For a moment Ryder stared at him, speechless. Then he found his voice. 'A fair price, General?'

'At the end of the last harvest the price of dhurra in the souks of this city was six shillings a sack. It was a fair price, and still is, sir.'

'At the end of the last harvest there was no war and no siege,' Ryder retorted. 'General, six shillings does not take into account the extortionate price I was forced to pay. Nor does it compensate me for the difficulties I experienced in transporting the sorghum and the fair profit to which I am entitled.'

'I am certain, Mr Courtney, that six shillings will

18

return you a handsome profit.' Gordon stared at him hard. 'This city is under martial law, sir, and profiteering and hoarding are both capital crimes.'

Ryder knew that the threat was not an idle one. He had seen many men flogged or summarily executed for any dereliction of their duty, or defiance of this little man's decrees. Gordon unbuttoned the breast pocket of his uniform jacket and brought out his notebook. He scribbled in it swiftly, tore out the sheet and passed it to Ryder. 'That is my personal promissory note for the sum of four hundred and fifty Egyptian pounds. It is payable at the treasury of the Khedive in Cairo,' he said briskly. The Khedive was the ruler of Egypt. 'What is the rest of your cargo, Mr Courtney?'

'Ivory, live wild birds and animals,' Ryder replied bitterly.

'Those you may offload into your godown. At this stage I have no interest in them, although later it may be necessary to slaughter the animals to provide meat for the populace. How soon can you have your steamer and the barges ready to depart, sir?'

'Depart, General?' Ryder turned pale under his tan: he had sensed what was about to happen.

'I am commandeering your vessels for the transport of refugees downriver,' Gordon explained. 'You may requisition what cordwood you need to fuel your boilers. I will reimburse you for the voyage at the rate of two pounds per passenger. I estimate you might take five hundred women, children and heads of families. I will personally review the needs of each and decide who is to have priority.'

'You will pay me with another note, General?'

19

Ryder asked, with veiled irony.

'Precisely, Mr Courtney. You will wait at Metemma until the relief force reaches you. My own steamers are already there. Your famed skill as a river pilot will be much in demand in the passage of the Shabluka Gorge, Mr Courtney.'

Chinese Gordon despised what he looked upon as greed and the worship of Mammon. When the Khedive of Egypt had offered him a salary of ten thousand pounds to undertake this most perilous assignment of evacuating the Sudan, Gordon had insisted that this be reduced to two thousand. He had his own perception of duty to his fellow men and his God. 'Please bring your barges alongside the jetty and my troops will guard them while they are offloaded, and the dhurra is taken to the customs warehouse. Major al-Faroque, of my staff, will be in command of the operation.' Gordon nodded to the Egyptian officer at his side, who saluted Ryder perfunctorily. Al-Faroque had soulful dark eyes, and smelt powerfully of hair pomade. 'And now you must excuse me, sir. I have much to attend to.'

*   *   *

As the official hostess to Her Britannic Majesty's consul general to the Sudan, Rebecca was responsible for the running of the palace household. This evening, under her supervision, the servants had laid the dinner table on the terrace that overlooked the Blue Nile so that David's guests might enjoy the breeze off the river. At sunset the servants would light braziers of eucalyptus branches and leaves. The smoke would keep the mosquitoes at bay. The entertainment would be provided with the compliments of General Gordon. Every evening the military band played and there was a fireworks display: General Gordon intended the show to take the minds of Khartoum's population off the rigours and hardships of the siege.

Rebecca had planned a splendid table. The consular silver and glassware had been polished to dazzling brilliance and the linen bleached white as an angel's wing. Unfortunately the meal would not be of comparable quality. They would start with a soup of blackjack weeds and rose hips from the ruins of the palace garden. This would be followed by a pâté of boiled palm-tree pith and stoneground dhurra, but the *pièce de résistance* was supreme of pelican.

Most evenings David took his station on the terrace above the river with one of his Purdey shotguns at the ready, and waited for the flights of waterfowl to pass overhead as they flew in to their roosts. Behind him the twins waited with the other guns. Such a matching trio of firearms was known as a garnish of guns. David believed that any woman who lived in Africa, that continent of wild animals and wilder men, should be competent in the use of firearms. Under his tutelage Rebecca was already an expert pistol shot. At ten paces she was usually capable with six shots from the heavy Webley revolver of knocking at least five empty bully-beef cans off the stone wall at the bottom of the terrace to send them spinning out across the waters of the Nile.

The twins were still too small to withstand the recoil of a Webley or Purdey, so he had trained

21

them to serve the spare shotguns until they had become as quick and dexterous as a professional loader on a Yorkshire grouse moor. The moment her father had fired both barrels, Amber snatched the empty gun from him and, at almost the same instant, Saffron thrust the second into his hands. While he picked his birds and fired again, the girls reloaded the empty weapon and were ready to serve him with it as soon as he reached for it. Between them they could keep up an impressive rate of fire.

David was a celebrated shot and seldom wasted a cartridge. While the girls squealed encouragement he might on occasion bring down five or six birds in quick succession from a flight of teal speeding high overhead. In the first weeks of the siege wild duck had regularly come within range of the terrace, teal, shovellers and more exotic species, such as Egyptian geese and garganey, all of which had provided important additions to the palace larder. But the surviving duck learnt quickly, and now the flocks habitually gave the terrace a wide berth. It was only the more stupid and less palatable birds that could still be brought to table by David's marksmanship. A brace of heavily billed pelicans were his most recent victims.

The accompanying dish Rebecca planned to serve was the boiled leaves and stems of the sacred Egyptian water-lily. When he had recommended this plant to her Ryder Courtney had told her that its botanical name was *Nymphaea alba*. He had a vast fund of knowledge of all the natural world. She used the lovely blue blossoms as a salad—their peppery flavour helped to disguise the pervading

22

fishy taste of pelican flesh. These plants grew in the narrow canal that cut off the city from the mainland. At this season the water in the canal was waist deep, but in the Low Nile period it dried out. General Gordon had set his troops to widening and deepening the canal into a moat to bolster the city's fortifications and, much to Rebecca's annoyance, they were destroying the source of this nutritious delicacy in the process.

The consular cellars were almost bare, except for a single case of Krug champagne that David was saving to celebrate the arrival of the relief force from the south. However, when Ryder Courtney sent Bacheet up to the consulate to accept the dinner invitation, he also sent three calabash gourds of Tej, the powerful native honey beer, which tasted like poor-quality cider. Rebecca intended serving it in crystal claret decanters to give it an importance it did not normally warrant.

Now she was putting the finishing touches to the dinner arrangements, and the table's floral decoration of oleander from the neglected gardens. The guests would start arriving in an hour and her father had not yet returned from his daily meeting with General Gordon. She was a little worried that David might be late and spoil her evening. However, she was secretly relieved that General Gordon had refused the invitation: he was a great and saintly man, a hero of the Empire, but scornful of the social graces. His conversation was pious and arcane, and his sense of humour, to be charitable, was impaired if not totally lacking.

At that moment she heard her father's familiar tread reverberating down the cloisters and his voice raised as he summoned one of the servants. She

23

ran to greet him as he stepped out on to the terrace. He returned her embrace in a distracted, perfunctory manner. She stepped back and studied his face. 'Father, what is it?'

'We are to leave the city tomorrow night. General Gordon has ordered all British, French and Austrian citizens to be evacuated at once.'

'Does that mean you will come with us, Daddy?' These days she seldom used the childish term of endearment.

'It does indeed.'

'How are we to travel?'

'Gordon has commandeered Ryder Courtney's steamer and barges. He has ordered him downriver with all of us on board. I tried to argue with him, but to no avail. The man is intractable and cannot be moved from his chosen path.' Then David grinned, seized her round the waist and spun her into a waltz. 'To tell the truth, I am vastly relieved that the decision has been taken out of my hands, and that you and the twins will be conveyed to safety.'

An hour later David and Rebecca stood under the candelabrum in the reception lobby to greet their guests, who were almost entirely male. Months before, nearly all the white women had been evacuated north to the delta, aboard General Gordon's tin-pot steamers. Now those vessels were stranded far south at Metemma, awaiting the arrival of a relief force. Rebecca and the twins were among the few European females who remained in the city.

The twins stood demurely behind their father. They had prevailed on their elder sister to allow them to be there when Ryder arrived and to watch

24

the fireworks with him before Nazeera, their nurse, took them to the nursery. Nazeera had been Rebecca's nurse too and was a beloved member of the Benbrook household. She stood close behind the twins now, ready to spring into action at the first stroke of nine. Much to the twins' disappointment, Ryder Courtney was last to arrive, but when he did they giggled and whispered together.

'He's so handsome,' said Saffron, and did her swooning act.

Nazeera pinched her and whispered in Arabic, 'Even if you are never to be a lady, you must learn to behave like one, Saffy.'

'I have never seen him in full fig before.' Amber agreed with her twin: Ryder wore one of the new dinner jackets that the Prince of Wales had recently made fashionable. It had watered satin lapels and was nipped in at the waist. He had had it copied from a picture in the *London Illustrated News* by an Armenian tailor in Cairo, and carried it off with a casual elegance far from his rumpled workaday moleskins. He was freshly shaven and his hair shone in the candlelight.

'And, look, he has brought us presents!' Amber had seen the telltale bulge in his breast pocket. She had a woman's eye for such details.

Ryder shook hands with David and bowed to Rebecca. He refrained from kissing her hand in the Frenchified gesture that many members of the diplomatic corps, who had arrived before him, had affected. Then he winked at the twins, who covered their mouths to suppress giggles as they dropped him a curtsy in return.

'May I have the honour of escorting you two

beautiful ladies to the terrace?' He bowed.

'Wee wee, Moonseer,' said Saffron, grandly, which was almost too much for Amber's self-control.

Ryder took one on each arm, stooping a little so that they could reach, and led them out through the french windows. One of the servants in a white robe and blue turban brought them glasses of lemonade, made from the few remaining fruits on the trees in the orchard, and Ryder presented the twins with their gifts, necklaces of ivory beads carved in the shape of tiny animals: lions, monkeys and giraffes. He fastened the clasps at the backs of their necks. They were enchanted.

Almost on cue the military band down on the maidan beside the old slave market began to play. The distance muted the sound to a pleasing volume, and the musicians succeeded in embellishing the familiar repertoire of polkas, waltzes and marching tunes of the British Army with beguiling Oriental cadences.

'Sing for us, Ryder, oh, please do!' Amber begged, and when he laughed and shook his head, she appealed to her father, 'Please make him sing, Daddy.'

'My daughter is right, Mr Courtney. A voice would add immeasurably to the pleasure of the occasion.'

Ryder sang unselfconsciously, and soon had them all tapping their feet or clapping in time to the music. Those who fancied their own vocal prowess joined in with the chorus of 'Over the Sea to Skye'.

Then the firework display began, General Gordon's nightly treat. The sky cascaded with sheets of blue, green and red sparks from the ship's signal rockets, and the watchers oohed and aahed in wonder. Over on the far bank of the Nile the Dervish gunner whom David had dubbed the Bedlam Bedouin fired a few shrapnel shells at the point from where he guessed the rockets were being set off. As usual, his aim was awry and nobody sought shelter. Instead, everyone booed his efforts with gusto.

Then the twins were led away, protesting vainly, to the nursery, and the company was summoned to the table by one of the robed Arab footmen tapping on a finger drum. Everyone was in fine appetite: if not yet starving, they were at least half-way there. The portions were minuscule, barely a mouthful each, but Herr Schiffer, the Austrian consul, declared the blackjack weed soup to be excellent, the palm-pith pâté nourishing and the roast pelican 'quite extraordinary'. Rebecca convinced herself that this was meant as a compliment.

As the meal drew to a close, Ryder Courtney did something to confirm his status as the hero of the evening. He clapped his hands and Bacheet, his boatswain, came out on to the terrace grinning like a gargoyle and carrying a silver tray on which reposed a cut-glass bottle of VSOP Hine Cognac and a cedarwood box of Cuban cigars. With their glasses charged and the cigars drawing until the tips glowed, the men were transported into an expansive mood. The conversation was diverting, until Monsieur le Blanc joined in.

'I wonder that Chinese Gordon refused such fine entertainment.' He giggled in a girlish, irritating manner. 'Surely it is not possible to save the mighty

British Empire twenty-four hours of every day. Even Hercules had to rest from his labours.' Le Blanc was head of the Belgian delegation sent by King Leopold to initiate diplomatic contact with the Mahdi. So far his efforts had not been crowned by success and he had ended up a captive in the city like the rest of them. The Englishmen at the table looked upon him pityingly. However, as he was a foreigner and knew no better, he was excused the solecism.

'The General refused to attend a banquet while the populace was starving.' Rebecca rose to Gordon's defence. 'I think that was very noble-minded of him.' Then she hurried on modestly, 'Not that I claim my humble offering as a great banquet.'

Following her example David initiated a eulogy to the General's inflexible character and his marvellous achievements.

Ryder Courtney was still smarting from Gordon's last demonstration of his adamantine character and did not join in the chorus of praise.

'He wields an almost messianic power over his men,' David told them earnestly. 'They will follow him anywhere, and if they don't he will drag them by their pigtails, as he did with his Ever Victorious Army in China, or kick their backsides black and blue as he does to the Egyptian riff-raff with which he is forced to defend the city at the moment.'

'Your language, Daddy,' Rebecca chided him primly.

'I am sorry, my darling, but it is true. He is completely fearless. Alone, mounted on a camel and in full dress uniform, he rode into that murderous rogue Suleiman's encamped army of

28

rebels and harangued them. Instead of murdering him out of hand Suleiman abandoned the rebellion and went home.'

'He did the same with the Zulus in South Africa. When he walked alone among their warlike *impis*, and turned his extraordinary eyes upon them, they worshipped him as a god. At that, he thrashed their *induna* for blasphemy.'

Another spoke up: 'Kings and potentates of many nations have competed to secure his services—the Emperor of China, King Leopold of the Belgians, the Khedive of Egypt and the premier of the Cape Colony.'

'He is a man of God before he is a warrior. He scorns the clamour of men, and before he makes any fateful decision he enquires in solitary prayer what his God requires of him.'

I wonder that God required him to steal my dhurra, Ryder thought bitterly. He did not voice the sentiment but changed the direction of the conversation dramatically: 'Is it not remarkable that in many ways the man who faces him now across the Nile shares many characteristics with our gallant general?' A silence followed this remark, which was almost as bad as Le Blanc's gaucherie, not at all worthy of a man of the calibre of Ryder Courtney.

Even Rebecca was aghast at the idea of comparing the saint with the monster. Yet she noticed that when Ryder spoke other men listened. Even though he was the youngest man at the table, the others deferred to him for his fortune and reputation were formidable. He had travelled indefatigably where few men before him had ventured. He had reached the Mountains of the

Moon and sailed on all of the great lakes of the African interior. He was a friend and confidant of John, the Emperor of Abyssinia. The Mutesa of Buganda and the Kamrasi of Bunyoro were his familiars and had granted him exclusive trading rights in their kingdoms.

His Arabic was so fluent that he could debate the Koran with the mullahs in the mosque. He spoke a dozen other more primitive tongues and could bargain with the naked Dinka and the Shilluk. He had hunted and captured every known species of the wild beasts and birds of Equatoria, and sold them to the menageries of the kings, emperors and zoological gardens of Europe.

'That is an extraordinary notion, Ryder,' David ventured cautiously. 'It strikes me that the Mad Mahdi and General Charles Gordon stand at opposite poles. But perhaps you can point out some characteristics they have in common.'

'First, David, they are both ascetics who practise self-denial and abstain from worldly comforts,' Ryder replied easily. 'And both are men of God.'

'Different Gods,' David challenged.

'No, sir! One and the same God: the God of the Jews, Muslims, Christians and all other monotheists is the same God. It is simply that they worship Him in different ways.'

David smiled. 'Perhaps we can debate that later. But for now tell us what else they have in common.'

'They both believe that God speaks directly to them and that therefore they are infallible. Once their minds are set they are unwavering and deaf to argument. Then again, like many great men and beautiful women, they are both betrayed by their belief in the cult of personality. They believe that they are able to carry all before them by the blue of their eyes or by the gap between their front teeth and their eloquence,' Ryder said.

'We know who possesses the blue and compelling eye,' David chuckled, 'but to whom belongs the gap-toothed grin?'

'To Muhammad Ahmed, the Mahdi, the Divinely Guided One,' said Ryder. 'The wedge shaped gap is called the *falja* and his Ansar consider it a mark of the divine.'

'You speak as though you are familiar with him,' said Le Blanc. 'Have you met the man?'

'I have,' Ryder confirmed, and they all stared at him as though he had admitted to supping with Satan himself.

Rebecca was the first to rouse herself. 'Do tell us, Mr Courtney, where and when? What is he truly like?'

'I knew him first when he lived in a hole in the bank of Abbas Island, forty miles up the Blue Nile from where we now sit. Often when I passed the island I would go ashore to sit with him and speak of God and the affairs of men. I could not claim that we were friends, nor would I ever wish to do so. But there was something about him that I found fascinating. I sensed that he was different, and I was always impressed by his piety, his quiet strength and unruffled smile. He is a true patriot, as is General Gordon—another trait they have in common.'

'Enough of General Gordon. We all know of his virtues,' Rebecca interjected. 'Tell us rather of this terrible Mahdi. How can you say he has in him a grain of the same nobility?'

'We all know that the domination of the Sudan

by the Khedive in Egypt has been iniquitous and brutal. Behind the magnificent façade of imperial dominion has flourished unspeakable corruption and cruelty. The native population has been subject to greedy and heartless pashas, and an army of occupation forty thousand strong, which was used to collect the extortionate taxes the pashas imposed. Only half went to the Khedive in Cairo and the rest into the personal coffers of the pashas. The land was ruled by bayonet and kurbash, the vicious hippo-hide whip. The effete pashas sitting here in Khartoum delighted in devising the most savage tortures and executions. Villages were razed and their inhabitants slaughtered. Arab and black man alike cowered under the shadow of the hated "Turk", but no man dared protest.

'The Egyptians, while aspiring to civilization, fostered and encouraged the trade in slaves, for that was how the taxes were paid. I have seen such horrors with my own eyes, and I was amazed by the forbearance of the population. I discussed all this with the hermit in his hole in the riverbank. We were both young men, although I was by some years the younger. We attempted between us to discover why this situation persisted, for the Arab is a proud man and has not lacked provocation. We decided that two essential elements of revolution were missing, and the first of these was the knowledge of better things. General Charles Gordon, as the governor of the Sudan, provided this. The other missing element was a uniting catalyst among the oppressed. In the fullness of time Muhammad Ahmed provided this. It was how the new Mahdist nation was born.'

They were silent, until Rebecca spoke again, and

hers was a woman's question. The political, religious and military facets of the Mahdi's history interested her very little. 'But what is he really like, Mr Courtney? What of his appearance and his demeanour? How does his voice sound? And tell us more of this strange gap between his teeth.'

'He possesses the same vast charisma as Charles Gordon, another trait they have in common. He is of medium height and slim in stature. He has always dressed in robes of spotless white, even when he lived in the hole in the ground. On his right cheek is a birthmark in the shape of a bird or an angel. This is seen by his disciples and adherents as a touch of the divine. The gap between his teeth rivets your attention when he speaks. He is a compelling orator. His voice is soft and sibilant, until his ire is aroused. Then he speaks with the thunder of one of the biblical prophets, but even in anger he smiles.' Ryder drew out his gold pocket-watch. 'It lacks only an hour of midnight. I have kept you late. We should all get a good night's rest, for as you have been told it is my duty, allotted to me by General Gordon, to make certain that none of you here tonight will ever be forced to listen to the voice of Muhammad Ahmed. Remember, please, that you are to be aboard my steamer at the Old City wharf before midnight tomorrow. It is my intention to sail while it is still too dark for the Dervish gunners to pick us out clearly. Please restrict your luggage to the minimum. With good fortune we may run clean away from them before they get off a single shot.'

David smiled. 'That will require a certain amount of luck, Mr Courtney, for the city is crawling with Dervish spies. The Mahdi knows exactly what we are up to almost before we know it ourselves.'

'Perhaps this time we will be able to outwit him.' Ryder half rose and bowed to Rebecca. 'I apologize if I have overstayed my welcome, Miss Benbrook.'

'It is still far too early for you to leave. None of us will sleep yet. Please sit down, Mr Courtney. You cannot leave us high and dry. Finish the story, for you have intrigued us all.'

Ryder made a gesture of resignation and sank down again on his chair. 'How can I resist your command? But I fear you all know the rest of the story, for it has been often told and I do not wish to bore you.'

There were murmurs of protest down the length of the table.

'Go on, sir. Miss Benbrook is right. We must hear out your version. It seems that it differs greatly from what we have come to believe.'

Ryder Courtney nodded acquiescence, and went on: 'In our western societies we pride ourselves in glorious traditions and high moral standards. Yet in savage and uneducated peoples ignorance provides its own source of great strength. It engenders in them the overpowering stimulus of fanaticism. Here in the Sudan there were three giant steps on the road to rebellion. The first was the misery of all the native peoples of the country. The second was when they looked about them and recognized that the source of all their ills was the hated Turk, the minions of the Khedive in Cairo. It needed but a single step more before the mighty wave of fanaticism crashed over the land. That was the moment when there arose the man who would become the Mahdi.'

'Of course!' interjected David. 'The seed had been sown long ago. The Shukri belief that one day, in the time of shame and strife, a second great prophet would be sent by Allah, who would lead the faithful back to God and sustain Islam.'

Rebecca looked sternly at her father. 'It's Mr Courtney's story, Father. Please let him tell it.'

The men smiled at her fire, and David looked guilty. 'I did not mean to usurp your tale. Pray go on, sir.'

'But you are right, David. For a hundred years the people of the Sudan have always looked in hope to any ascetic who rises to prominence. As this one's fame spread, pilgrims began flocking to Abbas Island. They brought valuable gifts, which Muhammad Ahmed distributed to the poor. They listened to his sermons, and when they left to return to their homes they took with them the writings of this holy man. His fame spread throughout the Sudan until it reached the ears of one who had waited eagerly all his life for the coming of the second prophet. Abdullahi, the son of an obscure cleric and the youngest of his four brothers, journeyed to Abbas Island in wild expectation. He arrived at last on a saddle-galled donkey, and he recognized instantly the devout young hermit as the true messenger of God.'

David could not restrain himself longer: 'Or did he recognize the vehicle that would convey him to power and wealth undreamed?'

'Perhaps that is more accurate.' Ryder laughed in accord. 'But, be that as it may, the two men formed a powerful alliance. Soon news reached the ears of Raouf Pasha, the Egyptian governor of Khartoum, that this mad priest was preaching defiance to the Khedive in Cairo. He sent a messenger to Abbas to summon Muhammad Ahmed here to the city to justify himself. The priest listened to the messenger, then stood up and spoke in the voice of a true prophet: "By the grace of God and his prophet, I am the master of this land. In God's name I declare *jihad*, holy war, on the Turk."

'The messenger fled back to his master and Abdullahi gathered around him a tiny band of ragged wretches, then armed them with sticks and stones. Raouf Pasha sent two companies of his best soldiers by steamer upriver to capture the troublesome priest. He believed in the incentive method of conducting warfare. He promised promotion and a large reward to whichever of his two captains made the arrest. At nightfall the steamboat captain landed the soldiers on the island, and the two companies, now in competition with each other, marched by separate routes to surround the village in which the priest was reported to be sheltering. In the confusion of the moonless night the soldiers attacked each other furiously, then fled back to the landing. The terrified steamboat captain refused to let them embark unless they swam out to his boat. Few accepted this offer for most could not swim, and those who could feared the crocodiles. So the captain abandoned them and sailed back to Khartoum. Muhammad Ahmed and Abdullahi, with their tatterdemalion army, fell upon the demoralized Egyptians and slaughtered them.

'The news of this extraordinary victory spread throughout the land, that men with sticks had routed the hated Turk. Surely it must have been the Mahdi who led them. Knowing that more Egyptian troops would be sent to kill him, the newly self-proclaimed Mahdi began a *hegira*, very much like the exodus of the One True Prophet from Mecca a thousand years before. However, before the retreat began, he appointed the faithful Abdullahi as his *khalifa*, his deputy under God. This was in accordance with precedent and prophecy. Soon the retreat became a triumphal progress. The Mahdi was preceded by tales of miracles and prodigious omens. One night a dark shadow obliterated the crescent moon, the symbol of Egypt and the Turk. This message from God high in the midnight sky was plain for every man in the Sudan to see. When the Mahdi reached a mountain fastness far to the south of Khartoum, which he renamed Jebel Masa in accordance with the prophecy, he deemed himself safe from Raouf Pasha. However, he was still within striking distance of Fashoda: Rashid Bey, the governor of the town, was braver and more enterprising than most Egyptian governors. He marched on Jebel Masa with fourteen hundred heavily armed troops. But, scornful of this rabble of peasants, he took few precautions. The intrepid Khalifa Abdullahi laid an ambush for him. Rashid Bey marched straight into it, and neither he nor any single one of his men survived the day. They were slaughtered by the ragged ill-armed *Ansar*.'

Ryder's cigar had gone out. He stood up, took a glowing twig from the brazier of eucalyptus branches and relit it. When it was drawing brightly again he returned to his chair. 'Now that Abdullahi had captured rifles and vast military stores, not to mention the treasury of Fashoda in which was deposited almost half a million pounds, he had become a formidable force. The Khedive in Cairo ordered that a new army be raised here at Khartoum and gave the command of it to a retired British officer, General Hicks. It was one of the most abysmally inept armies ever to take the field, and Hicks's authority was diluted and countermanded by the bumbling Raouf Pasha, who was already the author of two military disasters.'

Ryder paused and as he poured the last of the Hine into his glass he shook his head sadly, 'It is almost two years to the day that General Hicks marched out of this city with seven thousand infantry and five hundred cavalry. He was supported by mounted artillery, Krupps guns and Nordenfelt machine-guns. His men were mostly Muslims and they had heard the legend of the Mahdi. They began to desert before he had covered five miles. He clapped fifty men of the Krupps battery in chains to encourage them to greater valour, but they still deserted and took their manacles with them.' Ryder threw back his head and laughed, and although the tale had been terrifying the sound was so infectious that Rebecca found herself laughing with him.

'What Hicks did not know and what he did not believe even when Lieutenant Penrod Ballantyne, his intelligence officer, warned him, was that by now forty thousand men had flocked to the Mahdi's green flag. One of the emirs who had brought his tribe to join the array was none other than Osman Atalan of the Beja.'

The men around the table stirred at the mention of that name. It was one to conjure with, for the Beja were the fiercest and most feared of all the fighting Arabs, and Osman Atalan was their most dreaded warlord.

'On the third of November 1883, Hicks's motley force ran headlong into the army of the Mahdi, and they were cut to pieces by the charges of the Ansar. Hicks himself was mortally wounded as he stood at the head of the last formed square of his troops. When he fell the square broke and the Ansar swarmed over it. Penrod Ballantyne, who had warned Hicks of the danger, saw the General empty his revolver into the charging Arabs before his head was sliced off by a swinging broadsword. Ballantyne's own superior officer, Major Adams, was lying shot through both legs, and the Arabs were massacring and mutilating the wounded. Ballantyne sprang to horse and managed to lift Major Adams up behind his saddle. Then he hacked his way out through the attackers, and broke clear. He caught up with the Egyptian rearguard, which was by this time in full flight for Khartoum. He was the only surviving European officer so he took command. He rallied them and led a fighting retreat back into Khartoum. Ballantyne brought back two hundred men, including the wounded Major Adams. Two hundred men—of the seven and a half thousand who had marched out with General Hicks. His conduct was the one single ray of light in an otherwise dark day. Thus the Mahdi and his *khalifa* became masters of all the Sudan, and they closed in with their victorious forty thousand on this city, bringing with them the captured guns that torment us to this day. And so the populace languishes and starves, or perishes from pestilence and cholera, while awaiting the fate that the Mahdi has in store for Khartoum.'

There were tears in Rebecca's eyes as Ryder stopped speaking. 'He sounds a fine and brave young man, this Penrod Ballantyne. Have you ever met him, Mr Courtney?'

'Ballantyne?' Ryder looked surprised by this abrupt change in the focus of his tale. 'Yes, I was here when he rode back from the battlefield.'

'Tell us more about him, please, sir.'

Ryder shrugged. 'Most of the ladies I have spoken to assure me that they find him dashing and gallant. They are particularly enamoured of his moustache, which is formidable. Perhaps Captain Ballantyne might agree rather too readily with the general feminine opinion of himself.'

'I thought you spoke of him as a lieutenant?'

'In an attempt to garner some tiny grain of glory from that terrible day the commander of the British troops in Cairo made a great fuss of Ballantyne's role in the battle. It just so happens that Ballantyne is a subaltern in the 10th Hussars, which is Lord Wolseley's old regiment. Wolseley is always ready to give a fellow Hussar a leg up, so Ballantyne was uplifted to the rank of a full captain, and if that was not sufficient he was given the Victoria Cross to boot.'

'You do not approve of Captain Ballantyne, sir?' Rebecca asked.

For the first time David detected in his daughter's attitude towards Ryder Courtney a definite coolness. He wondered at the rather excessive interest she was evincing towards Ballantyne, who presumably was a stranger to her, when suddenly, with a small shock, he recalled that young Ballantyne had visited the consulate some

40

weeks before Hicks's army had marched away to annihilation at El Obeid. The lad had come to deliver a despatch from Evelyn Baring, the British consul in Cairo, which had been too sensitive to be sent over the telegraph, even in cipher. Although nothing had been said at the time he had guessed that Ballantyne was an officer in the intelligence section of Baring's staff, and that his seconding to Hicks's motley army was merely a cover.

Damme, yes! It's all coming back, David thought. Rebecca had come into his office while he was engaged with Ballantyne. The two young people had exchanged a few polite words when he introduced them, and Rebecca had left them alone. But later, when he was showing Ballantyne to the door, David had noticed her arranging flowers in the hall. On glancing out of his office window a short time later, he had seen his daughter walking with Ballantyne to the palace gates. Ballantyne had seemed attentive. Now it all fell into place. Perhaps it was not pure chance that Rebecca had been lingering in the hall when Ballantyne emerged from his office. He smiled inwardly at the way his daughter had pretended never to have met Ballantyne when she asked Ryder Courtney his opinion of the man.

So young, but already so much like her mother, David reflected. As devious as a palace full of pashas.

Ryder Courtney was still responding to Rebecca's challenge: 'I am sure that Ballantyne is an authentic hero, and I am indeed impressed by his facial hair. However, I have never detected in him any excess of humility. But then again I am ambivalent about all military men. When they have

41

finished thrashing the heathen, storming cities and seizing kingdoms, they simply ride away, their sabres and medals clinking. It is left to administrators like your father to try to make some order out of the chaos they have created, and to businessmen like myself to restore prosperity to a shattered population. No, Miss Benbrook, I have no quarrel with Captain Ballantyne, but I am not entirely enamoured of that branch of the state apparatus to which he belongs.'

Rebecca's eye was cold and her expression severe as Ryder Courtney stood up again to leave, but this time with greater determination. Rebecca did not attempt to delay his departure any longer.

*   *   *

It was after midnight before Ryder rode back to his godown. He slept only a few hours before Bacheet woke him again. He ate his breakfast of cold, hard dhurra cakes and pickled salt beef while seated at his desk, working over his journal and cash book by the light of the oil lamps. He felt a sinking sense of dread as he realized how finely drawn were his business affairs.

Apart from six hundred pounds deposited in the Cairo branch of Barings Bank, almost all his wealth was concentrated in the besieged city. In his warehouse he had over eighteen tons of ivory, worth five shillings a pound, but only when it reached Cairo. In beleaguered Khartoum it was not worth a sack of dhurra. The same could be said of the ton and a half of gum arabic, the sap of the acacia tree, which had been dried into sticky black bricks. It was a valuable commodity used in the

42

arts, cosmetics and printing industries. In Cairo his stock would sell for several thousand pounds. Then he had four large storerooms stacked to the ceiling with dried cattle hides bartered from the pastoral Dinka and Shilluk tribes to the south. Another large room was filled with trade goods: rolls of copper wire, Venetian glass beads, steel axe and hoe heads, hand mirrors, old Tower muskets and kegs of cheap black gunpowder, rolls of calico and Birmingham cotton goods, with all the other trinkets and gewgaws that delighted the rulers of the southern kingdoms and their subjects.

In the cages and stockades at the far end of his compound he kept the wild animals and birds that formed an important part of his trading stock. They had been captured in the savannahs and forests of Equatoria and brought downriver in his barges and steamer. In the stockades they were rested, tamed and made familiar with their human keepers. At the same time the keepers learnt what food and treatment would ensure their survival until they were transported north up the Nile to be auctioned to the dealers and their agents in Cairo and Damascus, and even to Naples and Rome where prices were considerably higher. In those markets some of the rarer African species might fetch as much as a hundred pounds each.

His most valuable possessions were concealed behind the steel door of the strongroom, which was hidden by a large Persian wall-hanging: more than a hundred bags of silver Maria Theresa dollars, that ubiquitous coin of the Middle East, minted with a portrait of the buxom queen of Hungary and Bohemia. This was the only coinage acceptable to the Abyssinians in their mountainous kingdom and his other more sophisticated trading partners, such as the Mutesa in Buganda, the Hadendowa and the Saar of the eastern deserts. At the moment there would be little trading with the emirs of these desert Arab tribes. Almost all had gone over *en masse* to join the Mahdi's *jihad*.

He smiled sardonically in the lamplight. I wonder if the Mahdi might be open to an offer of Maria Theresa dollars, he thought. But I expect not. I hear he has already accumulated over a million pounds in plunder.

In the strongroom alongside the canvas bags of dollars were even greater treasures. Fifty sacks of dhurra corn, a couple of dozen boxes of Cuban cheroots, half a dozen cases of Hine Cognac and fifty pounds of Abyssinian coffee.

Chinese Gordon is shooting hoarders. I hope he offers me a last cheroot and a blindfold, he mused. Then he became deadly serious again. Before Gordon had commandeered the *Intrepid Ibis* Ryder had made plans to move as much as possible of his stock and stores downriver to Cairo. Then he would run the blockade of the river.

He had also planned that, while he was occupied with this voyage, Bacheet would take the bulkier and less valuable stocks by camel caravan to Abyssinia and perhaps even to one of the trading ports on the coast of the Red Sea. Although the Mahdi had deployed his armies along the western bank of the Blue Nile, and the northern bank of the Blue Nile, and was blockading the river, there were still many gaps in his besieging cordon. Principal of these was the broad wedge of open desert between the two rivers, at whose apex stood the city. Only the narrow canal protected this part of the city perimeter, and although General Gordon's men were deepening and widening it there was nothing beyond: no Dervish army, only sand, scrub and a few stands of acacia thorn for hundreds of miles.

Said Mahtoum, one of the few emirs who had not yet gone over to the Dervish, had agreed a price with Ryder to bring his camels close in to the city, just out of sight of it behind a low, rocky ridge. There, under Bacheet's supervision, he would load the cargo and smuggle it over the Sudanese border to one of Ryder's trading stations in the foothills of the Abyssinian mountains. All of those plans must now go by the board. He would be forced to leave all his possessions in the beleaguered city, taking only a boatload of refugees with him.

'Damn General bloody Chinese bloody Gordon!' he said, stood up abruptly and moved around the room. Apart from the cabin of the *Intrepid Ibis* this was his only permanent home. His father and his grandfather had been wanderers. From them he had learnt the itinerant lifestyle of the hunter and the African trader. But this godown was home. It needed only a good woman to make it complete.

A sudden image of Rebecca Benbrook opened in his mind. He smiled ruefully. He had a feeling that, for no good reason he could fathom, he had burned his bridges in that quarter. He crossed to a pair of massive elephant tusks that were fastened by bronze rings to the stonework of the wall and stroked one of the stained yellow shafts absently. The feeling of the smooth ivory under his fingers was as comforting as a string of worry-beads. With a single bullet through the brain, Ryder had killed the mighty bull who had carried these tusks at Karamojo, a thousand miles south of Khartoum on the Victoria Nile.

Still fondling the ivory, he studied the faded photograph in its ebony frame on the near wall. It depicted a family standing in front of an ox-wagon in a bleak but unmistakably African landscape. A team of sixteen oxen was inspanned and the black driver stood beside them, ready to crack his long whip and begin the trek towards some nameless destination out there in the blue yonder. In the centre of the picture Ryder's father sat in the saddle of his favourite mount, a grey gelding he had named Fox. He was a big, powerfully built man, with a full dark beard. He had died so long ago that Ryder could not remember if it was a reasonable likeness. He was holding the six-year-old Ryder on the pommel of his saddle with his long skinny legs dangling. Ryder's mother stood at the horse's head gazing serenely at the camera. He remembered every detail of her lovely features and, as always when he looked on them, he felt his heart squeezed by the memory. She was holding his sister's hand. Alice was a few years older than Ryder. On the other side of her stood Ryder's elder brother, with one arm protectively round their mother's waist. That day had been Waite Courtney's sixteenth birthday. He was ten years older than Ryder, and had been more a father to him than a brother after their own father had been killed by a wounded buffalo during the course of the journey on which the five in the photograph had been about to embark.

The last time Ryder Courtney had wept was when he received the telegraph from his sister Alice in London with the terrible news that Waite had been killed by the Zulus on some God-forsaken battlefield in South Africa under a hill called Isandlwana, the Place of the Little Hand. He had left his widow Ada with two sons, Sean and Garrick; fortunately they were almost grown men and could take care of her.

Ryder sighed and drove those sad thoughts from his mind. He shouted for Bacheet. Although it was still dark, there was much they must do today if they were to be ready to sail before midnight.

The two men walked past the ivory warehouse to the gate of the animal stockade. Old Ali met them coughing and grumbling.

'O beloved of Allah,' Ryder greeted him. 'May the wombs of all your beautiful young wives be fruitful. And may their ardour fire your heart and weaken your knees.'

Ali tried not to grin at this levity, for all three of his wives were ancient crones. When a chuckle almost escaped him he turned it into a cough, then spat a glob of yellow phlegm into the dust. Ali was the keeper of the menagerie, and although he seemed to hate all mankind he had a magical way with wild creatures. He led Ryder on a tour of the monkey cages. They were all clean, and the water and feed in the dishes was fresh. Ryder reached into the cage of Colobus and his favourite jumped on to his shoulder, bared his teeth and exposed his fangs. Ryder found the remains of the dhurra cake from his breakfast in his pocket and fed it to him. He stroked the handsome black and white coat as they went on down the row of cages. There were five different species of ape, including dog-faced baboons, and two young chimpanzees, which were hugely in demand in Europe and Asia, and would find eager buyers in Cairo. They clambered up and

47

hugged Ali round the neck; the youngest sucked his ear as though it were its mother's teat. Ali grumbled at them in soft, loving tones.

Beyond the monkeys there were cages full of birds, from starlings of vivid metallic hues to eagles, huge owls, long-legged storks and hornbills, with beaks like great yellow trumpets. 'Are you still able to find food for them?' Ryder indicated the carnivorous birds tethered by one leg to their posts. Ali grunted noncommittally, but Bacheet answered for him.

'The rats are the only animals that still thrive in the city. The urchins bring them in for two copper coins each.' Ali looked at him venomously for having divulged information that was none of his business.

At the far end of the stockade the antelopes were penned together, except for the Cape buffalo who were too aggressive to share with other animals. They were still calves, barely weaned, for young animals were more resilient and travelled better than mature beasts. Ryder had left for last the two rare and lovely antelope he had captured on his last expedition. They had lustrous ginger coats with stark white stripes, huge swimming eyes and trumpet-shaped ears, and were also still calves; when fully mature they would be the size of a pony. Buds bulged out between their ears, which would soon sprout into heavy corkscrew horns. Although the cured hides of the bongo had been described before, no live specimen had ever been offered for sale in Europe, as far as Ryder knew. A breeding pair like this would command a prince's ransom. He fed them dhurra cakes and they slobbered greedily into his palm.

As they walked on Ryder and Ali discussed how best to maintain a constant supply of fodder to keep their charges nourished and healthy. The bongos were browsing animals, and Ali had discovered that they accepted the foliage of the acacia tree. Al-Mahtoum's men regularly brought in camel loads of freshly cut branches from the desert in exchange for handfuls of silver Maria Theresa dollars.

'Soon we will have to capture another floating reed island because if we do not the other animals will starve,' Ali warned lugubriously. He relished being the bearer of worrisome tidings. When rafts of swamp weed and papyrus broke free from the dense masses in the lagoons and channels of the Sud they were carried downstream on the Nile. Some of the rafts were so extensive and buoyant that often they brought large animals with them from the swamps. Despite the best efforts of the Dervish, Ryder and his crew were able to secure these living rafts with long cables and heave them on to the bank. There, gangs of labourers hacked the matted vegetation into manageable blocks and moored them in the moat of the channel. The grasses and reeds remained green until they could be used as fodder.

There was scarcely enough daylight for Ryder to finish his preparations to leave Khartoum, and the sun was setting by the time he and Bacheeet left the compound with a string of baggage camels for the old harbour. Jock McCrump had steam up in the boilers of the *Intrepid Ibis* when they went aboard.

Ryder was painfully aware of the spying eyes of the city upon them as they loaded the last bundles of cordwood for the boilers into one of the barges. The sun had been down for two hours before they had finished but the heat of the day still held the city in a sweaty embrace as the moon began to show its upper limb above the eastern horizon and transform the ugly buildings of the city with its pale romantic rays.

*   *   *

Unremarked among the other sparse river traffic, a tiny felucca used the last of the evening breeze to leave the Omdurman bank and slip downriver. Under cover of darkness it passed not much more than its own length beyond the entrance to the old harbour. The captain stood on one of the thwarts and stared into the entrance. He saw that torches were burning, and with the rays of the moon he was able to make out all the unusual activity around the *ferenghi* steamer moored in the inner harbour. He heard the clamour and shouting of many voices. It was as he had been informed. The *ferenghi* ship was making ready to leave the city. He dropped back on to his seat at the tiller and whistled softly to his three-man crew to harden the big lateen sail so that he could bring her closer to the night breeze, then put the tiller hard up. The small boat shot away at an angle across the current and headed back for Omdurman on the western side of the river. As they came under the loom of the land the captain whistled again, but more piercingly, and was challenged almost immediately from the darkness: 'In the name of the Prophet and the Divine Mahdi, speak!'

The captain stood up again and called to the

50

watchers on the bank. 'There is no God but God, and Muhammad is his prophet. I bear tidings for the Khalifa Abdullahi.'

*   *   *

The *Intrepid Ibis* still lay at the Old City wharf. Jock McCrump and Ryder Courtney were checking the row of Martini-Henry rifles in the gun rack at the back of the open bridge, making certain they were loaded, and that spare packets of the big Boxer-Henry .45 calibre cartridges were to hand, should they run into the Dervish blockade when they left the harbour.

No sooner had they completed their final preparations than the first of the most important passengers came up the gangplank, Bacheet leading them to their quarters. The *Ibis* had only four cabins. One belonged to Ryder Courtney, but over Bacheet's protests he was going to relinquish it to the Benbrook family. There were only two bunks in the tiny cabin. They would be crowded, but at least it had its own bathroom. The girls would be afforded some privacy in the crowded steamer. Presumably one of the twins could sleep with her father, while the other would be with Rebecca. The foreign consuls had been allocated the remaining cabins, while the rest of the almost four hundred passengers must take their chances on the open decks, or crowded into the three empty barges. The fourth barge was laden with the cordwood so that they would not be forced to go ashore to cut supplies of this precious commodity.

Ryder looked towards the eastern horizon. The moon was only a few days from full, and would give

51

him just enough light to descry the channel down towards the Shabluka Gorge. Unfortunately it would also light up the target for the Dervish gunners. Their aim was improving each day as they had more practice and experience with the laying of the Krupps guns that they had captured at El Obeid. They seemed to possess an endless supply of ammunition.

Ryder looked back at the wharf and felt a prickle of irritation. Major al-Faroque of General Gordon's staff had lined up a company of his troops to guard the perimeter of the harbour. With fixed bayonets they were prepared to prevent a mob of refugees without General Gordon's pass trying to storm the little steamer and force themselves aboard. The desperate populace would go to any lengths and take any chance to escape the city. What annoyed Ryder was that al-Faroque had allowed his men to light torches so that they could examine the faces and papers of those would-be passengers who were lining up at the entrance. The torchlight now illuminated the entire expanse of the wharf to the scrutiny of the Dervish sentries across the river.

'In God's name, Major, get your men to douse those lights!' Ryder bellowed.

'I have General Gordon's strict orders to allow no one to pass until I have checked their papers.'

'You are calling the Mahdi's attention to our preparations to sail,' Ryder shouted back.

'I have my orders, Captain.'

While they argued, the crowd of passengers and hopefuls was swelling rapidly. Most were carrying infants or bundles of their possessions. However, they were becoming anxious and panicky at being forbidden entry. Many were shouting and waving passes over their heads. Those who had no pass stood stubborn and grim-faced, watching for their opportunity.

'Let those passengers through,' Ryder shouted.

'Not until I have examined their passes,' the Major retorted and turned his back, leaving Ryder fuming helplessly at his bridge rail. Al-Faroque was stubborn and the altercation was having no effect except to delay the embarkation interminably. Then Ryder noticed David's tall figure pushing through the throng with his daughters pressing close behind him. With relief he saw that al-Faroque had recognized them and was waving them through the cordon of his troops. They hurried to the gangplank, burdened with their most valued possessions. Saffron was lugging her paintbox and Amber a canvas bag stuffed with her favourite books. Nazeera pushed the girls up the gangplank for David had used all his influence and the dignity of his office to obtain a pass for her.

'Good evening, David. You and your family will have my cabin,' Ryder greeted him, as he stepped aboard.

'No! No! My dear fellow, we cannot evict you from your home.'

'I will be fully occupied on the bridge during the voyage,' Ryder assured him. 'Good evening, Miss Benbrook. There are only two narrow bunks. You will be a little crowded, I am afraid, but it's the best available. Your maid must take her place in one of the barges.'

'Good evening, Mr Courtney. Nazeera is one of us. She can share a bunk with Amber. Saffron can share with my father. I will sleep on the cabin floor.

53

I am sure we will all be very comfortable,' Rebecca announced with finality. Before Ryder could protest an ominous chanting and shouting came from the large crowd held back by the guards at the head of the wharf, like floodwaters by a frail dam wall. It provided him with a welcome excuse to avoid another confrontation with Rebecca. There was an ominous glitter in her dark eyes, and a mutinous lift to her chin.

'Excuse me, David. I will have to leave you to install yourselves. I am needed elsewhere.' Ryder left them and ran down the gangplank. When he reached Major al-Faroque's side he saw that the crowd beyond the line of soldiers was growing larger and more unruly with every minute that passed, and they were pressing right up to the points of the bayonets. Monsieur Le Blanc was the last of the diplomatic corps to arrive. Incongruously he was decked out in a flowing opera cloak and a Tyrolean hat with a bunch of feathers in the band. He was followed by a procession of his servants, each heavily laden with his luggage. Born aloft on the shoulders of his porters was a pair of brassbound cabin trunks, each the size of a pharaoh's sarcophagus.

'You cannot bring all that rubbish on board, Monsieur,' Ryder told him, as the guards allowed him to pass.

Le Blanc reached him with sweat dripping off his chin, fanning himself with a pair of yellow gloves. 'That "rubbish", Monsieur, as you call it, is my entire wardrobe of clothing and is irreplaceable. I cannot leave without it.'

Ryder saw at once the futility of arguing with him. He stepped past Le Blanc and confronted the

54

first party of trunk-bearers as they staggered through the cordon with their load.

'Put those down!' he ordered, in Arabic. They stopped and stared at him.

'Do not listen to him,' squealed Le Blanc, and rushed back to slap at their faces with his glove. 'Bring it along, *mes braves*.' The porters started forward again, but Ryder measured the huge Arab who was clearly the head porter, then stepped up to him and slammed a punch into the point of his jaw. The porter dropped as though shot through the head. The trunk slipped from his fellows and crashed to the stone flags. The lid flew open and a small avalanche of clothing and toiletries poured out on to the wharf. The rest of the porters waited for no more but dropped their load and fled from the wrath of the mad *ferenghi* captain.

'Now see what you have done,' cried Le Blanc, and fell to his knees. He began gathering up armfuls of his scattered possessions and trying to stuff them back into the trunk. Behind him the crowd sensed an opportunity. They pressed forward more eagerly, and the guards were forced back a few paces.

Ryder grabbed Le Blanc's arm and hauled him to his feet. 'Come along, you Belgian imbecile.' He tried to drag him towards the gangplank.

'If I am an imbecile, then you are an English barbarian,' howled Le Blanc. He reached back and grabbed a trunk's heavy brass handle. Ryder could not break his grip, although he hauled with all his strength.

From the back of the crowd a large rock was hurled at the head of the Major al-Faroque. It missed its target and struck Le Blanc's cheek. He

55

shrieked with pain, released the trunk handle and clutched his face with both hands. 'I am wounded! I am gravely injured.'

More stones flew out of the crowd to fall among the soldiers and bounce off the pavement. One struck an Egyptian sergeant, who dropped his rifle and went down on one knee clutching his head. His men fell back, glancing over their shoulders for a line of retreat. The crowd yammered like a pack of hounds and pressed them harder. Someone picked up the sergeant's fallen rifle and aimed it at Major al-Faroque. The man fired and a bullet grazed the major's temple. Al-Faroque dropped, stunned. His men broke and ran back, trampling his prostrate form. They had been transformed in an instant from guards to refugees. Ryder picked up Le Blanc and ran with him kicking, screaming and struggling in his arms like a child in a tantrum.

Ryder dumped the Belgian on the deck, then raced on to his bridge. 'Cast off!' he shouted to his crew, just as the first wave of rioters and half the Egyptian *askaris* scrambled on board. The decks were already so overcrowded that the crew were shoved from their positions and were unable to reach the mooring lines. More and more rioters raced down the wharf, and leapt on board the steamer or scrambled into the barges. Those already on board tried to beat them back and the decks were buried under a mêlée of struggling bodies.

Saffron popped her head out of the main cabin to watch the excitement. Ryder picked her up and thrust her bodily into her elder sister's arms, then pushed them both into the cabin. 'Stay out of the way,' he shouted, and slammed the door. Then he snatched the fire axe from its bracket at the head of the companionway. More rioters were coming out of the darkness, unending hordes.

Ryder felt the deck of the *Ibis* heel over under the uneven distribution of weight. 'Jock!' he shouted desperately. 'The bastards are going to capsize us. We have to get her off the jetty.' He and Jock fought their way through the throng. They managed to cut the mooring lines free, but by this time the *Ibis* was listing dangerously.

When Ryder reached his bridge again and opened the throttle, he could feel the enormous drag of the overloaded barges. He glanced back and saw that the nearest had less than two feet of freeboard. He spun the wheel towards the harbour entrance.

The *Ibis* was driven by a Cowper engine, a powerful unit with three cylinders. This modern design incorporated an intermediate steam reservoir for compound expansion that allowed much higher boiler pressure than previous models. The *Ibis* needed all this power to enable her to drag the string of heavily loaded barges up through the fast-flowing waters of the cataracts. Now, under the thrust of the Cowper, she built up speed and a white wave blossomed under the bows of each barge, faster still and the water curled over their bows. A chorus of despairing cries rose from the passengers in the barges as they began to flood and settle even lower in the water. Ryder cut back the power, and managed to con the *Ibis* and her tows out through the harbour entrance into the open river where he would have more space in which to manoeuvre—but the increased turbulence of the surface exacerbated the build-up of the bow waves.

Ryder was forced to throttle right back until he barely had steerageway. The ship was picked up by the current and slewed across the channel with her tow lines becoming fouled. The barges ran down on the *Ibis*. The first of the heavy vessels crashed into her stern, and she shuddered with the shock.

'Cut them loose!' Le Blanc screamed, his voice so shrill with terror that it cut through the din. 'Cut them loose! Leave them behind! This is all their fault!'

The tangle of vessels, still bound together by their tow lines, drifted past the last buildings of the city, then into the broad reach of the combined Niles. Ryder realized he would have to anchor to give himself time to adjust the trim of the barges so that they would tow obediently. He considered turning back to put the stowaway passengers ashore. As they were now, they might flounder in the Shabluka Gorge. Even if they won through, his legitimate passengers would not be able to endure this overcrowding during the heat of the passage through the Desert of the Mother of Stones. Ryder gave the orders to break out the heaviest anchor before they were carried beyond the protection of General Gordon's artillery. Suddenly there was a warning cry from Bacheet.

'Boats coming fast! Dervish boats from the other bank!' Ryder ran to him and saw a flotilla of dozens of small rivercraft appearing swiftly and silently out of the darkness from the direction of Omdurman, feluccas, nuggars and small dhows. He ran back to the bridge. The ten-thousand-candle-power lamp was mounted on the bridge coaming. He turned its brilliant white beam on the approaching craft. He saw that they were crammed with armed Ansar.

The Dervish must have been fully aware of their escape plans and had been lying in ambush for the *Intrepid Ibis*. As they closed with the steamer and her tangled string of barges the Ansar shrieked their terrible praise of God, and brandished their broadswords. The long blades glimmered in the light, and the passengers in the barges wailed with terror.

'Man the rail!' Ryder shouted to his crew. 'Stand by to repel boarders!'

His crew understood this drill well. They had practised it regularly for the Upper Nile was a dangerous place and the tribes who lived upon its banks and in its marshes were savage and wild. They struggled to reach their places at the ship's side to meet the enemy, but the passengers were packed shoulder to shoulder and they found it almost impossible to force their way through. The ruck of human bodies surged forward as they were shoved from behind, and some of those nearest the side were thrown overboard. They screamed and splashed on the surface until they were borne away on the current or sank beneath it. A young wife with her newborn infant strapped to her back went over and although she paddled desperately to keep her baby's head above the surface, they were sucked back into the *Intrepid Ibis*'s propeller.

It was fruitless to attempt to rescue any of those in the water. Nor was there time to anchor, for the Dervish boats closed in swiftly: as they reached the barges they hooked on to the sides and the Ansar warriors tried to clamber aboard, but they were unable to obtain a foothold on the packed decks. They hacked and stabbed at the screaming passengers with their swords, trying to clear a space. The barges rolled wildly. More bodies splashed overboard.

The next wave of Dervish boats came at the *Ibis* from her starboard side. Ryder dared not open the throttle of his engines for fear of swamping the leading barge. If that happened the drag on the tow line would be so powerful the barge might drag *Ibis* under with her. He could not run from them so he must fight them off.

By this time Jock McCrump and Bacheet had passed out the Martini-Henry rifles from the gun rack. Some of the Egyptian *askaris* had brought their Remington carbines on board with them and stood shoulder to shoulder with the crew at the rail. Ryder played the spotlight on the approaching boats. In its stark beam the faces of the Ansar were murderous with battle lust and religious ardour. They seemed as inhuman as a legion from the gates of hell.

'Aim!' shouted Ryder, and they levelled their rifles. 'One round volley. Fire!'

The hail of heavy lead slugs ripped into the closely packed Arabs in the feluccas, and Ryder saw one Dervish flung backwards into the river, the sword spinning from his hands and half of his skull blown away in a bright cloud of brains and blood, sparkling crimson in the spotlight beam. Many more were struck down or hurled overboard by the impact of the 450-grain bullets at such close range.

'Load!' Ryder yelled. The breech-blocks snickered metallically, and the spent cases pinged away. The riflemen thrust fresh cartridges into the open breeches, and snapped the loading handles closed. 'One round volley. Fire!'

Before the men in the small boats had recovered

from the first volley, a second smashed into them, and they sheered away from it.

At that moment Ryder heard David's voice carry above the wails and shrieks of the other passengers. 'Behind you, Mr Courtney!' David had climbed up on to the roof of the cabin. He was balanced there with one of his shotguns held at high port across his chest. Ryder saw Rebecca at his side. She held one of her father's Webley revolvers in each hand, and handled them in a businesslike manner. Behind them stood the twins, each with a loaded shotgun ready to pass forward to their father. Their faces were moon pale but determined. The Benbrook family made a heroic little group above the struggling turmoil on the deck. Ryder felt a quick upthrust of admiration for them.

David pointed over the opposite rail with the barrel of his shotgun, and Ryder saw that another wave of Dervish boats was closing in from that side. He knew he could not get his men back across the crowded deck before the attackers came aboard. If he did he would leave the starboard side undefended. Before he could make the decision and give the order, David took matters into his own hands. He raised the Purdey shotgun and let fly right and left into the crew of the nearest boat. The spreading cloud of goose shot was, at this range, more potent than the single Boxer-Henry bullet. The instant carnage in the felucca stunned the Dervish attackers. Four or five had gone down and were struggling on the deck in puddles of their own blood. Others had been knocked over the side and, flotsam, washed away on the stream.

Saffron slipped the second Purdey into her father's hands while Amber reloaded the empty gun. Rebecca fired the Webley revolvers into the nearest felucca. The recoil from each shot threw the heavy weapons high above her head, but their effect was deadly. David fired again in such quick succession that the shots seemed to blend together in a single jarring concussion. As this havoc of lead pellets and revolver bullets sprayed over the boats, and they saw the tall white man on the cabin roof raise a third gun and aim at them, two of the felucca captains put their helms over, and turned away, unwilling to accept such punishment.

'Good man!' Ryder laughed. 'And well done, you lovely ladies!'

The Dervish feluccas gave up on such dangerous, vicious prey and turned on the overladen and defenceless barges. Now that all the attackers were concentrating on them, their fate seemed sealed. Dervish Ansar hacked their way on board and the passengers were driven like sardines before a barracuda to the far rail of the ungainly craft. The bulwark was driven under by their combined weight and the river rushed in and flooded her. The barge foundered and rolled over. Her weed-carpeted bottom pointed for a moment towards the moon. Then she plunged under and was gone.

Immediately the sunken barge acted like a great drogue on the tow line, and the *Intrepid Ibis* was cruelly curbed, like a horse pulled on to its haunches. The tow line had been made by twisting together three ordinary hawsers. It was immensely powerful, far too strong to part and release the barge. The *Ibis*'s stern was dragged down irresistibly and the water flooded the afterdeck in a rush.

Ryder tossed his rifle to one of the *Ibis*'s stokers and seized the heavy fire axe from him. He sprang down on to the flooding deck and shouldered his way to the stern. He was already knee deep in water, which cascaded in over the transom. Soon it would flood the engine room and quench the boiler fire. Ryder gathered himself and balanced over the tow line, which was now stretched tight as an iron bar through its fairlead in the stern plating. It was as thick as a fat man's calf, and there was no give or elasticity in the water-laid strands.

Ryder swung the axe from full reach above his head with all his strength and, with a crack, a dozen strands parted at the stroke. He swung the axe high once more and put every ounce of muscle behind his next stroke. Another dozen strands gave way. He kept swinging the axe, grunting with the power behind each stroke. The remaining strands of the cable unravelled and snapped under the fierce drag of the submerged barge and the *Ibis*'s driving propeller. Ryder jumped back just before the rope parted and slashed at him like some monstrous serpent. Had the parting cable end caught him squarely it might have broken both his legs, but it missed him by a few inches.

He felt the *Ibis* lurch under him as she was freed of the drag, then spring back on to an even keel. She seemed to shake the water off her decks as a spaniel shakes when it comes ashore with a dead duck in its jaws. Then the propeller bit in hard and *Ibis* surged forward. Saffron was shaken from her perch on the cabin roof. Her arms windmilled and Rebecca tried to catch her, but she slipped through her fingers and fell backwards with a shriek. If she had struck the steel deck she might have caved in the back of her skull, but Ryder threw aside the axe, dived under her and snatched her out of the air. For a moment he held her to his chest.

'A bird you certainly ain't, Saffy.' He grinned at her, and ran with her towards his bridge. Although she tried to cling to him, he dumped her unceremoniously in Nazeera's arms. Without a backward glance, he jumped behind the *Ibis*'s wheel, and pushed the twin throttles wide open. With a rush of steam from her piston exhausts, she tore away, rejoicing to be free of her towing cable, building up swiftly to her top speed of twelve knots. Ryder brought her round to port in a narrow arc of 180 degrees until he was rushing straight back towards the tangled mass of barges and feluccas.

'What are you going to do?' David asked, as he appeared at Ryder's side with his shotgun over a shoulder. 'Pick up swimmers?'

'No,' Ryder replied grimly. 'I am going to add to, not subtract from, the number of swimmers.' The bows of the *Ibis* were reinforced with a double thickness of half-inch steel plate to withstand contact with the rocks of the cataracts. 'I am going to ram,' he warned David. 'Tell the girls that we will hit with an almighty thump and they must hang on tight.'

The Dervish boats were thick as vultures round an elephant carcass. Ryder saw that some of the Ansar were freeing the tow lines that held the barges together and passing the cables down to the dhows. Obviously they intended dragging them one at a time into the shallows of the west bank where they could complete the slaughter and plundering at their leisure. The rest were still hacking at the cowering bodies on the crowded decks or leaning over the sides to stab at those who were struggling in the water and screaming for mercy. In the beam of the *Ibis*'s spotlight the waters of the Nile were stained the colour of mulberry juice by the blood of the dead and dying, and rivulets of blood trickled down the sides of the barges.

'The murderous swine,' Rebecca whispered. Then, to Nazeera, 'Take the twins to the cabin. They should not witness this.' She knew it was a forlorn command. It would require more bodily strength than Nazeera possessed to remove them from the bridge. In the reflection of the spotlight's beam their eyes were huge with dreadful fascination.

The capsized barge was floating bottom up, but sinking swiftly. Suddenly its stern rose, pointed at the moon, then slid below the surface and was gone. Ryder steered for a cluster of three big feluccas, which had tied on to the side of the nearest surviving barge. The Ansar were so busy with their bloody work on the deck that they did not seem to notice the *Ibis* bearing down on them. At the last moment one of the dhow captains looked up and realized the danger. He shouted a warning, and some of his comrades were scrambling back into the feluccas as the *Ibis* struck.

Ryder brought her in so skilfully that her steel bows tore through the wooden hulls in quick succession, the timbers shrieking and exploding with the sound of cannon fire as the boats capsized or were driven under the bloody waters. Although the *Ibis* touched the side of the barge as she tore past, it was a glancing blow and the vessel spun away.

Ryder looked down into the terrified faces of the

65

surviving refugees and heard their piteous entreaties for rescue. He had to harden his heart: the choice before him was to sacrifice all or rescue some. He left them and brought the *Ibis* around, still under full throttle, then aimed at the next group of Dervish attack boats as they wallowed helplessly without steerageway alongside another drifting barge.

Now the Ansar were fully aware of the danger. The *Ibis* bore down on them and the blazing Cyclops eye of the spotlight dazzled them. Some threw themselves overboard. Few could swim and their shields and broadswords drew them under swiftly. The *Ibis* crashed at full throttle into the first felucca, shattered it, and ran on with scarcely a check. Beyond was one of the largest Dervish dhows, almost the length of the *Ibis* herself. The steamer's steel bows sliced deeply into her, but could not severe her hull. The impact threw her back on her heels and some of those on her deck were hurled overboard with the crew of the dhow.

Ryder threw the *Ibis* into reverse, and as he backed off from the mortally stricken dhow he played the spotlight beam around her. Most of the Dervish boats had recovered their boarding parties from the barges, abandoning their prey in the face of the *Ibis*'s ferocious onslaught. They hoisted sail and steered back towards the west bank. The three surviving barges were no longer linked together, for the Ansar had succeeded in freeing the lines. Independently of each other they were spreading out and drifting in towards the west bank, thrust across the wide bend of the river by the current. In the powerful beam Ryder could just make out the Dervish hordes waiting to welcome them and complete the massacre. He swung the *Ibis* around in the hope that he could reach at least one and pick up the tow line again in time to drag it off the hostile shore.

As he tore towards the barges he saw that the one that contained the cordwood, heavier than the others, was being carried more slowly on the current. The remaining two were still in its teeth, their decks piled with the dead and wounded, blood painting their sides, glistening red in the spotlight beam. They would soon be into the shallows where the *Ibis* could not follow them.

Ryder knew every shoal and bend of the river as intimately as a lover knows the body of his beloved. He narrowed his eyes and calculated the angles and relative speeds. With a sinking feeling in the pit of his stomach, he realized he could not reach them in time to rescue them all. He kept the *Ibis* tearing downstream under full steam, but he knew it was hopeless. He saw first one barge, then the other check sharply and come to a halt, stranded on the shoals. From the shore the waiting Dervish warriors plunged into the river and waded out waist-deep to finish the slaughter. Ryder was forced to throttle back and watch helplessly in horror and pity as the Ansar scrambled aboard and their bloody work began again. In vain he directed the rifle fire of his crew at the hordes of Dervish still wading out to the stranded vessels, but the range was long and the bullets had little effect.

Then he saw that the cordwood barge was still floating free. If he acted swiftly he might still be able to salvage it before it, too, went aground. He opened the throttle and raced down to intercept it. It was of crucial importance to recover this stock of fuel for his boilers. With it, they might reach the first cataract without being forced ashore to cut more timber. Ryder shouted to Jock McCrump to prepare a new tow line, then brought the *Ibis* alongside the barge and held her in position while Jock and his boarding party jumped across to fix the fresh line.

'Quick as you like, Jock,' Ryder shouted. 'We're going to touch bottom at any moment.'

He looked anxiously at the enemy shore. They had now drifted within pistol shot, and even as he thought it he saw muzzle flashes as the Dervish riflemen opened fire on them from the bank. A bullet struck the bridge rail and ricocheted so close past David's ear that he ducked instinctively, then straightened, looking embarrassed. He turned sternly to Rebecca: 'Get the twins below immediately, and make sure they stay there until I tell you.'

Rebecca knew better than to argue with him when he used that tone. She gathered the twins and drove them off the deck with her fiercest tone and expression. Nazeera needed no urging and scuttled down to the cabin ahead of them.

Ryder played the spotlight along the bank, hoping to intimidate the Ansar marksmen or, at least, to illuminate them so that his own crew could return fire more accurately. Although Jock worked fast to rig the new tow line, it seemed like an eternity as they drifted swiftly towards the shallows and the waiting enemy. At last he bellowed across, 'All secure, Captain.'

Ryder reversed the *Ibis* slowly until the gap between the two vessels was narrow enough for Jock and his team to leap back on board the steamer. As soon as his feet hit the *Ibis*'s steel deck he yelled, 'Haul away!'

With a rush of relief Ryder eased the throttles ahead and gently drew the barge after him until she was following like an obedient dog on a leash. He began to haul her off into the main stream of the river, when a rushing sound filled the air and something passed so close above him that his hat spun off his head. Then, immediately afterwards, there followed the unmistakable boom of a six-pounder cannon, the sound following the shell from the west bank.

'Ah! They've brought up one of their artillery pieces,' David remarked, in a conversational tone. 'Only wonder is that it has taken them so long.'

Quickly Ryder doused the spotlight beam. 'They could not fire before for fear of hitting their own ships,' he said. And his last words were drowned by the next shell howling overhead. 'That was not so close.' He kept his right hand pressing down on the throttle handles to milk the last turn of speed out of his vessel. The weight and drag of the barge cut at least three knots off their speed.

'They are close enough to be using open sights,' David said. 'They should be able to do better than that.'

'They will—oh, I am sure they will.' Ryder looked up at the moon, hoping to see the shadow of a cloud fall across it. But the sky was brilliant with stars and the moon lit the surface of the Nile as if it were a stage. For the gunners the *Ibis* would stand out against the silver waters like a granite hillock.

The next shell fell so close alongside that a shower of river water fell over the bridge and

69

soaked those on it so that their shirts clung to their backs. Then there were more cannon flashes along the shore behind them as the Dervish gunners dragged up gun after gun and unlimbered to bring the *Ibis* under fire.

'Jock, we will have to give them the best of it and cut the barge loose,' Ryder called to the engineer.

'Aye, skipper. I had a notion ye would say just that.' Jock picked up the axe and started towards the stern.

Another Dervish gun-carriage galloped along the bank until it was slightly ahead of the straining *Ibis* and her burden. Though neither Ryder nor David was aware of it, the master gunner commanding the mounted battery was the Ansar whom David had dubbed the Bedlam Bedouin.

From astride the lead horse of the team, he gave a sharp command and they wheeled the gun carriage into line with the gun's muzzle pointing out across the river, and unlimbered. The number two and three loaders stamped the heavy steel base plate into the soft earth of the riverbank. They set the point of the trail into its slot in the plate. While they worked the master gunner was shrieking orders, wild with excitement: he had never in all his brief career been offered such a fine target as the *ferenghi* ship now presented. It was almost broadside on. Its silhouette stood out crisply against the shimmering waters. It was so close that he could hear the terrified voices of the passengers raised in prayer and supplication, and the peremptory commands of the captain speaking in the infidel language the gunner could not understand.

He used a hand-spike to traverse the gun round

the last few degrees until the long barrel was aiming directly at the ship. Then he wound down the elevation handle until he was gazing over the open iron sights at his target.

'In the Name of Allah, bring the bomboms!' he screamed at his loaders. They staggered up with the first ammunition box and knocked off the clips that held the lid in place. Inside, four shells lay in their wooden cradles, sleek and glistening ominously. The gunner, self-taught in the art of gunnery, had not yet fathomed the arcane principle of fuse delays. In fumbling haste, he used the Allen key he wore round his neck to screw the fuses to the maximum setting in the belief that this imparted to each missile the greatest amount of destructive power. The *Ibis* was a mere three hundred yards off the bank. He set his fuses at two thousand yards.

'In God's Name let us begin!' he ordered.

'In God's Name.' His number two flung open the breech of the Krupps with a flourish.

'In God's Name,' intoned the number three, and slid one of the long shells deep into the chamber until it was snug against the lands. The number two slammed the breech-block shut.

'God is great,' said the Bedlam Bedouin, as he squinted over his sights to make certain of his aim. He traversed the mount four degrees left until he was aiming at the base of the *Ibis*'s funnel. Then he jumped back and seized the lanyard. 'Allah is mighty,' he said.

'There is no other God but God,' chorused his team.

'And Muhammad and the Mahdi are his prophets.' The gunner jerked the lanyard, and the

Krupps slammed back against its base plate. The discharge deafened the crew with its report and blinded them with the muzzle flash and the flying dust.

On an almost flat trajectory the shell howled over the river and struck the *Intrepid Ibis* two feet above the waterline and just astern of midships. It passed obliquely through her hull as readily as a stiletto through human flesh, but by virtue of the maximum fuse setting it did not explode.

Had it been three inches higher or lower it would have done minimal damage, nothing that Jock McCrump with his gas welding equipment could not have repaired within a few hours. But that was not to be. In passing it slashed through the main steam line from the boiler. Steam heated to twice the temperature of boiling water and under pressure of almost three hundred pounds to the square inch erupted in a shrieking jet from the ruptured pipe. It swept over the nearest stoker as he bent to thrust a faggot of timber into the open firebox of the boiler. He was naked in the heat, except for a turban and loincloth. Instantly the steam peeled the skin and the flesh off his body in great slabs to expose the bones beneath. The agony was so terrible that the man could not utter a sound. Mouth gaping in a silent scream, he fell writhing to the deck and froze into a sculpture of the utmost agony.

Steam filled the engine room and boiled in dense white clouds from the ventilation ports to pour over the decks, shrouding the *Ibis* in a dense white cloud. Rapidly the ship lost power and swung idly broadside to the current. The Bedlam Bedouin and his gun-crew howled with excitement and triumph as they reloaded. But their quarry was now obscured by her own steam cloud. Although shells from many Krupps batteries along the bank plunged into the water alongside, or ripped the air overhead as though a giant was tearing a canvas mainsail in two, no more struck the little *Ibis*.

Jock McCrump had been on the bridge with Ryder when the shell struck. He grabbed a heavy pair of working gloves from the locker beside the forward steam winch, and pulled them on as he ran back to the engine-room hatchway. The steam that billowed through the opening stung his face and the bare skin of his arms, but the pressure in the boiler had dropped as the steam bled off through the ruptured pipe. He ripped the heavy canvas curtain that covered the hatch from its rail, and snapped at Ryder, 'Wrap me, skipper!'

Ryder understood instantly what he was going to do. He shook out the thick curtain, then wound Jock in it, cloaking his head and every part of his body but for his arms.

'The grease pot!' Jock's voice was muffled by the folds of canvas. Ryder seized it from its hook beside the winch, scooped out handfuls of the thick black grease and spread it over the exposed skin of Jock's muscular arms.

'That will do,' Jock grunted, and opened a slit in his canvas head cover to draw one last deep breath. Then he covered his face and plunged blindly down the steel companion ladder. He held his breath and closed his eyes tightly. But the steam scalded the exposed skin, melting away the coating of black grease from his bare arms.

Jock knew every inch of his engine room so intimately that he did not need to see it. Guiding himself with a light touch of gloved fingers over the familiar machinery, he moved swiftly towards the main pressure line. The shrieking of high-pressure steam escaping from the rupture threatened to burst his eardrums. He felt his arms cooking like lobsters in the pot and fought the impulse to scream, lest he use the last air in his aching lungs. He stumbled over the stoker's corpse, but recovered his balance and found the main steam line. It was wrapped with asbestos rope to prevent heat loss so he was able to run his gloved hands along it until he found the wheel of the stopcock that controlled the flow of steam into the line. Swiftly he spun the wheel and the rushing sound of escaping steam rose sharply, then was snuffed out as the valve closed.

It took ineffable pain to make a man like Jock McCrump sob, but he was crying like an infant as he staggered back to the foot of the companion ladder, then clambered painfully up to the deck. He stumbled out into the night air, which felt cold after the hellish atmosphere of the engine room, and Ryder caught him before he fell. He stared in horror at the huge blisters hanging from Jock's forearms. Then he roused himself and scooped more grease from the pot to cover them, but Rebecca had appeared suddenly and pushed him aside.

'This is woman's work, Mr Courtney. You see to your boat and leave this to me.' She was carrying a hurricane lamp and, by its feeble light, examined Jock's arms, pursing her lips grimly. She set the lamp on the deck, crouched beside Jock and began to work on his injuries. Her touch was deft and gentle.

'God love you, Jock McCrump, for what you've done to save my ship.' Ryder lingered beside Jock. 'But the Dervish are still shooting at us.' As if to underline the fact another Krupps shell plunged into the river, so close alongside that the spray rained down on them like a tropical cloudburst. 'How bad is the damage? Can we get power on at least one of the engines to get us out of range of the guns on the bank?'

'I couldnae see much at all down there, but at the best odds the main boiler will not have as much pressure in her as a virgin's fart.' Jock glanced at Rebecca. 'Begging your pardon, lassie.' He stifled a groan as Rebecca touched one of the pendulous blisters, which burst open.

'I'm sorry, Mr McCrump.'

'It's naught at all. Dinna fash yourself, woman.' Jock looked up at Ryder. 'Maybe, just maybe, I can knock together some kind of jury-rig and get steam to the cylinders. It just depends on the damage she's suffered down there. But at the best I doubt we'll get more than a few pounds of pressure into the line.'

Ryder straightened up and looked around. He saw the dark shape of Tutti Island no more than a cable's length downstream from where they wallowed, powerless, under the Dervish guns. What the Dervish cannon fire lacked in accuracy, it made up for in rapidity. From the sheer weight of shells being hurled at them, it could not be long before they received another direct hit.

He watched the changing bearing of the island for a moment longer. 'The current is carrying us past the island. If we anchor in its lee it will screen us from the guns.' He left them and shoved his way through the passengers, shouting for Bacheet and his mate Abou Sinn. 'Clear this rabble out of the way, and prepare to anchor at my command.'

They jumped to their stations, shoving and kicking aside the bewildered *askari* and stowaways to give themselves room to work. Bacheet freed the retaining tackle from the ring of the heavy fisherman's anchor that hung at the bows. Abou Sinn stood over the chain where it emerged through the fairlead of the chain locker with the four-pound hammer ready.

Ryder peered back at the land, watching the muzzle flashes of the Dervish guns and judging his moment. For a few minutes he held his breath while it seemed that they would be driven ashore on the island, then an eddy in the current pushed them clear and they drifted so close to the eastern side of the island that they were sheltered from the Dervish batteries.

'Let go!' Ryder shouted to Abou Sinn, and with a blow of the sledge-hammer he knocked the pin out of the anchor shackle. The anchor splashed into the river, the chain roaring out after it, and found the bottom. The chain stopped running and Bacheet secured it. The *Ibis* came up hard and short, and spun round in the current to face upstream, with the timber barge behind her on her tow line. The Dervish cannon fire tapered off as the gunners found themselves deprived of their target. A few more shells screeched high overhead or burst ineffectually into the sandbanks of the screening island, then the gunners gave up and silence descended.

Ryder found Jock sitting on the bunk in the cabin, being attended to by all the Benbrook ladies.

76

'How are you feeling?' he asked solicitously.

'Not so bad, skipper.' He indicated his arms: 'These bonny little lasses have done a fine job on them.' Rebecca had bandaged both arms with strips that the twins had torn from one of the threadbare cotton bedsheets, then fashioned a double sling from the same material. Now she was brewing a mug of tea for him on the stove in the tiny galley next door. Jock grinned. 'Home was never so good. That's why I ran away.'

'Sorry to interrupt your retirement, but can I trouble you to take a peek at your engine?'

'Just when I was really enjoying meself,' Jock grumbled, but rose to his feet.

'I'll bring your mug down to the engine room for you, Mr McCrump,' Amber promised.

'And I'll bring one for you, Ryder,' Saffron called.

Jock McCrump followed Ryder down to the engine room. Bacheet and Abou Sinn carried away the stoker's corpse, and by the light of a pair of hurricane lamps they assessed the damage. Now that Jock was able to examine his beloved engine more closely, he grumbled bitterly to disguise his relief. 'Bloody heathens! Can't trust them further than you can throw one of them. No sense of common decency, doing this to my bonny Cowper.' However, only the main steam line shot was through; the engine itself was untouched.

'Well, there's naught I can do for the steam line this side of my workshop in Khartoum. In the meantime, though, perhaps I can cobble something together to get a mite of steam through to the engine, but I reckon we'll not be breaking any speed records with the old girl.' Then he held up his bandaged arms. 'You'll have to do the donkey work, skipper.'

Ryder nodded. 'While we're at it, I'm going to send Bacheet to move all our uninvited passengers across to the barge. That will correct my trim and give me a little more manoeuvrability and control. It will also give the crew more room to work the ship properly.'

While the passengers were transhipped, Ryder and his engineer began the repairs. Working quickly but carefully, they bled off the remaining steam from the boilers and drew the fires from the grate. Then they used the in-line valve cocks to isolate the damaged section of the main steam line. Once this was done, they could begin rigging a bypass line to carry steam through to the power plant. They had to measure the lengths they needed and cut the new pipe sections to length by hacksaw, then clamp them into the heavy vice on Jock's workbench and cut threads into the ends of the pipes with the hand dies. They packed the joints with asbestos thread and tightened the elbows and connectors with their combined weight on the long-handled pipe wrench. They ended up with a mare's nest of convoluted improvised piping.

The work took the rest of the night, and by the time they were ready to test its integrity dawn was showing through the engine-room portholes. It took another hour to set the fires in the grates and work up a head of steam in the boiler. When the needle of the pressure gauge touched the green line Jock gingerly eased open the cock of the steam valve. Ryder stood beside him and watched anxiously, hands black with grease, knuckles bruised and bleeding from rough contact with steel pipes. They held their breath as the needle on the secondary pressure gauge rose, and watched the new pipe joints for the first sign of a leak.

'All holding,' Jock grunted, and reached across to the port-engine throttle. With a suck and a hiss of live steam the big triple pistons began to pump up and down in their cylinders, the rods moved like the legs of marching men, and the propeller shaft rotated smoothly in its bearings.

'Power up and holding.' Jock grinned with the pride of accomplishment. 'But I cannae take the chance and open her full. You'll have to take what you get, skipper, and thank the Lord and Jock McCrump for that much.'

'You're a living, breathing miracle, Jock. I hope your mother was proud of you.' Ryder chuckled. When he wiped the sweat off his forehead, the back of his fist left a black smear. 'Now, stand by to give me everything you can just as soon as I can get the anchor weighed and catted.' He charged up the ladder to the bridge. Abou Sinn followed him and ran to the controls of the steam winch.

As the *Ibis* pushed slowly forward against the river current, the anchor chain came clanking in through the hawserhole. The flukes broke free from the riverbed and Ryder eased open the throttle. The *Ibis* responded so sluggishly that she made little headway against the four-knot current. Ryder felt a cold slide of disappointment. He glanced over the stern at the barge. Drawing deeply under its cargo of cordwood and uninvited passengers, it was behaving with mulish recalcitrance. Dozens of pathetic faces stared across at him.

By God, I've half a mind to cut you free and

leave you to the mercy of the Mahdi, he thought venomously, but with an effort set the temptation aside. He turned instead to David, who had joined him silently. 'She'll never be able to hold her own in the Shabluka Gorge. When the entire flow of the combined Niles is forced through the narrows the current reaches almost ten knots. With only half her power the *Ibis* will be helpless in its grip. The risk of piling up on the rocky cliffs is too great to accept.'

'What other choice do you have?'

'Nothing for it but to battle our way back to Khartoum.'

David looked worried. 'My girls! I hate to take them back to that death-trap. How long will Gordon be able to hold out in the city before the Dervishes break in?'

'Let's hope it's long enough for Jock to finish his repairs so that we can make another run for it. But now our only hope is to get back into the harbour.' Ryder turned the *Ibis* across the current and headed her for the east bank. He tried to keep the bulk of Tutti Island between the ship and the Dervish batteries, but before they were half-way across the first shells were howling above the river. However, with the current giving him some assistance Ryder opened the range swiftly, and the skill of the Bedlam Bedouin and his comrades was not up to the task of hitting a target as small as the *Intrepid Ibis* at a range of over a mile, except by the direct intervention of Allah. This day, however, their prayers went unanswered, and although there were a few encouraging near misses the *Ibis* and her barge made good their crossing of the mainstream, then turned south for the city, hugging

80

the furthest edge of the channel at extreme range for the Krupps.

The Dervish feluccas sallied out from the west bank and made another attempt to intercept the steamer, but by now the sun was high. General Gordon's artillery on the riverfront of Khartoum was able to direct furious and remarkably accurate fire upon the enemy flotilla as it came within easy range. Ryder saw four small boats blown into splinters by direct hits with high explosive and correctly fused shells. The severed limbs and heads of the crews were hurled high in the yellow clouds of lyddite fumes. This discouraged all but a few of the bravest, most foolhardy captains, and most of the small boats turned back for the shore.

Three of the attack boats pressed on across the river, but the wind blew strongly from the south and the current was at five knots from the same direction. Two of the feluccas were swept downstream and were unable to make good a course to intercept the *Ibis*. Only one of them stood in her way. But Ryder had been given plenty of time to prepare a reception for it. He ordered all the deck passengers to lie flat, so as to offer no target to the attackers. As the enemy vessel raced towards them, heeled over by the wind and pushed along by the current, Bacheet and Abou Sinn were crouched below the starboard bulwark.

'Let them get close,' Ryder called down from the bridge, as he judged the moment. Then he raised his voice to full pitch: 'Now!' he bellowed.

Bacheet and Abou Sinn sprang up from hiding and aimed the brass nozzles of the steam hoses down into the undecked hull of the felucca. They opened the valves and solid white jets of live steam from the *Ibis*'s boiler engulfed the warriors crowded into the open boat. Their bloodthirsty war cries and angry challenges turned to screams of anguish as the dense clouds of steam flayed the skin and flesh from their faces and bodies. The hull of the felucca crashed heavily against the steel of the *Ibis*'s hull, and the impact snapped off the mast at deck level. The felucca scraped down the steel side of the steamer, then spun out of control in her wake. She now wallowed directly in the path of the heavily laden barge. The Ansar were so blinded by the steam that they did not see her coming. The barge smashed into the frail craft and trod her under the surface. None of her crew surfaced again.

'That takes care of that,' Ryder murmured, with satisfaction, then forced a smile at Rebecca. 'Forgive me for depriving you of the comfort of the cabin floor, but tonight you will have to make do with your own bed in the palace.'

'That is a hardship I am determined to endure with the utmost stoicism, Mr Courtney.' Her smile was almost as unconvincing as his, but he was amazed at how pretty she looked in the midst of so much mayhem and ugliness.

*   *   *

General Charles Gordon stood on the steps above the harbour entrance and watched the *Ibis* limp in. When Ryder looked up at him from the bridge, his regard was cold and cutting as blue ice, with no trace of a smile nor any hint of sympathy. When the steamer was tied up at the stone jetty Gordon turned away and disappeared.

Major al-Faroque remained to welcome the bedraggled passengers as they staggered ashore from the barge. His head was swathed in a white bandage, but his expression was ferocious as he picked out those of his men who had deserted their posts and attempted to escape. As he recognized them he lashed each offender across the face with the kurbash whip he carried, and nodded to the squad of *askari* who were lined up behind him. They seized the marked men and locked manacles on their wrists.

Later that afternoon, when Ryder was summoned to the general's office in the consular palace to make his report, Gordon was distant and dismissive. He listened without comment to all that Ryder had to say, condemning him with his silence. Then he nodded. 'I am to blame as much as anybody. I placed too much responsibility on your shoulders. After all, you are not a soldier, merely a mercenary trader.' He spoke scornfully.

Ryder was about to make an angry retort when a volley of rifle fire rang out from the courtyard of the palace below. He turned quickly to the window and looked down.

'Al-Faroque is dealing with the deserters.' Gordon had not risen from his chair. Ryder saw that the ten men of the firing squad were leaning nonchalantly on their weapons. Against the wall of the courtyard facing them sprawled an untidy row of corpses. The dead men were all blindfolded with their wrists tied behind their backs, their shirts bloodsoaked. Major al-Faroque was walking down the line, his service revolver in his right hand. He paused over a body that was twitching spasmodically and fired a single shot into the

83

blindfolded head. When he reached the end of the line he nodded to a second squad of men, who ran forward and piled the corpses into a waiting cart. Then another group of condemned men were led up from the cells into the courtyard and lined up along the wall. While a sergeant tied their blindfolds, the firing squad came to attention.

'I hope, General, that the consul's daughters have been warned of these executions,' Ryder said grimly. 'It is not something that young gentlewomen should witness.'

'I sent word to him that they should keep to their quarters. Your concern for the young ladies does you credit, Mr Courtney. However, you might have been of greater service to them by affording them safe passage downriver to a place of security.'

'It is my intention to do so, General, as soon as I am able to effect repairs to my steamer,' Ryder assured him.

'It might already be too late for that, sir. Within the last few hours I have received the most reliable intelligence that the Emir Osman Atalan of the Beja tribe is in full march with his array to join the Mahdi's besieging force out there.' General Gordon pointed out of the window across the White Nile at the Omdurman bank of the river.

Ryder was unable to conceal his alarm. With the notorious Osman Atalan opposing them, the nature of the siege would change. Any escape from Khartoum would become incalculably more difficult.

As if to endorse these grim thoughts, the next volley from the execution squad crashed out, and immediately afterwards Ryder heard the soft sounds of human bodies flopping lifelessly to the ground.

*   *   *

The Emir Osman Atalan, beloved of the Divine Mahdi, was riding at large. In response to the Mahdi's summons to Khartoum, he had been for many weeks on the march up from the Red Sea Hills with his army. His warrior spirit chafed at the monotony and drudgery of the pace set by the great agglomeration of animals and people. The baggage train of camels and donkeys, the columns of slaves and servants, women and children was strung out over twenty leagues, and when they camped at night it was like a city of tents and animal lines. Each of Osman's wives rode in a curtained litter on the back of her own camel, and slept at night in her own commodious tent, attended by her slaves. In the van and in the rearguard rode the legions of the forty thousand fighting men he commanded.

All the subservient tribes had massed to his scarlet and black banner: the Hamran, the Roofar of the hills and the Hadendowa of the Red Sea littoral. These were the same warriors who, within the last few years, had annihilated two Egyptian armies. They had slaughtered Baker Pasha's superior numbers at Tokar and El Teb and left a wide road of bleached bones across the desert. When the wind came from the west the inhabitants of Suakin on the coast twenty miles away could still smell the unburied dead.

Many of the tribes under Osman Atalan had played a major role at the battle of El Obeid where General Hicks and his seven thousand had perished. They were the flower of the Dervish army, but in their multitudes they moved too slowly for a man such as Osman Atalan.

He felt the call of the open desert and the silence of wild lands. He left the teeming legions to continue the march towards the City of Infidels while he and a small band of his most trusted aggagiers ranged out on their horses to indulge in the most dangerous sport known to the bravest of the tribes.

As he reined in his steed on the crest of a long wooded ridge that overlooked the valley of the Atbara river, Osman Atalan cut a romantic, heroic figure. He wore no turban, and his thick black hair was parted down the middle and drawn into a long plait that hung to the level of the blue silk sash that girt the waist of his ornately patched *jibba*. He held the scabbard of his broadsword clamped under his right knee against the saddle. The hilt was exquisitely fashioned from rhinoceros horn with a patina like amber, and the blade was inlaid with gold and silver. Under the fine loose cloth of his *jibba* his body was lean and wiry, the muscles of his legs and arms like the woven sinews of a bowstring. When he swung down from the saddle he stood tall beside his horse's head and stared out across the wide land below, searching for the first glimpse of the chase. His eyes were large and dark with the thick, curling lashes of a beautiful woman, but his features seemed carved in old ivory, hard flesh and harder bone. He was a creature of the desert and the wild places, and there was no soft flesh on him. The inexorable sun had gilded but not blackened his skin.

His aggagiers rode up behind him and dismounted. The title of honour was reserved for those warriors who hunted the most dangerous game on horseback, armed only with the broadsword. They were men carved from the same stone as their lord. They loosened the girths of their horses' saddles, then tethered the animals in the shade. They watered them, pouring from the waterskins into leather buckets, then spread mats of plaited palm fronds before them and put down a small heap of dhurra meal for them to feed. They themselves did not drink or eat, for abstinence was part of their warrior tradition.

'If a man drinks copiously and often, he never learns to resist the sway of the sun and the sand,' the old men said.

While the horses rested the aggagiers took down their swords and shields from where they were tied to the saddles. They sat in a small, companionable group in the sunlight, and began to strop their blades on the cured giraffe hide of their shields. The hide of the giraffe was the toughest of all wild game, yet not so heavy as that of the buffalo or hippopotamus. The shields were round targes, unadorned with image or emblem, marked only by the blade of the enemy, or the claw and fang of the chase. Blade-honing was a pastime with which they filled their leisure, as much part of their life as breathing, more so than eating or drinking.

'We will sight the quarry before noon,' said Hassan Ben Nader, who was the emir's lance-bearer, 'praised be the Name of God.'

'In Allah's Name,' the others chorused softly.

'I have never seen a spoor such as this lead bull leaves upon the earth,' Hassan went on, speaking softly so that he did not offend his master or the djinns of the wilderness.

'He is the bull of all bulls,' they agreed. 'There will be sport for a man before the sun sets.'

They glanced sideways at Osman Atalan, showing respect by not staring at him directly. He was deep in contemplation, squatting with his elbows on his knees and his smooth-shaven chin in the cup of his hands.

There was silence except for the susurration of steel on leather. They paused in this endless activity only to test an edge with a thumb. Each blade was about three and a half feet in length, and double-edged. It was a replica of the broadswords of the crusaders that, centuries before, had so impressed the Saracens before the walls of Acre and Jerusalem. The most treasured blades had been forged from the steel of Solingen, and handed down from father to son. The marvellous temper of this metal imparted immense power to the blade, and it was capable of taking an edge like that of a surgeon's scalpel—the lightest stroke would split hide and hair, flesh and sinew to the deepest bone. A full stroke could divide an enemy at the waist, cutting him in two as effortlessly as though he were a ripe pomegranate. The scabbards were fashioned from two flat pieces of soft mimosa wood, held together and covered by the skin of an elephant's ear, dried hard and strong as iron. On the flat of the scabbard were two raised leather projections about twelve inches apart, which held the weapon securely under the horseman's thigh. Even at full gallop it would not flap and bounce in the ungainly manner of the swords of European cavalry.

The aggagiers rested while the high sun moved through an arc of three fingers across the sky. Then Osman Atalan rose to his feet, in a single flowing, graceful movement. Without a word the others rose also, went to their mounts and tightened the girths. They rode on down the slope of the valley, through open savannah in which the stately flat-topped acacia trees stood along the banks of the Atbara river. They dismounted beside one of the deep green pools. The elephant had been there before them. They had filled their bellies with water, then bathed riotously, hosing powerful jets from their trunks over themselves and the surrounding sandbanks. They had scooped up cartloads of thick black mud and plastered it on their heads and backs as protection against the sun and the swarms of biting insects. Then the three mighty grey beasts had wandered away along the bank, but the sand and mud they had left on the edges of the pool were so fresh that they were still damp.

The aggagiers whispered excitedly together, pointing out the huge round tracks of the largest bull. Osman Atalan laid his war shield upon one of the pad marks. The circumference exceeded the giraffe-skin targe by the breadth of his finger.

'In God's Name,' they murmured. 'This is a mighty animal, and worthy of our steel.'

'I have never seen a greater bull than this,' said Hassan Ben Nader. 'He is the father of every elephant that has ever lived.' They filled the waterskins and let the horses drink again, then mounted up and followed the trail through the open acacia forest. The three bulls were moving head on to the faint breeze so that they would detect any danger ahead. The aggagiers moved up quietly and intently behind them.

The lead bull had dropped a pile of bright yellow

dung in a clearing. It was stringy with chewed bark that he had stripped from the acacias, and lumpy with the stones of the Doum palm tree. A swarm of bright butterflies hovered over it. The scent was so strong that one horse snorted nervously. His rider calmed him with a reassuring touch on his neck.

They rode on, with Osman Atalan a length ahead. The trail was plain to see even from the distance of a hundred paces or more, for the bulls had ripped long slabs of bark from the boles of the acacias. The pale wounds were so raw and recent that they glistened with the running sap, which would dry into sticky black lumps of the precious gum arabic.

Emir Osman rose high in the stirrups and shaded his eyes to gaze forward. Almost half a mile ahead, the shaggy head of a tall Doum palm rose above the lesser trees of the savannah. Although the breeze was so faint as to be barely palpable the distant palm top was whipping from side to side as though it were being battered by a hurricane.

He looked back at his companions and nodded. They smiled, because they understood what they were witnessing. One of the bulls had placed his forehead against the bottle-shaped trunk of the palm and was shaking it with all his massive strength as though it were a sapling. This brought the ripe Doum nuts showering down on his head.

They reined in their steeds to a walk. The horses had scented the chase and were sweating and trembling with fear and excitement, for they knew what would happen next. Abruptly Osman laid his hand on his mount's withers. She was a creamy honey-coloured mare. She lifted her lovely Arabian head and flared the wide nostrils that were the mark of her breed, but stopped obediently. Her name was Hulu Mayya, Sweet Water, the most precious substance in this thirsty land. She was six years old and in her prime, swift as an oryx and as gentle as a kitten, but with the heart of a lioness. In the clamour of battle and the fury of the chase she never faltered.

Like her rider she stared ahead for the first glimpse of their quarry. Suddenly there he was, one of the lesser bulls standing separated from his companions, dozing under the spreading branches of a mimosa tree. The dappled shadows blurred his outline.

Osman gestured with his right hand, and they went forward, the horses stepping warily as though they expected a cobra to rear up under their hoofs. Almost imperceptibly the shapes of the other two beasts emerged from among the trees. One, tormented by the stinging flies, shook his head violently so that his ears clapped thunderously against his shoulders. His tusks gleamed dully in the shade, darkened by sap and vegetable juices to the colour of a meerschaum pipe stained by tobacco smoke. The curved and tapered pillars of ivory were so vast that the aggagiers grunted with satisfaction, and touched the hilts of their broadswords. The third bull was almost hidden by a patch of kittar thornbush. From this angle it was impossible to judge how his tusks compared with those of his companions.

Now that Osman Atalan had placed the position of each bull, he could plan his attack on them. First they must deal with the nearest, for if they passed across his wind their scent would be carried to him. The smell of man and horse would send him away at a rush, trumpeting the alarm to the others, and only hard riding would bring them up to the herd again. In a whisper that was barely a movement of his lips, but with expressive gestures of the hands Osman Atalan gave his commands to the aggagiers. From long experience each man knew what was expected of him.

The bull under the mimosa tree was angled half away from them, so when Osman led them forward again he circled out to the right, then came in more directly from behind. The eyesight of the elephant is poor, when compared with that of other creatures of the wild, such as the baboon and the vulture. But if it has difficulty distinguishing shape it picks up movement readily enough.

Osman dared not approach closer while he was mounted. He slipped from the saddle and girded up the hem of his *jibba* with the blue sash, leaving his legs covered only with baggy breeches. He tightened the straps of his sandals, then drew his broadsword. Instinctively he tried the edge and sucked the drop of blood that welled from the ball of his thumb. He tossed Sweet Water's reins to Hassan, and started towards the massive grey shape in the shade of the mimosa tree. The bull seemed as majestic as a three-decked man-o'-war. It seemed impossible that such a mighty beast could fall to the puny blade.

Osman stepped lithely and lightly with the grace of a dancer, carrying the sword in his right hand. However, he had bound the first hand's breadth of the blade above the cruciform crosspiece of the hilt with a strip of skin from the ear of a freshly killed elephant: now that this had dried and cured it formed a double grip for his left hand.

As he approached the bull he heard the soft rumbling of its belly—the animal was sharing its contentment and pleasure with the rest of the herd, who were also dozing in the somnolent midday heat nearby. The bull was swaying gently, and swishing lazily at the flies with his stubby tail; the wiry bunch of hair at the end was almost worn away with age. The gigantic stained tusks were so long and thick that the bull was resting the blunt tips on the hard-baked earth. His weathered, corrugated trunk hung slackly between the ivory shafts. He was fondling the sun-dried, bleached femur bone of a long-dead buffalo with the tip, rolling it against his front foot, then lifting it to his lips as if to taste it, rubbing it between the fleshy finger-like projections on each side of the nostril openings, much as an ancient Coptic priest might play with his beads as he sat dreaming in the sun.

Osman changed his grip, two-handed now for the fatal stroke, and moved down the bull's flank close enough to touch him with the point of the sword. The riven grey hide hung down in bunches around the bull's knees, and in loose flaps under his sagging belly, like the clothing of an old man, too baggy for his wizened body.

His aggagiers watched him with awe and admiration. A lesser warrior would have chosen to hamstring his quarry, approaching the unsuspecting beast from behind and, with swift double strokes, severing the main tendons and arteries in the back of the legs above the huge, splayed feet. That injury would allow the hunter to escape, but cripple and anchor the bull until the severed arteries had drained the life from him, a slow death that might take up to an hour. However,

93

to attempt the head-on approach as their emir was doing, increased the danger a hundredfold. Osman was now well within the arc of the trunk, which was capable of delivering a blow that would shatter every bone in his body. Those huge ears picked up the smallest sound, even a carefully controlled breath, and at such close quarters the rheumy little eyes would detect the slightest movement.

Osman Atalan stood in the bull's shadow, and looked up at one of those eyes. It seemed much too small for the huge grey head, and was almost completely screened by the thick fringe of colourless lashes as the bull blinked sleepily. The dangling trunk was also shielded by the thick yellow tusks. Osman had to entice the bull into extending it towards him. Any untoward movement, any incongruous sound would trigger a devastating response. He would be clubbed down by a blow from the trunk, or trampled under the pads of those great feet, or transfixed by an ivory tusk, then knelt upon and ground to bloody paste under the bulging bone of the bull's forehead.

Osman twisted the blade gently between his fists and, with the polished metal, picked up one of the stray sunbeams that pierced the leafy canopy above his head. He played the reflected sunbeam on to the bull's gently flapping ear, then directed it forward gradually until it shot a tiny diamond wedge of light into the bull's half-closed eye. The elephant opened his eye fully and it glittered as it sought out the source of this mild annoyance. He detected no movement other than the trembling spot of sunlight, and reached out his trunk towards it, not alarmed but mildly curious.

There was no need for Osman to adjust his

double grip on the hilt. The blade described a glittering sweep in the air, fast as the stoop of the hunting peregrine. There was no bone in the trunk to turn the blow so the silver blade sliced cleanly through it and half dropped to the ground.

The elephant reeled back from the shock and agony. Osman jumped back at the same instant and the bull spotted the movement and tried to lash out at it. But his trunk lay on the earth, and as the stump swung in an arc towards Osman, the blood hosed from the open arteries and sprayed in a crimson jet that soaked his *jibba*.

Then the bull lifted the stump of his amputated trunk and trumpeted in mortal anguish, his blood spraying back over his head and into his eyes. He charged into the forest, shattering the trees and thornbushes that blocked his path. Startled from the brink of sleep by his trumpeting screams, the other bulls fled with him.

Hassan Ben Nader spurred forward with Sweet Water on the rein. Osman snatched a lock of her long silky mane and leapt into the saddle without losing his grip on the hilt of his broadsword.

'Let the first bull run,' he cried. The pumping of the massive heart would drive the blood more swiftly out of the open arteries. The bull would weaken and go down within a mile. They would return for him later. Without checking his horse, Osman passed the spot where the dying animal had turned sharply aside. He rose in the stirrups more clearly to descry the trails of the two unwounded bulls. He followed them until they reached the first hills of the river valley where they parted company. One bull turned southwards and stormed away through the forest, while the other clambered straight up the rocky slope. There was no time to study the spoor and decide which was the larger animal, so Osman made an arbitrary choice.

He signalled with his raised sword and the aggagiers separated smoothly into two bands. The first party rode on up the escarpment after one animal, and Osman led the rest after the other. The dust of its flight hung in the still hot air, so there was no need to slow down to read the spoor. Sweet Water flew on for another mile until, four hundred paces ahead, Osman made out the dark hump of the bull's back crashing through the grey kittar thorn scrub, like a whale breaching in a turbulent sea. Now that he had the chase in sight Osman slowed Sweet Water to an easy canter, to save her strength for the final desperate encounter. Even at this pace they gained steadily on the bull.

Soon the gravel and small pebbles thrown up by the bull's great pads rattled against his shield and stung his cheeks. He slitted his eyes and rode in still closer, until the bull sensed his presence, and turned upon them with speed and nimbleness astonishing in such a massive beast. The horsemen scattered before his charge, but one of the aggagiers was not quick enough. The bull reached out with his trunk and, at full gallop, plucked him from the saddle. The broadsword with which he might have defended himself spun from his grip, throwing bright reflections of sunlight before it pegged into the hard earth and oscillated like a metronome. The bull turned aside and, with his trunk coiled round the aggagier's neck, swung the man against the trunk of a Doum palm with such force that his head was torn from his body, then knelt over the corpse and gored it with his tusks, driving the points through and through again.

Osman turned Sweet Water back and, although she tossed her long mane with terror, she responded to the pressure of his knees and his touch upon the reins. He rode her in directly across the bull's line of sight, and shouted a challenge to attract the animal's full attention, 'Ha! Ha!' he cried. 'Come, thou spawn of Satan! Follow me, O beast of the infernal world!'

The bull leapt up with the corpse dangling from one of his tusks. He shook his head and the dead man was hurled aside. Then he charged after Osman, squealing with rage, shaking his great head so that the ears flapped and volleyed like the mainsail of a ship-of-the-line taken all aback.

Sweet Water ran like a startled hare, carrying Osman swiftly away before the charge, but Osman slowed her with a lover's touch on the bit. Though he lay forward over her neck he was looking back under his arm. 'Gently, my sweetest heart.' He moderated her speed. 'We must tease the brute now.'

The bull realized he was gaining and thundered after them like a squadron of heavy cavalry. He thrust his head forward and reached out with his trunk. But the mare ran like a swallow skimming the surface of a lake to drink in flight. Osman kept her streaming tail an arm's length ahead of the tip of the waving trunk. The bull forced himself to even greater speed, but as he was about to snatch down the horse and her rider Osman pushed her gently so that she ran tantalizingly ahead, just beyond the bull's reach. Osman spoke softly into her ear and she turned it back to listen to his voice.

'Yes, my lovely. They are coming on.' Through

97

the dust of the bull's run he could make out the shapes of his aggagiers closing in. Osman was offering himself and his mount like the cape to the bull, giving his men the opportunity to ride in and deliver the lethal strokes. The elephant was so absorbed with the horseman in front of him that he was unaware of the men who rode up under his out-thrust tail. Osman watched Hassan Ben Nader leap lightly from the saddle to the ground right at the bull's pounding heels. His outrider seized the loose reins and held the head for the instant that Hassan needed.

As he touched the earth he used the impetus of his horse's gallop to hurl himself forward. As the bull placed his full weight on the nearest leg, the rope of the tendon bulged tightly under the thick grey hide. Hassan slashed his blade across the back of the fetlock, a hand's span above the point where the straining tendon was attached to the joint. The gleaming steel edge cut down to the bone, and the main tendon parted with a rubbery snap that, even in the uproar of the chase, carried clearly to Osman's ear. In the same instant Hassan Ben Nader snatched back the reins from his outrider and leapt into the saddle. His horse plunged into full gallop once more. It was a marvellous feat of horsemanship. With three lunges his horse had carried him clear of the bull's tusks and trunk.

The bull lifted his wounded leg from the earth and swung it forward to take the next pace, but as his full weight came down on to the pad, the leg buckled and the fetlock joint gave way. An elephant is unable to run on three legs, as other four-legged creatures can, so he was instantly crippled and anchored to the spot. Squealing with agony and rage he groped for his tormentor. Osman spun Sweet Water about and, with his heels, drove her back almost under the outstretched trunk, shouting at the bull to keep his attention riveted, turning just out of reach. The bull tried to chase him, but stumbled heavily and almost went down as the crippled leg gave way under his weight.

In the meantime Hassan had circled back and, again undetected by the struggling animal, rode in now under his tail. He jumped down once more, and then, to demonstrate his courage, let his steed run on as he stood alone at the bull's heel. He waited an instant for the bull's full weight to come down on its uninjured leg, and when the tendon stood out proud beneath the skin he severed it with the skill of a surgeon. Both of the bull's back legs gave way under him and he sank helplessly on to his haunches, screaming his anguish to the pitiless sky and the triumphant African sun.

Hassan Ben Nader turned his back on the struggling animal and walked away unhurriedly. Osman jumped down from Sweet Water and embraced him. 'Ridden like a man, and killed like a prince.' He laughed. 'This very day you and I shall take the oath and eat the salt of brotherhood together.'

'You do me too much honour,' Hassan whispered, and fell to his knees in homage, 'for I am your slave and your child, and you are my master and my father.'

They rested the horses in the shade and watered them from the skins while they watched the last struggles of their quarry. The blood spurted from the gaping arteries in the back of the bull's legs, in rhythm with the pulse of his heart. The earth beneath his pads dissolved into a bath of mud and blood, until his crippled legs slipped and slid as he shifted his weight. It did not take long. The bright crimson flow shrivelled, and the lassitude of approaching death settled over him. At last the air rushed out of his lungs in a long, hollow groan and he toppled on to his side, striking the earth with a sound that echoed off the hills.

'Five days from now I will send you back here with fifty men, Hassan Ben Nader, to bring in these tusks.' Osman stroked one of the huge ivory shafts that thrust up into the air higher than his head. It would take that long for the cartilage that held them in the bony sockets of the skull to soften with decay so that the great shafts could be drawn out undamaged by careless axe strokes. They mounted and rode easily back along their own spoor to find the first beast that Osman had attacked. By this time he, too, would have bled to death from the terrible wound. It would be easy to track him down to the spot where he had fallen, for he must have left a river of blood for them to follow.

They had not gone half a league before Osman held up a hand to halt them and cocked his head, listening. The sound that had alerted him came again from across the rocky ridge over which the other band of aggagiers had pursued the third bull. The intervening hills must have damped down the echoes so that they had not heard them before. The sound was unmistakable to these experienced hunters: it was the sound of an angry elephant, one that was neither crippled nor weakened by its wounds.

'Al-Noor has failed to kill cleanly,' said Osman. 'We must go to his aid.'

He led them up the slope at a gallop, and as they crossed the ridge the sounds of conflict were loud and close. Osman rode towards them, and found a dead horse lying where it had been struck down, its spine shattered by a blow from the bull's trunk. The aggagier had died upon its back. They rode past them without drawing rein, and found two more dead men. At a glance Osman read the signs: one had been unhorsed in the face of the charging animal. The hooked, red-tipped thorns of the kittar had plucked him from the saddle as he had tried to escape the bull's charge. The other dead man was his blood-brother, and he had turned back to save him. As they had lived so they died, their blood mingled and their broken bodies entwined. Their horses had run free.

The elephant trumpeted again. The sound was closer now, and sharper. It rang out from a forest of kittar not far ahead. They slammed their heels into the flanks of their mounts and galloped towards the kittar. As they approached, a rider broke at full gallop from out of the thorn barrier into the open. It was al-Noor on his grey, which was in the extremes of terror and exhaustion. Al-Noor was almost naked: his *jibba* had been ripped from his body by the thorns and his skin was lacerated as though it had been clawed by a wild beast. The grey was staggering, throwing out its hoofs sloppily at each stride, and was too far gone to see and avoid the antbear burrow in its path. It stumbled and almost went down, throwing al-Noor over its head, then ran on, leaving its rider stunned, in the track of the great bull elephant that burst out of the thorn forest behind him. This was the patriarch bull, whose tracks had first astounded them. There

101

was blood on one back leg but too high and too far forward to have struck the tendon. Al-Noor had inflicted a flesh wound that did not slow or impede the animal. As he came on, he held his head high to keep his long tusks clear of the thorn scrub and stony earth. They extended from his lip twice as far as a tall man could reach with both arms spread wide. They were as thick as a woman's thigh with almost no taper from lip to tip.

'Ten cantars a side!' Hassan shouted, amazed. This was a legendary animal, with almost two hundred pounds of ivory curving out on each side of his great grey head. Still dazed al-Noor rose shakily to his feet and stood, swaying drunkenly, with blood and dust coating his face. His back was turned to the charging bull, and he had lost his sword. The bull saw him, squealed again, and rolled his trunk back against his chest. Al-Noor turned. When he saw death descending upon him he raised his right hand, index finger extended as a sign that he died in Islam, and cried, 'God is great!' It was his moment of acceptance. He stood without fear to meet it.

'For me and for Allah!' Osman called to his mare, and Sweet Water responded with her last reserves of strength and speed. She dashed in under the vaulted arch of tusks, Osman flat on her neck. The bull's trunk was rolled. There was no target for his blade. He could only hope to draw the charge off the man. The bull's gaze was so focused on al-Noor that he was unaware of the horse and rider coming in from the flank until they flashed past, so close that Osman's shoulder glanced off one of the tusks. Then they were gone, like the darting flight of a sunbird. The bull wheeled aside, forsaking the standing man and following the more compelling focus of his rage. He charged after the horse.

'O beloved of Allah,' al-Noor shouted his gratitude after the emir who had saved him, 'may God forgive all your sins.'

Osman smiled grimly as the words floated to him above the murderous trumpeting, the clash of hoofs and bursting thorn scrub. 'God grant me a few more sins before I die,' he shouted back, and led the bull away.

Hassan and the other aggagiers rode in his wake, shouting and whistling to attract the bull's attention, but he held on after Sweet Water. The mare had run hard but she was not yet spent. Osman looked back under his arm and saw that the bull was coming on apace, so swiftly that neither Hassan nor any other could get into position to attack his vulnerable back legs. He looked ahead and saw that he was being driven into a trap. Sweet Water was running into a narrow open lead between dense stands of the kittar thorn, but her path was blocked by a solid wall of thorn. Osman felt her check under him. Then she turned her head, gazed back at her beloved rider, as if seeking guidance, and rolled her eyes until the red linings showed. White froth splattered from the corners of her mouth.

Then horse and rider ran into the kittar, which closed round them in a green wave. The thorns hooked into hide and cloth like eagle's talons, and almost at once Sweet Water's graceful run was transformed into the struggles of a creature caught in quicksand. The bull thundered down upon them, its mighty progress unchecked by the kittar.

'Come, then, and let us make an end.' Osman called the challenge, dropped the reins and kicked his feet out of the stirrups. He stood up, tall, upon the saddle, facing back over Sweet Water's rump, his eyes on the level of the bull's. Man and beast confronted each other over a rapidly dwindling gap.

'Take us if you are able,' Osman called to the bull, knowing how the sound of his voice would infuriate the animal. The bull flattened his ears against the sides of his skull, and rolled the tips in rage and aggression. Then he did what Osman had been waiting for: he unrolled his trunk and reached out to seize the man and lift him high off the back of his horse.

Balancing to Sweet Water's violent lunges and struggles, Osman held the long blade poised, and as the serrated grey trunk was about to close round his body, he struck. The steel whickered in flight, and dissolved into a silver blur of light. The stroke was full, and seemed to meet no resistance: the steel sliced through hide, flesh and sinews, as though they were mist. It severed the trunk close to the lip as smoothly as the guillotine blade takes off a condemned man's head.

For an instant there was no blood, just the sheen of freshly exposed flesh and the gleam of nerve ends and white tendons. Then the blood burst forth, engulfing the great grey head in a crimson cloud as the arteries erupted. The bull screamed again, but now in agony and dismay. Then he lurched to one side as he lost his balance and sense of direction.

Osman dropped back into the saddle and guided Sweet Water with his knees, steering her out of the arc of the bull's blood-dimmed eyesight. The animal blundered in a wide uncertain circle as Hassan rode in behind him to make the cut in the back of his left leg. Then he jumped back into the saddle, leaving the bull anchored by his crippled leg. Osman slipped down from Sweet Water's back and, with another stroke of his blade, cut through the other hamstring.

The heart blood pumped from the terrible wounds in his back legs and trunk, but the bull remained upright for as long as a mullah might take to recite a single *sura* of the Koran. Osman Atalan and his aggagiers dismounted and stood at their horses' heads to watch his death throes and pray for him, praising his might and courage. When at last he fell with a crash to the stony earth, Osman cried, 'Allah is almighty. Infinite is the glory of God.'

*   *   *

The word flashed through the alleys and souks, and was shouted from the rooftops and minarets. As it spread, a sombre, funereal mood descended on the city of Khartoum. Whispering dolefully as they came together, the inhabitants hurried to find a vantage-point from which they could gaze across the river and behold their fate.

Ryder Courtney was in the workshop in his compound behind the hospital and the red mud walls of Fort Burri when a servant brought him a note from David Benbrook, scribbled on a torn sheet of consular paper. Since first light that morning Ryder had been working with Jock McCrump on the repairs to the *Intrepid Ibis*. When they had disconnected the punctured steam piping they discovered more damage than they had first suspected. Some of the metal fragments had been carried into the cylinders and had scored the liners. It was surprising that they had been able to make the return trip to the harbour.

'Damn good job I didnae let you go tearing away at full throttle,' Jock muttered morosely. 'We would have had a right ballocks if I had.'

They had been obliged to sway the heavy engine out of the *Ibis*'s hull on to the stone jetty. Then they transported it to the compound by ox-wagon, taking a circuitous route to avoid the narrow alleyways. They had been working on it for the last ten days, and the repairs were almost completed. Ryder wiped his hands on a ball of cotton waste, then glanced through the note. He handed it to Jock. 'Do you want to come and watch the Lord Mayor's show?'

Jock grunted. With long tongs he lifted a glowing sheet of metal from the forge and carried it to the anvil. 'Like as not we'll be having a gutful of that worthy Oriental gentleman Osman bloody Atalan without running out to stare at him now.' He hefted the heavy blacksmith's hammer and began to pound the metal to shape. He ignored Ryder as he plunged it into a trough of water. It cooled in a hissing cloud of steam and Jock measured it critically. He was shaping a patch for one of the shell holes in *Ibis*'s hull. He was not satisfied with the result, and whistled tunelessly as he returned it to the forge. Ryder grinned and went out to the stables for his horse.

He crossed the canal on the earthen causeway, and rode through the scurrying crowds to the gates of the consular palace. He hoped to avoid running into General Gordon, and was pleased to see his unmistakable khaki-uniformed silhouette on the upper parapet of Mukran Fort with half a dozen members of his Egyptian staff gathered around him. Each man had either a telescope or a pair of field-glasses focused on the north bank of the Blue Nile, so Ryder was able to ride past the fort and reach the consulate without drawing their attention. He handed his horse over to one of the syces at the gate of the stableyard and strode through the barren gardens to the legation entrance of the palace. The sentries recognized him at once and saluted him as he entered the main foyer.

An Egyptian secretary came hurrying to meet him. Like everyone else he wore a nervous, worried expression. 'The consul is on top of the watch-tower, Mr Courtney,' the man told him. 'He asked you to be good enough to join him there.'

When Ryder stepped out on to the balcony the Benbrook family did not notice him immediately. They were grouped around the big telescope on its tripod. Amber was taking her turn, standing on a cane-backed chair to reach the eyepiece. Then Saffron looked round and let out a squeak of delight. 'Ryder!' She ran to seize his arm. 'You must come and see. It's so exciting.'

Ryder glanced at Rebecca, and felt a tightening in the pit of his stomach. She showed no ill effects from their recent curtailed voyage downstream. On the contrary, she looked cool, even under the layers of green georgette petticoats that ballooned out over her crinoline. There was a bright yellow ribbon around the crown of her straw hat, and her hair was arranged in ringlets over her shoulders. It caught the sunlight.

'Don't let that child pester you, Mr Courtney.' She gave him a demure smile. 'She has been in an overbearing mood since breakfast.'

'Overbearing means regal and queenly,' said Saffron, smugly.

'It does not.' Amber looked back at her from the telescope. 'It means bumptious and insufferable.'

'Peace be unto both of you.' Ryder chuckled. 'Sisterly love is a beautiful thing.'

'Glad you could come,' David called to him. 'Sorry to tear you away from your work, but this is worth a look. You have had enough of the telescope, Amber. Let Mr Courtney have a turn.'

Ryder stepped up to the parapet, but before he stooped to the eyepiece he stared out across the river. It was an extraordinary spectacle: as far as he could see the land seemed to be on fire. It took a moment to realize that this was not smoke that gave the sky a dun, fuming aspect, but the dustcloud thrown up by a vast moving mass of living things, human and animal, that stretched away to the eastern horizon.

Even at such a distance there was a low reverberation in the air, like the muted hum of the beehive, or the murmur of the sea on a windless day. It was the sound of braying donkeys, lowing herds, fat-tailed sheep and thousands of hoofs, marching feet, the creaking of camel burdens and the squeal of axles. It was the clatter of giraffe-hide war shields, of spears and blades rattling in their scabbards, the rumble of the gun-carriages and the ammunition train.

Then, more clearly, he heard the trumpeting of

the *ombeyas*, the Sudanese battle trumpets carved from a single ivory tusk. The warlike call of these instruments carried an immense distance in the desert airs. Underlying it was the throbbing bass beat of hundreds of huge copper drums. Each emir rode at the head of his tribe with his drummers, trumpeters and banner-bearers preceding him. He was closely surrounded by his *mulazemin*, his bodyguards, his brothers and blood-brothers, and his aggagiers. Though they rode united now by the holy *jihad* of the Divine Mahdi most of these tribes carried their centuries-old blood feuds, and none trusted another.

The banners were of rainbow hues, embroidered with texts from the Koran, and exaltations to Allah. Some were so large that it took three or four men to hold them aloft, rippling and snapping in the hot desert breeze. The banners and the harlequin-patched *jibbas* of the warriors made a gorgeous show against the drab landscape.

'How many do you estimate there are?' David asked, as though he was speaking about the race-day crowd on Epsom Down.

'The devil alone knows.' Ryder shook his head doubtfully. 'From here, we can't see the end of them.'

'Fifty thousand, would you hazard?'

'More,' said Ryder. 'Maybe many more.'

'Can you make out the entourage of Osman Atalan?'

'He will be in the van, naturally.' Ryder placed his eye to the telescope and trained it forward. He picked out the scarlet and black banners. 'There is the devil himself. Right at the forefront!'

'I thought you said you had never before laid

eyes upon him,' David said.

'No introduction necessary. That's him, I tell you.'

In all that hubbub and bustle the slim figure on the cream-coloured horse was unmistakable for its dignity and presence.

At that moment there was a sudden commotion among the vast congregation on the far bank. Through the telescope Ryder saw Osman rise in the stirrups and brandish his broadsword. The front ranks of his *mulazemin* broke into a furious charge, and he led them straight at a small group of horsemen that rode to meet them from the direction of Omdurman. As the masses of cavalry and camels dashed forward they discharged volleys of joyous gunfire into the air. The blue smoke mingled with the dustcloud, and the spearheads and sword blades twinkled like stars in the murk.

'Who is that they are riding to meet?' David asked sharply.

Through the lens Ryder concentrated on the small group of horsemen, and exclaimed as he recognized the green turbans of the two leading horsemen. 'Damme, if it's not the Divine Mahdi himself and his *khalifa*, the mighty Abdullahi.' Ryder tried to make his tone sardonic and pejorative, but no one was deceived.

'With that merry band of cut-throats sitting across it, the road to the north is firmly closed.' Although David said it breezily, there was a shadow in his eyes as he looked to his three daughters. 'There is no longer any escape from this wretched place.' Any retort that Ryder could make would have been fatuous, and they watched in silence the meeting of the men who held the fate of

110

the city and all its inhabitants in their bloody hands.

*   *   *

With bared sword and his long plait thumping against his back, Osman Atalan charged straight at the mounted figure of the Mahdi. The prophet of Allah saw him coming in a whirlwind of dust, to the deafening bray of the war horns and the pounding of drums. He reined in his white stallion. Khalifa Abdullahi stopped his horse a few paces behind his master, and they waited for the emir to come on.

Osman brought Sweet Water to a plunging, skidding halt and shook his broadsword in the Mahdi's face. 'For God and his Prophet!' he screamed. The blade that had slain men and elephants in their hundreds was now only a finger's breadth from the Mahdi's eyes.

The Mahdi sat unmoved with that serene smile on his lips and the *falja* showing between them.

Osman spun Sweet Water round and galloped away. His bodyguard and banner-bearers followed him at the same wild gallop, firing their Martini-Henry rifles into the air. At a distance of three hundred paces Osman rallied his men and they regrouped at his back. He lifted his sword high, and again they charged in a serried phalanx, straight at the two lone figures. At the last instant Osman pulled up the mare so violently that she came down on her haunches.

'*La ilaha illallah!* There is but one God!' he yelled. 'Muhammad Rasul Allah! Muhammad is the prophet of God!'

Five times the horsemen retreated and five times they charged back. At the fifth charge Muhammad

111

Ahmed, the Divine Mahdi, raised his right hand and said softly, '*Allah karim!* God is generous.'

Immediately Osman threw himself from Sweet Water's back and kissed the Mahdi's sandalled foot in the stirrup. This was an act of the utmost humility, a rendering up of one man's soul to another. The Mahdi smiled down at him tenderly. He emanated a peculiar perfume, a mixture of sandalwood and attar of roses, known as the Breath of the Mahdi. 'I am pleased that you have come to join my array and the *jihad* against the Turk and the infidel. Rise up, Osman Atalan. You are assured of my favour. You may enter with me into the city of Allah, Omdurman.'

*   *   *

On the flat roof of his house, the Mahdi sat cross-legged on a low *angareb*, a couch covered with a silk prayer rug and strewn with cushions. There was a screen of reed matting over the terrace to shield them from the sun, but the sides were open to the cooling breeze off the river and to provide a view across the wide expanse of the Victoria Nile to the city of Khartoum. The ugly square blockhouse of Mukran Fort dominated the defences of the besieged city. Emir Osman Atalan sat facing him, and a slave maid knelt before him with a dish of water on which floated a few oleander petals. Osman dipped water from it and made the ritual ablutions, then dismissed the woman with a wave. Another lovely Galla slave girl placed between them a silver tray that bore three jewelled long-stemmed silver cups: chalices looted from the Roman Catholic cathedral in El Obeid.

112

'Refresh yourself, Osman Atalan. You have travelled far,' the Mahdi invited him.

Osman made an elegant gesture of refusal. 'I thank you for your hospitality, but I have eaten and drunk with the dawn and I will not eat again until the setting of the sun.'

The Mahdi nodded. He knew of the emir's frugality. He was well aware of the peculiar religious enlightenment and the sense of dedicated purpose brought on by fasting and denial of the appetite. The memories of his sojourn on Abbas Island were as fresh as if it had taken place the previous day, and not three years before. He lifted a silver cup to his lips, displaying for an instant the gap between his front teeth, sign of his divinity. Of course, he never drank alcohol but he was partial to a drink made from date syrup and ground ginger.

Once he had been lean and hard as this fierce desert warrior, but he was no longer a solitary hermit. He was the spiritual leader of a nation, chosen by God. Once he had been a barefoot ascetic who had denied himself all sensual pleasures. Not long ago it had been boasted through all the Sudan that Muhammad Ahmed had never known a woman's body. He was virgin no longer and his harem contained the first fruits of all his mighty victories. His was first choice of the captured women. Every sheikh and emir brought him gifts of the most lovely young girls in their territory, and it was a political imperative that he accept their largesse. The numbers of his wives and concubines already exceeded a thousand, and increased each day. His women fascinated him. He spent half his days among them.

They were dazzled by his appearance, his height and grace, his fine features, the winged birthmark and the angelic smile that disguised all his emotions. They loved his perfume and the gap between his teeth. They were intoxicated by his wealth and power: his treasury, the Beit el Mal, held gold, jewels and millions in specie, the spoils of his conquests and the sack of the principal cities of the Nile. The women sang, 'The Mahdi is the sun of our sky, and the water of our Nile.'

Now he set aside the silver cup and held out his hand. One of the waiting girls knelt to offer him a scented silk cloth with which to dab the sticky syrup from his lips.

Behind the Mahdi, on another cushioned *angareb*, sat the Khalifa Abdullahi. He was a handsome man with chiselled features and a nose like the beak of an eagle, but his skin was dappled, like a leopard's, with the scars of smallpox. His nature was also that of the leopard, predatory and cruel. Emir Osman Atalan feared no man or beast, except these two men who sat before him now. These he feared with all his heart.

The Mahdi lifted one gracefully shaped hand and pointed across the river. Even with the naked eye they were able to make out the solitary figure on the parapets of the Mukran Fort.

'There is Gordon Pasha, the son incarnate of Satan,' said the Mahdi.

'I will bring his head to you before the beginning of Ramadan,' said his *khalifa*.

'Unless the infidel reaches him before you do,' suggested the Mahdi, and his voice was soft and pleasant to hear. He turned to Osman. 'Our scouts report to us that the infidel army is at last on the

114

move. They are sailing southwards in a flotilla of steamers along the river to rescue our enemy from my vengeance.'

'At the beginning they will move at the pace of the chameleon.' The *khalifa* endorsed his master's report. 'However, once they pass through the cataracts and reach the bend of the river at Abu Hamed, they will have the north wind behind their boats and the current will abate. The speed of their advance will increase six-fold. They will reach Khartoum before Low Nile, and we cannot assault the city before the river falls and exposes Gordon Pasha's defences.'

'You must send half of your army northwards under your most trustworthy sheikhs and stop the infidels on the river before they reach Abu Klea. Then you must annihilate them, just as you destroyed the armies of Baker Pasha and Hicks Pasha.' The Mahdi stared into Osman's face, and Osman's spirits stirred. 'Will you deliver to me my enemy, Osman Atalan?'

'Holy One, I will give him into your hands,' Osman replied. 'In God's Name and with the blessing of Allah, I will deliver to you that city and all those within.' The three warriors of God gazed across the Nile like hunting cheetahs surveying herds of grazing gazelle upon the plains.

*   *   *

Captain Penrod Ballantyne had been waiting in the antechamber of Her Britannic Majesty's consulate in Cairo for forty-eight minutes. He checked the time on the clock above the door to the inner office of the consul general. On the left-hand side of the massive carved door hung a life-sized portrait of Queen Victoria as she had been on her wedding day, pure and pretty with the bloom of youth still on her and the crown of Empire on her head. On the opposite side of the door there was a matching portrait of her consort, Albert of Saxe-Coburg and Gotha, handsome and marvellously bewhiskered.

Penrod Ballantyne shot a glance at himself in the gilt-framed ceiling-high mirror that adorned the side wall of the antechamber and, with satisfaction, noted his own likeness to the young Prince Consort, now long dead while Penrod was young and vital. The captain's epaulettes on his shoulders and the frogging of his uniform jacket were bright new gold. His riding boots were polished to a glassy sheen, and the fine glove leather creased around his ankles like the bellows of an accordion. His cavalry sabre hung down along the scarlet side stripe of his riding breeches. He wore his dolman slung over one shoulder and clasped at his throat with a gold chain, and carried his Hussar's bearskin busby under his right arm. On his left breast he wore the purple watered silk with the bronze cross inscribed 'For Valour', which had been cast from the Russian guns captured at Sebastopol. There was no higher military decoration in the Empire.

Sir Evelyn Baring's secretary came in. 'The consul general will see you now.'

Penrod had been standing to preserve the pristine appearance of his uniform—creases at the elbows, down the back of his tunic and at the knees of his breeches were unsightly. He replaced the tall busby on his head, glancing in the mirror to make certain it was centred low on his eyebrows with the chain across the chin, then marched through the carved doors into the inner office.

Sir Evelyn Baring was seated at his desk, reading from a sheaf of despatches in front of him. Penrod came to attention and saluted. Baring beckoned him in without glancing at him. The secretary closed the door.

Sir Evelyn Baring was officially the agent of Her Britannic Majesty's Government in Egypt, and her consul general in Cairo with plenipotentiary powers. In truth he was the viceroy, who ruled the ruler of Egypt. Since the Khedive had been saved from the mobs of rebellion by the British Army and the fleet of the Royal Navy in Alexandria harbour, Egypt had become, in all but name, a British protectorate.

The Khedive Tawfig Pasha was a weak youth and no match for a man like Baring and the mighty Empire he represented. He had been forced to abdicate all his powers, and in return the British had given him and his people the peace and prosperity they had not known since the age of Pharaoh Ptolemy. Sir Evelyn Baring possessed one of the most brilliant minds in the colonial service. The Prime Minister, William Gladstone, and his cabinet were aware of and highly appreciative of his qualities. However, towards his underlings, his manner was patronizing and condescending. Behind his back they called him 'Sir Over Bearing'.

Now he ignored Penrod as he went on with his reading, making notes in the margins with a gold pen. At last he stood up from his desk, and left Penrod standing while he went to the windows that overlooked the river to Giza and the stark silhouettes of the three mighty pyramids on the far bank.

That damned idiot, Baring mused to himself. He has got us into this pretty pickle of rotten fish. From the outset he had opposed the appointment of Chinese Gordon. He had wanted to send Sam Baker, but Gladstone and Lord Hartington, the Secretary of War, had overruled him. It is in Gordon's nature to provoke conflict. The Sudan was to be abandoned. His job was to bring our people out of that doomed land, not to confront the Mad Mahdi and his Dervishes. I warned Gladstone of precisely this, Gordon is trying to dictate terms and force the Prime Minister and the cabinet to send an army to reoccupy the Sudan. If it were not for the unfortunate citizens that he has incarcerated with him, and for the honour of the Empire, we should let Chinese Gordon stew in his own juice.

As Baring turned away from the window and the contemplation of those immemorial monuments across the Nile, his eye fell on a copy of *The Times* of London that lay on the table beside his favourite armchair. He frowned more deeply. And then we have also to take into account the uninformed and sentimental opinions of the sweating masses, so readily manipulated by those petty potentates of the press.

He could almost recite the leading article from memory: 'We know that General Gordon is surrounded by hostile tribes and cut off from communication with Cairo and London. Under these circumstances the House has the right to ask Her Majesty's Government whether they are going to do anything to relieve him. Are they going to remain indifferent to the fate of the one man on whom they have counted to extricate them from their dilemmas, to leave him to shift for himself, and make not a single effort on his behalf?' was what Lord Randolph Churchill had said to the Commons, as reported on 16 March 1885. Damned demagogue! Baring thought now, and looked up at the Hussar captain. 'Ballantyne, I want you to go back to Khartoum.' He spoke directly to Penrod for the first time since he had entered the room.

'Of course, sir. I can leave within the hour,' Penrod responded. He knew that the one word the master of Egypt liked to hear above all others was 'yes'.

Baring allowed himself a wintry smile, an extraordinary mark of his approval. His intelligence system was wide-reaching and pervasive. Its roots burrowed into every level of Egyptian society, from the highest levels of the government and the military to the forbidden councils of the mullahs in their mosques and the bishops in their cathedrals and Coptic monasteries. He had his agents in the palaces of the Khedive and the harems of the pashas, in the souks, bazaars and brothels of the greatest cities and the meanest villages.

Penrod was nothing but a tiny tadpole in the festering swamp of intrigue in whose waters Sir Evelyn Baring set his lines and into which he cast his net. However, recently he had become quite fond of the lad. Behind the good looks and dandified appearance, Baring had detected a bright, quick mind and an attention to duty that reminded him of himself at the same age. Penrod Ballantyne's family connections were solid. His elder brother was a baronet and had large estates on the Scottish Borders. He himself had a significant income from a family trust, and the purple ribbon on his chest bore ample witness to his courage. Moreover, the young dog had shown a natural aptitude for intelligence work. Indeed, he was gradually and subtly making himself valuable— not indispensable, for nobody was that, but valuable. The only possible weakness that Baring had so far detected in him he carried in his trousers.

'I will give you no written message, for the usual reasons,' he said.

'Naturally, sir.'

'There is one message for General Gordon, and another for David Benbrook, the British consul. The messages are not to be confused. It may seem to you that they are contradictory, but pray do not let that trouble you.'

'Yes, sir.' Penrod divined that Baring trusted Benbrook well enough because he lacked brilliance. Just as he trusted Chinese Gordon not at all because of his brilliance.

'This is what you are to convey to them.' Baring spoke for half an hour without consulting any slip of paper, barely pausing to draw breath. 'Have you got that, Ballantyne?'

'I have, sir.'

One of the fellow's assets is his appearance, Baring thought. No one can readily believe that behind those whiskers and those wonderfully pleasing features is a mind that can assimilate such a lengthy, complicated message at the first recital, then deliver it accurately a month later. 'Very well,' he said flatly. 'But you must impress on General Gordon that Her Majesty's Government has no intention whatsoever of reconquering the Sudan. The British Army now making its way up the Nile is in no way an expeditionary force. It is not an army of reoccupation. It is a rescue column of minimal strength. The objective of the desert column is to insert a small body of regular first-line troops into Khartoum to bolster the defences of the city long enough for us to evacuate all our people. Once this has been achieved we intend to abandon the city to the Dervish and come away.'

'I understand, sir.'

'As soon as you have delivered your messages to Benbrook and Gordon you are to return northwards and join Stewart's relief column. You will act as guide, lead him across the bight of the Nile to where Gordon's own steamers are waiting at Metemma to take them upriver. You will attempt to keep in contact with me. The usual codes, mind.'

'Of course, Sir Evelyn.'

'Very well, then. Major Adams of General Wolseley's staff is waiting for you on the second floor. I understand that you are acquainted with him.'

'I am, sir.' Of course Baring knew that Penrod had won his VC by rescuing Samuel Adams from the bloody battlefield of El Obeid.

'Adams will give you a more detailed briefing, and provide you with the passes and requisitions you will need. You can catch the Cook's steamer this evening and be in Assouan by Tuesday noon. From there you are on your own. How long to Khartoum, Ballantyne? You have made the journey many times before.'

'It depends on conditions in the Desert of the Mother of Stones. If the wells are holding I can cut the great S-bend of the river and reach Khartoum in twenty-one days, sir,' Penrod answered crisply. 'Twenty-six at the outside.'

Baring nodded. 'Make it twenty rather than twenty-six. Let yourself out.' Baring dismissed him, without offering to shake hands. He was lost in his despatches again before Penrod reached the door. It was not important to Baring that people liked him. Only that they did their job.

*   *   *

Colonel Sam Adams was delighted to see Penrod again. He was walking with only a single stick now. 'The sawbones tells me I'll be playing polo again by Christmas.' Neither mentioned the long ride back from the battlefield of El Obeid. All that needed to be said on that subject had been said long ago, but Adams glanced admiringly at the bronze cross on Penrod's chest.

Penrod composed a cipher telegraph to the intelligence officer with the vanguard of the Desert Column that was assembling at Wadi Halfa eight hundred miles up the Nile. Adams's adjutant took it to the telegraphist on the ground floor and returned with the confirmation that it had been sent and received. Then Colonel Adams invited Penrod to lunch at Shephard's Hotel, but Penrod begged a prior engagement. As soon as he had his travel papers he left. A groom had his charger at the gate and it was less than half an hour's ride along the riverbank to the Gheziera Club.

Lady Agatha was waiting for him on the Ladies' Veranda. She was just twenty and the youngest daughter of a duke. Viscount Wolseley, the commander-in-chief of the British Army in Egypt,

122

was her godfather. She had an income of twenty thousand a year. Added to this, she was blonde, petite and exquisite, but an enormous handful for any man.

'I would rather have the French clap than Lady Agatha,' Penrod had recently overheard a wag remark at the Shephard's bar, and had been undecided whether to laugh or call the fellow outside. In the end he had bought him a drink.

'You are late, Penrod.' She was reclining in a cane chair and pouted as he came up the steps from the garden. He kissed her hand, then glanced at the clock over the garden entrance to the dining room. She saw the gesture. 'Ten minutes can be an eternity.'

'Duty, I am afraid, my lovely. Queen and country.'

'How utterly boring. Get me a glass of champagne.' Penrod looked up, and a waiter in a long white *galabiyya* and tasselled fez appeared as miraculously as a genie from the lamp.

When the wine came, Agatha sipped it. 'Grace Everington is getting married on Saturday,' she said.

'A mite sudden?'

'No, actually, just in time. Before it begins to show.'

'I hope she enjoyed the chase.'

'She tells me no, not at all, but her father is being beastly and says she must go through with it. Family honour. It is to be quiet and discreet, of course, but I have an invitation for you. You may escort me. It might be fun to watch her making an ass of herself, and of him.'

'I am sorry to say it but by then I shall be far

away.'

Agatha sat up straight. 'Oh, God! No! Not again. Not so soon.'

Penrod shrugged. 'I was given no choice.'

'When are you leaving?'

'In three hours' time.'

'Where are they sending you?'

'You know better than to ask.'

'You can't go, Pen. The reception at the Austrian embassy is tomorrow evening. I have a new dress.' He shrugged again. 'When will you come back?'

'That is blowing in the wind.'

'Three hours,' she said, and stood up. The movement attracted the gaze of every man on the veranda. 'Come!' she commanded.

'Lunch?' he asked.

'I think not.' Her family kept a permanent suite at Shephard's, and Penrod rode beside her open gharry. As the door to the suite closed she pounced on him, like a kitten on a ball of wool, lithe, playful and earnest all at once. He picked her up easily and carried her through to the bedroom.

'Be quick!' she ordered. 'But not too quick.'

'I am an officer of the Queen, and an order is an order.'

Later, she watched him as he dressed again while she lay stretched full length, languid and replete, inviting his appraisal. 'You won't find better than this, Penrod Ballantyne.' She cupped her hands under her breasts. They were pale and large in comparison to her girlish waist. She squeezed out her nipples, and he paused to watch her. 'You see? You do like it. When will you marry me?'

'Ah! May we apply ourselves to that question at some later date?'

'You are an utter beast.' She combed her fingers through the mist of strawberry curls at the base of her belly. 'Should I pluck myself here? The Arab girls do.'

'Your information on that subject is probably more accurate than mine.'

'I heard that you like Arab girls.'

'Sometimes you are amusing, Lady Agatha. At other times you are not. Sometimes you behave like a lady, and at others not at all.' He slung his dolman over his shoulder and adjusted the chain as he turned to the door.

She flew off the bed like a wounded leopard, and he only just had time to turn and defend himself. She went for his eyes with her sharp, pearly talons. But he seized her wrists. She tried to bite his face, small white teeth clicking together an inch from his nose. He bent her backwards so she could not reach. She kneed at his groin, but he caught the blow on his thigh and turned her round. She was helpless in the circle of his arms with her back to his chest. She pressed her firm round buttocks into him, felt him swelling and hardening, and gave a breathless but triumphant little laugh. She stopped struggling, sank to her knees and lifted high the twin half-moons of her buttocks. She wriggled her thighs apart so that the nest of pink curls peeked out between them. 'I hate you!' she said.

He dropped down behind her, still booted and spurred, his sabre belted at his side. He ripped open the front of his breeches, and she screamed involuntarily as he transfixed her. When he stood up again she collapsed and lay panting at his feet.

'How do you always know what I want you to do? How do you always know what to say, and when to say it? That terrible name you called me a moment ago was like chilli powder on a sweet mango—it took my breath away. How do you know these things?'

'Some might call it genius, but I am too modest to agree.'

She looked up at him. Her hair was tangled and her cheeks were flushed rosily. 'Call me that again.'

'No matter how richly you deserve it, once is enough for now.' He went to the door.

'When will you come back?'

'Perhaps soon, perhaps never.'

'You beast. I hate you. I truly hate you.' But he was gone.

*   *   *

Three days later Penrod stepped off the fast steamer at the Assouan jetty. He was wearing tropical khaki uniform without decorations or regimentals. He had exchanged the busby for a pith helmet with a wide brim. There were at least another fifty soldiers and officers within sight who were dressed almost identically, so he excited no attention. A ragged porter in a filthy turban seized his kit-bag and ran ahead of him into the maze of streets of the old town. Striding out on long legs Penrod kept him in sight.

When they reached the gate in a nondescript mud wall at the end of the narrow, twisted alley, Penrod tossed the porter a piastre and retrieved his bag. He tugged the bell cord and listened to the familiar chimes. After a while there were footsteps beyond the gate, soft and faltering, and a voice quavered, 'Who is it that calls? There is nothing here for we are poor widows and deserted by God.'

'Open this gate, you houri of Paradise,' Penrod replied, 'and swiftly, before I kick it down.'

There was a moment's stunned silence, broken at last by a wild cackle of laughter and a fumbling at the bolts. Then they were shot back and the gate creaked open. An ancient head, like a turtle's but partly covered with a widow's veil peered round the jamb. The gaping grin exposed two crooked teeth widely separated by an expanse of pink gum. 'Effendi!' The old woman squealed, and her entire face puckered with wrinkles. 'Lord of a thousand virtues.'

Penrod embraced her.

'You are shameless,' she protested with delight. 'You threaten my virtue.'

'I am fifty years too late to pluck that fruit.' He let her go. 'Where is your mistress?'

Old Liala glanced significantly across the courtyard. In the centre of the garden a fountain splashed into a pool in which Nile perch circled tranquilly. Around its border stood statues of the pharaohs: Seti, Thutmose and great Rameses, lifted from their tombs by grave-robbers back in the mists of time. It never failed to amaze him that such treasures were displayed in so humble a setting.

Penrod strode across the courtyard. His heart beat faster. He had not realized until that moment how much he had been looking forward to seeing her again. When he reached the beaded curtain that covered the doorway he paused to regain his composure, then jerked it aside and stepped

127

through. At first she was merely a dim, ethereal presence, but then his eyes adjusted and her shape emerged from the cool gloom. She was slim as a lily stem, but her robe was shot with gold thread, and there was gold at her wrists and ankles. As she came towards him, her bare henna-painted feet made no sound on the tiles. She stopped in front of him and made obeisance, touching her fingertips to her lips and her heart.

'Master!' she whispered. 'Master of my heart.' Then she hung her head and waited in silence.

He lifted the veil and studied her face. 'You are beautiful, Bakhita,' he told her, and the smile that blossomed over her features enhanced that beauty a hundredfold. She lifted her chin and looked at him, and her eyes glowed so that they seemed to light the dimmest recesses of the room.

'It has been only twenty-six days, but it seems like all my life,' she said, and her voice quivered like the strings of a lute plucked by skilled fingers.

'You have counted the days?' he asked.

'And the hours also.' She nodded. Roses coloured the waxen perfection of her cheeks, and the long lashes meshed over her eyes as she glanced away shyly. Then her eyes crept back to his face.

'You knew I was coming?' he accused her. 'How could you when I did not know it myself?'

'My heart knew, as the night knows the coming of dawn.' She touched his face as though she were blind and trying to remember something with her fingertips. 'Are you hungry, my lord?'

'I am famished for you,' he replied.

'Are you thirsty, my lord?'

'I thirst for you as a traveller thirsts for the

waterhole when he has been hunting seven days in the desert under the relentless sun.'

'Come,' she whispered, and took his hand. She led him into the inner room. Their *angareb* stood in the centre of the floor and he saw that the linen upon it had been washed, bleached and smoothed with a hot iron, until it shone like the saltpan of Shokra. She knelt before him and removed his uniform. When he stood naked she rose and stepped back to admire him. 'You bring me vast treasure, lord.' She reached out and touched him. 'An ivory sceptre, tipped with the ruby of your manhood.'

'If this is treasure, then show me what you bring in exchange.'

Naked, her body was moon pale, and her breasts bulged weightily, the nipples as large as ripe grapes, wine dark and swollen. She wore only a slim gold chain round her waist, and her belly was rounded and smooth as polished granite from the quarries above the first cataract. Her hands and feet were decorated with fine acanthus-wreath patterns of henna.

She shook out the dark tresses of her hair, and came to lie beside him on their mattress. He gloated over her with his eyes and fingertips, and she moved softly as his hands dictated, raising her hips and twisting her shoulders so that her bosom changed shape and no secret part of her body was hidden from him.

'Your quimmy is so beautiful, so precious, that Allah should have set it in the forehead of a ravening lion. Then only the valiant and the worthy might dare to possess it.' There was wonder in his voice. 'It is like a ripe fig, warmed in the sun, splitting open and running with sweet juices.'

'Feast to your heart's content upon the fig of my love, dear lord,' she whispered huskily.

Afterwards they slept entwined and their own sweat cooled them. At last old Liala brought them a bowl of dates and pomegranates, and a jug of lemon sherbet. They sat cross-legged on the *angareb* facing each other and Bakhita made her report to him. There was much for her to relate, great and dire news from the south, from Nubia and beyond. The Arab tribes were all in a state of flux and change, new alliances forged and century-old ties broken. At the centre of all this turmoil sat the Mahdi and his *khalifa*, two venomous spiders at the centre of their web.

Bakhita was older than Penrod by three years. She had been the first wife of a prosperous grain merchant, but she was unable to bear him a child. Her husband had taken a younger woman to wife, a dull-witted creature with broad, childbearing hips. Within ten months she had given birth to a son. From this position of marital power she had importuned her husband. He had tried to resist her, for Bakhita was clever and loyal and with her business acumen he had doubled his fortune in five short years. However, in the end the mother of his son had prevailed. Sorrowfully he had spoken the dread words: '*Talaq! Talaq! Talaq!* I divorce thee!' Thus Bakhita had been cast into that terrible limbo of the Islamic world inhabited only by widows and divorced women.

The only paths that seemed open to her were to find an old husband with many wives who needed a slave without having to pay the headprice, or to sell herself as a plaything to passing men. But she had honed the wiles of a merchant while serving her husband. With the few coins she had saved she bought shards of ceramics and chipped, damaged images of the ancient gods from the Bedouin and from the orphans who scratched in the ruins, the dry riverbeds and nullahs of the desert, then sold them to the white tourists who came up the river on the steamers from the delta.

She paid a fair price, took a modest profit and kept her word, so soon the diggers and grave-robbers brought her porcelain and ceramics, religious statuettes, amulets and scarabs that, after four thousand years, were miraculously perfect. She learnt to decipher the hieroglyphics of the ancient priests on these relics, and the writings of the Greeks and Romans who came long after them; Alexander and the Ptolemy dynasty, Julius Caesar and Octavian who was also Augustus. In time her reputation spread wide. Men came to her little garden to trade and to talk. Some had travelled down the great river from as far afield as Equatoria and Suakin. With them they brought news and tidings that were almost as precious as the trade goods and the relics. Often the men talked more than they should have for she was very beautiful and they wanted her. But they could not have her: she trusted no man after what the man she had once trusted had done to her.

Bakhita learnt what was happening in every village along the course of the great river, and in the deserts that surrounded it. She knew when the sheikh of the Jaalin Arabs raided the Bishareen, and how many camels he stole. She knew how many slaves Zubeir Pasha sent down to Khartoum in his dhows, and the taxes and bribes he paid to

131

the Egyptian governor in the city. She followed intimately the intrigues of the court of Emperor John in high Abyssinia, and the trade manifests in the ports of Suakin and Aden.

Then one day a small ragged urchin came to her with a coin wrapped in a filthy rag that was like no coin she had seen before or since. It filled the palm of her hand with the weight of fine gold. On the obverse was the portrait of a crowned woman, and on the reverse a charioteer wearing a laurel wreath. The surfaces were so pristine that they seemed to have been struck the previous day. She was able to read the legend below each portrait readily. The couple on the coin were Cleopatra Thea Philopator and Marcus Antonius. She kept the coin and showed it to no one, until one day a man came into her shop. He was a Frank and for a while she was speechless, for in profile he was the image of the Anthony on her coin. When she recovered her tongue, they talked for a while with Bakhita veiled and old Liala sitting in close attendance as chaperone. The stranger spoke beautiful poetic Arabic, and soon he did not seem to be a stranger. Without knowing it she began to trust him a little.

'I have heard that you are wise and virtuous, and that you may have items to sell that are beautiful and rare,' he asked at last.

She sent Liala away on some pretext, and when she poured another thimble of thick black coffee for her guest she contrived to let her veil slip so that he could glimpse her face. He started, and stared at her until she readjusted it. They went on speaking but something hung in the air, like the promise of thunder before the first winds of the *khamsin*.

Bakhita was gradually overtaken by an overpowering urge to show him the coin. When she placed it in his hand he studied the portraits gravely, then said, 'This is our coin. Yours and mine.' She bowed her head in silence and he said, 'Forgive me, I have offended you.'

She looked up at him and removed the veil so he could look into her eyes. 'You do not offend me, Effendi,' she whispered.

'Then why do your eyes fill with tears?'

'I weep because what you said is true. And I weep with joy.'

'You wish me to leave now?'

'No, I wish you to stay as long as your heart desires.'

'That may be a long time.'

'If it is God's will,' she agreed.

In the years that followed that first meeting she had given him everything that was in her power to give, but in exchange had asked from him nothing that he would not give freely. She knew that one day he would leave her, for he was young and came from a world where she could never follow him. He had made her no promise. At their first meeting he had said, 'That may be a long time,' but he had never said, 'always'. So she did not try to exact a pact from him. The certainty of the ending added a poignancy to her love that was sweet as honey and bitter as the wild melon of the desert.

This day she sat with him and told him all she had learnt since they had last spoken twenty-six days before. He listened and asked questions, then wrote it all out on five pages from his despatch notebook. He did not need to consult a cipher for he had learnt by heart the code that Sir Evelyn

Baring had given him.

Old Liala covered her head with her widow's cloak and slipped out into the alley carrying the despatch tucked into her intimate undergarments. The sergeant of the guard at the British military base knew her as a regular visitor. He was under strict orders from the base intelligence officer, so he personally escorted her to the headquarters building. Within the hour the message was buzzing down the telegraph line to Cairo. The following morning it had been deciphered by the signals clerk at the consulate and the *en clair* text was on the consul general's silver tray when he came in from breakfast.

Once she had sent Liala to the base with the report, Bakhita came back to Penrod. She knelt beside his stool and began to trim his sideburns and moustache. She worked quickly and, with the expertise of long practice, had soon reduced his fashionable whiskers to the ragged shape of a poor Arab *fellah*. Then she turned to his dense wavy curls and the tears slid down her cheeks as she hacked them away.

'They will soon grow again, my dove.' Penrod tried to console her as he ran his hand over the stubble.

'It is like murdering my own child,' she whispered. 'You were so beautiful.'

'And I will be beautiful again,' he assured her.

She gathered up his uniform from where it lay in the corner of the room. 'I will not let even Liala touch it. I will wash it with my own hands,' she promised him. 'It will await your return, but never as eagerly as I.'

Then she brought the cloth bag in which she had

134

kept his stained and ragged clothing from his last journey to the south. She wound the filthy turban round his cropped head. He strapped the leather purse round his waist and tucked the service revolver into the light canvas holster, then slipped the curved blade of the dagger into its sheath beside the Webley. They would not show under his dirty *galabiyya*. Then he strapped on a pair of rough camel-hide sandals and was ready to leave.

'Stay with God, honoured lady.' He bowed obsequiously and she was amazed at how easily he had made the transformation from swaggering Hussar to humble peasant, from *effendi* to *fellah*.

'Return to me soon,' she murmured, 'for if you perish, I shall perish with you.'

'I shall not perish,' he promised.

*   *   *

The harbour master took only a glance at the military travel pass before he assigned Penrod to the gang of stevedores on the next ammunition ship to leave for the south. Penrod wondered again if the elaborate precautions he was taking to avoid recognition were truly necessary. Then he reminded himself that the owner of almost every black or brown face in the swarming docks was a sympathizer of the Dervish. He knew also that he was a marked man. His heroics at El Obeid had been widely discussed, for they were the one blemish on a perfect victory for the Mahdi and his *khalifa*. Bakhita had warned him that when his name was uttered in the souks along the riverfront it was with a frown and a curse.

The steamer's cargo was made up entirely of

military stores for the army, which was assembling at Wadi Halfa in preparation for the drive upriver. The loading continued all that night and most of the next day. It had been a long time since Penrod had indulged in such hard and debilitating labour. A pause to straighten an aching back or even the slightest hesitation invited the flick and snap of the kurbash whip from one of the overseers. It required all his self-restraint to grovel to the blows and not retaliate with a clenched fist. The ship settled lower into the water as the heavy ammunition cases were heaped on her decks. At sunrise as she left the wharf, pulled into the channel of the river and thrust her ugly round bows into the current she had less than two feet of free board.

Penrod found a space between the tall piles of crates and stretched out in it. He clasped his skinned knuckles and raw fingers under his armpits. He ached in every joint and muscle. It was almost twenty hours' steaming against the stream to the port of Wadi Halfa. He slept for most of the voyage, and was fully recovered by the time they arrived early the next morning. Fourteen larger steamers were anchored in the main stream of the river. On the south bank was a vast encampment, lines of white canvas tents and mountainous piles of military stores. Boatloads of helmeted troops were being ferried out to the steamers by nuggars and small dhows.

Sir Evelyn Baring had explained the rescue-expedition plan in detail. This was the River Division of the double-pronged advance southwards. The flotilla was preparing to set out on the detour around the great western bend of the river. They would be forced to negotiate three dangerous cataracts along the way. The men going on board would have to tow the steamers on long lines from the bank through those boiling rock-strewn narrows.

Ahead of them, the Desert Column would travel swiftly across the bend of the Nile to Metemma, where Chinese Gordon's four little steamers were waiting to carry a small detachment of hand-picked men to Khartoum, to reinforce the city until the arrival of the main relief column.

The ammunition ship moored against the riverbank and the porters were immediately roused to begin offloading. Penrod was one of the first ashore and again his travel pass, when displayed to the subaltern in charge of the detail, worked its small miracle. He was allowed through. He picked his way through the encampment and was challenged often before he reached the guardpost at the entrance to the zareba that contained the Desert Column.

Its four regiments, commanded by General Sir Herbert Stewart, were drilling and exercising on the parade ground in preparation for the long trek across the loop. But it might be weeks or even months before they received the final marching orders from London.

The sergeant of the guard must have been forewarned of Penrod's arrival for he did not quibble when the dirty Arab labourer addressed him in the idiom of the officers' mess, and demanded to be taken to the adjutant's tent.

'Ah, Ballantyne! I received the telegraph from Colonel Adams in Cairo, but I didn't expect you for three or four days yet. You have made good time.'

Major Kenwick shook hands, but refrained from mentioning Penrod's unusual garb. Like most of the senior officers he was rather fond of this young scamp, but a little envious of his escapades. He seemed to have a knack of popping up whenever the bullets were flying and promotion was in the air.

'Thank you, Major. Do you know, by any chance, if my men are here?'

'Yes, damn it! And that sergeant of yours has helped himself to five of my best camels. If I had not been firm he would have made off with a whole troop.'

'I'll be on my way, then, if you'll excuse me, sir.'

'So soon? I rather hoped that we might have the pleasure of your company in the mess for dinner this evening.'

Penrod saw that he was eaten up with curiosity about this mysterious visitation. 'I'm in rather a hurry, sir.'

'Perhaps we might see you in Khartoum, then?' The adjutant kept fishing resolutely.

'Oh, I doubt it, sir. Shall we agree to meet at the Long Bar of the Gheziera Club when this little business has been settled?'

Sergeant al-Saada was waiting for him at the camel lines. Many eyes were watching so his greeting was cold and dismissive, a measure of the wide social chasm between a sergeant in a regiment of the Queen, and a common *fellah*. They rode into the dunes, Penrod trailing behind him on the grey she-camel. His spirits surged as she moved under him: he knew at once that al-Saada had chosen a wind-eater for him. As soon as they were out of sight of the camp al-Saada reined in. As Penrod

138

came up alongside him his forbidding expression split in a flashing grin, and he snapped his clenched fist across his chest in the riding salute. 'I saw you on the deck of the steamer when she came round Ras Indera. You have travelled fast, Abadan Riji.' The name meant the One Who Never Turns Back. 'I told Yakub you would be here in less than five days.'

'Fast I came,' Penrod agreed, 'but even faster must we go.'

Yakub was waiting for them a mile further on. He had the other camels couched behind an outcrop of black rock. Their shapes were rendered grotesque by the waterskins they carried, like huge black cancerous growths on their backs. Each camel was capable of carrying five hundred pounds, but in the Mother of Stones desert each man needed two gallons of water every day to stay alive. As they dismounted Yakub hurried to greet Penrod. He went down on one knee and touched his lips and his heart. 'Faithful Yakub has waited for you since Kurban Bairam.'

'I see you, Beloved of Allah.' Penrod smiled back at him. 'But did you forget my pack?'

Yakub looked pained. He ran back, untied it from one of the camels and brought it to him. Penrod unrolled it on the baked earth. He saw that his *galabiyya* had been freshly laundered. Swiftly he changed his rags for the fine wool robe that would protect him from the sun. He covered his face with the black cotton headdress in the fashion of the Bedouin, and tied the black sash round his waist. He tucked the curved dagger and the Webley revolver into the sash over his right hip, and his cavalry sabre on the opposite hip to balance them.

139

Then he drew the sabre from its plain leather scabbard and tested the edge. It stung like a cut-throat razor and he nodded approval at Yakub. Then he made a few practice strokes with the steel, cutting to both sides, lunging high and low, recovering instantly. The sabre felt good in his hand and seemed to take on a life of its own. In this age of breech-loading rifles and heavy ordnance Penrod still revelled in the *arme blanche*.

Almost every Arab carried the long broadsword, and Penrod had observed their use of the blade in contrast to his own. The heavy weapon did not suit the Arab physique. Unlike the mailed crusaders from whom the heavy blade had been copied they were not big, powerful men: they were terriers rather than mastiffs. They were devils to cut and lunge, and the broadsword could inflict a terrible wound. But they were slow to recover their blade. They did not understand the parry, and they used their round leather shield almost exclusively to defend themselves. Against a skilled swordsman they were vulnerable to a feint high in the natural line. Their instinctive response was to lift the shield and to lose sight of the opponent's point, and they would not see the thrust that followed the feint like a thunderbolt. At El Obeid when the square had broken and the Dervish had swarmed in, Penrod had killed five in as many minutes with that ploy. He ran the blade back into its scabbard and asked Yakub, 'Is the Mother of Stones open?'

'There is water at Marbad Tegga.' In the Taka dialect, the well's name meant Camel Killer. 'Little and bitter, but just sufficient for the camels,' Yakub replied.

Yakub was a Jaalin Arab who had been driven

from the tents of his people by a blood feud that started in a quarrel over dishonour to Yakub's sister. Yakub was quick and expert with the blade and the man had died. However, he had been the son of a powerful sheikh. Yakub had been forced to flee for his life.

One of Yakub's eyes gazed in a different direction from the other. The ringlets that dangled from under his turban were greasy and his teeth, when he smiled at Penrod, were yellow and crooked. He knew and understood the desert and the mountains with the instinct of a wild ass. Before he had been driven out of the tribe he had taken a knife wound that had left him with a limp. Because of this affliction he had been refused service in the armies of the Queen and the Khedive. Thus, with no tribe and no other master, Penrod was all he had. Yakub loved him like a father and a god.

'So we can still cut the snake?'

When Penrod posed a question of such weight, Yakub gave it all his respect and attention. He tucked the skirts of his *galabiyya* between his legs and squatted. With his camel goad he scratched a large figure S in the dirt, but the upper loop was smaller by half than the lower. It was a rough charting of the course of the Nile from where they stood to the mouth of the Shabluka Gorge. To follow the riverbank through this serpentine meandering would add many weeks to the journey. This, of course, was the route that the flotilla of the River Division would be forced to take. The Desert Division, on their camels, would cut across the great loop and regain the river at Metemma. This shortcut was well marked by the caravans of the

141

ages and by the bleached bones they had left behind them. There were two wells along the way that gave the traveller just sufficient water to make the crossing. Once they reached Metemma they could follow the upper limb of the Nile, keeping always in sight of the river as it swung back west again, until eventually it settled once more on its southerly course and headed for Khartoum. It was a hard road, but there was a harder one yet. The caravan masters called it 'cutting the snake'.

Yakub made a bold slash with the goad, drawing a straight line from their present position directly to the city of Khartoum. The line cut the S bend of the river neatly in half. It saved hundreds of miles of bitter, gruelling travel. But the trail was unmarked and to take a wrong turning meant missing the single well of Marbad Tegga, and finding instead a certain, terrible death. The well lay deep in the furnace-hot belly of the Mother of Stones, and it was well hidden. It would be easy to pass it by a hundred paces and never know it was there. The camels could drink the water, but its caustic salts would drive a man mad. Once they had watered the camels at Marbad Tegga it was still another hundred miles to the bank of the Nile at Korti below the fourth cataract. Long before they reached the river all the water in the skins would be finished. They might be twenty-four hours without a drop before they saw the Nile again, longer than that if the *djinni* of the desert were unkind to them.

Once they reached the riverbank, they must cross the river. At this point the current was swift, the stream was a mile wide and the camels were reluctant swimmers. But there was a ford known to few. Once they had crossed, drunk their fill and

142

recharged the waterskins, they would be forced to leave the Nile again and face the Monassir desert on the other bank, another two hundred waterless miles. Yakub reiterated all this, drawing it all on the earth with his goad. Penrod listened without interruption: although he had cut the snake three times before and won through to the river crossing at Korti, there was always something fresh to learn from Yakub.

When he had explained it all Yakub announced, 'With the fearless and cunning Yakub to guide you, and angels to watch over you, perchance we may indeed cut the snake.' Then he rocked back on his haunches and waited for Penrod to make the decision.

Penrod had been considering the gamble while he was talking. He would never have attempted it without Yakub. With him to lead, the gains in time and distance to reach Khartoum were worth the gamble, but there was another even more telling consideration.

Bakhita had told him that the Mahdi and his *khalifa* were well aware of the British preparations to rescue Gordon. Their spies had kept them fully informed of the concentration of British regiments and the flotilla at Wadi Halfa. She said that the Mahdi had ordered a dozen of the most important emirs to leave the siege of Khartoum and take their tribes northwards along the river, to contest the way, to meet the enemy at Metemma, Abu Klea and Abu Hamed. She said that already both banks of the river from Khartoum down to the first great bend were swarming with Arab horsemen and camel troops.

'The Mahdi knows that he must stop the Franks

143

before they reach the city.' She used the word that described all Europeans. 'He knows that their army is small and poorly equipped with horses and camels. They say he has sent twenty thousand men northwards to meet the British and to hold the river line until Low Nile, when he can complete the destruction of Khartoum and send General Gordon's head to his queen.' She had added, 'Be careful, my dear lord. They have cut the telegraph lines to the north and they know that the generals in Cairo must send messengers to Khartoum to keep in contact with the general. The Mahdi will be expecting you to try to win through to the city. His men will be waiting to intercept you.'

'Yes, they will be looking for us to cross the loop, but will they guard the road to Marbad Tegga, I wonder?' Penrod mused aloud. Yakub shook his head for he had no English. Penrod switched back into Arabic: 'In God's name, brave Yakub, take us to the bitter well of the Camel Killer.'

* * *

They mounted up on the high wooden saddles. Penrod checked the rifle in its scabbard under his leg, and the bandolier of ammunition tied to the crosspiece of the saddle, then prodded the grey camel. Groaning and spitting, she lurched to her feet.

'In God's Name let us begin,' sang al-Saada.

'May He open our eyes to make the way clear,' Yakub cried. 'And may He make the Camel Killer plain for us to behold.'

'God is great.' Penrod said. 'There is no other God but God.'

144

Each led a pack camel and the water sloshed softly in the skins. At first, loose equipment squeaked or clattered to the rocking gait of the camels, but quickly they readjusted the straps and bindings that held the burdens. Once they stopped briefly and bled the air from the waterskins so that they no longer gurgled. When they went onwards it was in silence, a weird and unnatural silence in the void of heat and unfathomable horizons. The spongy pads of the camels' feet fell soundlessly on the sands. The men wrapped their heads so that only the slits of their eyes showed and they did not speak. They slumped low on the tall wooden saddles and gave themselves over to the rhythm of the camels' gait.

They followed the ancient caravan road across a level expanse of orange-coloured sand that glowed in the sunlight until their eyes ached with the glare. The way was only faintly marked by the pale bones and desiccated carcasses of long-dead camels, preserved by sun so that some might have lain there for centuries. The air they breathed scalded and abraded the lining of the throat. The horizon wavered and dissolved in the silver lake of the mirage. The camels and their riders seemed to hang in space and though they rode forward as soundlessly as wraiths, they seemed never to move against the shimmering background. The only point of reference was the tenuous outline of the caravan trail, but even that seemed not to be attached to the earth but to rise up before them like a drifting tendril of smoke.

Penrod let himself lapse into the mesmeric trance of the desert voyager. Time was suspended and lost all significance. His mind ranged free and

145

he thought how easy it would be to believe, as the Bedouin did, in the supernatural powers that inhabited this otherworldly landscape. He dreamed of the jinn, and of the ghosts of lost armies that had perished in these sands. Though Yakub was only half a pistol shot ahead of him he seemed at times to be as distant as the mirage, fluttering like a sparrow on the wings of his robe. At other times he loomed gigantically on the back of his elephantine beast, swollen and elongated by the treacherous play of light. On they went, and silently on.

Slowly something began to appear before them, a mighty pyramid that dwarfed the man-made constructions of the delta. It quivered in the silver mirage, detached from earth, hanging inverted above the horizon, balancing on its point with the flat base filling the southern sky. Penrod stared at it in awe, and again his credibility was taxed as it shrank swiftly, disappearing to a dark spot, then began to grow again, this time with its pointed summit uppermost and its base anchored to the earth.

They rode on and now it assumed its true form, a cone-shaped hill with two smaller ones standing close behind it. In a clairvoyant flash Penrod perceived that natural features such as these must have been the model for those other man-made pyramids that had astonished mankind over the ages. The caravan trail ran straight towards them, but before they reached the first Yakub turned aside, leaving the trail on the left hand. He led them forward into a wilderness that was no longer marked by the faintest trace of man or of his passing. This was the hidden way to Marbad Tegga.

Penrod was lulled back into the hypnotic

146

suspension of time and feeling, and the hours passed as the sun made its noon and began its fiery descent to earth. At last he was roused by the altered gait of his she-camel. He looked around quickly and saw how the landscape had changed. The sand was no longer orange but ashen grey and seared. On the horizon all around were heaps of volcanic ash and lava several hundred feet high, as though all the worlds of the universe had been cremated and their remains dumped in this infernal cemetery and covered by these forbidding tumuli. The breath of ancient volcanoes had charred the very desert. There was no vestige of vegetation or of any living thing, except the three men and their pacing beasts.

Penrod saw why his mount's gait had changed. The earth was thickly littered with boulders and stones. Some were as large and perfect as round shot for heavy cannon, and others as small as musket balls. It was like the detritus of some long-forgotten battlefield. But Penrod knew that these were not the munitions of war. These rocks were the efflorescence left over from the eruption of the volcanoes. The liquid lava had been expelled into the sky in a deadly rain. As it fell back to earth it had cooled and solidified into these shapes. The camels were forced to pick their way across this dangerous footing, and their speed was much reduced.

The sun sank, and as it touched the earth it seemed to erupt in an explosion of green and crimson light, then fall away to give the world over to sudden night.

'Sweet night!' Penrod whispered, and felt his lip crack. 'Blessed cool night!' They couched the camels and fed them a small ration of crushed dhurra meal, then checked their harness and saddles for any sign of galling or chafing. While the men laid out their prayer mats and prostrated themselves towards Mecca, Penrod walked out into the desolation to loosen his cramped muscles and stiff joints. He listened to the night, but the only sound was the evening breeze along the dunes, whispering with the voices of the jinn.

When he returned Yakub was brewing coffee on the tiny brazier. They drank three cups each, and ate dates with thin rounds of dhurra biscuit. They anointed their lips and exposed skin with mutton fat to prevent them flaking and cracking. Then they lay down beside the camels and slept. Yakub roused them after two hours' rest. They mounted and went on southwards in the night.

The heavens were brilliant with stars, such a profusion that it was difficult to find the major navigational bodies in the silver dazzle. The air was cool and tasted sweet, but it was so dry that it baked the mucus in Penrod's nasal passages into pellets hard as buckshot.

Hour after hour the camels paced on. At intervals Penrod swung down from the saddle and strode along beside his mount, to rest her and stretch his legs. They stopped again before dawn, drank hot, unsweetened coffee, slept for an hour, then remounted and went on with the sun coming up on their left hand. The first rays struck and they quailed beneath the tyranny, covering their heads.

The desert was never the same. It changed its character and aspect as subtly as a beautiful courtesan, but always it was dangerous and deceptive. At times the dunes were soft and fleshy, pale ivory as the breasts and belly of a dancing girl, then turned the colour of ripe apricots. They flowed like the rollers of the ocean, or writhed together as sinuously as mating serpents. Then they collapsed over jagged escarpments of rock.

The hours and the miles fell behind them. When they paused to rest in the shade of the waterskins, it was often too hot to sleep. They lay and panted like dogs, then went on. The camels groaned and bellowed softly when they were couched and again when they were forced to their feet to resume the march. Their humps shrivelled. On the fifth day they refused to eat the small ration of dhurra meal that Yakub offered on the straw feeding mats.

'That is the first sign that they are nearing the limit of their strength,' Yakub warned Penrod. 'We must reach the well before dusk tomorrow evening. If we do not they will begin to die.'

It was not necessary to speak of the consequences for the men if the camels failed. The following morning, as they paused on the rim of a deep saucer of ground, Penrod pointed ahead. Along the opposite rim a frieze of gazelle stood in silhouette. They were as tiny and dainty as creatures in a dream, the colours of cream and milk chocolate, with lyre-shaped horns and white masked faces. After a moment they disappeared down the far side of the ridge as silently as if they had never existed.

'They drink at Marbad Tegga. We are close now.' It was the first time Yakub had spoken in many hours. 'We will be there before sunset.' He squinted with satisfaction.

At noon the camels refused to couch. They grumbled and moaned and shook their heads.

'They have smelt the water. They are eager to go to it,' said Yakub happily. 'They will lead us to the well like hunting dogs to the quarry.' As soon as the men had prayed and drunk their coffee, all three mounted again and rode on.

The camels quickened their pace and moaned with excitement as the scent of the water grew stronger in their nostrils. When they stopped again in the late afternoon Penrod recognized the terrain ahead from the last time he had passed that way. It was a fantastic array of shale hillocks, sculpted by wind and the ages into a gallery of weird shapes and fanciful carvings. Some resembled marching armies of stone warriors, others were crouching lions, and there were winged dragons, gnomes and jinn. But above them all stood a tall, striking column of stone that resembled a woman in a long robe and a widow's veil in an attitude of mourning.

'There is the Widow of Ahab,' said Yakub, 'and she faces towards the well where her husband died.' He prodded his mount with the long goad and they started forward again, the camels even more eager than their riders.

'Wait!' Penrod shouted urgently, and when Yakub and al-Saada looked back he stopped them with a peremptory gesture. He turned his own camel into a shallow wadi that hid them completely. They followed him unhesitatingly. They had to wrestle with the camels to force them to couch, goading and twisting their testicles before they sank down, bellowing in protest. Then they hobbled them with rawhide ropes so they were unable to rise again. Al-Saada stayed to guard them, and make certain they did not try to break away to reach the water. Then Penrod led Yakub to

150

the top of the ridge and they found a vantage-point among the shale hills. Penrod lay stretched on his belly and panned his field-glasses over the rugged ground beyond the Widow of Ahab. Yakub lay beside him, squinting hideously into the sunset. After a long wait he muttered, 'There is nothing but the sand and the rocks. You saw a shadow, Abadan Riji. Not even a jinn would inhabit this place,' and he began to stand up.

'Get down, imbecile,' Penrod snapped. They were silent and unmoving for another half an hour. Then Penrod handed Yakub the field-glasses. 'There is your jinnee.'

Yakub stared through the lens, then started and exclaimed when he picked out the distant shape of the man. Sitting in the shade at the base of one of the shale monoliths, he had been invisible. Only the pinprick of reflected light on the blade of the sword he was honing had alerted Penrod to his presence. Now he came to his feet and walked out into the slanting sunlight, an alien shape in the brooding landscape.

'I see him, Abadan Riji,' Yakub conceded. 'Your eyes are bright. He wears the patched *jibba* of the Mahdists. Is there more than one?'

'You can be certain of it,' Penrod murmured. 'Men do not travel alone in this place.'

'A scouting party?' Yakub hazarded. 'Spies sent to wait for the soldiers to come?'

'They know that the well of the Camel Killer is too small and the waters too bitter to supply a regiment. They are waiting to intercept messengers carrying despatches to Gordon Pasha in Khartoum. They know there is no other road. They know that we have to come this way.'

151

'They are guarding the water. We cannot go on without water for the camels.'

'No,' Penrod agreed. 'We must kill them. None must escape to warn those men of our passing.' He stood up and, using the cover of the hillock, went back to where al-Saada waited with the camels. They dared not brew coffee while they waited for night to fall, for the smell of the smoke might carry to the enemy and betray their presence. Instead they drank water sparingly from the skins, and sharpened their blades as they ate the evening meal of dates. Then the Arabs spread their mats and prayed.

Darkness fell hot and heavy as a woollen cloak over the hills, but Penrod waited until Orion the Hunter was at his zenith in the southern sky before they left the camels and went forward on foot, Penrod leading with the Webley in the sash at his waist and the bared sabre in his right hand. They had done this many times before and they moved well separated but always in contact. Penrod circled downwind of the spot at which they had last seen the Dervish sentinel, and was grateful for the evening breeze, which covered any small sounds they might make as they closed in. He smelt them first, the smoke of their brazier, the sharp odour of burning camel dung. He snapped his fingers softly to alert Yakub and al-Saada, and saw them crouch obediently, dark blobs in the starlight behind him.

He crept forward again, into the wind, keeping the smoke directly ahead. He stopped when he heard a camel belch and grumble softly. He lay flat against the earth and peered ahead, waiting with the patience of the hunter. His eyes scanned slowly over the broken ground in front of him, picking out

152

every rock and irregularity. Then something changed shape and his eyes flicked back to it. It was small, dark and round, not twenty paces ahead. It moved again and he recognized it as a human head. A sentry was sitting just over the lip of a shallow nullah. Although it was after midnight the man was still awake and alert. Penrod smelt Yakub beside him, the odour of sweat, snuff and camels, and felt his breath warm in his ear. 'I have seen him, and it is past time for him to die.'

Penrod squeezed his arm in assent, and Yakub slithered forward silently as a desert adder. He was an artist with the dagger. His shape merged with the rocks and star shadows. Penrod watched the sentry's head, and suddenly another appeared behind it. For a moment they became a single dark patch. Then there was a soft exhalation of breath and both heads sank from view. Penrod waited but there was no outcry or alarm. Then Yakub came out of the nullah with his peculiar crablike limp. He sank down beside his master.

'There are five more. They are sleeping with their camels in the bottom of the nullah.'

'Are the camels in harness?' He needed not have asked. The men were warriors and would be ready to jump into the saddle and ride the moment they were roused.

'The camels are saddled. The men sleep with their weapons beside them.'

'Is there another sentry?'

'I did not see one.'

'Where is the well?'

'They have not been foolish enough to camp beside the water. It is three or four hundred paces in that direction.' Yakub pointed to the right end of the hidden nullah.

'So, if there is another man he will be there, watching the water.' Penrod thought for a few moments, then snapped his fingers again. Al-Saada came to crouch beside them.

'I will wait between the camp and the well to watch for another sentry. The two of you will go in and make a place in Paradise for these sons of the Mahdi.' Penrod tapped each of them on the shoulder, an affirmation and a blessing. They were better at this kind of close work than he was. He was never able to suppress his squeamishness when he had to kill a sleeping man. 'Wait until I am in position.'

Penrod moved out swiftly to the right. He reached the rim of the nullah and looked down into it. He saw the body of the man Yakub had killed lying under the lip. The man's knees were drawn up to his chest and Yakub had covered his head with his turban to make it appear that he had fallen asleep at his post. Further on, the men and animals on the floor of the nullah were a dark huddle, and he could not tell one from another. Yakub must have crawled in close to count them. He moved into the shadow of a boulder from where he could keep an eye on the nullah and cover any approach from the direction of the well.

He felt his nerves tingle as, first, Yakub and then al-Saada slipped over into the nullah below him. They blended with the mass of men and animals, and he could imagine the bloody knifework as they moved swiftly from one sleeping man to the next. Then, suddenly, there was a ringing scream and his nerves jumped tight. One had missed his stroke, and he knew it was not Yakub. There was instant

154

confusion as the quiescent mass of bodies exploded into violent movement and sound. Camels lurched, bellowing, to their feet, men shouted and steel clashed on steel. He saw a man spring on to the back of one of the animals and burst out of the camp, riding up over the far wall of the nullah. Another Dervish escaped from the mêlée and bounded to the bottom of the nullah; he had gone only a short way when a figure raced after him in the unmistakable crablike style that covered the ground with deceptive speed. The two disappeared almost at once.

Penrod was poised to run down into the nullah and join in the fighting, when he heard footsteps behind him and stayed low. In the starlight he saw another figure running towards him from the direction of the Widow of Ahab. This must be the second Dervish sentry. He was carrying his sword in his right hand and his shield on the other shoulder. When he was too close to escape, Penrod jumped into his path. The Dervish did not hesitate but charged at him, swinging with the long blade. Penrod parried easily, steel resounding on steel, and feinted at his head. The Dervish lifted his shield to counter the blow, and instantly Penrod sent his blade home, a classic straight thrust into the centre of his chest so that the blade went clean through, and shot out two hands' span from the back of his ribs. With almost the same movement he cleared and recovered his blade, and the Dervish dropped without a cry.

Penrod left him and raced down the bank into the nullah. He saw al-Saada stooped over a fallen body, slashing with his dagger across his victim's throat; black blood sprayed from the severed

155

artery. Al-Saada straightened and looked about him, but his movements were sluggish. Three corpses were lying where they had slept.

'Botched! Two have got away,' Penrod snapped angrily. 'Yakub has chased one, but the other is mounted. We must go after him.'

Al-Saada took a pace towards Penrod and the blood-smeared dagger fell from his hand. He sagged slowly to his knees. The starlight was bright enough for Penrod to make out his expression of surprise.

'He was too quick,' al-Saada said, his speech slurred. He took his other hand away from his chest and looked down at himself. The blood from the wound under his ribs darkened his robe to the knees. 'Chase him, Abadan Riji. I will follow you in a little while,' he said, and toppled on to his face. Penrod hesitated only a moment as he fought his instinct to aid al-Saada. But he could tell by the loose-limbed way in which he had fallen that he was already beyond any help that he could give, and if he allowed the Dervish to escape his own chances of getting through to the besieged city would be seriously threatened.

'Go with God, Saada,' he said softly, as he turned away. He ran to the nearest Dervish camel and mounted it. With his sabre he cut free the knee halter. The camel reared on to its feet and plunged into a gallop that carried them up over the rim of the nullah. He could just make out the shadowy shape of the other camel flitting ahead, like a moth in the starlight. Within a few hundred paces he had adjusted to the pace of the animal beneath him. It seemed strong and willing, and it must have been well watered and fed during the vigil at the Marbad

Tegga. He used his body to urge it forward, like a jockey pushing for the post. A quick glance at the stars confirmed what he already knew: that the fugitive was heading directly south towards the nearest point on the Nile.

They covered another mile, then Penrod realized that the Dervish had slowed his camel to a trot. Either he had been wounded in the skirmish, he was unaware that he was being followed or he was saving his mount for the long and terrible journey that lay ahead if he hoped to reach the river. Penrod urged his own camel to its top speed, and closed the gap swiftly.

He was beginning to think that he might still come up with the Dervish before he realized his danger, but suddenly he saw the pale flash of the man's face turned back over his shoulder. The moment he spotted Penrod he lashed out with his goad and urged on his mount with sharp cries. The two camels ran as though linked together, down through a dry wadi and up the stony ridge beyond. Then, gradually, Penrod's mount began to exert its superior speed and stamina and closed in remorselessly. Penrod angled slightly across the enemy's rear, planning to come in on his left, gambling on the chance that he was right-handed and would be least able to defend himself on this side.

Suddenly, unexpectedly, the Dervish swung his camel at a right angle from its track, and brought it plunging to a halt only a hundred paces ahead. As he swivelled on the high wooden saddle Penrod saw that he had a rifle in his hands, and was lifting it to level it at him. He had thought the Arab was carrying only his sword. and had not considered the possibility that there might be a weapon in the gun-scabbard behind the saddle.

'Come on, then, you eater of pork!' Penrod shouted, and reached for the Webley tucked into his sash. The range was too long for the weapon, and the back of a running camel was not a steady platform from which to fire, but he must try to spoil his opponent's aim so he could get close enough for the blade.

The Arab fired from the back of the standing camel. Penrod knew from the muzzle flash of black powder and the distinctive booming report that he faced a Martini-Henry carbine, probably one of those captured at El Obeid or Suakin. A fraction of a second later the heavy lead bullet tore into flesh and the camel stumbled beneath him. The Dervish whirled away, bowed over the carbine as he tried to feed another cartridge into the breech. Riding hard Penrod came up on his left-hand side with the sabre at cavalry point. The Arab realized he could not reload in time and let the carbine drop. He reached over his shoulder and drew the broadsword from the scabbard strapped across his back. He stared across at Penrod, and started back in the saddle with the shock of recognition.

'I know thee, infidel!' he shouted, 'I saw thee on the field of El Obeid. Thou art Abadan Riji. I curse thee and thy foul, three-headed God.' He aimed a heavy cross-bladed cut at the head of Penrod's camel. At the last moment Penrod checked his beast and the stroke went high. The blade lopped off one of the animal's ears close to the skull and the camel shied to one side. Penrod steadied it, but felt it stumble as the bullet wound in its chest began to weaken it. The Dervish was just beyond

158

the reach of his sabre and although he thrust at him he could not touch him. His camel groaned. Suddenly its front legs collapsed, and it went down in a tangle. Penrod kicked his legs clear and landed on his feet, managing to stay upright.

By the time he had recovered his balance the Dervish on his camel was a hundred paces ahead and drawing away swiftly. Penrod snatched the Webley revolver from his sash and emptied the magazine after the dwindling shapes of rider and camel. There was no thumping sound of a bullet strike to encourage him. Within seconds they had dissolved into the darkness. Penrod cocked his head to listen, but there was only the sound of the wind.

His camel was struggling weakly to regain its feet, but suddenly it emitted a hollow roar and rolled over on to its back kicking its huge padded feet convulsively in the air. Then it collapsed and stretched out flat against the earth, its head thrust forward. It was breathing heavily and Penrod saw twin streams of blood spurt from its nostrils each time it exhaled. He reloaded the Webley, stooped over the dying animal, he pressed the muzzle to the back of its skull and fired a single shot into its brain. He took another few minutes to search the saddle-bags for anything of importance, but there were no maps or documents, except for a dog-eared copy of the Koran, which he kept. He found only a bag of dried meat and dhurra cakes, which would supplement their frugal rations.

He turned away from the carcass and set off along his own tracks back towards Marbad Tegga. He had covered barely half a mile when he saw another camel and rider coming towards him. He knelt in ambush behind a patch of jagged black rock, but as the rider came up he recognized Yakub and called to him.

'Praise the Name of Allah!' Yakub rejoiced. 'I heard a shooting.'

Penrod scrambled up behind his saddle and they turned back towards Marbad Tegga. 'My man escaped,' he admitted. 'He had a rifle and he killed my mount.'

'My man did not escape, but he died well. He was a warrior and I honour his memory.' Yakub said flatly. 'But al-Saada is dead also. He deserved to die for his clumsiness.'

Penrod did not answer. He knew there had been little love lost between them, for although they were both Muslims, al-Saada was an Egyptian and Yakub a Jaalin Arab.

In the bank of the nullah beyond the enemy camp Penrod found a deep cleft in the rocks and laid al-Saada in it. He wrapped his head in his cloak and laid the captured Koran on his chest. Then they piled loose shale over him. It was a simple burial but in accord with his religion. It did not take long, and neither spoke as they worked.

When they were done, they hurried back to the Dervish camp, and set about making preparations to continue the journey. 'If we go swiftly we might still pass through the enemy lines before the alarm is spread by the one who got away.'

The captured camels were all fat, well watered and rested. They transferred their saddles to them, and turned loose their own exhausted animals to find the water in Marbad Tegga, then make their way to the distant river. In the Dervish waterskins they had more sweet Nile water than two men

160

needed. Among the provisions they found more bags of dhurra meal, dates and dried meat.

'Now we have supplies enough to win through to Khartoum,' Penrod said, with satisfaction.

'They will expect us to head for the ford of the river at Korti, but I know of another crossing further to the west, below the cataract,' Yakub told him.

They mounted two of the fresh animals and, leading three others loaded with bulging waterskins, rode on southwards.

*   *   *

They rested through the middle of each day, lying in the meagre strip of shade cast by the animals. The camels were couched in direct sunlight, which would have brought the blood of any other man or beast to the boil but they showed no discomfort. As soon as the tyranny of the sun abated, they rode on through the evening and the night. In the dawn of the third day, while the eternal lamp of the morning star still burned above the horizon, Penrod left Yakub with the camels and climbed to the top of a conical hill, the only feature in this burnt-out, desolate world.

By the time he reached the summit, day had broken, and an extraordinary sight awaited him. Two miles ahead, something white as salt and graceful as the wing of a gull glided across this ocean of sterile sand and rock. He knew what it was before he lifted the field-glasses to his eyes. He stared at the single bulging lateen sail, which seemed so out of place in such a setting. He wasted a little more time revelling in the sense of relief and accomplishment that settled over him: the white wing of the dhow sailed upon the waters of the Nile.

They approached the river with the utmost caution. While the terrors of the Mother of Stones were behind them, a new menace lay ahead: men. The dhow had passed out of sight downstream. When they reached the riverbank it was deserted, revealing no sign of human habitation. Only a flock of white egrets flew eastwards in an arrowhead formation, low across the steely waters. There was a narrow fringe of vegetation along each bank, a few clumps of reed, scraggy palms and a single magnificent sycamore tree with its roots almost planted in the mud at the edge. An ancient mud-brick tomb had been built in its shade. The plaster was cracked and lumps had fallen out of the walls. Faded coloured ribbons fluttered from the spreading branches above it.

'That is the tree of St al-Maula, a holy hermit who lived at this place a hundred years ago,' said Yakub. 'Pilgrims have placed those ribbons in his honour so that the saint might remember them and grant any boon they seek. We are two leagues west of the ford, and the village of Korti lies about the same distance to the east.'

They turned away from the riverbank so that they would not be seen by the crews of any passing dhows and made their way westward through wadis and tumbled hillocks until they reached a tall stone bluff that overlooked a long stretch of the Nile. For the rest of that day, they kept their vigil from the summit of the cliff.

Although the Nile was the main artery of trade and travel for an area larger than the whole of

162

western Europe, not another vessel passed, and there was no sign of any human presence along this section of the banks. This alone made Penrod uneasy. Something must have disrupted all commerce along the river. He was almost certain that this was what Bakhita had warned him of, and that somewhere close by a massive movement of the Dervish armies was under way. He wanted to get across into the wastes of the Monassir desert as soon as possible, and to keep well away from the banks until he was opposite the city of Khartoum and could make a final dash into Gordon's beleaguered stronghold.

When the angle of the sun altered, it penetrated the water, and the darker outline of the shallows was just visible. A submerged spur of rock pushed half-way across the stream, and from the opposite side an extensive mudbank spread out to meet it. The channel between the two shallows was deep green but narrow, less than a hundred and fifty paces across. Penrod memorized its position carefully. If they used the empty waterskins as life-buoys, they could swim the camels across the deeper section. Of course, they must cross in darkness. They would be terribly vulnerable if they were caught in midstream in broad daylight, should a Dervish dhow appear unexpectedly. Once they had reached the far bank they could refill the skins and press on into the Monassir.

In the last hour of daylight Penrod left Yakub with the animals on the heights of the bluff and went down alone to examine the bank for tracks. After casting well up- and downstream he was satisfied that no large contingents of enemy troops had passed recently.

163

As darkness fell Yakub brought down the string of camels. He had emptied the last of the water from the skins, blown them up and stoppered them again. Each camel had a pair of these huge black balloons strapped to its flanks. They were roped together in two strings so that they would not become separated in the water.

The camels jibbed at entering the water but Penrod and Yakub goaded them down the bank and out on to the spur. As they headed into the middle of the Nile the water rose until it reached the men's chins, and they had to cling to the camel harness. The long legs and necks of the beasts allowed them to cross almost to the far side before they lost their footing and were forced to swim awkwardly. But the waterskins buoyed them up, and Penrod and Yakub swam beside them, urging them on and pointing their heads in the right direction, taking care to keep clear of their driving front legs below the surface. They swam them to the mudbank on the far side, and when they had regained their footing led them out on to dry ground. Quickly they refilled the waterskins and gave the camels their last drink for many days.

The crossing had taken longer than Penrod had bargained on, and the eastern sky was already paling before they were ready to leave the Nile, the skins filled tight and the camels' bellies swollen with water. Before they set out they tried to obliterate their tracks from the riverbank, but with that number of heavily laden animals and working in darkness it was impossible. They had to take a chance that the wind and the river waters would wipe away their tracks before they were discovered by Dervish scouts.

However, a dark premonition of evil rode on Penrod's shoulders as they headed out into the Monassir desert. After a few hours' travel the feeling grew so pervasive that he knew he must sweep the back trail to reassure himself that their crossing had not been discovered. He picked out the fleetest, most willing animal from their string— by now they knew each beast well by temperament and capability. He sent Yakub ahead with the others while he returned along their back trail. When he was still some miles from the river, he left the trail and headed for a line of low hills he had noticed earlier that overlooked the river. He couched and tethered his mount below the skyline, then crept forward. As he neared the crest of the hill he dropped to his belly, slithered up behind an outcrop of rocks and peered down into the valley of the Nile. His heart jumped against his ribs, and his nerves whipped tight at what he saw below him.

A small party of Dervish scouts was dismounted on the near bank of the Nile, and it was obvious that they had discovered the spoor as it emerged from the water. Through the field-glasses he studied the enemy intently. There were six of them. He thought that one might be the man he had chased from Marbad Tegga, but he could not be certain. They were all lean, hard desert Arabs, probably of the Beja tribe. They wore the gaily patched *jibbas* of the Mahdists, and carried the distinctive round targes and long-sheathed swords. They were leaning on the shafts of their spears and animatedly discussing the tracks on the bank. One turned and pointed south along the run of the spoor, and they all looked in the direction he had indicated. They seemed to be gazing directly

165

towards the spot where Penrod lay.

He ducked behind the rocks while he assessed his situation. It seemed obvious that the man he had chased from Marbad Tegga, even if that was not him down there, had reached the river ahead of them. He must have spread the warning to the forward elements of the main Dervish army coming down from the north. Perhaps one of the commanding emirs had sent this scouting party ahead to reconnoitre the river crossings and intercept them. Penrod could tell at a glance that these were aggagiers, the finest Dervish warriors. He and Yakub were outnumbered by three to one, and the Dervish were on the alert. He put out of his mind any notion of a fight. Their only salvation lay in flight.

Now he switched his attention from the men to their mounts. Each rode a handsome horse. They had only one pack camel to carry the leather bags of small gear, food and ammunition, but there were no waterskins. Obviously they were a swift scouting party, but because they carried no water they were confined to the narrow strip of ground a few miles each side of the river. They were not equipped for a deep foray into the Monassir. To intercept Penrod's caravan they would have to ride hard round the great loop of the river and try to get ahead of them on the riverbank opposite Khartoum. That journey was almost two hundred miles longer than the one that faced him and Yakub. He felt a great wave of relief as he realized that even the swiftest horses would not be able to cut them off before they reached their goal.

'I leave you to the mercy of Allah,' he murmured, in sardonic blessing, then wriggled back

166

from the skyline to return to his mount and catch up with Yakub. Then an unexpected stir among the men below made him pause. Quickly he refocused the field-glasses. Two of the aggagiers had run back to the single pack camel and forced it to kneel. They unstrapped some equipment from the animal's back. One of the Arabs squatted cross-legged with what appeared to be a writing tablet on his lap. He wrote with great concentration and care.

The other man took down a small crate from the camel's load and removed the cotton cover that protected it. He opened a trapdoor in the lid and reached inside with both hands. Penrod quailed as he saw a small birdlike head bobbing and weaving between the man's fingers. The writer laid aside his pen, carefully folded his message and stood up. The other man proffered the creature he held, and they were busy for a moment longer.

Then the scribe stood back and nodded. With both hands the other tossed the sleek grey pigeon high into the air. The bird exploded into flight, its wings clattering softly as it rose higher and higher above the river. All the Arabs watched it, heads thrown back. Their faint cries of encouragement reached Penrod even at that distance.

'Fly, little one, on the wings of God's angels!'

'Swiftly to the bosom of the Holy Mahdi!'

Up and up the pigeon climbed, and then it described a series of wide circles in the sky, a speck against the blue, until at last it found its bearings and shot away in a straight, swift line, headed into the south across the loop towards the Dervish city of Omdurman.

Penrod watched it out of sight, longing to see the

knife-winged silhouette of one of the desert Saker falcons towering above it, then beginning the deadly stoop, but no predator appeared and the pigeon vanished.

Penrod ran down the back slope of the hill and sprang into his camel's saddle. He turned its head in the same southerly direction as the pigeon had taken and urged it into the pacing gait that it could maintain for fifty miles without rest. But the pigeon would reach Omdurman before nightfall, while he and Yakub still had at least two hundred and fifty miles to ride. He knew now what a terrible gauntlet they had yet to run before he could reach Khartoum and deliver his despatch to Chinese Gordon.

*　　　*　　　*

Osman Atalan marched in the horde of worshippers towards the great mosque of Omdurman. Over his head floated his personal banner, which had been awarded to him by the Mahdi. It was worked with texts from the Koran, and it was carried by two of his aggagiers. All around him throbbed the massive copper war drums. The *ombeyas* bleated and brayed, and the crowds shouted praises to God, to the Mahdi and his *khalifa*. The heat clamped down upon the moving mass of humanity and the dust rose in a cloud from the trampling feet and hung over their heads. As they approached the outer wall of the mosque the excitement built up steadily for they knew that today the Mahdi, the light of Islam, would preach the word of God and his Prophet. The Ansar began to dance. Once they had been called Dervish, but the Mahdi had forbidden the use of that name as demeaning.

'The Holy Prophet has spoken to me several times and he has said that whosoever calls my followers Dervish should be beaten seven times with thorns and receive a plague of stripes. For did I not give a proud name and a promise of Paradise to my own true warriors who triumphed on the battlefield of El Obeid? Did I not decree that they be known as my Ansar, my helpers and partisans? Let them be known only as Ansar, and let them glory in that name.'

The Ansar danced in the sunlight, whirling like dust devils, faster and faster, spinning so that their feet seemed barely to touch the earth, and the ranks of worshippers that pressed around them ululated and shouted the ninety-nine beautiful names of Allah: 'Al-Hakim, the Wise. Al-Majid, the Glorious. Al-Haqq, the Truth . . .' One by one the dancers were overtaken by holy ecstasy and fell to the ground, frothing at the mouth and twitching until their eyes rolled back in the sockets and only the whites showed.

Osman entered the gates of the mosque. It was a vast enclosure open to the sky, and surrounded by a twenty-foot-high wall of mud bricks. It was eight hundred paces square and the whole expanse was packed with the kneeling ranks of *jibba*-uniformed faithful. At the far end of the mosque an opening was screened off by a rank of black-robed Ansar, the Mahdi's executioners.

Osman made his way slowly through the crowds towards this space. The ranks of kneeling figures gave way to him and called his praises as he passed, for he was the foremost of all the great emirs. In the first row of worshippers his aggagiers spread out his prayer mat of fine dyed wool. Beside it they piled the six great tusks that they had taken in the hunt in the Valley of the Atbara. Osman knelt on the mat and faced the narrow gate in the wall, which led to the private compound of the Mahdi.

Gradually the wild hubbub of the worshippers descended to a hum, and then to a charged, expectant silence. This was shattered by a ringing blast on an *ombeya* and through the gateway appeared a small procession. At the head were the three *khalifas*. In appointing these men as his successors the Mahdi had simply followed the precedent set by the first Prophet Muhammad.

There should have been a fourth *khalifa*, Al Senussi, the ruler of Cyrenaica. He had sent an emissary to the Sudan to report to him on this person who claimed to be the Mahdi. The man had arrived while the sack of the city of El Obeid was in full swing. He had watched in horror the massacre, the pillage, the torture, the children being chopped into pieces by the Ansar. He did not tarry to meet the Mahdi and fled from the carnage to report back to his master the inhumanities he had witnessed.

'This monster cannot be the true Mahdi,' Al Senussi decided. 'I want no truck with him.'

Thus there were only three *khalifas*, of whom Abdullahi was the first. Compared to him the other two were of no significance. Abdullahi led them to the prayer mats that had been laid out for them on the raised dais. When they had taken their places there was another expectant pause.

The *ombeya* shrieked once more and the Mahdi's sword-bearer entered through the

170

gateway. He carried before him the symbol of the Mahdi's temporal powers: a sword with an extraordinarily long, bright blade. Its gold hilt and guard were worked with jewelled stars and crescents, and the steel was inlaid in gold with the double-headed eagle of the Holy Roman Empire, beneath which was the legend 'Vivat Carolus'. It was not an Islamic relic but must once have belonged to a Christian crusader. It was an heirloom that had been passed down over the centuries until it had become the sword of the Mahdi. Behind his sword-bearer came the prophet of God himself.

The Mahdi was dressed in a spotlessly clean and beautifully quilted *jibba*. On his head he wore a gold casque with chain mesh cheekpieces that might once have belonged to one of Saladin's Saracens. He began a slow, dignified progress through the congregation of kneeling worshippers. Their ranks opened before him, and sheikhs, warriors, priests and emirs crawled forward to kiss his feet and proffer gifts.

They held up handfuls of pearls and gold jewellery, of precious stones and beautifully wrought objects of silver. They laid bolts of silk and pure gold embroidery at his feet. The Mahdi smiled his angelic smile and touched their heads in acceptance of each gift. While his Ansar followed behind him and gathered up the offerings, the Mahdi preached to them.

'Allah has spoken to me many times, and he has told me that you should be forbidden to wear fine clothes and jewellery, for this is conceit and pride. You should wear only the *jibba*, which marks you as a lover of the Prophet and the Mahdi. Therefore it

171

is right and wise that you should deliver these trinkets and fripperies into my keeping.'

Those close enough to hear the words shouted them aloud so that all might hear and know the wisdom of the Mahdi, and others further on repeated them so by the end they had been shouted to the furthest reaches of the vast enclosure. The worshippers praised God that they should be allowed to hear such wisdom.

They lifted up leather bags of gold and silver coins and poured them at his feet, glittering piles of Maria Theresa dollars, gold mohurs and English sovereigns, the currency of the Orient and the Occident. Osman Atalan crawled forward under the weight of the largest of the six tusks and his aggagiers followed him with similar offerings. The Mahdi smiled down on Osman and stooped to embrace him.

The watchers hummed with amazement at such favour bestowed.

'You know that these riches cannot buy you a place in Paradise. If any man hold back treasures and does not bring them to me freely and of his own accord, Allah will burn him with fire and the earth will swallow him. Repent and obey my words. Return to me all that you have taken for yourselves. The Prophet, grace be upon him, has told me many times that any man who still keeps the spoils of looting in his possession shall be destroyed. Believe the revealed word of the Prophet.'

They shouted again with joy to hear the word of God and his Prophet and the Divine Mahdi, and shoved their way to the front to deliver up their treasure.

Once the Mahdi had completed his progress round the mosque he returned to the dais and took his seat on his silk prayer mat. One at a time, his three *khalifas* knelt before him and offered their gifts. One clapped his hands and his grooms led in a black stallion that shone like washed obsidian in the sunlight. Its saddle was carved from ebony, while its bridle and reins were of gold lace, tasselled with the feathers of marabou and eagles.

The second *khalifa* offered him a royal *angareb* bed, whose frame was cunningly carved of ivory and inlaid with gold.

Abdullahi was the *khalifa* who knew his master best. He offered the Divine Mahdi a woman, but no ordinary woman. He led her into the enclosure himself. She was cloaked from head to ankles, but her outline beneath the silk was as graceful as that of a gazelle, and her bare feet were elegantly shaped. The *khalifa* opened the front of her cloak, but held it so that she was screened from all eyes other than those of the Mahdi. She was naked under the cloth.

The Mahdi leant forward on one elbow and stared at her. She was a lovely child of the Galla who, at fourteen years, had eyes as dark as pools of oil, and skin as smooth as butter. She moved like a newly woken fawn. Her breasts were small and girlish, but shaped like ripe figs. Every hair had been meticulously plucked from her sex, so that the pink tips of her inner lips peeked out at him shyly from the plump little cleft. This emphasized her tender age. The Mahdi smiled at her. She hung her head, covered her mouth with a tiny hand and giggled coyly. The Khalifa Abdullahi covered her again and the Mahdi nodded at him. 'Take her to

173

my quarters.'

Then he rose, spread his arms and began to speak again.

'The Prophet has told me many times that my Ansar are a chosen and blessed people. Thus He has forbidden you to smoke or chew tobacco. You shall not drink alcohol. You shall not play a musical instrument except the drum and the *ombeya*. You shall not dance, except in praise of God and his Prophet. You shall not fornicate, nor shall you commit adultery. You shall not steal. Behold the fate of those who disobey my laws.'

He clapped his hands, and from the side gate his executioners led in an elderly man. He was barefoot and dressed only in a loincloth. His turban had been stripped off and his unwashed hair was a dirty white. He looked confused and hopeless. He had a rope round his neck. When he stood in front of the dais one of the executioners jerked it and threw him to the ground. Then four surrounded him with their whips poised.

'This man has been seen smoking tobacco. He must suffer a hundred blows with the kurbash.'

'In the Name of God and his victorious Mahdi!' the congregation assented, with a single voice, and the executioners laid on together.

The first stroke raised a red welt across the man's back, and the second drew blood. The victim writhed and shrieked as others followed in quick succession. At the end he moved no more and they dragged him out of the gate through which he had entered. Behind him the dust was damp with his blood.

The next offender was brought in at the rope's end, and the Mahdi gazed down on him with a mild and benign smile. 'This man stole the oars from his neighbour's dhow. The Prophet has decreed that he shall have one hand and one foot cut off.'

The executioner standing behind him swung his broadsword low and hard, and lopped off the right foot at the ankle. The man collapsed in the dust and as he put out a hand to save himself, the executioner stood on it to pin it to the ground, then hacked down and cut through the wrist bone. Quickly and expertly they cauterized the stumps by dipping them into a small pot of boiling pitch from the brazier. Then they tied the severed hand and foot around the man's neck and dragged him out through the side gate.

'Praise the justice and mercy of the Mahdi,' howled the worshippers. 'God is Great and there is no other God but God.'

Osman Atalan watched from his seat in the front rank of the mosque. He was amazed by the wisdom and perception of the Mahdi. He knew instinctively that new religious orders are not forged by granting luxurious indulgences but by enforcing moral austerity and devotion to the word of God. No man who witnessed the rule of this prophet could doubt that he wielded the authority of God.

The Mahdi spoke again: 'My heart is as heavy as a stone with sorrow, for there is a couple in our midst, a man and a woman, who have been taken in adultery.'

The congregation roared with anger and waved their hands above their heads, crying, 'They must die! They must die!'

They brought in the woman first. She was little more than a child, a waiflike figure with stick-thin arms and legs. Her hair had come down in a tangle

175

over her face and shoulders, and she wailed piteously as they tied her arms and legs to the stake below the dais.

Then they led in the man. He also was young, but tall and proud, and he called to the woman, 'Be brave, my love. We will be together in a better place than this.'

Despite the rope round his neck he strode forward towards the edge of the dais as if he wished to address the Divine Mahdi, but the executioner pulled him up short. 'No closer, thou foul beast, lest your blood soil the raiment of the Victorious One.'

'The penalty for adultery is that the man suffer beheading,' said the Mahdi, and his words were repeated and shouted across the wide enclosure. The executioner stepped up behind his victim and touched the back of his neck with the blade of the sword, marking his aim. Then he drew back and struck, and the blade fluted through the air. The girl at the stake screamed in despair as her lover's head seemed to spring from his shoulders. He stood a moment longer as a bright stream fountained into the air, then cascaded over his torso. The Mahdi stepped back fastidiously but a single drop splashed the skirt of his white *jibba*. The dead man fell in an untidy tangle of limbs and his head rolled to the foot of the dais. The girl wailed and struggled with her bonds to reach him.

'The penalty for the woman taken in adultery is that she be stoned,' said the Mahdi.

The Khalifa Abdullahi rose from his cushion and went to the girl at the stake. With a strangely tender gesture he swept the hair back from her face and tied it behind her head, so that the believers could see her expression as she died. Then he paced back to the pile of stones that had been placed ready to hand. He selected one that fitted neatly into his hand and turned back to face the girl-child. 'In the Name of Allah and the Divine Mahdi, may they have mercy on your soul.'

He hurled the stone with the strength and speed of a spearman, and it caught the girl in the eye. From where he sat Osman Atalan heard the rim of the socket crack. The eye popped out and hung by the vine of its nerve on her cheek, like some obscene fruit.

One after the other the *khalifas*, the emirs and the sheikhs came forward, took up a stone from the pile and threw it. By the time Osman Atalan took his turn the front of the girl's skull had been crushed and she was hanging lifelessly against her bonds. Osman's stone struck her shoulder but she did not move. They left her hanging there while the Mahdi finished delivering his sermon.

'The Prophet, grace and eternal life be upon him, has said to me on many occasions that he who doubts that I am the true Mahdi is an apostate. He who opposes me is a renegade and an infidel. He who wages war against me shall perish from this life and be destroyed and obliterated in the next world. His property and his children shall become the property of Islam. My war against the Turks and the infidel is by the order of the Prophet. He has made me privy to many terrible secrets. The greatest of these is that all the countries of the Turks, the Franks and the infidels who defy me and who defy the word of Allah and his Prophet shall be subdued by the holy religion and law. They shall become as dust and fleas and small things who

177

crawl in the darkness of night.'

*   *   *

When Osman Atalan returned to his tent in the palm grove beside the waters of the Nile and looked across at the fortress of the infidel, he felt exhausted in the flesh as though he had fought a mighty battle, but he was as triumphant in the spirit as though the victory had been granted to him by Allah and the Divine Mahdi. He sat on the precious carpet of silk from Samarkand and his wives brought him a gourd of sour milk. After he had drunk, his principal wife whispered to him, 'There is one who awaits you, my lord.'

'Let him come to me,' Osman told her. When he came he was an old man but straight of limb with bright young eyes. 'I see you, Master of the Pigeons,' Osman greeted him, 'and may the grace of Allah be with you.'

'I see you, mighty emir, and I pray the Prophet to hold you to his heart.' He proffered the grey pigeon he held gently against his breast.

Osman took the bird from him and stroked its head. It cooed softly, and he untied the silk thread that held a tiny roll of rice paper to its scaly red leg. He smoothed it against his thigh and as he read it he began to smile and the weariness slipped from his shoulders. Carefully he reread the last line of the tiny script on the note.

'I have seen his face in the starlight. Verily, it is the Frank who escaped your wrath on the battlefield of El Obeid. The one who is known as Abadan Riji.'

'Summon my aggagiers and place the saddle on

178

Sweet Water. We ride for the north. Mine enemy has come.' They scurried to do his bidding.

'By God's grace we do not need to search the length and breadth of the Monassir Desert,' he told Hassan Ben Nader and al-Noor, who stood outside the tent with him while they waited for the grooms to bring their horses. 'We know when and where he crossed the loop, and there is only one place to which he can be headed.'

'It is two hundred and fifty miles from where he crossed to where he aims to reach the river here opposite Khartoum,' said al-Noor.

'We know he is a tough warrior for we all saw him at El Obeid. He will travel fast,' said Hassan Ben Nader. 'He will murder his camels.'

Osman nodded in agreement. He knew the type of man he was hunting. Hassan was right: this one would have no qualms about riding his camels to death. 'Three days, four at most, and like a little fish he will swim into our net.' The groom brought Sweet Water to him and she whinnied when she recognized Osman. He fondled her head and gave her a dhurra cake to crunch while he checked her bridle and girth. 'He will keep well away from the bank of the river until he is ready to cross.' Osman was thinking aloud with the mind of the chase. 'Will he cross south of Omdurman or to the north?' he mused, as he came back to the mare's head, and before any of his companions could speak he answered himself: 'He would not cross to the north, for as soon as he entered the water the current would push him back and away from the city. He must cross to the south so that the flow of the Bahr El Abiad,' he used the Arabic name for the White Nile, 'will carry him down to Khartoum.'

A man coughed and shuffled his feet in the dust. Osman glanced at him. Only one of his aggagiers would dare question his words. He turned to the most trusted of his men. 'Speak, Noor. Let your wisdom delight us like the singing of the heavenly cherubim.'

'It comes to me that this Frank is as wily as a desert jackal. He may reason as you have just done and, knowing your mind, decide to do the opposite. He may choose to cross far to the north, then swing wide towards the mountains and cross the Bahr El Abiad rather than the Bahr El Azrak.'

Osman shook his head. 'As you have said, he is no fool and he knows the lie of the land. He also knows that the danger for him will not be in the empty desert but on the rivers where our tribes are concentrated. You think he will choose to cross two rivers rather than one? No, he will cross the Bahr El Abiad to the south of the city. That is where we will wait for him.'

He swung up easily into the saddle, and his aggagiers followed his example. 'We move south.'

They rode into the cool of the evening, and a long veil of red dust spread behind them. Osman Atalan was in the van, with Sweet Water striding out in a flowing canter. They had covered only a few miles when he reined in the mare, and stood in the stirrups to survey the terrain ahead. The tops of the palm trees that marked the course of the river were just visible on the left, but on the right stretched the great void of the Monassir, which after two thousand miles would give way to the infinite wastes of the Sahara.

Osman swung down from the mare's back and squatted at her head. Immediately his aggagiers did the same. 'Abadan Riji will circle out wide to the west to keep well clear of the river until he is ready to make the crossing. Then he will come out of the wilderness, and in the night try to slip through our lines. We will lay our net thus and thus.' He sketched out the lines of his pickets in the dust and they nodded their agreement and understanding as they watched. 'Noor, you will take your men and ride thus and thus. You, Hassan Ben Nader, will ride thus. I shall be here in the centre.'

*　　　*　　　*

Penrod drove the camels at a pace that not even the hardiest men and beasts could keep up for long. They covered the ground at eight miles an hour, and kept it up for eighteen hours without rest, but it taxed even their endurance to the limit. Both men were also exhausted when he called the first halt. They rested for four hours by his pocket watch, but when they tried to rouse the camels to go on the oldest and weakest refused to come to his feet. Penrod shot him where he lay. They distributed the water that the dead beast was carrying among the other camels, then mounted up and went on at the same pace.

When they reached the end of the next eighteen-hour stage of the march Penrod calculated that they had roughly another ninety to one hundred miles to go to reach the Nile ten miles south of Khartoum. Yakub agreed with this estimate, although his calculations were based on different criteria. They had broken the back of the journey, but it had cost them dear. Thirty-six hours' hard going, and only four hours of rest. When they tried

181

to feed them, the camels refused to eat their meagre ration of dhurra.

Once the six camels were couched Penrod went to each waterskin and lifted it to judge the remaining contents. Then he pondered over the equation of weights and distances and the condition of each beast. He decided on a deliberate gamble. He explained it to Yakub, who sighed, picked his nose and lifted the skirts of his *galabiyya* to scratch his crotch, all symptoms of doubt. But in the end he nodded lugubriously, not trusting himself to voice approval.

They selected the two strongest camels and took them out of sight of the other four weaker animals. They watered them from the skins they carried, pouring the sweet water into leather buckets. The animals' thirst seemed unquenchable, and they sucked down bucketful after bucketful. They drank almost thirty gallons each. The change in their condition was startlingly swift. They rested them another hour, then fed them all the rations of dhurra that their companions had refused. The two chosen beasts devoured it gluttonously. Now they were strong and alert again. The resilience of these extraordinary creatures never failed to amaze Penrod.

When the four hours of rest ended they led the two camels back to where the other four lay listlessly. They forced the used-up animals to their feet. Now when they began the next stage of the journey the two pampered animals carried nothing but their saddles. Between them the exhausted camels carried all the remaining water and equipment as well as the two riders. One collapsed after three more gruelling hours. Penrod shot it.

He and Yakub drank as much of the water from its skins as their bellies would hold. Then they shared the rest between their two strong beasts.

They pushed on at the same pace, but within another ten miles the remaining two weaker beasts went down in quick succession. Half-way up the slip-face of a low dune one fell as though shot through the brain, and half an hour later the other groaned and its back legs gave way. It knelt to die and closed the thick double rows of lashes over its swimming eyes. Penrod stood over it with the Webley in his hand. 'Thank you, old girl. I hope your next journey is less arduous.' And he put her out of her misery.

They allowed the surviving camels to drink what they could of the water, then drank themselves. What remained they loaded up. The two camels were strong and willing. Yakub stood beside them, and studied the terrain that lay ahead, the outline of the dunes and the shape of the distant hills. 'Eight hours to the river,' he estimated.

'If my backside lasts that long,' Penrod lamented, as he climbed into the saddle. He ached in every nerve and muscle, and his eyeballs felt raw and abraded by the sand and the glare of sunlight. He abandoned himself to the pacing gait of the beast under him, the legs on each side swinging in unison, so that he pitched and rolled in the saddle. The desolate landscape fell away behind them, and the dunes and bare hills were so monotonously similar that at times he had the illusion they were making no progress but repeating the same journey endlessly.

Still clinging to the saddle, he slipped into a dark, leaden sleep. He slid sideways and almost fell off, but Yakub rode up alongside him and shook him awake. He lifted his head guiltily, and looked at the height of the sun. They had been riding for only two hours.

'Six more to go.' He felt lightheaded, and knew that at any moment sleep would overtake him again. He slipped to the ground and ran beside his camels' head until the sweat stung his eyes. Then he mounted up again and followed Yakub through the shimmering wasteland. Twice more he had to dismount and run to keep himself awake. Then he felt the camel under him change its pace. At the same time Yakub shouted, 'They have smelt the river.'

Penrod pushed up alongside his camel. 'How far?'

'An hour, perhaps a little longer, before it will be safe for us to turn eastwards and head straight towards the river.'

The hour passed slowly, but the camels paced on steadily until they saw another low ridge of blue shale appear out of the heat haze ahead. To Penrod it seemed identical to hundreds of others they had passed since they had crossed the loop, but Yakub laughed and pointed at it: 'This place I know!' He turned his camel's head and the beast quickened its pace. The sun was half-way towards the western horizon, and their shadows flitted ahead over the barren earth.

They came up over the ridge, and Penrod stared ahead eagerly for a glimpse of greenery. The wasteland was unrelieved and unrelenting. Yakub was undismayed, and shook his lank curls in the hot wind, as the camels ran on across the plain.

Ahead another low shale bank seemed to rise no

184

more than head high above the level ground. Yakub brandished his goad and leered across at Penrod with a satanic squint. 'Place your trust in Yakub, the master of the sands. Brave Yakub sees the land as a vulture from on high. Wise Yakub knows the secret places and the hidden pathways.'

'If he is wrong brave Yakub will have need of a new neck, for I will break the one on which he balances his thick skull,' Penrod called back.

Yakub cackled and pushed his mount into a cumbersome gallop. He reached the top of the bank fifty paces ahead of Penrod, stopped and pointed ahead dramatically.

On the horizon they saw a line of palm trees stretched across the landscape, but it was difficult to judge the distance in the flat, uncertain light. The bunches of palm fronds on each long bole reminded Penrod of the ornate hairstyles of the Hadendowa warriors. He estimated that it was under two miles to the nearest grove.

'Get the camels down,' he ordered, and jumped to the ground. Surprisingly he felt strong and alert. At first sight of the Nile the weariness of the journey seemed to have left him. They took the camels behind the ridge and couched them out of sight from the river plain.

'In which direction lies Khartoum?' Penrod asked.

Without hesitation Yakub pointed to the left. 'You can see the smoke from the cooking fires of Omdurman.'

It was so faint on the horizon that Penrod had taken it for dust or river haze, but now he saw that Yakub was right. 'So we are at least five miles upstream of Khartoum,' he observed. They had reached the precise position he had aimed for.

He went forward cautiously and squatted on the high ground with the field-glasses. He saw at once that he had overestimated the distance to the riverbank. It was probably closer to one mile than two. There was no cover on the river plain, which was flat and featureless. It seemed that there was some cultivation under the palm trees, for he made out a line of darker green below the untidy fronds. 'Probably dhurra fields,' he muttered, 'but no sign of a village.' Again he checked the height of the sun. Two hours until dark. Should we make a run for the river before sunset, or wait for darkness? He felt impatience building in him, but he held it in check. While he considered the choice he kept the binoculars to his eyes. The riverbank could be far beyond the first trees of the grove, or it might be right there at the edge.

Movement caught his eye and he concentrated on it. A faint shading of pale dust was rising from among the palms. It was moving from left to right, in the opposite direction of Omdurman. Perhaps it was a caravan, he thought, following the road along the riverbank. But then he realized it was moving too fast. Riders, he decided, camels or horsemen. Suddenly the dustcloud stopped moving, hung for a few minutes at the same point, then gradually settled. They have halted in the grove, right between us and the riverbank. Whoever they were they had made the decision for him. Now he had no alternative but to wait for darkness. He went back to where Yakub sat with the camels. 'Mounted men on the riverbank. We'll have to wait for darkness when we can sneak past them.'

'How many?'

'I'm not certain. A large band. Judging by the dust there are maybe twenty or so.' There was little water left in the skins, no more than a few gallons. With the river in sight they could afford to be profligate so they drank their fill. By this time it was slimy with green algae and had taken on the taste of the crudely tanned leather, but Penrod drank it with relish. What they could not consume they gave to the camels.

Then they inflated the empty skins. This was a laborious job: they held each skin between their knees and blew into the nozzle, holding it closed between breaths by clamping a hand over the opening. When each skin was full and tight they stoppered it. Then they strapped them to the backs of the kneeling camels. All was ready for the river crossing, and Yakub looked at Penrod. 'Yakub the tireless will keep watch while you rest. I will wake you at the setting of the sun.'

Penrod opened his mouth to refuse the offer, then recognized the sense of it. The elation was wearing off, and he realized that, without sleep, he was nearly at the end of his tether. He knew, too, that Yakub was almost indefatigable. He handed him the field-glasses without protest, stretched out on the shady side of his camel, wrapped his scarf round his head and was almost instantly asleep.

'Effendi.' Yakub shook him awake. His voice was a hoarse whisper. With a single glance at his face Penrod knew that there was trouble. Yakub's squint was hideous, one eye fixed on Penrod's face but the other roved and rolled.

As Penrod sat up his right hand closed on the butt of the Webley. 'What is it?'

'Riders! Behind us.' Yakub pointed back along

the way they had come. Far out on the sun-seared plain a tight bunch of horsemen was coming on fast. 'They are on our tracks.'

Penrod snatched the field-glasses from him and stared back at them. They wore the *jibba*. He counted nine. They were covering the ground at a canter. The leaders were leaning forward in their saddles to watch the ground ahead.

'They were waiting for us,' said Yakub. 'It was the pigeon that warned them.'

'Yes! The pigeon.' Penrod leapt to his feet. He took a last glance at the height of the sun. It was squatting wearily on the horizon and little daylight remained. The camels were ready to run, eager for water, and lunged to their feet at the first touch of the goad.

Penrod leapt into the saddle and pointed his mount's head at the distant line of palm trees. He used the goad and it lumbered into a gallop. From behind he heard the distant thud of a rifle shot and a bullet ricocheted off the stony ground in a puff of dust and chips, but it was fifty yards out on the left. Even at such long range it was poor shooting, but the Dervish favoured the sword and the spear above the gun. They considered any expertise in the use of firearms to be effete and unmanly. The true warrior killed with the blade, man to man.

Within seconds the camels had crossed the ridge and were screened by the shale bank from further enemy fire. Penrod knew that they were no match for a good horse over the short run, but he pushed his on with cries of 'Ha! Ha!', the sting of the goad and urgent movements of his body. Yakub was lighter, though, and his mount drew gradually ahead.

As they raced for the edge of the palm groves Penrod searched for any sign of the horsemen he had spotted earlier. He hoped they might have ridden on towards Omdurman, and left their path open to the river. Even the best of us needs a little luck, he thought, then heard faint but excited cries from far behind. He looked back under his arm, and saw the nine horsemen sweeping over the shale bank they had just crossed. They were strung out but riding hard. There were more shots, but they flew wide. The palm groves drew closer, and he felt his confidence burgeoning. They had a clear run to the bank of the Nile.

'Come, Effendi, watch Yakub and you will learn how to ride a camel.' The little Jaalin tribesman laughed with delight at his own sense of humour. Both their animals were extended in full gallop, and Penrod ducked as loose pebbles flew back from the pads of the camel in front of him and flicked past his ears.

Suddenly there was a different sound of gunfire, much sharper and clearer. The band of riders he had seen earlier raced out of the grove. They must have been halted and resting among the trees, but now they had been alerted by the shots of the pursuers. All of them wore the *jibba* of the Dervish and were armed with spear, sword, targe and rifle. They were on a converging course, racing in from the right along the edge of the grove to cut them off from the river. Penrod narrowed his eyes as he judged their speed and the distance to where their paths would cross.

We will make it, but with little to spare, he decided. At that moment a heavy Boxer-Henry .45 calibre bullet struck Yakub's camel in the head and killed it instantly. It dropped onto its nose and the long legs flew over its head as it tumbled. Yakub was thrown high, then struck the hard ground heavily.

Penrod knew that he must be either killed or knocked senseless. He dared not stop to help him. Baring's messages were more important than the life of one man. None the less he was filled with dismay at the thought of leaving Yakub to the mercy of the Dervish. He knew they would give him to their women to play with. The Hadendowa woman could castrate a man, then flay every inch of skin from his body without allowing him to lose consciousness, forcing him to endure every exquisite cut of the blade. 'Yakub!' he bellowed, with little hope of any response, but to his astonishment Yakub clambered shakily to his feet and looked about groggily.

'Yakub! Make ready.' Penrod leant out sideways from the saddle. Yakub turned and ran in the same direction, to lessen the shock as they came together. They had often practised this trick in preparation for just such a moment on the battlefield or the hunting ground. Yakub was looking back over his shoulder to judge his moment. As the camel swept by him he reached up and linked arms with Penrod. He was jerked clean off his feet, but Penrod used the momentum to swing him back over the camel's croup.

Yakub grabbed him round the waist and stuck to him like a tick to a dog. The camel ran on without check. The moment Penrod was sure that Yakub was secure he twisted in the saddle and saw that the closest Dervish was only two hundred yards out on their right flank. He rode a magnificent cream mare with a flowing golden mane. Although he wore the green turban of an emir, he was not a greybeard but a warrior in his prime, and he rode with the menace of a couched lance, slim, supple and deadly.

'Abadan Riji!' To Penrod's astonishment the emir challenged him by name. 'Since El Obeid I have waited for you to return to Sudan.'

Then Penrod remembered him. His face and figure were not easily forgotten. This was Osman Atalan, emir of the Beja.

'I thought I had killed you there,' Penrod shouted back. The emir had chased him as he carried the wounded Adams out of the broken square, just as the Dervish charge overwhelmed it. Osman had been riding another mount, not that lovely mare. Penrod had been up on a big strong gelding. Even burdened with Adams it had taken Osman a good half-mile to catch him. Then they rode stirrup to stirrup and shoulder to shoulder, as though riding each other off the ball in a game of polo, Osman slashing and hacking with that great silver blade, and Penrod meeting it with parries and stop hits, until his moment came. Then he feigned a straight thrust at Osman's eyes. The Dervish threw up his targe to catch the point, and Penrod dropped his aim and hit him, driving hard under the bottom rim of the targe. He had felt his steel go well in. Osman reeled back in the saddle and his mount had swerved aside, breaking out of the trial of strength.

Looking back under his arm as he carried Adams away, Penrod had seen that Osman's mount had slowed to a walk, and that his rider was hunched over and swaying. He had thought he was

191

probably mortally wounded.

But that was clearly not the case, for now Osman shouted, 'I swear on my love of the Prophet that today I will give you another chance to kill me.'

Osman's men rode close behind him and Penrod saw that they were as dangerous as a pack of wolves. One of the aggagiers aimed his carbine and fired. The black powder smoke erupted from the muzzle and the bullet parted the air so close to Penrod's cheek that he felt its kiss. He ducked instinctively, and heard Osman shout behind him, 'No guns! Blades only. I want this one for my sword, for he has tainted my honour.'

Penrod faced ahead, giving all his concentration to wringing the utmost from the camel under him. They rushed towards the palm grove, but behind him he could hear the thunder of hoofs riding to a crescendo. As they rode past the first trees of the grove, he saw that he had been mistaken; this was not a field of dhurra but a dense stand of second-growth palmetto. The long needle spines could stab through the hide of a horse, but not that of a camel. He turned his mount's head and it charged straight at the thicket.

He heard the hoofs closer behind him and the hoarse breathing of a horse at full gallop, then saw the mare's golden head appear in the periphery of his vision.

'Now is your chance, Abadan Riji!' Osman called, and pushed the mare alongside the camel. Penrod leant across the narrow gap and thrust at his turbaned head, but Osman swayed back and kept his targe low, sneering at Penrod over the rim. 'The fox never comes twice to the snare,' he said.

'You learn swiftly.' Penrod conceded, and caught

the great crusader sword on his own slim blade, turning it in the air so that it flew past his head. He steered the camel with his toes against its neck into the thicket of spiny palmetto. The camel crashed through, but Osman turned aside, breaking off his attack rather than lame or cripple the mare.

He galloped furiously round the edge of the thicket while the camel ran straight through. He had lost at least a hundred paces as he came back into the camel's tracks and rode hard to catch up with it again.

Penrod saw the wide expanse of the Nile directly ahead, a shimmering luminescence in the fading light. The camel bounded forward under him as it, too, saw the river. Penrod carried the sabre in his right hand, with the goad and the reins in the left. 'Yakub, take my pistol!' he said softly. 'And for the love and mercy of Allah, try this time to aim fair and shoot straight.'

Yakub reached round his body and pulled the Webley from his sash. 'The remarkable Yakub will slay this false emir with a single shot,' he cried, took deliberate aim and closed both eyes before he fired.

Osman Atalan did not flinch at the crack of the shot: he came on swiftly, but he had seen how close they were to the riverbank. He swung the mare in across the camel's rump, and stood in the stirrups with the long sword poised.

Penrod saw that he had changed his attack, and that he meant to cripple the camel with a deep cut through the hamstrings. With a stab of the goad and a hard tug on the reins he swung the beast's shoulder into the mare. Standing off balance in his stirrups Osman could not respond swiftly enough to counter the turn, and the two animals came together with the impetus of their combined weights. The camel was almost twice the height of the mare at the shoulder, and half again as heavy. She reeled and went down on her front knees. Osman was thrown on to her neck.

With the skill and balance of an acrobat he retained his seat, and kept a grip on his sword. However, by the time the mare had found her feet again, the camel had pulled too far ahead for her to catch up before it reached the riverbank.

As he raced towards it Penrod had only a moment to survey the river before him. He saw that the bank was a sheer drop of ten feet and that the water below it was green and deep. It was at least a mile across to the opposite bank and three large islands of reeds and papyrus were floating down in stately procession towards Khartoum in the north. That was all he had time to observe. With Osman and his aggagiers racing up behind them he urged the camel straight to the top of the bank.

'In God's Name!' shrieked Yakub. 'I cannot swim.'

'If you stay here the Dervish women will have your balls,' Penrod reminded him.

'I can swim!' Yakub changed his mind.

'Sensible Yakub!' Penrod grunted, and as the camel hesitated he stabbed hard into its neck with the goad. It leapt outwards so violently that Yakub lost his grip on the Webley as he snatched at a handhold. With a gut-wrenching sensation they dropped to hit the water with a splash as high as the bank above their heads. The aggagiers reined in their horses and milled about on top of the bank, firing down at the two men floundering on the surface.

'Stop!' Osman shouted angrily, and knocked up the barrel of al-Noor's carbine. His intervention came too late, for a bullet fired by one of the others hit the camel and damaged its spine. The terrified beast swam desperately with its front feet, but its paralysed back legs anchored it so that it turned in small circles, bellowing and hissing with terror. Despite the crippling injury it rode high in the water, buoyed by the inflated waterskins.

'You think you have cheated me yet again,' Osman shouted across the water, 'but I am Osman Atalan, and your life belongs to me.'

Penrod guessed immediately from the emir's tone of false bravado that, like most desert Arabs, he could not swim. For all his wild courage on land, he would never expose himself and his beautiful mare to the attack of the jinn and the monstrous Nile crocodiles that infested these waters. He would not follow his enemy over the bank into the swift green river.

For a minute longer Osman wrestled with his chivalrous instincts, his passionate desire for single combat, to avenge himself on his enemy with the sword. Then he gave way to expediency, and made an abrupt, eloquent chopping gesture with his right hand.

'Kill them!' he ordered. At once his aggagiers jumped to the ground and lined the top of the bank. They aimed volley after volley at the group of bobbing heads. Penrod seized Yakub by one arm and dragged him behind the struggling camel, using it as a shield. The current carried them swiftly downstream and the aggagiers followed, running along the bank, and keeping up a hail of carbine fire. All the time the current was carrying them away from the bank and the range was opening. At last a lucky shot struck the camel in the head, and it rolled over like a log in the water.

Penrod drew the dagger from his sash, and cut loose one of the inflated skins from its saddle. 'Hold here, brave Yakub,' he gasped, and the terrified Arab seized the tag of rawhide rope. They abandoned the camel's carcass, and Penrod swam them slowly out across the current towards the middle of the river.

As darkness dropped over them, with the suddenness of the African night, the shape of the Dervish on the bank faded away and only the muzzle flashes of their rifles still showed. Penrod swam with a gentle sidestroke, kicking with both legs, paddling with one hand and towing Yakub with the other by the scruff of his neck. Yakub was clinging to the skin bladder, and shivering like a half-drowned puppy. 'There are crocodiles in this cursed river so large they could swallow a buffalo, horns and all.' His teeth chattered and he choked on a mouthful of water.

'Then they would not trouble themselves with a skinny little Jaalin,' Penrod comforted him. A huge dark shape loomed out of the gloom and bore down on them. It was one of the floating islands of papyrus and reeds. He caught a handful of reeds as it drifted by, and dragged himself and Yakub up on to it. The vegetation was so densely matted and intertwined it could have supported a herd of elephants. It undulated softly under their feet as they crawled across it to the side nearest Khartoum. They squatted there, regaining their strength and gazing across at the eastern bank.

Penrod was worried that, on such a moonless night, he might not see the city when they reached it and stared into the darkness until his eyes ached. Suddenly he thought he could make out the ugly square shape of Mukran Fort, but his eyes were playing tricks and, when he stared at it, it dissolved. 'After such a journey, it would be the height of stupidity to sail past Khartoum in the night,' he muttered, and then his doubts were dispelled.

From downstream there came the crash of artillery fire. He leapt to his feet and peered through the papyrus stems. He saw the brilliant orange muzzle flashes of cannon demarcating the Omdurman side of the river. Seconds later the shells burst on the east bank and illuminated Khartoum's waterfront. This time there was no mistaking the stark outline of Mukran Fort and, beyond it, the consular palace. He smiled grimly as he remembered the nightly artillery bombardment by the Dervish gunner, whom David Benbrook had dubbed the Bedlam Bedouin. 'At least he has not run out of ammunition yet,' he said, and explained to Yakub what they had to do.

'We are safe here,' Yakub demurred. 'If we stay here the river will push us in time to the bank and we can walk ashore like men, not swim like iguanas.'

'That will not happen until you reach the Shabluka Gorge, where this raft will surely be destroyed. You know well that the gorge is the lair of all the most evil river djinni.'

Yakub thought about that for a few minutes, then announced, 'Brave Yakub fears no jinnee, but he will swim with you to the city to watch over you.'

The skin bladder had leaked half its air, and they blew it tight again while they waited for the raft to reach the most advantageous point. By then the moon had risen, and although the Dervish bombardment had petered out, they could make out the city skyline clearly, and even see a few small cooking fires. They slipped into the water. Yakub was becoming more courageous by the minute and Penrod showed him how to kick with his legs and help to drive the bladder across the current.

After a laborious swim Penrod felt the bottom under his feet. He let the bladder go and dragged Yakub ashore. 'Fearless Yakub defies all the crocodiles and jinn of this little stream.' Yakub posed boldly on the bank and made an obscene gesture towards the Nile.

'Yakub should close his fearless mouth,' Penrod advised, 'before one of the Egyptian sentries puts a bullet in his defiant backside.' He wanted to get into the city secretly. Apart from the danger of being shot by the guards, any contact with the troops would result in him being taken immediately to General Gordon. His orders from Sir Evelyn Baring were to deliver his message to Benbrook first, and only then to report to Gordon.

Penrod had spent months in Khartoum before and after the disaster of El Obeid, so he was intimately aware of the layout of the defences and fortifications, which were concentrated along the riverfront. Keeping well outside the walls and the canal, he worked his way swiftly around the southern outskirts. When he was almost opposite the domed roof of the French consulate, he approached the canal bank. Once he was certain that it was clear, they waded across, the water only chin deep.

When they reached the other side they lay up in the palm grove to wait for the patrol to pass. Penrod whiffed the smoke of Turkish tobacco before he saw them. They sauntered past along the footpath, rifles trailing, the sergeant smoking. It was behaviour typical of the slovenly Egyptian troops.

As soon as they were gone he dropped into the drainage ditch that led to the outer city wall. The ooze stank of raw sewerage, but they crawled through the tunnel, past the back wall of the French consulate and into the old town. Penrod was perturbed at how easily they had got through. Gordon's defences must be stretched to breaking point. At the beginning of the siege he had commanded seven thousand Egyptians, but that number must have been much reduced by the attrition of disease and desertion.

They hurried through the deserted alleys, stepping round the bloated carcasses of men and animals. Even the appetite of the crows and vultures was inadequate to the task of devouring such an abundance. The stench of a city under siege assailed his nostrils, death and putrefaction. He had heard it called the cholera bouquet.

Penrod paused to pull his pocket watch from its pouch and held it to his ear. It had not survived the dousing in the river. He looked at the moon, judged that it was well after midnight, and hurried on unchallenged through the deserted streets. When they reached the gates of the consular palace there was still lamplight in a few windows. The sentry at the front gate was asleep, curled like a dog in his box. His rifle was propped against the wall, and Penrod took charge of it before he kicked him awake. It took some time and a great deal of argument with the sergeant of the guard, but despite his appearance and the smell of sewerage that wafted from his robes Penrod was able at last to convince him that he was a British officer.

When he was led to David Benbrook's office, the consul was reading by lamplight. He looked annoyed by the intrusion, as he removed the reading glasses from his nose and stood up. He was dressed in a velvet smoking jacket and had been poring over a sheaf of documents. 'What is it?' he snapped.

'Good evening, Consul.' Penrod saluted him. 'I'm sorry to trouble you at this time of night, but I've just arrived from Cairo with messages from Sir Evelyn Baring.'

'God bless my soul!' David stared at Penrod in amazement. 'You're English!'

'I am, sir. I have had the pleasure of your previous acquaintance. I am Captain Ballantyne of the 10th Hussars.'

'Ballantyne! I remember you well. As a matter of fact we were speaking about you just the other day. How do you do, my dear fellow?' After they had shaken hands David held his handkerchief to his nose. 'First thing is to get you a bath and some fresh clothes.' He rang for the servants. 'I am not sure that there will be hot water at this time of night,' he apologized, 'but it should not take long to get the boiler going.'

Not only was the bathwater scalding, David Benbrook even produced half a cake of perfumed soap from Paris and lent Penrod a razor. While he shaved David sat on the lid of the commode across

200

the tiled bathroom. He seemed oblivious to Penrod's nudity, and scribbled notes in a little red leatherbound book, as Penrod repeated Baring's long and involved message. Then he questioned Penrod avidly about General Stewart's preparations for the rescue expedition. 'Hasn't even left Wadi Halfa yet?' he exclaimed, with alarm. 'By Gad, I hope we'll be able to hold out until he gets here.'

David was of almost the same build as Penrod. Even a pair of his boots fitted as though they were made for the younger man. Penrod had considerably less girth, but he belted in the trousers and tucked in a freshly ironed white shirt. When he was dressed David led him back to his study. 'I cannot even offer you brandy to wash it down,' he said, as a servant placed a beautiful Sèvres plate before Penrod. On it sat a small portion of dhurra cake and a lump of goat's milk cheese no larger than the first joint of his thumb. 'Hard commons, I'm afraid.'

'Very nourishing, sir.' Penrod nibbled the dhurra.

'Damned pleased to have your despatches, Ballantyne. We've been completely in the dark here for months. How long did it take you from Cairo?'

'I left there on the nineteenth of last month, sir.'

'Damn me, but that was good going.' David nodded. 'Now, tell me what the London newspapers are saying.' He was eager for every scrap of news that Penrod could tell him.

'They are quite openly reporting the bad blood between General Gordon and Mr Gladstone, sir, and public opinion is strongly on General Gordon's side. They want Khartoum relieved, the General rescued, and the savages taught to mind their manners.'

'What is your opinion, Captain?'

'As a serving officer I do not allow myself an opinion on such matters, sir.'

'Very wise.' David smiled. 'But as a member of the public, do you think that the Prime Minister has shown lack of resolve?'

Penrod hesitated. 'May I speak frankly, sir?'

'That is what I am inviting you to do. Whatever you say will remain between us. You have my word on it.'

'I think that Mr Gladstone has shown neither cowardice nor indecision in refusing to send an army upriver to save the life of General Gordon, as most of the British public believes. The general had only to embark on one of his steamers and come home. I believe that the Prime Minister did not feel justified in involving the nation in costly and risky operations here in the heart of Sudan merely to vindicate the personal honour of one man.'

David drew a deep breath. 'My goodness me! I asked for your frank opinion and I got it. But tell me, Ballantyne, don't you think that there is not some personal resentment in Whitehall for an officer whose rash and intractable actions have brought so much odium upon them?'

'It would be remarkable if that was not the case. It is clearly demonstrated in the despatches from Sir Evelyn that I deliverd to you.'

David considered Penrod seriously. He was not just a pretty fellow, he thought, he had a thinking head on his shoulders. 'So you would oppose the despatch of Wolseley's force to our relief?'

'Oh, never!' Penrod laughed. 'I'm a soldier, and

soldiers thrive on war. I hope to be in the thick of it, even if it doesn't make good sense, which is apparent, and if matters turn nasty, which is highly likely.'

David laughed with him. 'War seldom makes good sense,' he agreed. 'It is refreshing to hear a military man say it. But why has Gladstone changed his mind, and agreed to send an army?'

'The expressed desire of the nation is a force to which Mr Gladstone has always acceded. I understand from Sir Evelyn Baring that the Prime Minister was advised that only a single brigade would be needed for the expedition. Only after he had reluctantly taken the decision, and announced it to the nation, did the war ministry ask for a much larger force. It was too late then to reverse the decision so the relieving army has become not a single brigade but ten thousand men.'

The hours sped away as they talked until the grandfather clock in the corner chimed again. David stared at it in astonishment. 'Two o'clock, upon my soul! We'll have to give you a few hours' sleep before you meet Gordon. I imagine you're in for a torrid time with him.'

The servants were waiting up for him but David dismissed them and personally showed Penrod to one of the guest suites. The night was so sultry and he was so tired that he could not bother himself to don the thick flannel nightshirt that David provided. Instead he stripped naked and before he crawled beneath the single sheet he placed his dagger under the pillow. Then he went out like a candle in a high wind.

He awoke without a change in his breathing, and was immediately aware that someone was in the bedroom with him. While he feigned sleep, he tried to remember where he was. Through his eyelashes he saw that the curtains were drawn and the light in the room was muted. It was still early in the morning. He moved his hand infinitesimally slowly under the pillow until his fingers curled around the hilt of his dagger. He waited like a coiled adder for the strike.

There was a light footstep beside his bed, and someone coughed softly, nervously. The small sound gave him direction and he launched himself off the bed. He bore the intruder to the floor, held him by the throat with one hand, and with the other touched him with the point of the dagger. 'If you move I will kill you,' he whispered ferociously in Arabic. 'Who are you?'

Then he became aware that his captive smelt of rosebuds and the throat he held was silken smooth and warm. The body under him was clad in taffeta bodice and skirts and there were marvellous protuberances and hollows under the fine cloth. He released his hold and sprang to his feet. He stared down in astonishment and consternation as his captive sat up. It took him some seconds to grasp that he had assaulted and threatened a young woman with shining blonde hair. And that sitting on the floor, with her skirts in disarray around her, her eyes were at the same level as his naked groin, her gaze was fixed upon an object that happened to be a part of his anatomy seldom exposed to public scrutiny.

Still gripping the dagger, he spun round to grab the sheet from the bed. Before he could wrap it round himself he realized that he was offering the reverse view to the young woman. Haste made him clumsy, and he fumbled until at last, modestly covered, he faced her again.

'I am mortified, Miss Benbrook. I had no idea it was you. You startled me.'

Her pale cheeks were slowly suffused with a rosy blush, but she was still panting for breath, as though she had run a distance. The effect this had on what lay beneath her bodice was riveting. 'If I startled you, sir, then you have no idea how you have alarmed me. Who are you and what are you doing—' Her hand flew to her mouth as she recognized him, despite his unflattering new haircut. 'Captain Ballantyne!'

'Your servant, madam.' His bow was spoilt by the need to retain a grip on both the dagger and his sheet. She scrambled to her feet, stared at him a moment longer with wide eyes, then fled from the room. He stared after her. He had forgotten how pleasing she was to the eye, a condition not at all spoilt by her confusion and dismay. Then he grinned. 'That alone was worth the journey,' he said to himself.

He whistled as he shaved and dressed, then winked at himself in the mirror and said aloud, 'Perhaps next time she will recognize me more readily, now that she has more to remember me by.' Then he went down the stairs.

David was already seated at the breakfast table, but apart from the white-robed servants he was alone. 'Have some of this.' He placed a spoonful of an amorphous pale green substance on Penrod's plate. 'The taste is execrable, but I have it on excellent authority that it is highly nutritious.'

Penrod peered at it suspiciously. It looked like green cheese. 'What is it?'

'I understand that it is the curds of papyrus and reed weeds, made by my daughters. We eat a lot of it. In fact, since the official rations were reduced to one cup of dhurra corn a day, we eat little else.'

Penrod put a morsel cautiously into his mouth. 'My compliments to your daughters. It is very palatable.' He tried to sound convincing.

'It's not bad really. Try it with Worcester sauce or Gentleman's Relish. You will soon grow accustomed to it. Now, shall we go and call upon General Gordon?'

*   *   *

General Gordon turned from the window through which he had been staring across the river at the enemy emplacements. He stared at Penrod with that disconcerting blue gaze as he saluted. 'At ease, Captain. I believe you made the journey from Cairo in record time,' he said.

How did he know that? Penrod wondered, and then it was obvious. We have the boasting of the fearless Yakub to thank.

In silence General Gordon listened to his report and the messages he had brought from Sir Evelyn. When he had finished speaking, Gordon did not reply immediately. He paced up and down the long room, finally stopping to stare at the large-scale map of the Sudan that was spread on the table under the windows. The view from them was unrestricted: the glass panes had been blown out by shrapnel from the Dervish artillery across the river, but Gordon had taken no steps to fortify his headquarters or to protect his person. He seemed to be concerned only for the safety of the city and the well-being of its people.

'I suppose that we must be grateful to the Prime Minister for coming to the rescue of the populace, even though he is several months too late,' he remarked at last. Then he looked up at Penrod. 'The only consolation for me is that now I have at least one British officer on my staff.'

At those words, Penrod felt the first chill breeze of unease blow down his spine. 'My orders from General Stewart, sir, are to return to Wadi Halfa as soon as I have delivered my despatches to you. I am seconded to the new Camel Corps with orders to assist in guiding them across the loop of the Nile to the assault upon Metemma.'

Gordon thought about that for a moment, then shook his head. 'If General Stewart has not yet left Wadi Halfa it will be months before he reaches Metemma. You will be more useful here than sitting at Wadi Halfa. Besides, there must be hundreds of other guides qualified to bring the Camel Corps across the loop. When the rescue column reaches Abu Hamed, I shall reconsider. But in the meantime I need you here.'

He said it with such finality that Penrod knew argument was futile. His dreams of action and glory were shattered. Instead of riding into the city at the head of his corps after fighting his way up from Metemma, he was now sentenced to the dreary monotony of the siege.

I must bide my time, and choose my moment, he decided, and did not let his expression betray his true feelings. 'It will be an honour to serve under you, General, but I would appreciate having those orders in writing.'

'You shall have them,' Gordon promised, 'but

207

now I must bring you up to date with the situation here, and our immediate and most pressing problems. Take a seat, Ballantyne.'

Gordon spoke quickly, almost with agitation, flitting from subject to subject, chain-smoking cigarettes from a silver case. Slowly Penrod began to understand the enormous strain under which he had been working, and to gain an inkling of the terrible loneliness of this command. He sensed that before his arrival, there had been nobody Gordon could trust to share with him some of the burden. If Penrod was not an equal in rank, at least he was an officer of a first-line British regiment, and as such was worth a dhow full of Egyptian staff officers.

'You see, Ballantyne, I have here the responsibility and duty without full control. I am daily afflicted not only by the incompetence of the Egyptian officers but by their unconscionable behaviour and total lack of morality or sense of duty. They wilfully disobey orders, if they think they can escape the consequences, they neglect their duties and spend most of their time with their concubines. Unless I chivvy them they seldom bother to visit the front-line defences. I am aware that they conspire and intrigue with the Dervish in the hope that they may win advantage when the city falls, which they are convinced it will. They steal from their own men. The troops fall asleep at their posts, and in their turn steal from the populace. I suspect that large quantities of dhurra have been stolen from the granary. The women and children of the city spit at me and revile me in the streets when I am forced to reduce the rations yet again. We are down to a cupful of grain per person per day.' He lit another cigarette and the flame of the match fluttered in his cupped hands. He puffed rapidly, then smiled coldly at Penrod. 'So you can imagine that your assistance will be welcome. That is especially true since you are so well acquainted with the layout of the city.'

'Of course you may rely on me, General.' Despite his cold, almost messianic gaze, Penrod wondered how close Gordon was to breaking point.

'I am going to delegate to you the following responsibilities at the outset. Until now Major al-Faroque has been in charge of the storage and distribution of food. His efforts have been at best pathetically inadequate. I suspect, though I cannot prove it, that he knows something of the missing grain. You will take over from him immediately. I want you to let me have an inventory of all the available supplies as soon as possible. Under the rule of martial law, you have the power of seizure. You may commandeer any stores you need. Any transgressions are to be treated with the utmost severity. You may flog or shoot looters and black-marketeers without reference to me. The troops and the populace must be forced to accept the unpleasant laws—you will make them fully aware that the alternatives are even worse. Do you understand that?'

'Of course, General.'

'Do you know a Ryder Courtney?'

'Only in passing, sir.'

'He is a trader and merchant of this city. I was obliged to requisition a shipment of his dhurra. As a mercenary without an altruistic bone in his body, he resents it. He has his own compound within the city, and behaves as though he is independent of all authority. I want you to make the true position

209

clear to him.'

'I understand, sir,' said Penrod, and thought sourly, So now I am no longer a Hussar but a policeman and quartermaster.

Gordon was watching his expression, and saw the reaction, but he went on unruffled: 'Among other enterprises, he owns and operates a large river steamer. At present it is undergoing repairs in his workshop. Once it is serviceable again, it will be useful in future military operations and possible evacuation of our populace, should Stewart's column fail to arrive in time. Courtney also has horses and camels, and much else that will be vital to us as the Dervish noose tightens around us.' Gordon stood up as a signal that the meeting was at an end. 'Find out what he is up to, and what he knows of the missing dhurra, Ballantyne. Then report back to me.'

*   *   *

Penrod knew of Ryder Courtney's reputation: David Benbrook had spoken of him and even Sir Evelyn Baring had taken note of him. It seemed that he was a resourceful and formidable character. If Penrod was to carry out Gordon's orders he would gain nothing by marching up to the front gate of Courtney's compound and announcing himself and his intentions. First, he thought, a little scouting expedition is called for.

He left the palace gardens by the river gate. It was unguarded, and he made a note of that. He moved swiftly along the waterfront, to prevent warning of his arrival being telegraphed ahead. At the first redoubt of the defences the sentries were recumbent, resting weary limbs and eyes. Penrod had heard of Gordon's swift justice, and he had no wish to precipitate a massacre and decimation of the Egyptian garrison, so he used cane and boot to remind them of their duty.

He went on along the line of fortifications and gun emplacements that had been erected since his last visit to the city. It was evident that these had been planned by General Gordon, for they had been laid out with a soldier's eye and understanding of terrain. He inspected the field guns, and though he was no artilleryman, he picked out the deficiencies in care and handling of the weapons. The shortage of ammunition was painfully apparent. When he questioned them, the gunners told him they were not allowed independent fire but had to wait for orders from their officers before they were allowed to send a single shell across the river. The Dervish on the opposite bank were under no such limitation, and morning and evening they indulged in uninhibited barrages, which made up in enthusiasm for any lack of accuracy. Usually the middle of the day was calm and peaceful while both sides rested from the heat of the sun.

Penrod moved quickly past the harbour, where he noticed a white river steamer with most of her machinery stripped out and spread on the stone wharf for repair. Her hull and superstructure were peppered with shrapnel hits. A gang of Arab workers was busy patching and painting over the damage. A white engineer supervised them, encouraging his crew with a chorus of oaths and imprecations that carried clearly across the water in the accents of the Glasgow docks. It was obvious

211

that it would be weeks, if not months, before the steamer was ready to sail. Penrod moved on along the river frontage of the Blue Nile towards Fort Burri and the arsenal.

As he picked his way through the alleyways, which were almost clogged with shell debris and filth, brown faces looked down at him from the windows and rickety balconies that almost met overhead. Women held up their naked infants so that he could see the swellings and bruising of scurvy, the skeletal limbs. 'We are starving, Effendi. Give us food,' they pleaded. Their cries alerted the beggars, who hobbled out of the gloomy depths of the alleyways to pluck at his clothing. He scattered them with a few shrewd cuts of his cane.

The guns on the parapets of Fort Burri covered the north bank of the Blue Nile, and the Dervish fortifications facing them. Penrod paused to study them, and saw that the enemy were taking few precautions. Even with the naked eye he could see figures across the river moving about in the open. Some Dervish women were washing their laundry on the riverbank and spreading it out to dry in full view of Fort Burri. They must have realized how perilously depleted was Gordon's stock of shot and shell.

Behind Fort Burri stood the squat and ugly blockhouses of the arsenal and the munitions store. General Gordon was using them as the city granary. There were sentries at the entrance and at each revetment that supported the crumbling walls. From what Gordon had told him, even those guards and the repairs to the walls had been no match for the ingenuity of Ryder Courtney or the Egyptian officers, or whoever was to blame for the depredations in the granary. However, this was not the time to visit the arsenal or to conduct an audit of the stores. That would come later. Penrod was headed towards the sprawling complex of Ryder Courtney's compound, which lay a short way beyond, almost on the canal that defended the city from an assault out of the southern desert.

As he approached he saw that there was unusual activity in progress on the canal banks behind the walls of the compound. This puzzled him, so he left the road and followed the towpath that ran along the embankment. At first he thought that the many men working in the canal were constructing some form of fortification. Then he realized that women were carrying bundles on their heads from the embankment into the rear gate of Courtney's compound.

As he came closer he saw that a huge raft of river weed almost blocked the canal. It was similar to the mass of vegetation on which he and Yakub had escaped from Osman Atalan the previous day. Dozens of Arabs swarmed over the raft, clad only in loincloths and armed with scythes and sickles. They were cutting the papyrus and river weed and tying it into bundles for the women to carry away.

What the devil are they up to? He was intrigued. And how did that raft of weed get into the canal so conveniently placed for Courtney to harvest? Then the answer occurred to him. Of course! He must have captured and roped it in the main river, then used muscle power to drag it up the canal. They warned me that he is crafty.

The workers hailed Penrod respectfully, invoking Allah's blessing on him. They looked impressed when he returned the greeting in fluent, colloquial Arabic. Although he wore no uniform, they knew his name was Abadan Riji, and that he had ridden off Osman Atalan and all his most famous aggagiers to reach Khartoum. Yakub had seen to it that all the city knew of their heroics.

When Penrod followed the line of Sudanese women through the rear gate of the compound, no one challenged him. He found himself in a large walled enclosure, which swarmed with activity. The women piled their bundles in the centre and returned to the canal for the next load. Another team was seated in groups, chattering as they picked over the cut stems and sorted them into piles. They discarded all the dead and dried-out material, and chose only that which was still green and succulent. This they sorted into the various types of vegetation. The largest heap comprised the common papyrus, but there was also water-hyacinth, and three other types of grass and reed. The *nymphaea* was obviously the most prized plant for it was not piled on the dusty ground like the papyrus and hyacinth but carefully packed into sacks and carried away for pulping by another team of women. They were working over a long line of stamp mortars that usually crushed dhurra into flour. The women worked in unison, thumping the heavy wooden pole they used as a pestle into the bowl-shaped mortar, pounding the water-lilies with a little water into pulp. They sang as they swayed and rocked to the rhythm of the swinging poles.

Once the contents of the mortars were reduced to a thick green paste, another party of women collected it in large black clay pots, and carried it through the gate of a second enclosure. Penrod was interested and followed them. No sooner had he

214

stepped through the gate when, for the first time, he was challenged in a peremptory treble. 'Who are you and what are you doing here?'

Penrod found himself confronted by two young females, neither of whom stood much taller than his belt buckle. One was dark brunette and the other was golden blonde. One had eyes the colour of molten toffee, while the smaller girl's were the bright blue of petunia petals. Both gazed up at him with a severe expression and pursed lips. The taller child had her fists on her hips in a pugnacious attitude. 'You're not allowed in here. This is a secret place.'

Penrod recovered from his surprise, gallantly lifted his hat and bowed deeply. 'I beg your pardon, ladies, I did not mean to trespass. Please accept my apologies and allow me to introduce myself. I am Captain Penrod Ballantyne of Her Majesty's 10th Royal Hussars. At present I am on the staff of General Gordon.'

Both girls' expressions softened as they continued to stare at him. They were unaccustomed to being addressed in such polite terms. Furthermore, like most other women, they were not impervious to Penrod's charms.

'I am Saffron Benbrook, sir,' said the taller girl, and curtsied. 'But you may call me Saffy.'

'Your servant, Miss Saffy.'

'And I am Amber Benbrook, but some people call me Midget,' said the blonde. 'I don't really like the name, but I suppose I am a little shorter than my sister.'

'I agree entirely. It is not a fitting name for such a lovely young lady. If you will permit me, I shall address you as Miss Amber.'

'How do you do?' Amber returned his bow with a curtsy, and when she straightened up she found herself in love for the first time. It was a sensation of warmth and pressure in her chest, disturbing but not altogether unpleasant.

'I know who you are,' she said, just a trifle breathlessly.

'Do you, indeed? And, pray, how is that?'

'I heard Ryder speaking to Daddy about you.'

'Daddy, I presume, is David Benbrook. But who is Ryder?'

'Ryder Courtney. He said you had the finest pair of whiskers in Christendom. What happened to them?'

'Ah!' replied Penrod, his face suddenly touched with frost. 'He must be a noted comedian.'

'He is a great hunter and very, very clever.' Saffron rushed to his defence. 'He knows the name of every animal and bird in the world—the Latin names,' she added portentously.

Amber was determined to wrest back Penrod's attention from her twin. 'Ryder says that the ladies find you dashing and gallant.' Penrod looked slightly better pleased, until Amber went on innocently, 'And that you agree wholeheartedly with their opinion.'

Penrod changed the topic. 'Who is in charge here?'

'We are,' the twins chorused.

'What are you doing? It looks very interesting.'

'We are making plant curds to feed our people.'

'I would be most grateful if you could explain the process to me.' The twins seized upon the invitation and competed vigorously for his attention, interrupting and contradicting each

216

other at every opportunity. Each grabbed one of Penrod's hands and dragged him into the inner courtyard.

'When the most succulent leaves are crushed, then they have to be filtered.'

'To get rid of the pith and rubbish.' There was no longer any thought of safeguarding secrets.

'We strain it through trade cloth from Ryder's stores.'

'We have to squeeze it to get out all the goodness.'

Pairs of Sudanese women were pouring the green pulp into lengths of printed cloth, then twisting it between them. The juices dribbled into the huge black cast-iron pots, which stood on three legs over the smouldering cooking fires.

'We measure the temperature—' Saffron brandished a large thermometer importantly.

'—and when it reaches seventy degrees,' Amber cut in, 'the protein coagulates—'

'I am telling it,' said Saffron, furiously. 'I am the oldest.'

'Only by one hour,' Amber retorted, and gabbled out the rest of the explanation. 'Then we sieve off the curds and make them into bricks and dry them in the sun.' She pointed triumphantly at the long trestle tables laden with square blocks set out upon them in neat rows. This was what Penrod had eaten for breakfast, and he remembered David's warning that there was precious little else.

'We call it green-cake. You can taste some if you like.' Amber broke off a morsel and stood on tiptoe to place it between his lips.

'Scrumptious!' Penrod exclaimed, and swallowed manfully.

'Have some more.'

'Excellent, but enough for now. Your father says it is even tastier with Worcester Sauce,' he said hurriedly, forestalling delivery of the next mouthful, which was already on its way in Amber's grubby little hand. 'How much green-cake can you make in a day?'

'Not enough to feed everybody. Just enough for ourselves and our own people.'

The efficacy of the green-cakes was apparent. Unlike the rest of the malnourished populace, none of the inhabitants of the compound was showing signs of starvation. In fact, the twins were blooming. Then he remembered his brief meeting with their elder sister that morning. Nothing wrong with her either. He smiled at the memory, and the two children took it as a sign of his approval and smiled with him.

Penrod realized that he now had staunch allies in the Courtney stronghold. 'You really are two very clever young ladies,' he said. 'I would be most obliged if you were to show me around the rest of the compound. I hear that there are all sorts of fascinating things here.'

'Would you like to see the animals?' cried Amber.

'The monkeys?' said Saffron.

'The bongos?'

'Everything,' agreed Penrod. 'I would like to see everything.'

It was soon apparent that the twins were the favourites of everyone and that they had the run of the Courtney compound. They were particular friends and intimates of Ali the animal-keeper. It was only with the greatest difficulty that the old man prevented himself grinning with delight as soon as he laid eyes on them. They led Penrod from cage to cage, calling to the animals by name and feeding them by hand when they responded.

'They didn't like the green-cake at all when we first tried to feed them with it, but now they all love it. Just look how they gobble it up.' Amber pointed.

'What about dhurra? They must like that too?' Penrod set a bait for her.

'Oh, I suppose they do,' Saffron cut in, 'but there isn't enough for the people, let alone the animals.'

'We only get a cupful a day,' Amber confirmed.

'I thought your friend Ryder had plenty of dhurra and that he was selling it.'

'Oh, yes! He had a whole boatload. But General Gordon took it all from him. Ryder was furious.'

Penrod was grateful that the girls' innocent disclosures virtually guaranteed that, despite the general's suspicions, Courtney was not guilty of the theft of grain from the arsenal. He had no reason to feel any warmth for the man, especially after his remarks about Penrod's whiskers and his good opinion of himself, but he was an Englishman and it would have been distasteful for Penrod to have to confirm Gordon's suspicions.

'I would very much like to meet your friend Ryder,' he suggested tentatively. 'Would you introduce me?'

'Oh, yes! Come with us.'

They dragged him from the menagerie, and across an inner courtyard until they reached a small door at the far end. The twins let go of his hands and raced each other to the door. They threw it open and burst into the room beyond. Penrod stepped up close behind them and, from the doorway, surveyed the room swiftly.

It was obviously both an office and the private living quarters of the owner of the compound. A massive pair of elephant tusks were mounted on the far wall, the largest Penrod had ever seen. The other walls were covered with magnificently woven Persian carpets, and dozens of murky yellowing photographs in dark wooden frames. More carpets covered the floors, and in a curtained recess, a large *angareb* bed was spread with golden leopardskins, dappled with black rosettes. The chairs and the massive desk were hewn from polished native teak. The bookcases held rows of leatherbound journals, and scientific books on flora and fauna. A row of rifles and muzzle-loading guns stood in a rack between the curves of the thick yellow tusks. Penrod's gaze slid over this untidy masculine display, then riveted on the couple who stood in the middle of the room. Even the tumultuous twins were frozen with shock at the sight.

Man and woman were locked in a passionate embrace, oblivious to everything and everyone around them. Saffron broke the silence with a wail of accusation: 'She's kissing him! Becky is kissing Ryder on his mouth!'

Ryder Courtney and Rebecca Benbrook sprang apart guiltily, then stood, frozen, staring at the group in the doorway. Rebecca turned ice pale and her eyes seemed to fill her face as she looked at Penrod. He cut her a mockingly appreciative salute. 'We meet again so soon, Miss Benbrook.'

Rebecca dropped her gaze to the floor and now her cheeks turned the bright crimson of live coals. Her mortification was so intense that she felt dizzy and swayed on her feet. Then, with an enormous effort, she rallied. Without looking at either man she rushed forward and seized her little sisters by the wrists. 'You horrible children! How many times have you been told to knock before you enter a room?'

She dragged them out of the open door, and Saffron's voice receded in the distance: 'You were kissing him. I hate you. I'll never speak to you again. You were kissing Ryder.'

The two men faced each other as though neither had heard the sisterly accusations of betrayal. 'Mr Courtney, I presume. I hope my visit has not come at an inconvenient time.'

'Captain Ballantyne, sir. I heard that you arrived in our lovely city late last night. Your fame precedes you.'

'So it appears,' Penrod conceded. 'Though for the life of me I know not how.'

'Simple enough, I assure you.' Ryder was relieved that there was to be no heavy-handed banter regarding the romantic episode that Ballantyne had witnessed—it might have led to an outbreak of hostilities. 'Your outrider, Yakub of the Jaalin, is the intimate friend of the nursemaid of the Benbrook twins and a stalwart of their household, a good lady by the name of Nazeera. Her busy tongue is one of her most apparent failings.'

'Aha! Now I understand. Perhaps you were even expecting my visit.'

'It comes as no great surprise,' Ryder admitted. 'I understand that General Gordon, may all his enterprises flourish, has some questions for me regarding the dhurra missing from the arsenal.'

Penrod inclined his head in acknowledgement. 'I see you keep yourself well informed.' He was appraising Ryder Courtney with a penetrating gaze, cloaked by a disarming smile as they sparred.

'I try to keep abreast of affairs.' Ryder was not at all disarmed by the smile, and his own gaze was just as shrewd. 'But please do come in, my dear fellow. It is perhaps a little early, but may I offer you a cigar and a glass of first-rate Cognac?'

'I was convinced those two marvellous commodities no longer existed in this naughty world.' Penrod moved across to the chair Ryder indicated.

When their cigars were drawing evenly they regarded each other over their charged glasses. Ryder gave the toast: 'I congratulate you on your speedy journey from Cairo.'

'I wish I were already on my way back.'

'Khartoum is hardly a spa,' Ryder agreed. They sipped the brandy and talked guardedly, still sounding each other out. Ryder knew Penrod by sight and reputation so there were no real surprises for him.

Penrod learnt swiftly that he had not been misinformed, and that Ryder was a formidable character, tough, quick and resilient. He was also good-looking in a rugged, forthright style. No wonder the lovely Miss Benbrook had shown herself susceptible to his advances. I wonder just how susceptible. It might be amusing to test her commitment to this fellow, man to man and hand to hand, so to speak. Penrod smiled urbanely, masking the glint of steel in his eyes. He dearly loved a contest, pitting his skills and wits against another, especially if a handsome prize were at

222

stake. There was more to it than that. The nubile Miss Benbrook's involvement with Ryder Courtney added a new dimension to the sharp attraction he had previously felt towards her. It seemed that, despite appearances, she was not made of ice, that there were depths beneath the surface, which might be fascinating to plumb. He was amused by his own choice of metaphor.

'You mentioned the missing dhurra,' Penrod broached the subject again.

Ryder nodded. 'I have a proprietary interest in that shipment,' he said. 'It once belonged to me. It was transported at great expense and no little hardship several hundred miles down the river, then commandeered, some might even say stolen, by the redoubtable Chinese Gordon the minute I landed it safely in Khartoum.' He fell silent and brooded on the injustice.

'Naturally you have not the faintest notion what happened to it once it passed out of your hands?' Penrod suggested delicately.

'I have made some enquiries,' Ryder admitted. Under his instructions Bacheet had spent several weeks pursuing them. Even the rabbit warren of ancient buildings and alleyways of Khartoum could not hide five thousand ardebs of grain indefinitely.

'I would be fascinated to known the results of those investigations.'

Ryder regarded the tip of his cigar with a frown of annoyance. The lack of humidity in the desert air desiccated the tobacco leaf and caused it to burn like a grass fire. 'Did you hear if, by any chance, the good general has offered a reward for the return of the missing dhurra?' he asked. 'Lord knows, he paid little enough for it on the first purchase. Six shillings a sack!'

'General Gordon has not spoken to me of a reward,' Penrod shook his head, 'but I will suggest it to him. I would think that a reward of six shillings a sack might bring forth information, don't you?'

'Perhaps not,' Ryder replied. 'However, I believe that an offer of twelve shillings would be almost certain to produce results.'

'I shall speak to him at the first opportunity.' Penrod nodded. 'Although that does seem a trifle steep.'

'None of his promissory notes, either,' Ryder warned. 'It is common knowledge that the Khedive has given him drawing rights of two hundred thousand pounds on the Cairo treasury. A few gold sovereigns would sing sweeter than all the paper canaries ever to come out of the forest.'

'A sentiment most poetically expressed, sir,' Penrod commended him.

*   *   *

Rebecca sat in her secret place in a hidden corner of the battlements in the consular palace. She was hidden by an ancient hundred-pounder cannon, a monstrous rusting relic that had probably never been fired in this nineteenth century, and would certainly never be fired again. She had covered her head and nightgown with a dark woollen cloak, and she knew that not even the twins would find her there.

She looked up at the night sky and could tell by the height of the Southern Cross above the desert horizon that it was well after midnight, but she felt as though she would never be able to sleep again.

In a single day her whole existence had been thrown into uproar and confusion. She felt like a captive wild bird, battering its wings against the bars, bleeding and terrified, falling to the floor of the cage with heart racing and body trembling, only to launch itself at the bars again in another futile attempt to escape.

She did not understand what was happening to her. Why did she feel this way? Nothing made sense. Her mind darted back to that morning when, as soon as she had seen the twins bathed and dressed, she had begun her weekly housekeeping inspection. As soon as she entered the blue guest suite she had seen the strange figure occupying the four-poster bed. She had not been informed by the staff of the arrival of any guests and Khartoum under siege was the last place to attract casual visitors. Knowing this, she should have left the bedroom immediately and raised the alarm. What had made her approach the bed she would never know. As she stooped over the sheet-covered figure, it had launched itself at her with the suddenness of a leopard dropping out of a tree on its prey. She found herself borne to the floor by a stark naked man with a dagger in his hand.

Remembering that terrible moment, she bowed her head and covered her face with her hands. It was not the first time that she had seen the male body. When Rebecca turned sixteen her parents had taken her on a tour of the capital cities of Europe. She and her mother had gone to see Michelangelo's *David*. She had been struck by the statue's unearthly beauty but the cold white marble had invoked in her no troublesome emotions. She had even been able, unblushingly, to discuss it with

225

her mother.

Her mother often described herself as emancipated. At the time Rebecca thought that this merely meant she smoked Turkish cigarettes in her boudoir and spoke frankly of the human anatomy and its functions. After her suicide Rebecca realized that the word had deeper significance. At the funeral in Cairo she had overheard some of the older women whispering together, and one had remarked tartly that Sarah Benbrook had made David a cuckold more often than she cooked him breakfast. Rebecca knew her mother never cooked breakfast. Nevertheless, she looked up the word 'cuckold' in her father's dictionary. It took her a while to work out the true meaning, but when she did she had decided that she did not want to be emancipated like her mother. She would be true to one man for life.

Rebecca had next seen the male body only last year. David had taken her and the twins with him on an official visit to the upper reaches of the Victoria Nile. The Shilluk and Dinka tribesmen who inhabited the banks of the river wore no clothing of any description. The girls recovered from the first surprise when their father remarked that it was merely custom and tradition for them to adopt the state of nature, and they should think nothing of it. From then onwards Rebecca looked upon the enormous dark appendages as a rather ugly form of adornment, rather like the pierced lips and nostrils on the tribes of New Guinea that she had seen illustrated.

However, when Penrod Ballantyne had leapt upon her that morning the effect had been devastating. Far from leaving her uninterested and rather pitying, she found emotions and feelings of whose existence she had never dreamed until that moment erupting into her consciousness. Even now in the darkness, with the cloak over her head and her face covered with both hands, she was blushing until her face felt as though it was on fire.

I won't think about it ever again, she promised herself. 'It' was as fully as she allowed herself to describe what she had seen. Never. Never again. She even eschewed that description on the second attempt. Then immediately she found herself thinking about it with all her attention.

After that long-ago visit to Europe, Rebecca had overheard her mother discussing the subject with one of her friends. They agreed that a woman in a state of nature was beautiful, while a man was not, except Michelangelo's *David*, of course.

'It wasn't ugly or obscene,' Rebecca contradicted her mother's shade. 'It was . . . it was . . .' But she wasn't sure what it had been, except very disturbing, fascinating and troubling. What had happened later between her and Ryder Courtney was connected with the first episode in some strange way that she could not fully understand.

Over the previous months she and Ryder had gradually become friends. She had realized that he was strong, clever and amusing. He had an inexhaustible fund of marvellous stories and, as Saffron had often remarked, he smelt and looked good. She came to find his company reassuring and comforting in the days of the siege, when death, disease and starvation gripped the city. As her father had observed, Ryder Courtney was a man of accomplishment. He had built up a thriving business enterprise and sustained it even though the world seemed to be falling apart. He took good care of his own people and his friends. He had shown them how to make the green-cake, and he could make her laugh and forget her fears for a few hours. She felt safe when she was with him. Of course, once or twice he had made physical contact with her—a light touch on the arm when they were talking, or his hand brushing hers as they walked together. But always she had pulled away. Her mother had warned her often about men: they just wanted to ravish you, then leave you sullied for ever so that you could never find a husband. That was bad enough but, worse, ravishment was painful and, in her mother's experience, only childbirth more so.

Then that very morning after her horrible experience in the Blue Bedroom when her emotions had been in turmoil, she had gone alone to Ryder's quarters. She had never done that before. She had always taken at least one of the twins with her as a chaperone. But this morning she had been confused. She felt guilty about her strange and ambivalent thoughts of Captain Penrod Ballantyne. She was terrified that she had inherited the bad seed from her mother. She needed to be comforted.

As always, Ryder had been pleased to see her, and ordered Bacheet to brew a pot of the precious coffee. They had chatted for a while, at first discussing the twins and their lessons, which, since the beginning of the siege, had fallen sadly into default. Suddenly and unexpectedly, even to herself, Rebecca had begun to sob as though her heart would break. Ryder had stared at her in astonishment: he knew she was neither a whiner nor a weeper. Then her had put his arms round her and held her tight. 'What has happened to you? I have never seen you like this. You have always been the bravest girl I know.'

Rebecca was surprised by how good it felt to be held by him. 'I'm sorry,' she whispered, but made no effort to pull away. 'I'm being very silly.'

'You're not silly. I understand,' he told her, in the deep, gentle tone he used when he was comforting a frightened animal or a hurt child. 'It is getting too much for all of us. But it will soon be over. The relief column will be here before Christmas, mark my words.'

She shook her head. She wanted to tell him that it was not the war, the siege, the Dervish or the Mad Mahdi, but he stroked her hair and she quietened, pressing her face to his chest, his warmth and strength, and his rich man-smell. 'Ryder,' she whispered and lifted her face to explain how she felt to him. 'Dear, dear Ryder.' But before she could say more he kissed her full on the lips. The surprise was so complete that she could not move. When she had recovered her wits sufficiently to pull away, she found that she did not want to. This was something so new and different that she decided to indulge herself a few moments longer.

The few moments became a few minutes and when at last she opened her mouth to protest, an incredible thing happened: his tongue slipped between her lips and stifled her protest. The sensation this produced was so overwhelming that her knees threatened to give way and she had to cling to him to hold herself up. The full muscular length of his body was pressed hard against her, and her protest came out as mewing sounds, like the cries of a newborn kitten seeking the teat. Then, to her consternation, she felt a monstrous hardness growing up between their lower bodies, something that seemed to have a life of its own. It terrified her, but she was powerless. Her will to escape evaporated.

A shrill high voice sundered the bonds that held her and set her free: 'She's kissing him! Becky is kissing Ryder on his mouth!'

Thinking about that moment now, she spoke aloud in the darkness under the great cannon: 'Now even Saffy hates me, and I hate myself. It is all such a terrible mess, and I wish I could die.'

She did not realize how far the words had carried until a voice answered her from the darkness: 'So there you are, Jamal.' The name meant the Beautiful One.

'Nazeera, you know me too well,' Rebecca murmured, as the plump, familiar shape appeared.

'Yes, I know you well and I love you more than I know you.' Nazeera sat beside her on the carriage of the cannon, and placed her arms round her. 'When I found that you were missing from your bed, I knew I would find you here.' Rebecca rested her head on Nazeera's shoulder and sighed. Nazeera was as soft and warm as a feather mattress and smelt of attar of roses. She rocked Rebecca gently. After a while she asked, 'Now, do you still wish to die?'

'I did not mean you to overhear me,' Rebecca answered ruefully. 'No, I do not want to die. Not for a while yet. But life is difficult sometimes, isn't it, Nazeera?'

'Life is good. It is men who are difficult most of

the time,' said Nazeera.

'Bacheet and Yakub?' Rebecca teased her. Nazeera's admirers were no secret within the family. 'Why don't you choose one of them, Nazeera?'

'Why don't you make a choice, Jamal?'

'I don't understand what you mean.' Rebecca lifted her cloak off her head and stared at Nazeera, her eyes large and dark in the starlight.

'I think you do. Why is it that the day the beautiful captain returns to Khartoum you rush for safety to al-Sakhawi, and when you find out that he does not think of himself as just your old friend, you decide you want to die?'

Rebecca covered her face again. Nazeera knew nearly everything, and had guessed the rest. In a few words she had helped Rebecca understand her turmoil. Nazeera went on rocking her. She started to croon a lullaby, an old tune with new words: 'Which one will it be? How will you choose, and who will it be?'

'You make it seem like a child's game, Nazeera.' Rebecca tried to sound stern.

'Oh, it is. Life is just a child's game, but often the games of children, like those of grown-ups, end in bitter tears.'

'Like poor little Saffy,' Rebecca suggested. 'She says she hates me, and she won't speak to me.'

'She thinks you have stolen her love from her. She is jealous.'

'She is so young.'

'No. She will soon be a woman and at least she knows what she wants.' Nazeera smiled tenderly. 'Unlike some older women I know.'

'Twelve shillings?' Ryder Courtney insisted. 'There can be no misunderstanding?'

'Twelve shillings. The word of an officer and a gentleman.'

'That description might be debated,' Ryder grunted.

'Will you not carry a weapon?'

'Yes.' Ryder hefted the heavy ironwood club.

'I meant a sidearm or an edged weapon.' Penrod touched the sabre in its scabbard on his belt.

'In the dark it will not be easy to tell friend from foe. I prefer denting heads with a fist or a club. Not so irrevocable.'

They were stepping out, shoulder to shoulder, along one of the sordid alleys of the native quarter of the city. They both wore dark clothing. The sun had set little more than an hour ago, but it was already dark. Just enough daylight lingered for them to pick their way along. Bacheet was waiting for them near the Ivory Tower, one of the more notorious brothels of the most dangerous section of the city. He whistled softly to attract their attention, then beckoned them into the ruins of a building that had been destroyed by Dervish cannon fire from across the river. The three found seats on the piles of masonry and shattered roof beams. The intermittent glow of Penrod's cigar shed just enough light for them to make out each other's features.

'Has Aswat arrived yet?' Ryder asked in Arabic.

'Yes,' replied Bacheet. 'He came an hour ago, at sunset.'

'Who is he?' asked Penrod. 'Who is responsible

for this business?'

'I can't be certain yet. Bacheet has heard his men call him Aswat but he wears a mask, to keep his face well hidden. Nevertheless, I have my suspicions. We will know for sure before the night is out.' Ryder turned back to Bacheet. 'How many men with him?'

'I counted twenty-six. That includes six armed guards. They will work late tonight. They always do. There is a lot of dhurra, and the sacks are heavy to move about. Aswat divides them into two gangs of about twelve men each. When the curfew falls, and the streets are deserted, they carry the sacks to the customers in other parts of the city. Two of Aswat's armed men who know the password of the night go ahead of each gang to make sure the road is clear of patrols. Two others bring up the rear to make sure they are not followed. Aswat waits at the tannery. It seems he won't take a chance on the street.'

'How many sacks does Aswat distribute every evening?' Ryder asked.

'About a hundred and twenty.'

'So by now he has sold a few thousand,' Ryder calculated. 'Probably less than three thousand left in his store. Do you know what he is charging for a sack?'

'At first it was five, but he has raised it to ten Egyptian pounds. He takes only gold, no notes,' Bacheet told him.

Ryder shook his head. 'Chinese Gordon is getting another bargain. The going rate is ten pounds. He is offering me but twelve shillings reward.'

'I'll cry for you tomorrow,' Penrod promised.

233

'Where is Aswat storing the stolen grain?'

'At the end of this street,' Bacheet explained. 'He is using an abandoned tannery.'

'Who have you left to watch the building?' Penrod asked Bacheet.

'Your man, Yakub. He is a Jaalin. The most treacherous of all tribes. Even that slithering of snakes have driven him out from their nest. I do not trust Yakub at all. He has no sense of honour, especially with women,' said Bacheet, bitterly. It was well known that he and Yakub were rivals for the favours of the widow Nazeera.

'But he is a good man in a fight, is he not?' Penrod defended Yakub.

Bacheet shrugged. 'Yes, if you do not turn your back on him. He is waiting behind the tannery, on the canal bank. My men are hidden in the courtyard of the Ivory Tower. The mistress of the house is a good friend.'

'She should be,' Ryder murmured drily. 'You are one of her best customers.'

Bacheet ignored such a fatuous remark. 'I chose this place to wait because from these windows we will be able to keep watch on the alley.' He nodded at the empty window openings. The glazing had been blown out by the shell blast, and the frames had been stolen for firewood. 'It is the only way to reach the tannery.'

'Good,' Ryder said. 'Two of your best men must follow the gangs. I want the names of all the merchants dealing with him. As soon as we have them we shall drop in on Effendi Aswat at the tannery.'

At that moment they heard the muffled tramp of feet. Bacheet slipped out through a shell hole in the rear wall to carry out Ryder's orders. Penrod stubbed out his cigar and wrapped the butt in his handkerchief, then joined Ryder at the empty window. They stayed well back in the shadows so that they were not spotted from the alley. A group of dark, furtive figures moved past the window. The two guards were first: they wore khaki Egyptian uniform with a flowerpot fez. They carried their rifles, bayonets fixed, slung over the shoulder. The porters followed them, bowed under the heavy dhurra sacks. The two armed men of the rearguard followed a short distance behind.

When they had disappeared Penrod remarked, 'Now I understand why you would not allow me to bring any of the garrison troops, and why you insisted that we use only your Arabs. Gordon's Egyptians are in this up to their necks.'

'Deeper than their necks,' Ryder corrected him. Within a short time the unburdened porters and their escorts came hurrying back down the alley towards the tannery. Bacheet appeared again, with the suddenness of the genie from the lamp. 'Ali Muhammad Acrani, who has a house behind the hospital, has bought all twenty-four sacks of the first delivery,' he reported. They waited for the next delivery to pass the windows. It was after midnight before the heavily laden porters left the tannery for the sixth time and staggered down the alley.

'That will be the last delivery,' Bacheet told Ryder. 'In God's Name, it is time at last to catch the jackal while he is still gobbling up the chickens.'

'In God's Name,' Ryder agreed.

When they slipped out of the rear of the shelled building, Bacheet's band was waiting for them in the shadows of the rear wall, armed with broadswords and spears. None carried firearms. Ryder led them quietly down the alley, keeping close to the dark buildings on each side. The silhouette of the tannery rose against the starbright desert sky. It was a three-storeyed building, dark and derelict, that blocked the end of the alleyway.

'Very well, Captain Ballantyne. I think it's time for you to go and find your man, Yakub.'

While they waited in the ruined building they had discussed the last details of the raid, so now there was no hesitation or misunderstanding. They had agreed that, as this was Ryder's affair, he would make the decisions and give the orders. However, Yakub was Penrod's man and would take orders only from him.

Penrod touched Ryder's shoulder in acknowledgement and moved quickly to the enclosing wall of the tannery's yard. The gate was closed and locked, but Penrod sheathed his sabre and jumped up to grab a handhold in a crack in the masonry. He pulled himself up with a single lithe movement, swung his legs over the top of the wall and dropped out of sight.

Ryder gave him a few minutes to get clear, then led Bacheet and the rest of the party to the high gate. He knew the layout of the building. Before the siege he had sent almost all of the hides he brought up from Equatoria to be processed by the old German who had owned the factory. The tanner had fled Khartoum with the first exodus of refugees. Ryder knew that the gate led into the loading yard. He tried it, but found it locked from the inside. It was unpainted, dry and cracked. He drew out his knife, whose point sank into the wood

236

as though it were cheese.

'Dry rot,' he grunted. He ran the blade through the narrow gap between the edge of the door and the jamb, and located the staple of the lock on the far side. He backed off a few paces, lined up, then stepped forward and slammed the flat of his right boot into the door. The screws that held the lock on the far side were ripped from the rotten wood and the gate swung open.

'Quickly now! Follow me.' Across the yard there was a raised loading platform with the main doors of the warehouse leading off it. This was where he had unloaded his bundles of raw hides for curing, and where he had collected the finished product. A broken-down wagon still stood against the platform. The entire place stank of half-cured leather. The glimmer of lamplight showed through slits in the boarded-over ground-floor windows, and beneath the main doors to the warehouse.

Ryder ran up the steps of the loading platform. Rats scurried into their holes as he crossed to the main door. He paused to listen and heard muffled voices through the woodwork. Gently he put his weight on the door, which eased open an inch, and peered through the gap. A man was leaning against the door frame with his back turned to Ryder. He wore the long dark cassock of a Coptic Christian priest and the hood covered his head. Now he turned quickly and stared at Ryder with astonishment in his eyes.

'Ah, Effendi Aswat,' Ryder greeted him, as he lifted the ironwood club. 'Do you have any dhurra for sale?' He swung the club with the power of his wide shoulders behind it, aiming at the cloaked head. It should have cracked on the priest's skull, but the down stroke crashed into the top frame of the door above Ryder's head with a force that numbed his wrist. The club flew from his grip and struck the cloaked figure a glancing blow on the shoulder that sent him reeling backwards with a howl of pain.

'To arms! Stand to arms! The enemy is on us!' the priest shouted, as he raced away across the open floor of the warehouse.

Ryder wasted a few moments retrieving his club from where it had rolled against the wall. As he straightened he glanced around the cavernous warehouse. It was lit by a dozen or more oil lamps hanging from the railing of the catwalk that ran round the high walls, just below the roof beams. In the dim light he saw that Bacheet had underestimated the strength of the opposition: at least twenty other men were scattered around the warehouse. Some were slaves, naked except for turbans and loincloths, but others wore the khaki uniforms and red fez of the Egyptian garrison troops. All had frozen in the attitude in which the priest's cry had caught them.

The slaves were stacking mountainous heaps of sacks in the centre of the warehouse and the floury smell of ripe dhurra blended with the ancient reek of raw hide and tannin. An Egyptian lieutenant and three or four non-commissioned officers were overseeing their efforts. It took them all some moments to gather their wits. They stared, aghast, at Ryder as he advanced on them brandishing his club. Then, with warlike shouts, Bacheet and his Arabs burst in through the main doors.

The Egyptian non-commissioned officers came to life and rushed to where their rifles were stacked against the far wall. Their lieutenant pulled his revolver from its holster and loosed off a shot before Bacheet and his gang were upon them, swinging swords and thrusting spears. The shouting, hacking, cursing mêlée surged back and forth across the warehouse floor. One of the slaves threw himself at Ryder's feet and clung to his knees, screaming for mercy. Impatiently Ryder tried to kick him away, but he clung like a monkey to a fruit tree.

At the far end of the long building Aswat was getting away. With the robes of his cassock billowing behind him, he jumped over a pile of loose dhurra sacks and darted to the foot of one of the vertical steel ladders that led up to the overhead catwalk. As he started to climb, his skirts flapped around his legs, hampering his movements. Despite this handicap, he climbed with agility. All the while he kept up cries of encouragement and exhortation to his men: 'Kill them! Let none escape! Kill them all!'

Ryder tapped the clinging slave across the temple with the club, and he released his grip and crumpled to the floor. Ryder jumped over his inert body and ran to the foot of the ladder. He stuffed the club under his belt and leapt on to the first rungs, following the priest and gaining on him rapidly. He saw that beneath the skirts of his cassock the fugitive wore polished riding boots and spurs, and that his legs were clad in khaki riding breeches.

The priest reached the catwalk, and clung to the handrail, heaving for breath. He peered back down the ladder. His voice shrilled with panic when he saw Ryder coming up fast behind him. 'Stop him!

Shoot him down like a dog!' But his men were too occupied with their own problems to take any notice. He struggled with the skirts of his cassock, trying to hoist them high enough to reach the sidearm that bulged on his hip, but he could not free it. Now Ryder was almost on him and Aswat abandoned the effort. Instead he snatched one of the oil lamps that hung from the handrail. He lifted it high over his head. 'Stop! In God's Name, I warn you! I will burn you alive.'

The hood of the cassock fell off to reveal the khaki tunic of the Egyptian Army, with the epaulettes and scarlet tabs of a major on the shoulders. His curls were dark and wavy, lustrous with pomade. Ryder caught a whiff of a pungent eau-de-Cologne. 'Major Faroque. What a pleasant surprise,' Ryder said cheerfully.

Al-Faroque's expression was frantic. 'I warned you!' he screamed. With both hands he hurled the lamp at Ryder, who flattened himself against the rungs of the ladder. As the lamp flew past his shoulder, it spun a meteor's tail of burning oil through the air behind it. It struck the steel ladder near the bottom and exploded, spraying a sheet of fire over the closest stack of dhurra sacks. Rivulets of flickering blue flames poured over the tinder dry sacks, which caught swiftly and burned as brightly as candles.

'Don't come near me!' al-Faroque yelled down at Ryder. 'I warn you. Don't—' He grabbed the second lamp off its hook, but Ryder was ready for it and pulled the club from his belt. The major threw with all his strength, sobbing with the effort as the lamp left his hand.

It flew straight towards Ryder's face. He

watched it coming and, at the last moment, swatted it aside. It spun down into the body of the warehouse, and burst over another stack of dhurra. The grain went up in a leaping conflagration.

Al-Faroque turned to run, but Ryder threw himself up the last few feet and seized him by the ankle. He squealed and tried to kick himself free, but Ryder held him easily and hauled him towards the edge of the catwalk. Al-Faroque grabbed on to the handrail, and clung to it, squealing like a pig being dragged to slaughter.

At that moment a pistol bullet, fired from below, grazed Ryder's shoulder and struck the steel ladder six inches in front of his eyes. It left a bright smear of lead on the steel. The sting of the passing shot was so intense and unexpected that he slackened his grip on al-Faroque's ankle. Al-Faroque felt him give, and kicked backwards. The rowel of the spur on his other riding boot ripped across Ryder's temple, and knocked him off balance. Ryder let go of the man's leg, and grabbed at the ladder rung before his eyes. Al-Faroque pounded away along the catwalk.

Another shot from the tannery floor hissed past Ryder's head and kicked a slab of plaster and cement dust from higher up the wall. He glanced down in time to see the Egyptian guards who had escorted the last delivery of grain run back into the warehouse. He realized they must have seen the flames and heard the gunfire. They were blazing away wildly, stabbing with bayonet and sword at Bacheet's men. The one who had fired at Ryder reloaded his carbine, then swung up the stubby barrel and took deliberate aim at him. Helpless, Ryder watched the flash of the muzzle blast, and the swirling bouquet of black powder smoke. Another bullet clanged on the steel footplate inches above his head. It galvanized him and he hauled himself up the last few feet on to the catwalk. He jumped to his feet and raced after al-Faroque.

The Egyptian had disappeared through the low door at the far end of the catwalk. Ryder reached the opening, expecting another bullet from the marksman below, but when he glanced down he saw the trooper flopping about on the concrete floor like a fresh-caught catfish in the bottom of the boat. Bacheet was standing over him with one foot on his throat, trying to pull the buried spearhead out of his chest. Just then one of the enemy charged at him. Bacheet gave one last heave, the spear came free and he levelled it at his new assailant.

Ryder saw that his own men on the floor below were heavily outnumbered, and although they were fighting like gladiators they were gradually being overwhelmed. He was on the point of letting al-Faroque escape and turning back to join them when another two men ran into the warehouse through a rear door.

'More power to the glorious 10th!' Ryder roared, as he recognized Penrod Ballantyne and Yakub with him, dagger in hand. Penrod parried the bayonet thrust that the Egyptian lieutenant levelled at his face, then caught him with the riposte, sabring him cleanly through the throat; the silver blade parted the lieutenant's vertebrae, and was blurred with pink blood as it came out through the back of his neck. Penrod recovered his blade smoothly, and the Egyptian fell to the ground. His heels drummed spasmodically on the concrete as he went into his death throes. Penrod had a moment to wave casually at Ryder, who pointed through the door at the end of the catwalk.

'It's al-Faroque!' he yelled at Penrod. 'He went that way. Try to cut him off.' That was all he had time for, and he did not know if Penrod had heard, let alone understood. The flames were roaring like a mighty waterfall, and the entire contents of the warehouse were burning furiously, flames racing up the dry timber beams that supported the walls and roof.

So much for my reward, Ryder thought bitterly. Coughing in the smoke, he ran on after al-Faroque. He reached the low door at the end of the catwalk through which the man had disappeared, and stuck his head through it. He sucked in a deep breath of sweet night air and, through streaming eyes, saw that beneath him another ladder ran down the rear wall of the tannery, to the towpath of the canal.

Al-Faroque was still struggling with the folds of his cassock on the bottom rungs of the ladder, but when he saw Ryder's head he let go and dropped the last six feet to land on his hands and knees. He scrambled up, unhurt, and looked up at Ryder. 'Get back!' he shouted. 'Don't try to stop me.' He tried again to hoist the tangled skirts of his cassock, and succeeded in reaching the holster on his belt. He drew the revolver and aimed it at Ryder. The light of the flames through the rear windows of the tannery lit the towpath brightly. Ryder saw that the major's hand was shaking. Oily drops of sweat ran down his cheeks and dripped from his double chins. He fired two quick shots, which struck the wall on each side of the door. Ryder ducked back inside and heard al-Faroque's footsteps running away along the towpath.

If he reaches the alley, he might get away, Ryder thought, as he clambered out of the door and swung on to the top rungs of the escape ladder. He went down it swiftly, dropped the last ten feet and landed with such force that he bit his tongue. He spat out the blood, and saw that al-Faroque had a lead on him of at least a hundred yards. He had almost reached the corner of the building.

Still carrying his club Ryder raced after him, but al-Faroque dodged round the corner and was gone. Seconds later Ryder reached it, and saw he was half-way down the alley, moving with amazing speed for such a portly figure. Ryder launched himself after him. Once al-Faroque reached the end of the alley he would disappear into the tangled maze of streets beyond. He'll not wait for us to catch him. He'll clear out of Khartoum tonight, Ryder thought grimly. By dawn he will be across the river and converted into the Mahdi's most faithful disciple. What mischief he can do us over there! He was starting to gain on him. But not fast enough, he thought.

As al-Faroque reached the end of the alley, an elegant figure stepped out of a dark doorway and kicked his back foot across the other. Al-Faroque crashed to earth with a force that drove the air from his lungs. However, he wriggled forward on his plump belly and tried to reach the revolver that had flown from his hand as he went down, but as his fingers closed over the butt Penrod stamped hard on his wrist, pinning his hand.

Ryder came up, stooped over him, and cracked him across the back of his skull with the club.

244

Al-Faroque's face dropped and he snored into the filth of the alley floor.

'A perfect flying trip,' Ryder said to Penrod, with admiration. 'Doubtless perfected on the rugger fields of Eton.'

'Not Eton but Harrow, my dear fellow. And don't confuse the two,' Penrod corrected him. Then, as Yakub appeared at his side, he changed easily into Arabic: 'Tie him up tidy and tight. Gordon Pasha will be interested to talk to him.'

'Perhaps he will allow me to watch the execution?' Yakub asked hopefully, as he unbuckled al-Faroque's belt and used it to strap his arms behind his back.

'Gentle Yakub,' said Penrod, 'I have no doubt that he will prepare a place for you in the very front row of the entertainment.'

By now the sky and the rooftops of the city were brightly lit by the blazing tannery. They left al-Faroque to Yakub, and ran back to the main gate. The heat of the flames was so intense that the combatants were being driven out of the building into the open. As they emerged from the doors or jumped from the windows, Bacheet and his Arabs were waiting for them. There were pugnacious shouts and bellows, the clash of blades and a few shots, but gradually most of the renegade Egyptian garrison troops were rounded up. A few managed to escape into the alleys, but Yakub went after them.

Dawn was breaking as the survivors were marched in clanking chains up to the gates of Mukran Fort. General Gordon watched their arrival from the battlements, and sent for Penrod. His benign expression turned to cold fury when he learnt of the destruction of three thousand sacks of his precious dhurra. 'You let a civilian take command of the raid?' he demanded of Penrod, and his blue eyes blazed. 'Courtney? The trader and black-marketeer? A shabby fellow without a patriotic scruple or a shred of social conscience?'

'I beg your pardon, General, but Courtney was every bit as committed to the recovery of the missing grain as we were. In fact, his agents discovered where it was hidden,' Penrod pointed out mildly.

'His commitment went as far as twelve shillings a sack, and not a penny further. If you had taken command this fiasco might well have been avoided.' Gordon stood on tiptoe to glare at him. Penrod stood rigidly to attention and, with an effort, kept his mouth grimly shut.

With an obvious effort Gordon regained his equanimity. 'Well, at least you were able to apprehend the ring leader. I am not at all surprised to find that it was Major al-Faroque. I am going to make an example of him to stiffen the remainder of the garrison. I am going to have him and his accomplices shot from the mouth of a cannon.'

Penrod blinked. This was a particularly savage military punishment reserved for the most outrageous crimes. As far as he knew, it had last been performed on the captured sepoys after the suppression of the mutiny in India almost thirty years ago.

'I would shed no tears if that scoundrel Courtney were to share the same fate.' The little general stamped to the window of his headquarters and scowled across the river at the enemy lines. 'However, I don't suppose I can do that to an

246

Englishman,' he growled, 'more's the pity. But I will decide on something that will leave him in no doubt of my true estimate of his conduct and his moral worth. It will have to be something that affects the contents of his purse. That is where he keeps his conscience.'

Penrod knew that by far his best policy was silence. The good Lord knows I cherish no great affection for Ryder Courtney, he thought. No doubt we will soon be at daggers drawn over the favours of a young lady of our mutual acquaintance. Yet it is difficult to suppress a sneaking admiration for the fellow's brains and courage.

Gordon turned back from the window and pulled his gold hunter from his pocket by its chain. 'Eight o'clock. I want this rogue al-Faroque and his minions tried, sentenced and ready for execution by five this afternoon. I want it done in public on the maidan to make the deepest impression on the populace. I cannot abide black-marketeering in this city where most of the populace is starving. You are in charge, Ballantyne, and I want it done properly.'

*   *   *

It had all gone off very well, Penrod decided, as he wandered down the terrace of the consular palace before he retired for the night. He came to a stately tamarind tree whose branches overshadowed half the terrace and leant against the trunk. He was smoking the Cuban cigar that Ryder Courtney had pressed upon him when they parted. Courtney had declined the invitation to attend the executions. 'I don't blame him. I myself would rather have been employed elsewhere,' he murmured.

He felt slightly queasy as he thought about it now, and he took a long, deep draw on the cigar. At five o'clock that afternoon almost the entire garrison of Khartoum had paraded on the maidan to witness punishment. Only the minimum strength was left to man the defences of the city. Although they had not been ordered to do so, it seemed that the entire civilian populace, too, lined the perimeter of the parade ground three and four deep. The eight Krupps guns were lined up wheel to wheel and aimed at maximum elevation toward the besieging Dervish hordes in Omdurman. The ammunition shortage was too severe to waste even these eight rounds: after they had completed the primary destruction they would fly on across the river to burst among the legions of besiegers and, with luck, kill a few more of the enemy.

The first to be marched out were the black-marketeers and merchants of the city who had been caught red-handed with stocks of al-Faroque's grain. Ali Muhammad Acrani was at the head of the file. When Penrod had searched his premises behind the hospital he had found six hundred sacks hidden in the slave cells under the barracoons.

The prisoners were lined up close behind the guns. Gordon Pasha had sentenced them to watch the executions. In addition all their possessions, including the contraband dhurra, were confiscated. Finally they were to be expelled from the city to take their chances on the clemency of the Mahdi and his Ansar across the river. Penrod considered their fate. Given the same choice, I think I would have preferred the kiss of the gunner's daughter, he decided.

His mind went back to that afternoon's programme of entertainment on the maidan. When all the spectators were assembled, Penrod had given the order and Major al-Faroque and the seven other condemned men were marched out from the cells of Mukran Fort. They wore full dress uniform. Each man stood to attention in front of the artillery piece to which he was allocated. The regimental sergeant major read out the charges and sentences in a stentorian voice that carried to every one of the spectators. They craned forward to catch the words ' . . . that they shall be shot from guns.' A hum of anticipation went up from the packed ranks. This was something none of them had ever witnessed. They held up their babies and young children for a better view.

They watched the sergeant major roll up the charge sheet and hand it to a runner, who carried it to where Gordon Pasha and Captain Ballantyne stood. The man saluted and handed the roll to the general. 'Very well.' Gordon returned the salute. 'Carry out the sentences.'

The sergeant marched smartly down the rank of condemned men, halting before each in turn and ceremoniously ripping the insignias of rank and merit from their shoulders and the breasts of their tunics. He threw the golden crowns, chevrons and medals into the dust.

When the eight men stood in their torn clothing, forlorn and dishonoured, he gave another order. One at a time the condemned were led to the waiting guns and spreadeagled over them. The gaping muzzles were aimed into the centre of their chests and their arms strapped along each side of the shining black barrels. From this grotesque

249

embrace they would receive the kiss of the gunner's daughter. Al-Faroque threw himself down in the dust of the parade ground. He howled, wept and drummed his heels. Finally he had to be carried to his gun by the soldiers.

'Prepared to carry out the sentence,' the sergeant major bellowed.

'Carry on, Sergeant Major!' Penrod snapped back, his face and voice expressionless.

The sergeant major drew his sword and raised the bare blade. The drummer-boy at his side raised his sticks to his lips, then dropped them to the drumhead in a long roll. The sergeant major dropped his sword blade, and the drummer stopped abruptly. There was a momentary silence and even Penrod drew a sharp breath. The first gun bellowed.

The victim disappeared for an instant in a cloud of dense grey powder smoke. Then the separate parts of his torso were spinning high in the air. There was a stunned silence after the explosion, then a spontaneous burst of cheering from the spectators as the head fell back to earth and rolled across the sun-baked clay.

The sergeant major raised his sword again. The drum rolled, and was again abruptly cut short. Another thunderous discharge. This time the spectators were anticipating the result and the wild applause was mixed with hoots of laughter. Al-Faroque was last in the line and as his turn came closer he screamed for mercy. The crowd yelled in imitation, and al-Faroque's bowels voided noisily. Liquid faeces stained the back of his breeches. The hilarity of the watchers swelled to a bellow as the drum rolled for the eighth and last time.

Al-Faroque's head leapt higher in the air than that of any man who had preceded him.

Penrod examined the stub of his cigar and decided regretfully that he could not take another draw without scorching his fingertips. He dropped it on to the flags of the terrace and ground it out under his heel. Although it was late and he had already made his nightly rounds of the city's defences, he still had a pile of paperwork to complete before he could think of bed. Gordon would want all his lists and reports first thing in the morning. The little martinet made no allowances for the contingencies of the siege and the heavy load he had already placed on Penrod's shoulders: 'We have to keep up to scratch, Ballantyne, and set an example.'

At least he spares himself even less than he does me, Penrod thought.

He straightened up from the tree, preparing to make his way up to the quarters that David Benbrook had allocated to him, when a small movement on one of the second-floor balconies caught his eye. The door to the balcony had opened and he was able to see into the room beyond it. The interior was lit by an oil lamp that stood on a ladies' dressing-table, and he could just make out the upright posts and canopy of the bed. The wallpaper was patterned with red roses and sprigs of greenery.

A slim feminine figure appeared in the doorway, back-lit by the lamp, which spun a golden nimbus about her head, like a medieval painting of the Madonna. Even though he could not see her face, he recognized Rebecca immediately. She wore a robe of some lustrous material with a pale blue sheen, probably crêpe-de-Chine. It fitted her closely, emphasizing the curve of her waist and hip, and leaving her arms bare below the elbows. She came to the front of the balcony where the moonlight added subtle silver tones to the golden lamplight behind her.

She gazed down on to the garden and terrace below her but did not see him, half concealed by the wide branches of the tamarind. She gathered her skirts and, with a graceful movement, swung her lower body up until she was sitting on the balcony wall. Her feet were bare, and her legs exposed to the knees. Her calves were shapely, her feet small and girlish. Penrod was enthralled by their elegance. Now the lamplight struck her in profile and left the other half of her face in mysterious moon shadow. She held an ivory-backed brush in one hand, and her long blonde hair was loose. She stroked the brush through it, beginning at the pale parting that ran down the centre of her scalp and ending at her waist, where the tresses danced and rippled. Her expression was serene and lovely.

Penrod wanted to move close enough to study every plane and angle of her face and perhaps even to catch a trace of her perfume. Despite the gloves, the long sleeves and the wide-brimmed straw hat that she wore habitually during the day, the skin of Rebecca's bare arms and legs was not fashionably milky but a light gold. Her neck was long and graceful, her head tilted at a beguiling angle. She began to hum softly. He did not recognize the tune, but it was a siren song he could not resist. He moved closer to the balcony with the caution of a hunter, waiting for her to close her eyes briefly at the completion of each brush stroke before he took another small step towards her. Now he could hear the intake of her breath at the end of each bar of the tune and almost feel the warmth and texture of her lips under his own. He imagined the tremulous way in which they would part to allow him to taste the apple-sweet juices of her mouth.

At last she set aside the brush, twisted her hair into a thick rope and coiled it on top of her head. She drew a long hairpin with a jewelled head from the lapel of her gown and reached up to secure her hair. As she did so she turned her head away and Penrod took advantage of this to step forward again.

She froze like a gazelle sensing the stalk of the leopard. He stood still and held his breath. Then she turned to face him and her eyes flew wide. She stared down at him for a moment, then swung her legs back into the balcony and sprang to her feet. Her lips framed a silent accusation: 'You were spying!'

Then she whirled away through the open door and closed it behind her, with just a faint click of the latch, as though she did not want anyone else to hear. As though the fact that he had been spying on her was a secret between them. Penrod's heart was drumming and his breath came faster. He regretted that he had frightened her away. He wished he had been able to watch her a little longer, as though he might have learnt some secret by studying her unsuspecting face.

He left the terrace and, as he mounted the main spiral staircase to his own quarters, his predatory instinct, which, for a brief interlude, had been replaced by an almost reverential awe, reasserted itself. He smiled. At least we now know where to find Mademoiselle's boudoir, should the need arise, he thought.

*   *   *

Unlike her twin, Amber was unperturbed by what they had witnessed when they burst in upon their elder sister and Ryder. She was the only one of the Benbrook sisters who returned to his compound the following day. She arrived at the usual hour with Nazeera in tow and immediately took charge of the team of three dozen Sudanese women who were manufacturing the precious green-cake. She relished not having to share the authority with Saffron.

*   *   *

Bacheet found his master in the workshop at the harbour and whispered his report.

Ryder looked up from the *Ibis*'s main steam line, which he and Jock McCrump were welding. 'Her sisters?' Ryder demanded. 'Miss Saffron and Miss Rebecca?'

Bacheet shook his head. 'Only Miss Amber.' This was not a conversation that Ryder wanted to share with Jock McCrump and the *Ibis*'s stokers and oilers. He jerked his head towards the door and Bacheet followed him out.

They were half-way back to the compound before Ryder broke the silence. 'What happened, Bacheet?' Bacheet looked innocently uncomprehending, but Ryder was certain that he had shared Nazeera's mattress last night and knew every detail

254

of what had transpired during the past twenty-four hours in the ladies' quarters of Her Britannic Majesty's consular palace.

'Tell me what you know,' he insisted.

'I am a simple man,' said Bacheet. 'I know horses and camels, the cataracts and currents of the Nile. But what do I know of a woman's heart?' He shook his head. 'Perhaps you should enquire of these mysteries from one much wiser than I.'

'Send Nazeera to me.' Ryder stifled a smile. 'I shall wait for her at the monkey cages.'

Nazeera approved of Ryder Courtney. Of course, he had the parboiled look of most *ferenghi*, and his eyes were a disconcerting and unnatural shade of green, but a man's looks and age counted for little if he was a good provider. This one's wives would never starve: he was a man strong in body and resolve, and he would protect his own. Yet there was a gentleness in him. He would never beat his women, unless their behaviour truly invited it. Yes, she approved of him. It was to be regretted that, so far, al-Jamal had not displayed equal good sense.

She came to the animal compound, and whispered to old Ali that he should stay within call but out of earshot. She might be a widow and almost forty years of age, but she was a devout, respectable woman. She had convinced herself that she was the only one who knew of her discreet friendships with Yakub and Bacheet.

She greeted Ryder, asked the blessings of the Prophet for him, touched her heart and lips, then squatted at a polite distance from him. She drew her shawl over the lower part of her face and waited for him to speak.

Ryder asked after her health, and she assured him that she was well. Then he asked after the health of her charges.

'Al-Jamal is well.'

'I am happy to hear that. I was worried about her. She has not come to help the women today.'

Nazeera inclined her head slightly but made no comment.

'Nazeera, is she angry with me?' he asked.

She drew a sharp breath of disapproval. The question lacked even a semblance of subtlety. She should not dignify it with a reply. However, this time she would make allowances for him: after all, he was an infidel.

'Al-Jamal feels that you took advantage of her trust. She was in need of comfort and counsel so she came to you as a friend, but you behaved like a lecher.'

Bacheet saw Ryder's face crumple with dismay.

'Lecher?' he asked. 'She is wrong. I bear her great respect and affection. I am not a lecher.'

Nazeera was balanced on a knife edge of loyalty. She could not tell him that the real offence was that they had been discovered not only by the twins but also by the pretty captain. But she liked him enough to give him a light word of comfort. 'I love her like my own daughter, but she is a young girl and understands nothing, not even her own heart. She will change with the moon and the wind and the current, like a dhow without a captain. When she says she wishes never to see someone again, she means at least until midnight, but probably not until noon tomorrow.'

Ryder pondered this as he offered a morsel of green-cake through the bars of the cage to Lucy, the vervet monkey. She was due to give birth at any moment. She seized his wrist and licked the last crumbs from his fingers.

'What should I do, Nazeera?' He asked.

She shook her head. Men were such children. 'Anything you do now will only make matters worse. Do nothing. I will tell her how much you are suffering. Most young girls like to hear that. When it is time to do so we will speak again.'

Ryder was much cheered, by this offer of assistance. 'But what of Saffron? Why has she not come to help Amber?'

'Filfil feels as strongly about your behaviour as her eldest sister.' Filfil was the Arabic word for pepper, and also Saffron's nickname. 'She also has expressed an intention never to speak to you again. She says that she wishes to die.'

Ryder looked alarmed again. 'A single kiss, and a fairly chaste one at that. Now she wants to die?'

'Long ago she chose you as her future husband. She has even discussed the details with me. I should warn you now that she will never allow you to have more than one wife.'

Ryder burst out in incredulous laughter. 'What a sweet and funny child she is, but a child nevertheless.'

'In a few short years she will be of marriageable age,' Nazeera did not smile, 'and she has made her plans.'

Ryder laughed again, but this time with a note of trepidation. 'Nazeera, I do not wish to encourage her to believe in the impossible, but nor do I wish to hurt her. Will you give her my message? Will you tell her that there is important work for her to do? I need her here.'

'I will tell her, Effendi,' Nazeera rose to her feet and bowed, 'but she will need more encouragement than that to forgive your infidelity. But now I must go to help al-Zahra,' Amber's Arabic name meant 'the Flower'. 'We can never make enough of the green-cake to feed so many hungry mouths.'

After she had gone Ryder lingered a few minutes longer at the monkey cage, pondering his predicaments. Lucy perched at the bars, belly bulging between her knees, and offered her head to his caress. She loved to be scratched behind the ears, and to have her fur searched for vermin. At last Ryder sighed and made to leave the cage. Lucy seized his hand as he tried to pull it out through the bars, and sank her sharp white fangs into his thumb.

'You creature, you!' He cuffed her lightly. She shrieked, as though in mortal anguish, and shot to the top of the cage where she gibbered at him furiously.

'A plague on you, and all female wiles!' he scolded, and sucked his thumb as he left the enclosure to go down to the harbour. Today Jock McCrump hoped to complete the repairs to the hull and engine, and he was planning to take the *Ibis* out on her trials.

*   *   *

Penrod stood on the parapet of the forward redoubt on the riverbank opposite Tutti Island. He stamped on the sandbags to test their solidity. As the stores of dhurra were used up he had the empty sacks filled and worked into weak points in the fortifications. 'That will do!' he told the Egyptian

258

sergeant in charge of the work detail. 'Now we need a few more timber baulks in the embrasures of the gun pits.' Under General Gordon's orders, he was stripping the abandoned buildings, and using their timbers to strengthen the fortifications.

He strode along the top of the sandbagged wall, pausing every fifty or hundred paces to survey the riverbank below. He had placed marker pegs in the strip of muddy earth between the foot of the wall and the edge of the water. A month ago the Nile had lapped the wall three feet from the top. Two weeks ago a few inches of mud had appeared at the foot of the wall. Now the strip of bank was six feet wide. Each day the river was falling. Within the next few months it would enter the stage of Low Nile. This was what the Dervish were waiting for. The wide banks would dry out to give a safe mooring for the dhows ferrying their legions across the river, and a firm footing from which to launch a final assault on the city.

Penrod jumped down on to the mudflat and moved his pegs out to the edge of the receding river. In places there were now fifteen or twenty feet of exposed bank. They will need a lot more ground from which to launch a full-scale attack, he decided, but the river is falling rapidly. The Mahdi had shrewd and experienced warlords commanding his army, men like Osman Atalan. Soon they would start probing the defences with midnight raids and sorties. Where will they strike us first? he wondered. He walked on along the perimeter, looking for the weak spots. By the time he reached Mukran Fort he had picked out at least two points where he could expect the first raids to strike.

He found General Gordon at one of his

259

favourite lookouts on the parapet of the fort. He was seated under a thatched sunshade at a camp table on which were laid out his binoculars, notebooks and maps. 'Sit down, Ballantyne,' he said. 'You must be thirsty.' He indicated the earthenware water jug on the table.

'Thank you, sir.' Penrod filled a glass.

'You may rest assured that it has been boiled the full half-hour.' It was a barbed jest. Under threat of flogging, Gordon had ordered all the garrison water to be boiled to those specifications. He had learnt the necessity of this during his campaigns in China. The results were remarkable. Although at first Penrod had believed this was another whim of Gordon's he had since become a fervent believer. Cholera was raging among the civilian populace of the city, who openly flouted Gordon's decrees and filled their waterskins from the river and the canal, into which discharged the city sewers. By contrast the garrison troops had suffered only three cases, and all of those had been traced to disobedience and the use of unboiled water. All three victims had died. 'Damned lucky for them,' Penrod had remarked to David Benbrook. 'If they had lived Gordon would have had them shot.'

'The death of the dog, they call it. Reeking torrents of your own hot excrement and vomit, every muscle and sinew of your body knotted in agonizing cramps, a desiccated skeleton for a body and a head like a skull!' David shuddered. 'Not for me, thank you very much. I'll take my water boiled.'

Penrod felt his skin crawl as he recalled that description: it was so accurate. Yet thirst could kill as swiftly as the cholera. The heat and the desert air sucked the moisture from his body so his throat was parched. He raised the mug, savoured the smell of woodsmoke, which proved it was safe, then drained it in four long swallows.

'Well, now, Ballantyne, what about the north bank?' Gordon never wasted time in pleasantries.

'I have marked a number of weak spots in the line.' Penrod spread his field map on the table and pinned down a corner with the water jug. They pored over it together. 'Here and here are the worst. The river level is dropping sharply—it's down another three inches since noon yesterday. Each day exposes us more. We will have to strengthen those places.'

'Heaven knows, we are hard pressed for men and material to keep pace with the work.' Gordon looked up shrewdly at Penrod. 'Yes? You have something to suggest?'

'Well, sir, as you say, we cannot hope to maintain the entire line impregnable . . .' Gordon frowned. He could not abide those he referred to as 'dismal Johnnies'. Penrod hurried on before he could level the accusation. '. . . so it occurred to me that we should deliberately leave some gaps in our outer defences to entice the Dervish to attack them.'

'Ah!' Gordon's frown lifted. 'Poisoned gifts!'

'Exactly, sir. We leave an opening, then behind it we set a trap. We run them into one of the blind alleys, and cover it with enfilading fire from the Gatlings.'

Thoughtfully, Gordon rubbed the silver stubble on his chin. They had only two Gatling guns, the rejects of Hicks's expedition. He had declined to take them with him on the march to El Obeid as he had considered them too cumbersome. Each weapon was mounted on its own heavy gun-carriage, a sturdy axle and two iron-shod wheels. It needed a span of at least four oxen to drag it into action. The mechanisms were fragile and prone to stoppages. Hicks had believed in traditional volley fire from squares of infantry, rather than sustained fire from a single exposed position. He conceded that the Gatlings might be useful in a static defensive position, but he was convinced that there was no place for them in a flying offensive column. He had left the two guns and a hundred thousand rounds of the special .58 bore ammunition in the arsenal at Khartoum when he marched away to annihilation at El Obeid.

Penrod had found them stored in a dark recess of the arsenal, where he had collected a pistol to replace the one Yakub had lost, under dusty tarpaulins. He was familiar with the Gatling. He had selected two teams of the most likely Egyptian troopers under his command, and within a week had taught them to serve the weapons. Even though it was a complicated firing mechanism, they had learnt swiftly. The copper-cased rimfire .58 bore cartridges were fed by gravity from a hopper on top of the weapon. The gunner turned a hand crank, and the six heavy brass barrels rotated around a central shaft. As each bullet dropped from the hopper it was seized by one of the six cam-operated bolts, locked into the breech, fired and ejected by gravity. The rate of fire depended on the vigour with which the gunner turned the crank handle. It required strength and stamina to keep up a sustained fire for longer than a few minutes, but in practice Penrod timed one gun at nearly three hundred rounds in a half a minute. Of course, as soon as it heated it jammed. There was no machine-gun he knew of that did not.

In one respect Hicks had been correct, the Gatling guns were not very mobile. Penrod had realized that, in the event of a surprise night attack, it would not be possible to move them swiftly from one position to another on the ten-kilometre perimeter of the city's defence works.

Penrod summarized his plan: 'Suck them through the pretended weak spots on to the Gatlings and cut them up, sir.'

'First rate!' Gordon beamed. 'Show me again where you propose to set your traps.'

'Well, sir, I thought that here below the harbour would be the most obvious point.' Gordon nodded approval. 'The other spot would be here, opposite the hospital.' Penrod prodded the map with his forefinger. 'Behind both those positions there is a maze of narrow streets. I will block them with piles of rubble and timber baulks, then site the Gatlings behind strong brickworks . . .' They discussed the plan over the next hour.

'Very well, Ballantyne. Carry on.' At last Gordon dismissed him.

Penrod saluted and headed for the ramp that led away from the parapet of the fort. Half-way down he paused to peer into the north. Only eyes as sharp as his could have picked out the tiny dark speck in the cloudless steel blue sky. At first he thought it was one of the Saker falcons coming in over the wastes of the Monassir desert from the north. He had noticed that a pair of the splendid birds were nesting under the eaves of the arsenal roof. He watched the tiny shape approaching, then shook his head. 'Not the typical falcon wingbeat.'

263

The distant shape grew in size and he exclaimed, 'Pigeon!'

He was reminded sharply of his last ride down from the north when he and Yakub had cut the loop of the river. He watched the pigeon's approach with keen interest. As it approached the river, it began a wide circle high in the steely sky with the city of Omdurman as its centre.

'Pigeon returning to loft.' He recognized the manoeuvre. A pigeon nearly always began a long flight with a number of circles to orient itself, and ended in the same way before it descended to its home. This bird swung wide over the river, then passed almost directly overhead where Penrod stood.

'It's another bloody Dervish carrier!' He had seen the tiny roll of rice paper tied to its leg. He pulled his watch from his hip pocket and checked the time. 'Seventeen minutes past four.' He had bought the watch from Consul Le Blanc at an exorbitant price to replace the one that had been doused on his last crossing of the river.

He watched the pigeon come round in another sweeping circle that carried it over the grounds of the consular palace, then begin a long, slanting descent across the broad waters of the Nile. The last glimpse he had of it was as it dropped in steeply towards the whitewashed dome of the small mosque on the southern outskirts of Omdurman.

As he slipped the watch back into his pocket he had the feeling he was being watched and looked round. General Gordon's head showed above the parapet. 'What is it, Ballantyne?' he called down.

'I can't be certain, General, but I would wager a gold sovereign to a pinch of dry pigeon droppings

264

that the Mahdi is running a regular bird mail with his army in the north.'

'If you are right, I would give more than a gold sovereign to get my hands on one of his messages.' Gordon stared grimly across the river at the mosque where the pigeon had landed. It was almost a month since Penrod had arrived in the city. Since then they had received no news from Cairo. There was no way of guessing what had happened to General Stewart and his relief column. Had they begun the march? Had they been beaten back? On the other hand perhaps they were only days away.

'Ballantyne, how can you get me one of those pigeons?' Gordon asked quietly.

A little before four the following afternoon Penrod was waiting on the terrace of the consular palace with his head thrown back to watch the northern sky.

'Right on time!' he exclaimed, as the speck appeared in the north sky, slightly to the east of where he had expected it. As it passed over his head he estimated the bird's speed and height with narrowed eyes. 'Two hundred feet if it's an inch, and going like its tail's on fire. A long call!' he murmured. 'But there is no wind, and I have taken pheasant higher than that.' He stroked his moustache, which was approaching its former glory.

*   *   *

The consular dinner that evening was formal. There were a dozen guests, all that remained of the diplomatic corps and the civil administrators of the

265

Khedive in Cairo. As usual, Rebecca was her father's hostess. David had sent an invitation to Ryder Courtney, without consulting either Rebecca or Saffron, either of whom would surely have exercised a veto if they had had the chance.

Ryder had been cherishing a young buffalo heifer in the expectations of selling it for an enormous profit when the city was relieved. The prospect of salvation was becoming daily more remote, and the buffalo had a voracious appetite that was increasingly difficult to satisfy. When he received David's invitation he slaughtered the animal and sent a haunch with two bottles of Cognac to the consular kitchens.

Rebecca recognized the gift as a peace-offering, and it placed her in a terrible quandary. Could she refuse it, when it would make the evening a triumphant success? It would mean acknowledging Ryder's existence, which she was not yet prepared to do. She solved the dilemma by sending him a note, delivered by Amber, accepting the gift on behalf of her father. She knew this was weakness on her part, but she salved her conscience by determining not to address a single word to him if he attended the dinner.

Ryder, as was his wont, was the last guest to arrive. He was looking so elegant in his dinner jacket, and seemed so at ease with himself and the world that Rebecca's anger was exacerbated.

Nazeera lied, she thought, as she watched from the corner of her eye as he chatted affably with her father and Consul Le Blanc. He isn't suffering in the least.

At that moment she became aware that she, in her turn, was being watched. She glanced round sharply to see Captain Ballantyne studying her from across the room with the knowing smile that had begun to infuriate her. He is always spying, she thought. Before she recovered her poise and looked away, she noticed that his hair and his whiskers had grown out in a rather fetching fashion. She felt her cheeks burn and that disconcerting sensation in her lower belly. She turned to Imran Pasha, the former governor of Khartoum who was now subservient to General Gordon.

Ten minutes later she glanced around surreptitiously to see whether Captain Ballantyne was still spying on her, and felt a twinge of annoyance when she saw that he was engrossed with the twins—or they were with him. Both Amber and Saffron were shrieking with laughter in a most unladylike fashion. She regretted that she had given in to their blandishments and allowed them to join the company instead of making them eat their dinner with Nazeera in the kitchen. She had scored a small point by seating Saffron beside Ryder Courtney: the child would have difficulty holding firm to her vow never to speak to him again. She had placed Captain Ballantyne as far away from herself as possible, at her father's end of the table.

The buffalo haunch was a glorious pink in the centre, and running with juices. The company fell upon it in ravenous silence. No sooner were the plates removed than Captain Ballantyne whispered a few words to her father, stood up, bowed to her and strode from the room. She knew better than to expect an explanation for his departure. After all, they were at war, and he was responsible for the city's defences. However, she regretted that she was to be deprived of the opportunity to snub him more profoundly.

She glanced down the table at the second object of her disapproval, and saw that Saffron had obviously forgiven Ryder. At the beginning of the meal he had ignored her haughtiness and had concentrated all his attention on Amber at his right hand. This had brought Saffron close to tears of jealousy. Then he had switched tactics and turned all his charm on her. She had been unprepared for this. 'Saffron, did you know that Lucy has had her babies?' Before she realized the trap, she was listening avidly as he told her Lucy had given birth to twins, what the babies looked like, how proud Lucy was of them. He had named them Billy and Lily.

'Oh, can I come and see them tomorrow? Oh, please, Ryder,' Saffron cried.

'But Saffy, Nazeera told me you were not feeling well,' Ryder said.

'That was yesterday. I *was* feeling rather peaky.' Ryder gathered that 'peaky' was one of her new words. 'But I am very well now. Amber and I will be with you at seven o'clock tomorrow morning.' The trial of wills had ended with a complete capitulation on her part.

Rebecca made a small *moue* at the silliness of the child, and turned her attention back to Consul Le Blanc. She had overheard her father remark to Ryder that he was as queer as a duck with four legs. It was a pity that she was unable to ask Ryder what that meant. It sounded intriguing, and Ryder knew everything. I suppose I will have to forgive him in time, she thought, but not just yet.

The dessert was pâté of green-cake with warm honey sauce: at David Benbrook's instigation Bacheet had robbed the nest that wild bees had built in the palace roof. He had been sternly restricted to the removal of a single honeycomb—David had a sweet tooth and was hoarding the bees' output. This dish was also warmly received, and the Limoges porcelain dessert bowls were scraped clean.

'I have not enjoyed a meal as much since my last visit to Le Grand Véfour in eighty-one,' Le Blanc assured Rebecca.

Despite his four legs, he is rather a dear old ass, she thought. In this new mood of benevolence she glanced back at Ryder, caught his eye, then nodded and smiled. His obvious relief was really quite gratifying. Am I becoming fast? she questioned herself. She was not certain what being fast entailed, but her father disapproved of fast women, or said he did.

After their guests had departed and they had climbed the spiral staircase to the bedroom floor her father placed his arm round her shoulders, hugged her and told her how proud he was of her, and what a lovely woman she was growing into.

So he does not think I am becoming fast, Rebecca thought, but nevertheless she felt strangely discontented. As she prepared for bed she whispered, 'There is something missing. Why should I feel so unhappy? Life is so short. Perhaps the Mahdi will storm the city tomorrow and it will all be over, and I won't even have lived.'

As if the monster had heard her and stirred in his lair, there came the crash of artillery fire from across the Nile. She heard a shell shriek overhead, then burst somewhere in the native quarter near the canal. With her hair in a golden cloud upon her shoulders she threw on her silk dressing-gown, turned the lamp down low and opened the door to the balcony. She hesitated, feeling guilty and uncertain. 'There won't be anybody there,' she told herself firmly. 'It's after midnight. If he's still awake, he'll be at the waterfront with those Gatlings.'

She stepped out on to the balcony and before she could stop herself she glanced down and searched beneath the outspread branches of the tamarind tree. She felt a nasty twinge of disappointment when she realized she had guessed right. Nobody was there. She sighed, leant her elbows on the wall and stared out across the river.

The Bedlam Bedouin is having an early night, she thought. Since sunset there had been only that single cannon shot, and now all was silent. In the moonlight she watched the bats diving and circling as they hunted insects in the top branches of the ficus tree at the bottom of the terrace. After a few minutes she sighed again and straightened up. I'm not sleepy, but it's late. I should go to bed, she thought.

A vesta flared in the shadows beneath the tamarind tree, and her heart tripped. The flame settled to a yellow glow, and she saw his face lit like the portrait in a cameo, while the rest of him remained shrouded in darkness. He had a long black cigar between his teeth. He placed the tip of it to the match and drew deeply. The flame burned up brightly. 'Oh, sweet Jesus, he is so beautiful.' The blasphemy was out before she could quell it. Still holding the burning match in front of his face he looked up at her. She stared back. He was fifty yards away but she was mesmerized, like a bird by a cobra.

He blew out the vesta, and the image of his face was gone. Only the glow of his cigar remained, brighter then fading as he drew on it. The pain came over her again, pervasive and debilitating, until she no longer had control of her emotions. Like a woman in a trance she turned slowly, went back through her bedroom and out into the corridor beyond. She passed the door to her father's suite, and her bare feet danced faster over the silken carpet that led her to the head of the staircase. She ran down, and was suddenly stricken with the fear that he would be gone by the time she reached the terrace. She fumbled with the latch of the front doors—it seemed an eternity before they opened. She ran across the lawn, then stopped dead when she saw his dark shape exactly where it had been.

He took the cigar from his mouth, dropped it on to the stone flags and waited. Her feet moved again, of their own accord, slowly at first then faster. 'I don't—I won't—' she stammered.

'Don't talk,' he commanded. And she was overwhelmed by deep gratitude although she did not understand why. She went into his arms, which closed round her. She lost all contact with reality. His mouth tasted of cigar smoke mingled with precious musk, a distillation of masculine ambergris, a rare elixir of desire. She felt terrified and helpless, yet as safe and secure as though she had been spirited into the keep of a fairy fortress.

Her silk robe and the light cotton nightgown offered no obstacle to him. Her skin beneath them

271

was burning hot, but his cunning fingers ignited deeper and more intense fires within her. She closed her eyes, threw back her head and surrendered to his touch. Suddenly she gasped and her eyes flew open at a sensation almost too exquisite to be borne. The painful knot in the pit of her stomach burst, and a new, wonderful sensation replaced it and diffused through her whole being. She looked down and realized that the front of her gown was open to her navel and his mouth was pressed to her breast. She could feel his teeth upon her nipple, and thought he might bite through to her very heart.

He picked her up and she felt weightless. He laid her on the lawn, and the grass felt cool and soft under her back. He lifted the skirts of her robe and the night air caressed her thighs and belly. She felt his weight come over the top of her. He was touching her where she had never been touched before. Her thighs fell apart.

The cannon across the river roared. She heard the shriek of the approaching shell, and her legs snapped together like the blades of a pair of scissors. The shell flew so close overhead that it took her breath away so that she could not scream. It crashed into the east wing of the palace, and burst in a cloud of flame, dust, flying plaster and bricks.

With all her strength she thrust him away and rolled out from under him. She jumped up and, long pale legs flashing, ran like a fawn startled from its forest bed, back across the terrace and up the stairs. Frantically she raced to the twins' room, beside her father's suite. The door was never locked. She ran in to them, gathered them up and held them tight. She was sobbing with relief to find them safe, and for her own escape. 'Are you all right, my darlings? Oh, dear Jesus, thank you for keeping us all safe.' She hugged them closer, but the twins were sleepy and grumpy.

'Why did you wake us up?' demanded Saffron.

'What's wrong with you, Becky? Why are you crying?' Amber yawned and rubbed her eyes. 'Why are you being so silly?'

Before she could reply her father came in through the door, carrying a lantern. 'Are you girls all right?'

'What happened? What is all the fuss about?' Saffron clamoured.

'Didn't even wake you up, what?' David laughed. 'The Bedlam Bedouin will be mortified. He's been shooting at the palace for months. The first time he manages to hit it, you go on sleeping as though nothing had happened. Shows a lack of respect, I'd say.'

'Oh, was it a shell?' Amber said. 'I thought it was a dream.'

'Where, Daddy? Where did it hit?'

'The east wing, but it's deserted. Nobody hurt. No fires. Everything safe.'

The twins were asleep before Rebecca left them, but after she got back to her own bed she could not drop off. She tried a prayer. 'Gentle Jesus, meek and mild, thank you for looking after Papa and the twins. Thank you saving me from . . .' She did not think it necessary to elaborate: He knew everything. '. . . for saving me from a fate worse than death.' She had read that expression somewhere, and now seemed an appropriate time to use it. 'Please keep me from temptation.' But the prayer did not seem to help. She did not truly feel as though she had been saved; on the contrary, she felt as though she had been cruelly deprived of something of great value, something as dear as life itself.

She thought about how he had touched her and began to ache again, where his fingers had been. Timidly she ran her own hand down to make sure he had not hurt her. She started with panic as she felt that she was bleeding, all hot and running wet. She pulled away her hand and held it up to the moonlight streaming in through the window. Her fingers were indeed damp but not with blood. She replaced her hand, and felt the pain swelling up inside her. She was panting, and wicked images flashed before her tightly shut eyelids. Penrod Ballantyne standing over her, naked, with the knife in his hand. She imagined his fingers where hers were now.

The huge ball inside her exploded, and the pain was gone. She felt a wonderful sense of elation and freedom. She felt herself falling backwards through the mattress, sinking down into a warm dark nest of sleep. When Nazeera woke her, sunlight was streaming in through the open balcony door.

'What happened to you, Becky? You are glowing like a ripe peach on the bough with the morning sun upon it.'

Arabic is such a romantic language, Rebecca thought. It suits my mood perfectly. 'Darling Nazeera, I feel as though this is the very first morning of my life,' she replied, in the same language, and wondered why Nazeera suddenly looked so worried.

Penrod understood David's reluctance to part for even a few hours with his precious double-barrelled twelve-bore London best guns by James Purdey & Sons. They were extraordinary weapons and had probably cost him as much as fifty pounds each, he guessed. 'One hundred and fifty,' David corrected him. 'Tsar Alexander of all the Russias and Kaiser William of Germany both have guns almost identical to mine.'

'I assure you that they are needed in the furtherance of an excellent cause, sir. I give you my solemn word of honour that I will look after them as though they were my firstborn,' Penrod wheedled.

'I hope you treat them better than that. It is always possible to beget brats. Purdeys like mine are another matter entirely.'

'Perhaps I should explain why I need to borrow them,' Penrod suggested.

David listened attentively. He became more intrigued as Penrod continued. In the end he sighed with resignation. 'Very well, but there is a condition. The twins go with them.' As he saw Penrod's nonplussed expression he went on, 'They are my loaders and I have taught them to pay proper respect to my guns.'

Both girls were delighted to be chosen for the commission, Amber even more so than Saffron. This was an opportunity for her to have her hero to herself for a while. They were ready and waiting on the palace terrace an hour ahead of the appointed time.

When Penrod arrived they insisted on coaching

him in the skills of passing and handing the guns. He soon saw how seriously they took their duties: to humour them he pretended ignorance and asked a few asinine questions. 'Where do you put the bullets in?'

'They are not bullets, silly. They are cartridges,' Amber explained importantly. She was chief instructress. She and Saffron had debated this issue the previous night, when the lights were out and they were supposed to be asleep. Finally Amber had settled the matter: 'Saffy, you can have Ryder as your special friend, but Captain Ballantyne is mine. Remember that!'

When it came to handling the guns, Penrod was deliberately clumsy and slow so that he did not deprive Amber of the pleasure of correcting him.

'When I pass it to you, you must try to remember to hold out your left hand with the palm up, Captain Ballantyne, so I can place the fore-end into your hand.'

'Like this, Miss Amber?' He managed to keep a straight face, as he reflected that he had been about the same age that Amber was now when he had first been allowed to attend his family's grand shoot at Clercastle on the Borders, and to take his place in the line like a man.

'Don't hold your hand so high, Captain Ballantyne, otherwise I can't reach.' She hated to draw attention to the discrepancy in their heights. At last she was satisfied. She even commended him on his progress: 'I must say, you do learn quickly, Captain Ballantyne.'

'I think that you and I make an excellent team, Miss Amber,' he replied seriously, and Amber felt quite giddy with gratification.

'Yes, but have you actually ever shot before?' Saffron was feeling left out, a sensation to which she was unaccustomed.

'Once or twice,' Penrod reassured her.

'My papa is one of the best shots in England,' Saffron informed him grandly.

'I am sure Captain Ballantyne will do very well.' Amber pulled a disapproving face at her twin. Could not Saffy keep quiet for once?

'Well, we shall see about that,' said Saffron haughtily.

All three waited impatiently on the terrace, the twins vying with each other to be the first to spot the pigeon. They saw it in the same instant, and squealed with excitement. The bird's wing tips were bone white. They flashed in the sunlight. It was high as it came in across the river, much too high as it passed overhead. The Purdeys were choked full and full, giving them an effective pattern of pellets at a range out to sixty yards, but this pigeon was at least three hundred feet high.

'Why didn't you shoot?' Saffron demanded, as it flew on.

'It was well out of range,' Penrod told her. 'If I prick the bird and send it wounded to its loft, the Dervish might tumble to what we are up to. They will stop using the birds. We must have a clean kill.'

'Daddy would have killed it easily.'

'Look, it's coming round again.' Amber tried to prevent her sister baiting the captain.

The pigeon turned wide beyond the scattered buildings of Omdurman, then came back across the river, angling in towards the waterfront, losing height gradually.

'That should do well enough,' Penrod

murmured, and brought up the gun. The movement was unhurried, almost casual. His left arm was extended almost straight in line with the barrels, his right cheek pressed to the comb of the butt-stock. He picked up the bird from behind its tail, and swung smoothly through its line of flight. At the final instant, as his forefinger tightened on the trigger, he gave the gun an extra forward flick. It fired and the muzzle kicked up at the recoil. Smoothly he remounted the gun, his hands, shoulder and head dropping into the same position as before. The gun thudded again and jumped with a spurt of black powder smoke from the right-hand muzzle.

'Miss!' cried Saffron.

The bird was so high that there was a perceptible delay after the sound of the shots before the pellets reached it. Then the pigeon lurched and tottered in the air. Its legs dropped and dangled down.

'Hit!' howled Amber.

Then the pattern of the second shot caught the wounded bird and they heard the pellets rattle on its plumage. One pellet struck it under the chin and it threw back its head as the lead cut through to its brain.

'Dead!' Amber shrieked. 'Stone dead in the air! Even Papa couldn't have done better.' The pigeon's wings folded and it plummeted to earth, but it still had the momentum of its flight and curled out towards the water.

'It's going to fall into the river,' Penrod shouted with alarm, and tossed the shotgun back to Amber. It took her by surprise but she caught it before it hit the earth. Penrod bounded away down the lawn towards the riverbank, and she ran after him, hampered by the heavy gun.

For a while it looked as though the dead bird might fall on firm ground, but then the breeze caught it. Penrod came up short on the muddy strip of ground above the water's edge and watched in dismay as the pigeon splashed in thirty yards offshore. The carcass floated in the centre of a spreading circle of ripples and loose blue breast feathers.

'Crocodile!' Amber screamed behind him. A hundred yards beyond the fallen pigeon Penrod saw the monstrous head push through the surface. The skin was gnarled and lumpy as the bark of an ancient olive tree. 'Big one!' Amber shouted.

'It's after the pigeon,' Saffron cried.

Penrod did not hesitate. He pulled off his boots and flung them aside, then ran to the water's edge ripping off his shirt so that the buttons flew away like sown wheat. His breeches went next and he was left with only his underpants, in a dashing crimson silk. He ran into the green water until it reached his waist, then linked his hands over his head and dived forward. The moment his head broke water again, he struck out in a powerful overarm stroke. The crocodile was drawn on by the commotion, and its great tail thrashed from side to side, driving it to meet Penrod.

'Come back!' wailed Amber. 'Leave the silly old bird!'

Penrod swam furiously, kicking hard with both legs, cleaving through the water. The crocodile moved much faster. This was its element, but it had three times further than Penrod to travel. He reached the carcass and thrust the pigeon's head into his mouth, then turned and started back towards the shore. 'Faster!' Amber shouted wildly. 'It's gaining on you! Faster, please! Please!'

The great saurian had fixed all its attention on the man. Instead of diving, it swam on the surface and the long tail drove from side to side, sending out a boiling wake behind it. It was so close that its eyes glittered like opaque yellow marbles. Long fangs protruded over its scaly lips, the rows interlocking with each other. It bore in on Penrod's naked legs.

'It's going to catch you!' Amber was wild with fear. She had not reloaded the shotgun, but now she pushed the slide across and broke open the breech. She fumbled a pair of cartridges out of the leather bag on her hip, thrust one into the breech, and dropped the other into the mud. There was no time to retrieve it or find another so she snapped the breech closed. As she ran into the water it rose to her knees, her hips, then her lower ribs.

Penrod was directly in front of her, crashing through the water like a maniac, kicking up a froth behind him. With cold horror Amber watched the monster close the gap between them. Suddenly it reared high out of the water, and its jaws gaped open. The lining of its mouth and throat was a lovely buttercup yellow. It was so close that she could clearly see the flap of skin at the back of its throat sealing off the opening of its gullet to keep the water from flooding into its lungs. The fangs were sharp and ragged. She could smell the obscene reek of its open maw. It lunged towards Penrod's legs.

Amber threw up the gun and thumbed back the ornate hammer. At any other time she would have needed both hands to work against the heavy spring of the sidelock, but she was possessed. The butt was too long to fit into her shoulder so she held it under her right armpit. She aimed, and kept her eyes open, as her father had taught her, as she pulled the back trigger. If she had pulled the front one the hammer would have fallen on an empty chamber. David had taught her well.

The gun bucked and bellowed and a blast of shot swept inches over Penrod's head. The muzzle blast deafened him. Amber and the gun were sent flying backwards by the recoil and she disappeared under the swirling river waters.

The full charge of shot flew down the crocodile's gullet. The great jaws shut with a clash like the slamming of steel gates, and its body arched into a drawn bow of agony. The glistening black snout almost touched its tail. Half out of the water it performed a backwards somersault, then dived below the surface and was gone in a mighty swirl of green waters.

Penrod found the bottom and staggered to where Amber had gone under. His ears were ringing painfully with the concussion of the shot, and as he shook his head to try to clear them the sodden pigeon carcass he was still holding in his teeth flopped against his cheeks. Golden tendrils of Amber's hair floated on the surface like some lovely water plant. Penrod seized a handful and dragged her head to the surface. She spluttered and choked, but she still had a firm grasp on her father's Purdey. Penrod changed his grip, swung her under his arm and he waded with her, an undignified tangle of sodden skirts, hair and kicking limbs, to the bank.

'Put me down!' she gasped. 'Please put me

281

down.'

He set her on her feet. 'Cough it all up,' he ordered, 'Don't swallow any.' He pounded her between the shoulder-blades. The city sewers spilled into the river upstream. He did not want to lose this little one to the blast of the cholera horn.

David and most of the palace staff had been watching from the terrace and were running down to the riverbank. Before they arrived Penrod knelt in front of her. 'Are you all right now?'

'Yes, I am,' she gasped, 'but Papa's gun is wet.'

'What a brave and wonderful girl you are.' Penrod hugged her hard. 'I'd choose you in a scrap every time.' As her father came running up, Penrod rose to his feet but he kept one arm round Amber's shoulders. 'Forgive the impropriety, sir, but I owe this young lady my life.'

'Quite right and proper, Captain. I'm going to give her a kiss myself.'

Before that could happen Nazeera and Rebecca arrived.

'That filthy river!' Rebecca avoided Penrod's eyes, and pulled Amber away from him. 'Nazeera, we're going to get her into a Lysol bath.' The two swept Amber away.

*   *   *

In the bathroom, as Rebecca and Nazeera stripped off Amber's bedraggled, mud-plastered clothing and Saffron poured another bucket of heated water into the porcelain hip-bath, Amber was in raptures, 'Did you hear what he said, Becky? He said he'd choose me in a scrap every time.'

Rebecca studiously avoided a reply, but went to

282

the bath and poured a liberal measure of Lysol into the steaming water.

Saffron was not so reticent. 'So now I suppose you think that makes him your beau,' she mocked.

'He jolly well will be one day. You wait and see.' Amber placed her hands on her bare hips and glared at her twin.

'Don't be so silly, Midget,' Rebecca rebuked her. 'Captain Ballantyne is old enough to be your father. Now, come and get into this bath at once.'

Nazeera felt a pang as she watched Amber clamber into the bath. Changes seemed to have taken place in the child's body. Soon there would be womanly hollows and swells where before all had been flat and featureless.

I am losing all my babies, she lamented inwardly.

*   *   *

Once he had buckled on his breeches, Penrod could examine the pigeon. It was a large bird with body plumage of bronze and wing tips of white, probably a female for they made the best homers. The message it carried had been folded and rolled tightly into a spill no larger than the first joint of his little finger and secured to the bird's leg with a fine silk thread. With his pocket-knife he cut the thread, and kept the carcass to take to the kitchens. He wrapped the roll of paper in his handkerchief to mop up as much moisture as possible, then pulled on his boots and, leaving David to mourn his waterlogged shotgun, set out for General Gordon's headquarters in the west wing of the palace.

*   *   *

283

'I understand that you have had some success with your shooting. There was a great deal of excitement on the riverbank,' Gordon greeted him.

'I managed to bring down a pigeon, sir, and it was a carrier.'

'You retrieved the message?' demanded Gordon eagerly.

'I have it, but it took a soaking in the river. I have not dared to unfold it, because the rice paper might disintegrate.'

'Let's take a look at it. Put it here.' Obediently Penrod placed his bundled handkerchief on the general's desk, and carefully unfolded it. They studied the tiny roll of paper.

'Seems it's still in one piece,' Gordon murmured. 'It's your prize. You unfold it.'

Careful Penrod nipped the silk thread with the point of his penknife blade. The rice paper was so fine that it tore along the folds as he tried to open it, but the inner part of the message had been kept almost dry by the tightness of the roll. The ink had run, and in spots the words were indecipherable.

'We need a book,' Penrod said, 'to press it while it dries completely.'

Gordon handed him his leatherbound copy of the Bible.

'Are you certain, sir?'

'The good book for good works,' Gordon told him.

Penrod opened the Bible and gingerly spread the damp sheet between the pages. He closed it and pressed the heel of his hand on the outer cover. Gordon was visibly impatient. He paced up and down the room puffing at one of his Turkish

284

cigarettes until he could contain himself no longer. 'Damned thing must be dry enough by now.'

Penrod opened the Bible carefully. The sheet of rice paper was still intact, flattened by the pressure, and it seemed that the ink had not run further. Gordon handed him a large magnifying glass. 'Your eyes, and your understanding of Arabic, are probably better than mine.'

Penrod carried the Bible across to the table below the window where the light was better. He pored over it, and after a moment began to read aloud the tiny flowing script: ' "I, Abdullah Sayid, son of Fahl, Emir of the Baggara, greet the Victorious Mahdi who is the light of my eyes, and call down upon him the blessing of Allah and his other Prophet, who is also named Muhammad." '

'Standard salutation,' Gordon grunted.

Penrod went on: ' "True to the orders of the Victorious Mahdi, I stand guard upon the Nile at Abu Hamed, and my scouts watch all the roads from the north. The infidel Frank and the despicable Turk approach on two separate routes. The Frankish steamers have this day passed through the cataract at Korti." '

Gordon slammed the flat of his hand on the desk. 'Praise God! This is the first hard intelligence I have had in six weeks. If Wolseley's steamers have arrived at Korti they should reach Abu Hamed before the end of Ramadan.'

'Sir!' Penrod agreed, though he was not so sure.

'Go on, man. Go on!'

'A trifle difficult here. The ink has run badly. I think it says, "The camel regiments of the Franks are still encamped at the Wells of Gakdul, where they have been now for twenty-eight days." '

'Twenty-eight days? What on earth does Stewart think he is playing at?' Gordon demanded. 'If only he had some gumption, he would make a bold dash for it. He could reach us within ten days.'

That is Chinese Gordon's own style—the bold dash and the grand gesture, Penrod thought, but he kept his expression neutral. 'Stewart is also a death-or-glory lad, but he has to bring up his supplies before he can make the final charge to the city.'

Gordon jumped up again, and flicked the butt of his cigarette through the open window. 'With two thousand of Stewart's first-line British troops I could hold the city until the desert freezes over, but still he shilly-shallies at Gakdul.' He spun on his heel and faced Penrod again. 'Go on, Ballantyne, what else is there?'

'Not much, sir.' He stooped over the tattered scrap of paper. ' "In the name of the Victorious Mahdi, and with the blessing of Allah, we will meet the infidel at Abu Hamed and destroy him." ' Penrod looked up. 'That's all. It seems that Sayid ran out of space.'

'Very little for our comfort,' Gordon observed, 'and the Nile is falling.'

'With a brace of Ryder Courtney's fast camels Yakub and I could be at the Wells of Gakdul in three days,' Penrod said. 'I could take Stewart your message.'

'You do not escape me so easily, Ballantyne.' Gordon laughed ironically, a short bark of sound. 'Not yet awhile. We will continue to follow the progress of the relief columns by intercepting the pigeons.'

'The Dervish might accept one or two missing

birds as prey of the falcons,' Penrod demurred, 'but we must not frighten them off by killing every one as it arrives.'

'Of course, you have a point. But I must have news. I want you to shoot every fourth pigeon that comes in.'

*   *   *

Muhammad Ahmed, the Victorious Mahdi, walked in the cool of the evening along the bank of the great river. He was attended by his *khalifa* and his five most trusted emirs. As he walked he recited the nine-and-ninety beautiful names of Allah and his entourage murmured the response after each was enunciated.

'Al-Ghafur, the concealer of faults.'

'God is great!'

'Al-Wali, the friend of the righteous.'

'Praise be to God!'

'Al-Qawi, the strong.'

'May his word triumph.'

They reached the tomb of the saint al-Rabb, and the Mahdi took his seat in the shade of the tree that spread its branches over it. When his warlords were assembled, he called upon each to report his order of battle, and give an account of the troops that he commanded. One after another they knelt before him and described their array. Then the Mahdi knew he had seventy thousand men gathered before the walls of Khartoum; another twenty-five thousand had gone two hundred miles north to Abu Hamed on the bend of the river to await the approach of the two British forces. These Ansar were of the finest, their religious ardour and their devotion to the *jihad* against the infidel at its fiercest. The Mahdi knew that no infidel army could prevail against them.

The Mahdi smiled at Osman Atalan. 'Tell me what we know of the enemy,' he ordered.

'O Mighty and Victorious Lord, beloved of God and the other Prophet, know you that each day Abdullah Sayid, Emir of the Baggara, sends a pigeon from his camp at Abu Klea on the bend of the Nile. Some of the birds do not reach my lofts, for there are birds of prey and other hazards along their flight path, but most come to my hand.'

The Mahdi nodded. 'Speak to me, Osman Atalan. Tell us what news of the enemy movements these birds bring us.'

'Sayid reports that the infidel steamers, seven in number, have passed through the last cataract below Korti, and now that the worst of their voyage is behind them, they come on apace. They are travelling almost five times faster than they did below the cataract. They carry many men and great guns.'

'God shall deliver them to my hand, and they shall be destroyed,' said the Mahdi.

'God is great!' Osman Atalan agreed. 'The second infidel column has reached the Wells at Gakdul. There they have stopped. We do not know why this is. I believe that there is not sufficient good fodder to feed the camels for the heavy work they must do. They wait at Gakdul for more supplies to be brought up from Wadi Halfa.'

'How many infidel troops are at Gakdul?'

'Divine One, Sayid has counted more than one thousand Franks, and about the same number of camel drivers, guides and servants.'

'Are these Franks mad?' the Mahdi demanded. 'How can they dream to prevail against my one hundred thousand Ansar?'

'It may be that they are waiting at Gakdul for reinforcements to join them,' Osman suggested delicately.

'These infidels shall be destroyed also. No mortal man can prevail against the will of God. All these things God has told me.'

'Allah is all seeing and all knowing.'

'Know you that on many nights Allah has come to me as an eagle of flame. He has told me many grave secrets that are too powerful for the common man to hear,' he said, in his soft mellifluous voice, and they bowed before him.

'Blessed is the Mahdi, for he alone hears and understands the word of Allah,' chanted Khalifa Abdullahi.

'Allah has told me that before the infidel and the Frank and the Turk can be driven for ever from the Sudan and the earthly kingdom of Allah and Islam, my enemy Gordon Pasha must be destroyed. Allah has told me that Gordon Pasha is the black angel, Satan, in the guise of a man.'

'May he be ever accursed, and never look upon the face of God,' they cried.

'Allah, the All Wise, has told me that the noble warrior of Islam who cuts the head of Gordon Pasha from his trunk, like some bitter and evil fruit, and brings it to me, and lays it at my feet, shall ever be blessed and that there shall be prepared for him a place in Paradise at God's right hand. He will also be given power and riches in this world of the flesh.'

'God is merciful! God is great!' they chanted.

'Allah has spoken to me, and he has told me the name of my servant who shall bring the head of the infidel to me,' quoth the Mahdi solemnly, and they prostrated themselves before him.

'Let the man be me!'

'If it be me, I shall want no other honour in this life or hereafter.'

The Mahdi held up his hands and they fell silent. 'Osman Atalan of the Beja, draw closer to me,' he said. On his hands and knees Osman crawled to his feet. 'Allah has told me that you are that man.'

Tears of joy streamed down the emir's cheeks. He bowed his head over the Mahdi's feet and washed the dust from them with his tears. Then he unwrapped his turban and, with the locks of his long dark hair, he dried the feet of the Chosen Prophet of God.

*　　*　　*

'The Nile is falling,' said Osman Atalan, 'and God and the Mahdi have prepared a task for us.' His aggagiers drew closer to the campfire and watched his face by the light of the flames. 'They have chosen us above all the warriors of Allah. We are blessed beyond all other men, for we have been given the wondrous chance to die for the glory of Allah and his Mahdi.'

'Let us seize Allah's bounteous gift. Command us, Great Lord,' his aggagiers pleaded.

He studied their fierce expressions with pride. These were not men, but man-eating lions. 'Our sacred task is to bring to the Divine Mahdi the head of Gordon Pasha, for omnipotent and mighty Allah has decreed that when we achieve this the infidel will be driven from this land for ever, and that Islam will prevail throughout all the world.'

Al-Noor asked: 'Shall we wait for the time of Low Nile, so that we may find a firm foothold on the city shore and a passage through the walls?'

'Every day we delay, the forces of Satan march down upon us from the north. Already their steamers laden with men and guns sweep up the river. Yes, the river is still high, but God has made clear a road for us.' Osman clapped his hands. An old man limped into the firelight and knelt before him. 'Have no fear, Beloved of God. No harm shall come to you. Tell these men what you know.'

'I was born and I have lived all my life in the City of the Elephant's Trunk, Khartoum. But since the Victorious Mahdi has invested the city and laid siege, the curse of Allah has been laid upon the city. Those infidels and Turks who have thought to resist his wisdom and his truth have been made to suffer as no men before them. Their empty bellies cling to their backbones, their children are eaten up by the cholera, the vultures gorge on their rotting corpses, the fathers club the birds and eat them half cooked while their crops bulge with the flesh of their own children.' The aggagiers moved restlessly as they listened to this recital. What an abomination to eat the flesh of the bird that had devoured your children. 'Those who are not too weak of starvation flee the doomed city, and the defences are every day denuded and weakened. I am one of those who has flown. But, like you, I wish to see the infidel banished for ever from the Sudan, and the son of all evil, Gordon Pasha, destroyed. Only then may I return in the peace of the Mahdi to my home.'

'Let Allah accomplish this,' they murmured. The man was old and frail but they admired his spirit.

'The Turks who fight for Gordon Pasha are so reduced in number by disease, starvation and desertion that the infidel can no longer guard the city walls. In their place Gordon Pasha has placed men of straw, mere scarecrows, to frighten off the timid among you.'

'What is this talk of straw men?' Hassan Ben Nader demanded. 'Is it true?'

'It is true,' Osman confirmed. 'I have sailed close to the harbour mouth in this brave old man's dhow. There is a place in the defences where a creek runs into the river through a stone gateway. This is the main outflow from the city sewers. Gordon Pasha has manned the gateway and the walls on either side with dummy soldiers to replace those who have died or run away. Only their heads show above the parapets. At intervals a few old women move them so that from this bank they seemed to live. There is none to resist our onslaught. With one rush we can be through the gap. Then the city and all those within will be ours.'

'There will be great stores of gold and jewels,' al-Noor mused.

'There are women in the city, hundreds of women. As his wives, concubines and slaves, the Turk has chosen the most beautiful women of the Sudan and all the surrounding lands. For each of us there will be a dozen women at least.' Hassan Ben Nader's eyes gleamed in the firelight. 'The women of the Franks have hair like yellow silk and their skin is like rich cream.'

'Speak not of gold and slaves. We fight for the glory of Allah and the Mahdi.' Osman reprimanded them for their greed. 'After that we fight for our own honour and a place in Paradise.'

'When will we attack these straw men?' Al-Noor laughed with excitement. 'I have sat too long with my harem, and I am growing fat. It is time to fight again.'

'Three nights from now it will be the dark of the moon, and in the night we will cross the river. At first we will land two hundred men on the beach—there is no space for more. When we have forced the breach a thousand more will follow us, and after them a thousand more. By dawn I will stand on the parapets of Mukran Fort with the head of Gordon Pasha in my hands, and the prophecy will be fulfilled.' Osman stood up and made a sign of blessing over them. 'Make certain that your swords are sharp and all your wives are with child before we cross the river.'

*   *   *

'The old fisherman, the uncle of Yakub, has given the signal. A handful of sulphur in the flames of his cooking fire, and the puff of yellow smoke that Yakub was watching for,' Penrod reported to the Chinese Gordon.

'Can we trust this fellow, Yakub? To me he seems an evil rogue.'

'I have trusted him often in the most dire circumstances and I am still alive, General.' Penrod kept his anger under control, but with difficulty.

'Has he been able to warn us when the Dervish will attack—if they do?'

'No, sir, we don't know that,' Penrod admitted, 'but I expect they will use the new moon.'

293

While Gordon consulted his almanac for the moon phases, David Benbrook, the third man in the room, gave his appraisal of the chances of success. 'He is a brave man, this uncle of Yakub. I know him well. He has been in my service ever since I arrived in Khartoum. His information has always been reliable.' David was sitting in a chair by the window. These days, he and the general spent much time together. They were unlikely companions, but as Gordon's tribulations increased he seemed to find solace with his own kind.

Without seeming to do so Penrod studied Gordon's face while he spoke to David. Even in repose, a nerve fluttered in his right eyelid. This was only a visible sign of how finely stretched Gordon was. One of the other deeper and more significant indications was in his behaviour: the brutal excesses of inhumanity. It seemed to Penrod that these were becoming more savage each day, as though by the kurbash, the firing squad and the noose he could delay the fall of the city. Even he must now see that our struggle is drawing towards the end, and the populace is beyond hope or caring. Does he believe that he can compel them to their duty by convincing them that the consequences of their disobedience will be far worse than anything that the Mahdi can do to them? Penrod studied Gordon's face as the general spoke to David Benbrook. At least Benbrook is a man of humanity, he thought. His influence on Gordon can only be for the good.

He put aside such considerations when Gordon stood up and addressed him abruptly. 'Let us go down to the harbour and inspect your preparations to meet this imminent attack, Ballantyne.'

Penrod knew it was unwise for Gordon Pasha to show himself on the walls where the attack was expected: too many spies were watching his every move, and the Dervish were too shrewd not to suspect that he was preparing something for their discomfort. However, he knew it was even more unwise to gainsay the little man.

But Penrod need not have concerned himself: Gordon was too sly an old fox to lead the hounds to the entrance of his earth. Before they left the palace, Gordon removed his distinctive fez and replaced it with a grubby turban, the tail of which concealed half of his face, then covered his uniform with a stained, nondescript *galabiyya*. From a distance he looked like any humble citizen of Khartoum.

Even when they reached the harbour Gordon did not show himself on the parapets. However, he was meticulous and painstaking in his inspection of Penrod's preparations. He peered through every embrasure that pierced the walls of the derelict buildings that overlooked the noisome sewerage-clogged creek. He stood behind a Gatling and traversed the gleaming multiple barrels from side to side. He was dissatisfied with the dead area directly under the muzzles. He climbed out of the Gatling's nest into the ooze of the creek and placed himself in the line of fire, then moved closer to the redoubt.

'Keep the gun trained on me,' he ordered.

The gunner kept depressing his aim until he shook his head with exasperation. 'You are too close, General. It can no longer bear.'

'Captain Ballantyne, if they reach this point the Dervish will be under the gun.' Gordon looked pleased that he had caught Penrod out.

Penrod realized it was no excuse that Gordon overloaded him with responsibilities: he had been negligent, and he rebuked himself silently. Such an elementary oversight is almost as bad as starving the gun for ammunition, he thought bitterly. He ordered the engineers to tear down the wall of sandbags and rebuild it with a lower sill.

'Where have you placed the second Gatling?' Gordon demanded. He had Penrod on the defensive now, and was pushing his advantage.

'It is still in the redoubt in front of the hospital. That is the other obvious weak point in our perimeter. I dare not leave that gap undefended, and place all our bets on the attack striking us here. The Dervish may even mount two simultaneous strikes at both positions.'

'They will strike here,' Gordon said, with finality.

'I agree that is the highest probability. So I have built another machine-gun nest over there, where it can cover the beach and enfilade both banks of the creek. As soon as the attack develops and the enemy is committed, I can rush the second gun across from the hospital to this side. Equally, if we are mistaken and they strike at the hospital I can move this gun over to cover that position.'

'How long will it take to move the guns.' Gordon demanded.

'I estimate about ten minutes.'

'No estimates, Ballantyne. Run an exercise and time it.'

On the first attempt the gun-crew encountered a pile of fallen masonry in the alley behind the harbour. They had to clear it before they could bring the heavy carriage through. The second attempt was more successful: it took twelve minutes to run it through the streets and resite it in the prepared nest to cover the beach and the banks of the creek.

'It will be in darkness,' Gordon pointed out. 'The crew must be able to do it with their eyes closed.'

Penrod kept them practising the manoeuvre late into the night. They cleared all obstacles and shell damage from the streets and alleys, and filled in the potholes and gutters. Penrod designed new gun tackles so that twenty men at a time could pull it.

By the morning of the second day they had cut the transit time down to seven and a half minutes. All this had to be done in darkness after curfew. If the Dervish learnt that they were practising moving the Gatlings from one point to another on the perimeter they would suspect a trap. Penrod was not sure that they knew of the existence of the two guns: while in the arsenal they had been stored away from prying eyes, and had probably been forgotten. In any event the Dervish had a deep scorn for firearms. It was unlikely they had ever seen the Gatlings in action so they could not guess at their destructive potential. Until now he had been careful to exercise the gun-crew where they were not under observation from the enemy bank of the Nile. They only fired the weapons into the empty desert on the southern perimeter of the city. When they were not in use he kept them covered with tarpaulins.

'With your permission, General, I intend to take up permanent quarters here at the harbour. I want to be on the spot when the enemy launch their attack. As things stand at present, it might all be over during the time it would take me to get here from the palace.'

'Good,' Gordon agreed. 'But if the Dervish spies discover that you have set up permanent headquarters here at the harbour our plan will be compromised.'

'I have thought about that, General, and I believe I will be able to conceal my whereabouts without causing suspicion.'

They enlisted the co-operation of David Benbrook in concealing from everybody, including the Benbrook sisters and consular staff, that he had moved only as far as the harbour. The story was put about that Penrod had secretly left the city, sent on a mission by General Gordon to carry a message to the British relief column at the Wells of Gakdul.

Penrod found his new quarters a far call from the luxury of his suite in the palace. He set up his *angareb* in a tiny dugout in the back wall of the Gatling emplacement. He had no mosquito net, and spent most of the night swatting the insects: at dusk they rose in clouds from the creek. Previously the palace's paltry food supplies had been augmented by the ingenuity of the Benbrook sisters, Nazeera, the kitchen staff and, of course, by David Benbrook's marksmanship. In his new headquarters Penrod shared the same rations as his men. Gordon had been forced to reduce the issue of dhurra to below starvation level, and hunger was now a constant spectral companion. Yakub was able to scrounge a few dried fish heads and skeletons from his uncle's house and these went into the stew pot that Penrod shared with his gunners. Some of the Egyptians were eating the pith of the palm trees and boiling the leather thongs of their *angarebs*. Much as he had once disparaged the taste of it, Penrod now sorely missed the rations of green-cake that the Benbrook sisters had regularly brought home from the compound of Ryder Courtney.

Penrod could not afford to be seen in the city, so he had to confine himself strictly to the harbour. This self-imposed incarceration was even more irksome than his cramped quarters and the disgusting food. It was a relief to direct all his energy and imagination into preparations for the coming conflict.

His plan was in two parts. First he had to lure the Dervish through the drainage ditch in the outer wall, and into the narrow creek. Then he had to ensure there was no way for them to get out, at least not alive. Gordon restricted his inspection tours to the hours of curfew. Penrod never expected praise from Chinese Gordon, but made certain that he gave the general no further cause for criticism.

Once all the preparations were completed, Yakub was more forthcoming in his praise than Gordon had been. 'With the help of clever Yakub you have built an abattoir.' He chuckled. 'A slaughter house for the pigs of Ansar.' Instinctively he fiddled with the hilt of his dagger as he looked around the stockade they had built. The men were stacking dry timber from the derelict buildings of the city on the bonfires that Penrod had ordered to be constructed on both banks of the creek. He had taken great care that once they were lit the flames would illuminate the enemy, but would not dazzle his gunners and riflemen. Each evening at nightfall his men soaked the bonfires with lamp oil so that their combustion would be almost instantaneous.

* * *

Penrod's sudden mysterious disappearance caused varying levels of consternation and concern among the Benbrook sisters. The one who suffered least was Saffron. She merely found herself deprived of a whip to torment her twin. It was no longer satisfactory to tease Amber about her beau, when he had absconded. Besides, Amber's distress whenever she raised the subject detracted from Saffron's enjoyment. Teasing was fun; inflicting pain was not.

On the other hand Rebecca was adept at concealing her true feelings so Saffron had no inkling as to how profoundly Penrod's disappearance had affected her. Had she guessed, she would have had richer fields to plough.

When Amber had almost convinced herself that she would never again set eyes upon Captain Ballantyne, and that suicide was the only solution to her tragic existence, Yakub saved her life. This was not a deliberate act of charity: it was in gratification of Yakub's baser instincts.

His strict confinement, by his master, to the harbour defences above the mosquito-ridden creek suited Yakub not at all. In the last months he had become accustomed to finer living. Each evening Nazeera had provided him with a bowl of the same food as the consul general and his family enjoyed. This was not a great feast, but it far surpassed the watery communal stew, which smelt and tasted of rotten fish and dried animal hides.

However, by far the most troubling element in this new existence was that each night he lay awake at the foot of his master's *angareb*, waiting for the Dervish attack and wondering if Nazeera was being faithful to him. If her previous behaviour was anything to go upon, this seemed highly unlikely. He brooded on the fact that the perfidious Bacheet, that illegitimate son of a Beja father and a Galla pleasure dancer, was under no restrictions as to his nocturnal movements. The thought of Bacheet creeping into his beloved's *angareb* each night kept Yakub from sleep more effectively than all the mosquitoes from the creek. He rose quietly, as if he was going to use the latrine bucket. One of the sentries challenged him at the harbour gate, but Yakub knew the password.

Amber was sitting sleepless at her bedroom window. It was three days since Captain Ballantyne had disappeared. She tortured herself with the thought that he might have been caught by the Dervish before he reached the British lines. She imagined him as a prisoner of the Mahdi. She had heard of the fate of those who fell into that monster's bloodstained hands, and knew she would not sleep that night.

Below her window someone moved in the shadows of the courtyard. She drew back quickly. It might be an assassin sent by the evil Mahdi, but at that moment the man glanced up towards her window and she recognized his squint. 'Yakub!' she breathed. 'But he should be with Penrod on the way to the Wells of Gakdul.' Yakub was Penrod's shadow: wherever he went Yakub followed.

The breathtaking truth dawned upon her. If Yakub is here, then Penrod is somewhere close by.

He did not go to Gakdul after all. It was only recently that she had allowed herself to think of him as Penrod, and not as Captain Ballantyne.

Amber's melancholy and foreboding dropped away. She knew exactly where Yakub was going. She sprang up from the window-seat, ran lightly to her wardrobe and threw a dark cloak over her nightdress. She paused only long enough to make certain that Saffron was still asleep, then slipped out of the bedroom and crept downstairs, making certain to avoid the twelfth step, which always creaked and woke her father. She let herself out of the kitchen side door and crossed the stableyard to the servants' compound.

Nazeera's window was lamp-lit. She found a lookout position in one of the empty stables and settled in to wait. She passed the next few hours by trying to imagine what Yakub and Nazeera found to keep themselves busy for such a long time. Rebecca had said that the two of them made love. Amber was not sure what this procedure entailed: her most diligent enquiries had not greatly increased her understanding of the subject. She suspected that Rebecca herself, despite her knowing airs, was just as ignorant as she was.

'It's when people kiss each other,' Rebecca had explained loftily, 'but it's not polite to talk about it.' Amber found this unsatisfactory. Most of the kisses she had observed were fleeting and usually planted on the cheek or the back of a hand, which could only be considered fairly dull entertainment. The one glaring exception was the exchange she and Saffron had witnessed between Ryder and Rebecca, which had caused such a brouhaha. That had been much more interesting. Both participants had obviously enjoyed the process, but even that had lasted less than a minute. In comparison, Yakub and Nazeera had been at it half the night.

I will ask Nazeera, she decided, then had a better idea. 'As soon as I find out where he is, I will ask Penrod. He's a man, so he must know how they do it.'

Shortly before dawn the lamplight in Nazeera's room was extinguished, and moments later Yakub crept out of the door and set off through the dark, silent streets in guilty haste. Amber kept him in sight until he reached the harbour, and she heard one of the sentries challenge him. Then she had to get back to the palace before they found out she was missing.

*   *   *

'Cat been at the cream?' Saffron demanded. Amber's ebullient mood was such a marked change from the days of gloom that had preceded it that she had to tackle her sister later that day as they worked side by side over the green-cake cauldrons in Ryder Courtney's compound.

Amber gave her a sweet but enigmatic smile, and would not be drawn.

That evening, an hour after curfew, Penrod Ballantyne was amazed to recognize Amber's voice arguing with the sentries at the entrance to his headquarters in the Gatling emplacement. He rushed out immediately, buckling on his sword belt. 'You silly child,' he scolded her severely. 'You know very well there is a curfew. You might have been shot.'

Amber had hoped for a warmer reception. 'I

303

brought you some green-cake. I knew you must be starving.' She unwrapped the small bundle she was carrying. 'And one of Papa's clean shirts. I can smell your old one from here.'

Penrod was about to demand how she had learnt of his whereabouts when, in the light of the bullseye lantern, he saw tears of humiliation in her eyes. But she blinked them back and faced him with her chin up. 'Furthermore, Captain Ballantyne, I will have you know that I am not a silly child.'

'Of course you are not, Miss Amber.' He relented instantly. 'You took me by surprise. I just did not expect you. I apologize.'

She perked up. 'If you give me your old shirt I will take it back to wash it for you.'

Penrod found himself in a dilemma. With the threat of an imminent Dervish attack on the harbour, he should not allow her to stay here another minute. For the same reason he dared not leave the emplacement to escort her back to the palace, and he could not let her wander through the city alone after curfew. He could send Yakub with her, but he needed him at his side. There was no one else he could trust. He chose the lesser of all evils.

'I expect that you will have to spend the night here. I cannot allow you to break curfew and go home alone,' he muttered.

Her face lit up with pleasure. This stroke of fortune far exceeded her remotest expectations. 'I can cook your dinner,' she said.

'There isn't much to cook, so why don't you and I share your very generous gift of green-cake?'

They sat on his *angareb* in the dugout. There

304

were no curtains to this alcove so the gunners were involuntary chaperones as they nibbled the green-cake and talked in low tones. It was the first time he had spent any time with her, and Penrod soon discovered that Amber was entertaining company. She had an impish sense of humour that appealed to him, and a quaint manner of expressing herself. She described her various travels with her father, which ranged from Cape Town to Cairo, and finally Khartoum. Then, abruptly, she fell silent, placed her chin in her hand and considered him thoughtfully. 'Captain Ballantyne, now that we have become friends, would you be civil enough to answer a question that has been troubling me lately? Nobody seems to know the answer.'

'I am honoured that you consider us friends.' Penrod was touched. She was such a funny little thing. 'I would be delighted to render you any assistance I can.'

'How do people make love?' she asked.

Penrod found himself deprived of words and the breath to speak them. 'Ah!' he said, and smoothed his moustache to win time. 'I think that it is done in various ways. There do not seem to be any fixed rules of engagement.'

Amber was disappointed. She had expected more of him. Obviously he knew as little as Rebecca. 'I suppose they kiss each other like you and I saw my sister kissing Ryder. Is that how they do it?'

'Indubitably.' He grabbed thankfully at the opening. 'I think that is exactly how they do it.'

'I should think that would become rather boring after a while.'

'It seems to grow on some people,' Penrod said.

'There is no accounting for taste.'

Amber changed the subject again, with disconcerting suddenness. 'Did you know that Lucy, Ryder's monkey, has had babies?'

'I had no idea. Boys or girls? What are they like?' He followed her thankfully on to firm ground.

Minutes later Amber's eyes closed, she subsided against his shoulder and, like a puppy, dropped into instant sleep. She did not stir even when he laid her on the *angareb* and covered her with the threadbare blanket. He was in a good mood, smiling to himself as he left her and went on his midnight inspection of the harbour defences. For once every one of the Egyptian sentries was wide awake. Either they were stimulated by the proximity of the enemy and their own exposure in this forward position, or their hunger drove away sleep.

He found a comfortable place to sit on the forward firing platform and listened to the drums across the river. Their monotonous tempo became soporific and he found himself nodding. He stirred guiltily: If Chinese Gordon finds me I'll be up before the firing squad myself. He took a turn along the parapet, and came back to his seat. He let himself relax and drift to the edge of sleep, but every few minutes he opened his eyes. He had trained himself to tread this tightrope without falling off it. Across the river the drums fell silent.

He opened his eyes again and looked up. Red Mars, the god of war, was hunting across the southern quadrant of the moonless sky with Sirius, the Dog, in leash. It was the darkest and loneliest hour of the night. He was close to the edge of sleep, but he kept his eyes open.

'Penrod.'

Cool fingers brushed his cheek. 'Are you asleep?' He turned his head to her. He was touched that she had used his baptismal name. She must truly think of him as her friend. 'No, I am not, but you should be.'

'I heard voices,' Amber whispered.

'A dream, perhaps,' he replied. 'There are no voices.'

'Listen!' said Amber.

Faintly he heard a dog bark on the west bank and another answered it from Tutti Island, further downriver. No dogs remained in the city. The last had been killed and eaten months before. 'Nothing.' He shook his head doubtfully, but she seized his arm and her sharp little fingernails dug in painfully.

'Listen, Pen. Listen!'

He felt his nerve ends jump tight, like the strike of a heavy fish on the deep-run fly. It was a whisper so faint, so insubstantial on the night breeze that only sharp young ears could have picked it up. It came from far out on the river. Sound carries over water, he thought, and stood up swiftly and silently. Faint as the breeze in the palm fronds, he had heard the traditional word of command to lower and furl the lateen sail of a dhow as it came in to its moorings. Now that he was straining his hearing to its limit, he heard the soft slap of bare feet on a wooden deck, and the slatting of canvas. Seconds later came the creak of a muffled rudder in its yoke as the dhow put up its helm. 'They have come,' he whispered, and moved swiftly along the firing platform to alert each of his men. 'Stand to! Stand to your guns. The Dervish are here. Hold your fire until my command.'

The sergeant gunner stripped the tarpaulin off the Gatling. The stiff material crackled softly and Penrod hissed him to silence. He looked into the ammunition hopper that sat on top of the glistening weapon. It was filled to the brim: six hundred rounds. He lifted the lids of the spare ammunition cases. They were all unlocked. At the Hill of Isandlwana when the Zulu *impis* had broken the British square the spare ammunition cases had been locked and the officer who had the Allen key had ridden out on patrol. Every white soldier in the camp had died that day under the Zulu blades. Ryder Courtney had told him that his elder brother had been among them. Tonight the ammunition cases were unlocked and the four Egyptian loaders were standing by to keep the hopper filled.

He ran to the rear of the firing platform. The corporal of signallers with a detail of four men had their crates of rockets open, and a line of ten flares ready for firing in their launching brackets, nose cones pointed skywards. 'Send up a flare at the first shot. Keep one burning in the sky until the last shot is fired. I want the whole area lit up like daylight,' Penrod ordered.

There was no time for anything else. Penrod started back towards the forward firing platform to take command there. He could not trust the jittery Egyptians to resist blazing away at their first glimpse of the enemy boats before the Dervish were disembarked upon the beach and well inside the trap.

He tripped over Amber, who was at his heels. 'Sweet Mary! I had forgotten about you.' He caught her by the arm and dragged her to the rear entrance of the redoubt. 'Run!' he ordered. 'You have to get out of here right away. This is no place for you now. Even the streets are safer. Run, Amber, and don't stop until you get home.' He gave her a firm shove through the doorway to send her on her way, and did not wait to see if she had obeyed before he turned back towards the forward firing platform.

Amber ran a few paces down the alley, then turned and crept back to the entrance of the redoubt. She watched Penrod disappear into the darkness. 'I am sick and tired of being treated like a baby,' she whispered. She hesitated only a moment before she followed him.

She moved quietly and self-effacingly along the back of the parapet so as not to attract the attention of the troopers who were manning the firing embrasures. They are all too busy to worry about me, she thought. Her confidence swelled, and she hurried forward to look for Penrod. What if he needs me? I will be no use sitting in my bedroom at the palace. She saw his tall figure just ahead.

Penrod was already standing at the parapet that overlooked the beach. The straw-filled decoys had been dragged away and now live riflemen leant on the firing sills, peering down upon the dark beach. He had his drawn sword in his right hand. Amber felt a prickle of pride. He is so brave and noble, she thought. She found a place to hide in a corner of the rear wall and sank down behind it. From here she could watch over him. A tight, brittle silence held all the men at the firing wall.

Suddenly Amber realized how few of them were

spread out thinly along the wall, twenty paces between them. These men did not seem enough to stop the hordes of the Dervish.

Then a man close to where Amber knelt whispered so softly that she could barely catch the words. 'Here they come.' His voice quavered with fear. The breech-block of his Martini-Henry snicked as he chambered a round. He lifted the weapon to his shoulder, but before he could press the trigger an open hand slapped across his face.

As he reeled sideways Penrod seized him by his collar and spoke close to his ear: 'Fire before my command, and I will have you blown from the cannon's mouth,' he promised. Al-Faroque's execution had left a deep impression on all the Egyptians who had witnessed it. Penrod pushed the man back to his position and they waited.

Then Penrod drew breath sharply. The first Dervish boat glided in towards the beach below. As it touched the sand a dark horde of Ansar clambered out into the waist-deep water and waded on to the narrow strip of mud below the walls. They carried their swords at shoulder height and moved with barely a sound. From the dark waters behind them appeared a flotilla of small dhows and feluccas, each packed with a mass of men.

'Hold your fire!' Penrod strode back and forth along the parapet, keeping his puny force under control with his savage whisper. The feluccas and dhows kept coming in until the beach was packed with hundreds of Ansar. There was not room for all of them on firm ground and the ones in the rear were still waist deep in the river. Those in front began to rip down the barricade that blocked the entrance to the drainage creek.

'Steady now! Steady!' Penrod exhorted them.

Part of the barricade crashed down and the Dervish swarmed through. Their war cry went up: 'There is no God but God!'

'Volley fire!' Penrod shouted and the rifles crashed out. The Dervish rushed on through the hail of bullets. Then the first rockets soared into the night sky, and the masses of Dervish swarmed like columns of ants in the weird greenish light. The riflemen fired down into them but there were so many that the bullets had little effect. When the front ranks reached the harbour wall they clambered up it, the rear ranks shoving from below. As they came over the top the defenders thrust with the bayonets.

Penrod strode along the wall, firing his new Webley pistol point blank into their bearded faces. In his right hand he carried his sabre and when the revolver was empty he slashed and hacked with the blade. The dead and wounded Ansar toppled back on to their comrades who were climbing up behind them. The Egyptian line was too flimsy to hold them in check much longer: all along the top of the wall knots of Dervish were gaining footholds. Their two-handed crusader blades hissed through the air with the sound of bats' wings. One of the Egyptians reeled back from the parapet with his right arm sliced off cleanly above the elbow. His blood was inky black in the light of the rockets.

'Back!' shouted Penrod. 'Fall back to the second line!' Even in her own terror, Amber was startled by how clearly his voice carried above the uproar. His men formed quickly into a skirmishing line, bayonets facing outwards, and they retreated

311

backwards along the top of the wall. For a terrible moment Amber thought she would be left behind, but she sprang up and ran like a startled hare. Instinctively she knew that the Gatling emplacement was the strongest point of the defence, and headed for it.

She reached it well ahead of Penrod and his men, and scrambled to the top of the wall of sandbags. As she hung there, someone grabbed her arm from the far side and dragged her over. She fell on top of her rescuer. He smelt of rotten fish heads, and glared at her with a horrific squint, his face green in the light of the flares. 'Nazeera will kill you with her bare hands if she finds out you are here.' He pushed her roughly into the dugout in the back wall, just as Penrod led his men back in a rush.

'Gatling gunner! Open fire!' Penrod had selected the man on the crank handle of the gun for his strength and stamina. Sergeant Khaled was a colossal black man from one of the Nubian tribes of upper Egypt. Men like him made the finest soldiers in all the army of the Khedive. He bobbed up and down like a marionette as he worked. The brightly burnished barrels spun, like the revolving spokes of a chariot wheel. The flickering glare of muzzle flashes lit the parapet as brightly as a stage.

With a sound like a giant ripping up a roll of heavy canvas, a continuous stream of bullets tore into the ranks of Ansar as they swarmed forward. The heavy lead bullets slogged into living flesh, and the ricochets screamed off the stone parapets, almost drowning the clamour of the Dervish force. Traversing back and forth the Gatling scythed them down, piling heaps of corpses along the front of the wall. Those who followed scrambled over them and grabbed at the barrels of the rifles that aimed at them through the embrasures, trying to tear the smoking weapons from the hands of the defenders on the far side of the wall. The soldiers thrust at them with their bayonets, screaming with battle rage, and the Dervish screamed back at the agony of the steel slicing deeply into their bodies. Then the barrels of the Gatling swung back and blew them away, like the *khamsin* wind. The last of the Dervish tumbled off the revetment, and lay in huddles or dragged themselves through the black slick of the creek bed.

Sergeant Khaled straightened up and the gun fell silent. His black face was split with a white and ferocious grin, and his barrel chest ran with rivers of sweat that gleamed in the green light of the flares.

'Reload!' Penrod shouted, as he filled the chambers of his own revolver from the loops on his belt. 'Get ready for the next wave.'

The loaders came running up with the ammunition buckets, and the shiny copper-cased cartridges cascaded into the Gatling hopper. Other ammunition boys ran along the parapet, doling out paper packets of Boxer-Henry ammunition to the riflemen. The water-carriers followed them, squirting water from the nozzles of the skins directly into the parched mouths of the soldiers.

'Be ready for them. They are not beaten. They will come back through the creek again.' Penrod moved down the parapet, talking to the men. The trooper whose arm had been hacked off had died from loss of blood. They laid his body against the rear wall and covered him with a blanket. Penrod started back towards the Gatling to bolster the courage of Sergeant Khaled and his gunners, but as he passed the doorway to his dugout he saw a small white face staring out at him. 'Amber! I thought you had gone.'

Now that she was discovered she decided to brazen it out. 'I knew you didn't mean to send me away. Anyway, it's too late now. I have to stay.'

He was about to debate this point with her, but from the depths of the creek bed rose the dread chorus of Dervish war cries. The hordes poured back in a flood that filled the creek from side to side.

Penrod drew the Webley from the holster on his belt and broke it open to check that it was fully reloaded. He snapped the breech closed. 'I know you can use this. I have seen you practising with your father.' He thrust the weapon, butt first, into her hands. 'Get back into the dugout. Climb under the bed. Stay there until this is over. Shoot anybody who touches you. This time do as you're told. Go!' He ran back to the parapet.

Two hundred Egyptian riflemen did not wait for his command to reopen fire. The volleys crashed down into the creek bed, and the Gatling ripped and rattled, a stream of spent cartridge cases spilling into a glistening mound on the floor of the redoubt beneath its carriage. A succession of coloured flares burst high above the arena, illuminating with garish light the Dervish struggling upwards through the reeking mud. Their ranks were so closely packed that every bullet must strike. Surely mortal men must break under such punishment, yet they came on, clambering over the torn and twitching corpses of their comrades, their multi-coloured *jibbas* plastered with reeking black mud, never wavering, each man trying to fight his way to the front rank of the attack, scornful of death, eager to seek it out in the smoking muzzles of the guns.

But there was a line at the foot of the wall across which even their courage could not carry them. The Gatling stopped them there, as though they had reached a wall of glass, building up taller piles of dead men. Wave after wave of warriors came on to add their own corpses to the growing heaps. Swiftly the creek was transformed into a ghastly charnel house. Then, as the attack wavered, the Gatling fire ceased.

'Captain! Stoppage!' Sergeant Khaled yelled. 'The gun is jammed.' As the import of those words struck the Egyptian troopers, horror dawned on their faces in the light of the flares. As the full extent of this disaster struck them their fire dwindled, stammered, and fell silent. Even the Ansar in the creek were caught up in the spell. A weird and unnatural quiet fell over the battlefield, broken only by the groans and cries of the wounded. It lasted but a few seconds.

Then a single voice spoke. *'La ilaha illallah! There is but one God!'* It was a voice Penrod recognized. He looked down into the grisly creek bed and saw Osman Atalan in the first rank of the Dervish horde. Their eyes locked. Then the battle cry went up from hundreds of throats and the attack swept forward again. As though the wall of glass that had contained them was shattered, they clawed their way up the steep, treacherous bank of the creek towards the redoubt.

The heads of the Egyptian riflemen turned as

315

they looked back to find a line of retreat. Penrod knew that gesture well. He had seen it before, on the terrible day when the square broke at El Obeid. It was the prelude to flight and rout. 'I will kill the first man who breaks,' he shouted, but one ignored him.

As he turned to run, Penrod stepped forward and thrust for his belly. The long blade of his sabre slipped in as though it had been greased, and the point sliced out through the back of the man's khaki tunic. He dropped to his knees, and clasped the blade of the sabre with his bare hands. Penrod pulled out the razor-sharp steel between his victim's fingers, severing skin and flesh and sinew. The man screamed and toppled backwards.

'Stand your ground, and keep firing.' Penrod held high his blood-wet blade. 'Or sing the same song as this cowardly creature.' They turned back to the firing embrasures and poured their volleys down into the mass of Dervish clambering up towards them.

Sergeant Khaled was hammering on the breech mechanism of the silent Gatling with his bare fists, leaving the skin of his knuckles on the sharp metal edges. Penrod grabbed his shoulder and pulled him aside. By the light of the flares he saw the crushed cartridge case jammed in the jaws of one of the six cam-operated bolts. It was a number-three stoppage, the most difficult to clear. There was a trick to it that Penrod had learnt from hard experience. He snatched the bayonet from the sheath on Sergeant Khaled's belt and, with the point of the blade, worked to prise open the jaws of the bolt.

The Dervish came up the walls, climbing like

316

squirrels up the trunk of an oak. The Martini-Henry rifles fell silent as the attackers wriggled through the embrasures and grappled hand to hand with those Egyptians who had stood their ground. The Gatling's bolt was still jammed solidly. Penrod glanced up: at that moment the fate of the city and all its inhabitants hung on him.

One of the many myths that had built up around the image of General Chinese Gordon was that his voice could carry above the din of any battlefield. Penrod heard it now in the uproar of this inevitable disaster. 'Number-two gun, open fire.' Penrod had never expected to welcome those harsh and hectoring tones. They carried clearly across from the secondary emplacement that Penrod had built in anticipation of just such a moment as this. His knees went weak with relief. Then he braced himself, and turned his mind back to the jammed gun.

*   *   *

Waiting, sleepless, on the glacis of the hospital fortifications, Gordon had heard the opening volleys of the battle, and seen the rocket flares sailing up from the harbour into the night sky. He had roused his gunners. They limbered up the second Gatling and ran it through the alleyways and byways of the city. It took them eight and a half minutes to reach the harbour and unlimber the Gatling in the empty emplacement that had been prepared for it. True to his nature, Gordon had timed them. He nodded approval and thrust the hunter back into his pocket.

'Number-two gun, open fire,' he grated, and the

317

monstrous thunder of the six rotating barrels smothered the frenzied war cries of the Dervish. A moving sheet of fire swept relentlessly across the revetment of the creek. From this angle he caught them in left flank and rear. His fire tumbled them off the walls like ripe apples from a wind-shaken tree. Most lost their weapons in the fall. Those who rose to their feet again were hurled forward by the press of bodies still surging up the creek, and were trapped against the footwall of the fortifications.

'Back! Go back! It is over,' shouted those in the forefront.

'Forward!' screamed those coming up from the beach, 'For God and His Ever Victorious Mahdi!' The creek became a massive log-jam of bodies packed so tightly that even the dead were held upright by their comrades.

Penrod could not witness all this taking place while he struggled with the jammed bolt. At last he forced the point of the bayonet behind the lug of the cam and hammered on the hilt with his palm. He ignored the pain, and shouted at Sergeant Khaled, 'Back up the crank!' Khaled heaved anticlockwise on the handle, taking the pressure off the cam and suddenly the lug flew back, with a clanging force that would have taken off Penrod's thumb, had he not jerked it away. The crushed and deformed cartridge case flew clear. As Khaled released the handle, the next round dropped from the hopper and was fed smoothly into the breech. The bolt cocked with a sweet, almost musical clank.

'Number-one gun cocked and ready, Sergeant.' Penrod slapped Khaled on the shoulder. 'Commence firing!' Khaled stooped to the crank, and Penrod himself took hold of the twin traverse handles and depressed the barrels so they were aimed down into the struggling confusion of mud-smeared Ansar. The gun jumped, hammered and shook in Penrod's hands.

Not even the bravest could withstand the combined fire of the two Gatlings. It rolled them back until they jammed in the portal of the drain tunnel, then decimated their ranks, piling their bodies like faggots of firewood on that narrow strip of beach. As the survivors staggered through the shallows towards the boats, the bullets kicked foam from the surface around them. When at last they clambered aboard, the heavy bullets splintered the deck timbers and struck down the crew cowering within the hulls. Their blood dribbled out of the bullet-holes and trickled down the outside of the hulls, like claret spilt from the goblet of a drunkard.

With their cargoes of broken bodies on the decks, the dhows steered back across the river in the first flush of day. As the last pulled out of the bight of the harbour the Gatlings ceased their dreadful clangour. The timid silence of the dawn was marred only by the lamentations of the new widows across the river on the Omdurman bank.

Penrod stepped back from the Gatling, whose barrels glowed as though they had been heated in a blacksmith's forge. He looked around him like someone awakening from nightmare. He was not surprised to find Yakub at his side. 'I saw Osman Atalan in the front rank of the enemy host,' he told him.

'I saw him also, lord.'

'If he is still on this bank of the river, we must find him,' Penrod ordered. 'If he is alive, I want him. If he is dead, his head shall be sent to the Ever Victorious Mahdi. It may discourage him and his Ansar from another attack on the city.'

Before he left the redoubt Penrod called to Sergeant Khaled, 'See to our wounded. Get them to the hospital.' He knew how futile that would be. Both the Egyptian doctors had deserted from Gordon's regiment months ago, but not before they had stolen and sold all the medical supplies. At the hospital building a few old Arab midwives still treated the wounded with herbs and traditional potions. He had heard that Rebecca Benbrook had tried to teach some of the Sudanese women how to take care of the wounded in a more orthodox fashion, but he knew that she had no medical training. She could do little more than attempt to staunch bleeding, and make sure the wounded had clean boiled water to drink, and extra rations of dhurra and green-cake.

Before the words were out of his mouth he heard a scream. He glanced in the direction it had come from and saw a woman dressed in black robes bending over a wounded Dervish. The Arab and Nubian women of the city had an instinct for death and loot. The first were arriving even before the crows and the vultures.

The wounded Dervish wriggled and writhed as the woman prodded him into position with the point of her little dagger. Then, with an expert stroke that started in his throat under the ear and raked forward, she opened both his carotid and jugular arteries and hopped back so the blood would not soak her skirts. Long ago Penrod had learnt not to interfere in this type of business. Arab women were worse than the men, and this one had made no attempt to conceal what she was about. He turned away. 'Sergeant, I need prisoners for questioning. Save as many as you can.' Then he jerked his head to Yakub. 'Come, All-seeing Yakub. Let us seek the Emir Osman Atalan. The last I saw of him, he was on the beach trying to rally his men as they ran for the boats.'

'Wait for me, Pen. I am coming with you.' Amber had crept out of the dugout.

Once again he had forgotten her presence. Her hair was in tangled disarray, her blue eyes were underscored with plum-coloured bruises, and her yellow frock was filthy with smoke and dust. The revolver was too big for the hand that held it. 'Will I never get rid of you? You must go home, Amber,' he said. 'This is no place for you, and it never was.'

'The streets are not safe,' Amber argued. 'Not all the Dervish got away in the boats. I saw hundreds of them escaping that way.' She waved the Webley in an indeterminate gesture over her shoulder. 'They will be waiting to ravish me or cut my throat.' 'Ravish' was one of her new words, although she was uncertain of its meaning.

'Amber, there are corpses and dying men down there. It's no place for a young lady.'

'I have seen dead men before,' she said sweetly, 'and I am not a lady yet, just a little girl. I only feel safe with you.'

Penrod laughed a little too harshly. He always felt lightheaded and detached from reality when fighting was over.

'Little girl? In stature, perhaps. But you have all the wiles of a fully fledged member of your sex. I am no match for you. Come along, then.'

They slipped and slid down the bank into the

creek. The first rays of the sun were gilding the minarets of the city, and the light improved every minute. Penrod and Yakub moved cautiously among the bullet-torn bodies of the fallen Ansar. Some were still alive, and Yakub leant over one with his dagger poised.

'No!' Penrod said sharply.

Yakub looked aggrieved. 'It would be merciful to help his poor soul through the gates of Paradise.' But Penrod indicated Amber, and shook his head again even more definitely. Yakub shrugged and moved on.

Penrod was looking for Osman Atalan's green turban. As he ducked out under the stone arch of the tunnel on to the muddy beach, he picked it out: it was on the head of a corpse floating face down in the lap and wash of the wavelets at the edge of the bank. Through the clinging folds of the *jibba* he saw that the corpse was lean and athletic. There were two bullet-holes in its back. The Gatling had inflicted massive damage—he could have thrust his fist into the holes. A few fingerling Nile perch worried the ragged tatters of raw meat that hung from the wounds. The end of the turban floated free, waving like a tendril of seaweed in the wash of the current. Osman Atalan's long dark hair was entwined with the cloth.

Penrod felt his spirits plunge when only moments before he had been intoxicated. He felt cheated and angry. There should have been more to it than this. He had sensed that he and Atalan were caught up together in the ring of destiny. This was no way for it to end. There was no satisfaction in finding his enemy floating like the carcass of a pariah dog in a drainage creek with fish nibbling his flesh.

Penrod sheathed his sabre and went down on one knee beside the floating body. With a strangely respectful gesture he took the dead man's arm and rolled the body face up in the shallows. He stared at it in astonishment. This was an older, less noble face, with brutish brows, thick lips and broken teeth stained by the smoke of the hashish pipe.

'Osman Atalan has escaped.' He spoke aloud in his relief. He was overtaken by a sense of prescience. It was not over yet. Fate had linked him and Atalan, as a serpentine liana binds two great forest trees to each other. There was more to follow, much more. He knew it in his heart.

There was a soft sound behind him, but it did not alarm him. He thought it was either Yakub or Amber. He went on studying the features of the dead emir, until Amber screamed, 'Pen! Behind you! Look out!' She was some way to his right. Even as he turned he knew it was not her he had heard so close behind him. And he knew he was too late. Perhaps, after all, this *was* where it ended, on this strip of mud beside the great river.

He completed the turn with his right hand on the hilt of his sabre, rising from his knees, but he knew he could not regain his feet and draw his sword in time. He had only a fleeting glimpse of his assassin. The Dervish had been feigning death: it was one of their tricks. Coiled like a poisonous adder he had waited his moment. Penrod had fallen into the trap: he had turned his back and sheathed his sabre. The Dervish had come to his feet with his broadsword drawn back like a forester about to make the first cut on the trunk of a tree. Now he swung all his wiry frame behind the stroke.

He was aiming a few inches above the point of Penrod's left hip bone.

Penrod watched the massive silver blade looping towards him, but it seemed that time had slowed. He was like an insect trapped in a bowl of honey, and his movements were sluggish. He realized that the blade would slice through the soft tissue of his midriff, until it struck his spinal column just above the pelvic girdle. That would not stop it. The entire circumference of his body would offer as little resistance as if it were the spongy stem of a banana tree. This single stroke of the blade would bisect him neatly.

The shot came from his right, a flat blurt of sound, the characteristic report of the Webley .44. Although he was not looking directly at her, Penrod was aware of Amber's small shape at the periphery of his vision. She was holding the weapon double-handed at the full reach of both her arms, but the heavy recoil threw it high above her head.

The assassin was a young man with a thin, unkempt beard, his pockmarked skin the colour of toffee. Penrod was staring at his face as the heavy Webley bullet struck him in the left temple and blasted through his skull just behind the eyes. It distorted his features as though they were an india-rubber mask. His lips twisted and elongated, and his eyelids fluttered like the wings of butterflies. His eyes bulged from their sockets, and the bullet erupted from his right temple in a cloud of bone chips and wet tissue.

Half-way through the sword stroke his fingers opened nervelessly and the weapon flew from his grip. It spun past Penrod's hip, missing it by a hand-span, and cartwheeled away to peg point first into the muddy bank. The assassin took a step back before his legs folded and he collapsed.

With his right hand on the hilt of his half-drawn sabre Penrod turned to stare in amazement at Amber. She dropped the revolver and burst into sobs. He went to her and picked up the Webley, thrust it into the holster on his belt and buckled the flap. Amber was sobbing as though her heart was breaking. She was shivering and her lips were quivering wildly as she tried to tell him something. He placed one arm round her shoulders and the other behind her knees and lifted her as though she were an infant. She clung to him with both thin arms round his neck.

'That is absolutely enough for one day,' he said gently. 'This time I shall take you home myself.'

Gordon was waiting for him in the Gatling redoubt as he came up the bank. 'A fair night's work, Ballantyne. The Mahdi will think once or twice before he comes again, and the populace will be much heartened.' He lit a cigarette and his hand was steady. 'We will throw the Dervish dead into the river, a floating warning to their comrades. Perhaps some may even be carried down through the gorge to our troops coming upriver. They will know that we are holding out. It may encourage them to a little more haste.' Now he glanced at Amber, who was still weeping silently. Her whole body shook with sobs, but the only sounds were small gulps of breath. 'I will take command here. You may escort the young lady back to her family.'

Penrod carried Amber into the street. She was still weeping. 'Cry if it makes you feel better,' he whispered to her, 'but, by God, you are as brave a little thing as any man I have known.' She stopped weeping but her grip tightened round his neck.

By the time he handed her over to Rebecca and Nazeera Amber had cried herself to sleep. They had to prise her arms from round Penrod's neck.

*   *   *

General Gordon used their little victory to counter the numbing despair of the civilian inhabitants of the city. He gathered up the corpses of the enemy, two hundred and sixteen, laid them out in rows on the harbour quay and invited the populace to view them. The women spat upon them, and the men kicked them and shouted abuse, calling down the curse of Allah and condemning them to the fires and torments of hell. They shouted with glee as the corpses were thrown into the river, where the crocodiles snapped at them and dragged them below the surface.

Gordon posted official bulletins in every square and souk of the city, announcing that the British relief columns were now in full march for the city and would almost certainly arrive within days. He also gave them the joyous tidings that the Dervish were so disheartened by their devastating defeat and the approach of the British columns that vast numbers were deserting the black flag of the Mahdi and marching into the desert to return to their tribal homelands. It was true that there was a large movement of Dervish troops on the enemy bank, but Gordon knew that they were being sent northwards in battle array to oppose the British relief columns.

More welcome bulletins announced that General Gordon had declared a double ration of dhurra from the stock he was holding in the arsenal. The same bulletin informed the people that the remaining stocks of grain were more than sufficient to feed the city until the arrival of the relief column. It assured them that when the steamers docked in the harbour they would offload thousands of sacks of grain.

That night Gordon lit bonfires on the maidan. The band played until midnight, and the night sky was lit up again by rockets and coloured flares.

Early the following morning he called a more sombre meeting in his headquarters. There were only two other participants: David Benbrook and Penrod Ballantyne.

Gordon looked at Penrod first. 'You have drawn up the latest inventory of the grain stocks?'

'It did not take long, sir. At ten o'clock last night there were four thousand nine hundred and sixty sacks remaining. Yesterday's issue of double rations expended five hundred and sixty-two. At the present rate of consumption, we have sufficient dhurra for another fifteen days.'

'In three days I will be forced to halve the ration again,' Gordon said, 'but this is not the time to tell the people.'

David looked shocked. 'But, General, surely the relief column will be here in two weeks. Your own bulletins gave that assurance.'

'I have to protect the people from the truth,' Gordon replied.

'What, then, is the truth?' David demanded.

Gordon contemplated the ash on his cigarette before he replied. 'The truth, sir? The truth is not a monolith cast in iron. It is like a cloud in the sky, constantly changing shape. From every direction that one views it, it offers a different aspect.'

'That description has great literary value, I have no doubt, but in this situation it is of little help.' David smiled bleakly. 'When can we expect the relief column to reach us?'

'The information I am about to disclose to you must not go beyond the four walls of this room.'

'I understand.'

'Six Dervish were taken prisoner at the harbour.'

'I thought there would have been more.' David frowned.

'There were.' Gordon shrugged. David knew better than to pursue the subject. This was the Orient where different standards prevailed. Interrogation under torture fell within those standards. 'The six prisoners were questioned by my Sergeant Khaled. We obtained much useful intelligence, none of it reassuring. The steamers of the River Division seem to have been delayed at Korti.'

'Good Lord! They should have been at Abu Hamed by now,' David exclaimed. 'What on earth is holding them back?'

'We do not know, and speculation is vain.'

'What of the Desert Division under Stewart?'

'Here it is the same sad story. Stewart is still encamped at the Wells of Gakdul,' Gordon told him.

'It does not seem possible that either of those divisions can reach us before the end of the month,' David mused, then looked at the others hopefully for a denial. Neither man responded.

Gordon broke the silence. 'What is the state of the river, Ballantyne?'

'Yesterday it fell five inches,' Penrod replied.

'Each day the pace of the ebb is accelerating.'

'Can one apply the word "ebb" to falling river waters?' David asked, as if to make light of the serious implications.

Gordon ignored the frivolous question. 'The prisoners had other information to give us. The Mahdi has ordered another twenty-five thousand of his élite fighting men northwards to reinforce his army. There are now fifty thousand Dervish gathered at Abu Hamed.' He paused, as though reluctant to continue. 'Stewart has two thousand. That means he is outnumbered twenty-five to one. The Dervish know exactly what route he must follow to reach the river. They will choose their ground with care before they attack.'

'Stewart is a fine officer.' David tried to sound confident.

'One of the best,' Gordon agreed. 'But twenty-five to one is long odds.'

'In God's Name we must warn Stewart of the danger.'

'Yes, that is what I intend.' Gordon looked across at Penrod. 'I am sending Captain Ballantyne to the Wells of Gakdul to warn him and guide him through.'

'How do you intend that he make the journey, General? As far as I am aware, there are no camels in the city. They have all been eaten. There is only one steamer, Ryder Courtney's *Intrepid Ibis*, but the engine is still out of commission. It is highly unlikely that a dhow will get through the Dervish lines.'

Gordon gave a chilly smile. 'I have discovered that Mr Courtney is the owner of a fine herd of at least twenty racing camels. He has been prudent

329

enough not to keep them in the city where I might have found them, but has sent them out into the desert, to a tiny oasis two days' travel to the south. They are grazing there under the care of some of his people.'

David chuckled. 'Ryder Courtney has more arrows to his bow than a monkey has fleas.'

'For somebody who recently queried my use of the language, that is as magnificently garbled an image as you are like to come across in a year of searching.' Penrod smiled with him.

'When taxed with the question of the camels, he at first denied ownership.' Gordon was not smiling. 'Then he denied that he had any intention of concealing them from me, and said that it was simply a matter of the availability of grazing for the beasts. I immediately commandeered them. If he had been honest with me from the beginning I might have considered compensation.'

'He may not comply with your orders,' David said. 'Ryder Courtney is a man of independent spirit.'

'And of avaricious instinct,' Gordon agreed. 'But in this case he would be unwise in the extreme to gainsay me. Even under martial law one would hesitate to shoot a subject of the Queen, but he has several warehouses full of ivory and a large menagerie of exotic but edible animals.' Gordon looked smug. 'My persuasive logic has prevailed. Courtney has sent word to his herdsmen at the oasis to bring the camels in, and I expect them to be at our disposal by the day after tomorrow.'

'I had no idea of the gravity of the situation,' David murmured. 'Had I done so I would have prevented my daughter arranging a celebration of your victory at the harbour. She has planned a soirée for tomorrow evening. Unfortunately our kitchens can no longer provide elaborate dinners. However, there will be piano recitals and singing. If you think this inappropriate, General, I shall ask Rebecca to cancel the evening.'

'Not at all.' Gordon shook his head. 'Although I shall not attend, Miss Benbrook's festivities will keep up pretences and spirits. She must go ahead, by all means.'

*   *   *

Amber and Saffron opened the musical programme with a piano duet of 'Greensleeves'. It mattered little that the consular palace's grand piano was in sorry need of tuning: the twins made up in enthusiasm for what they lacked in other areas.

This evening Rebecca was a gay and vivacious hostess, and her father could not help remarking her change of mood. Last week she had been sad and moping but now she sang 'Spanish Ladies' with Ryder Courtney, then prevailed on him to render a solo of 'My Bonnie Lies Over the Ocean.' This was well received by the company. Saffron, in particular, applauded him rapturously.

Then Amber dragged Penrod on to the floor. 'You have to sing also. Everybody has to sing or do something.'

Penrod gave in graciously. 'Can you play "Heart of Oak"?' he asked, and Amber ran to the piano. Penrod's voice startled and thrilled them all: it was easy, lyrical and true.

331

'Come, cheer up, my lads!
'Tis to glory we steer,
To add something more
To this wonderful year . . .'

When the song ended Rebecca tried to blink tears from her eyes, as she called gaily, 'Refreshments will be served before the next act.'

She served strong Abyssinian coffee in delicate Limoges porcelain demitasses. There was no milk or sugar. While she was serving Captain Ballantyne, she fumbled and spilt hot coffee on to his gleaming boots.

Her father watched her from across the room as she blushed bright scarlet, and thought her confusion was almost as uncharacteristic as her clumsiness. Suddenly he realized what it meant. *The pretty soldier has her deeply entangled in his web. She is all fluster and flutter whenever he is within fifty paces. When he disappeared she almost pined away, and now he is back she is dizzy with delight.* He frowned, and thrust his hands into his pockets. *She does not realize that in two days he will disappear again. I would hate to see her badly hurt. It is my paternal duty to warn her.* He thought about that for a moment. *And perhaps I shall. After all, the identity of the father of my grandchildren is very much my business.*

Rebecca recovered herself, and clapped her hands for attention. 'Ladies and gentlemen, I have a special treat for you this evening. All the way from Madrid, where she has danced before the King and Queen of Spain and other crowned heads of Europe, Señora Esmeralda Lopez Conchita Montes de Tête de Singe, the celebrated flamenco

332

dancer.' There was a brief but mystified spattering of applause as from behind the curtains a plump Spanish lady in lace mantilla, clattering bangles and earrings swept into the room on the arm of Ryder Courtney. In the centre of the floor she sank into a deep curtsy, then rose to her feet with unusual grace for such a portly female. She clicked castanets above her head, and as Rebecca struck up the opening bars of the 'March of the Toreadors' Señora Tête de Singe launched a drumfire salvo of heel stamps.

David let out a snort of laughter. He had been the first to recognize Consul Le Blanc beneath the tall wig and hectic makeup. Then a howl of laughter went up from the entire room, and did not subside until Le Blanc sank to the floor in another theatrical curtsy, his makeup running.

In the ensuing pandemonium David crossed to Rebecca and took her arm. 'What an inspired entertainment, my darling. Le Blanc was superb. I do so love a good impersonation.'

Rebecca was in such high spirits that when he led her towards the french windows she went without protest. 'Ah!' he said. 'My kingdom for a breath of fresh air.' He led her along the terrace. 'Of course, Ryder Courtney has a fine voice. A man of many talents. He will make some lucky lady a wonderful husband.'

'Papa, you are always so subtle.' She tapped his shoulder with her fan.

'I have no idea what you are talking about. But I must say I was surprised by Captain Ballantyne. He also has an extraordinary singing voice.' She went still, and looked away.

'What a pity he is leaving, this time for good, and

we shall probably never have the pleasure of listening to him again.'

'What are you saying, Daddy?' Her voice was small.

'Dear me, I should not have let that slip. Gordon is sending him north with despatches to Cairo. You know these military men. Ships in the night, all of them, I'm afraid. One can not rely on them.'

'Daddy, I think we should go in to entertain our guests.'

*   *   *

Rebecca looked at herself in the mirror of her dressing-table. Her face was so thin that the cheekbones cast shadows beneath them. There are no fat people in Khartoum, these days. Even Consul Le Blanc is skin and bones. She smiled at the exaggeration, and noted with pleasure the improvement the smile made. I must try not to frown. She dipped her powder puff in the crystal bowl and lightly dusted the hollows under her eyes. 'Better and better,' she whispered. She was thin but she still had the bloom of youth upon her skin. 'At least Daddy thinks I am beautiful. I wonder if he would agree.' Thinking of him brought a glow to her cheeks. 'I wonder if he is out there again.' She glanced towards the balcony doors. 'I am not going to look. If he is there, he will think I am encouraging him. He will think that I am a fast woman, which I am definitely not.'

She let her dress fall round her ankles, and reached for the crêpe-de-Chine gown. Before she slipped it on she looked at her reflection in the mirror. Then, on an impulse, she crossed the bedroom and locked the door. She had sent Nazeera away, but she did not want her to return unexpectedly. As she went back to the mirror she pushed the straps of her shift off her shoulders, and let it fall to the floor beside her dress. She looked at her naked body in the mirror. Her ribs showed beneath her white skin, and her pelvic bones stood proud. Her belly was concave as that of a greyhound. She touched her breasts. Nazeera said that men did not like small breasts. 'Are they too small?'

Then she remembered the feel of his lips upon them, the brush of his moustache and the sharpness of his teeth. As she stared, the tips swelled and darkened with heat. Suddenly she was aware of that wetness again, hot as blood, spreading slowly down the inside of her thighs. From her breasts her fingertips traced downwards, but as they brushed the gossamer cloud of golden hair at the base of her hollow belly, she jerked her hand away. 'I shall never do that again,' she told herself.

She reached for the gown, and belted it round her waist. She looked at the balcony door. 'I should not go out there. I should blow out the lamp and go to bed.' She moved slowly across the floor and hesitated at the door. 'This is silly and dangerous. Heaven knows where it will lead. I only pray that he is not there.'

She placed her hand on the door handle and drew a deep breath as though she was about to plunge into an icy pool. She turned the handle and stepped out on to the balcony. Her eyes turned instantly to the base of the tamarind.

He was there, leaning against the trunk. He

straightened and looked up at her. His face was in shadow and she stepped to the edge of the balcony to see him more clearly. They stood very quietly, staring at each other. Rebecca felt as though she might suffocate. Every breath was an effort. Her skin was hot and sensitive. Her whole body was on the rack, every nerve stretched to breaking point. The long sinews down the inside of her thighs were drawn tight as whipcord. She turned her head and gazed at a branch of the tamarind. It curled out from the trunk like a python, thick as her waist, and hung over the edge of the balcony beside where she stood. The twins used it as a ladder and a swing. The bark was lightly polished where they had slid along it. Now she laid one hand on it and looked down again at Penrod.

'I am not enticing him,' she told herself firmly. 'This is not an invitation. He must not think that it is.'

He went to the base of the tree, and began to climb upwards. No! she thought. He must not do that! I did not mean that!

She was alarmed by the rapidity with which he came up towards her. He reached the bough, and instead of sliding along it in an ungainly manner, with his legs dangling on either side, he stood up and ran lightly along it as though it were a gangplank. He was twenty feet above the ground, and she was terrified that he might slip. She was even more frightened that he would reach the balcony safely—and what then?

She ran back into her bedroom, and closed the door behind her. She reached for the latch to lock it but her fingers disobeyed her. She backed away from the door into the centre of the floor. She heard his footstep on the balcony and her breathing came faster. The door handle turned and her fists clenched at her sides. She wanted to call to him to go away and leave her alone. But no sound passed her lips.

He pushed open the door very slowly, and she wanted to scream. But her father was in the room across the landing and the twins' room was even closer. She did not want to wake them.

Penrod stepped into the room and shut the door quietly behind him. She stared at him, huge startled eyes in a thin pale face. He came to her slowly, with one hand outstretched as though to calm an unbroken filly. She began to tremble.

He touched her cheek. 'You are very lovely,' he whispered, and she thought she might burst into tears. He placed both hands on her shoulders, and she stood rigid. He leant gently towards her. She could not tear her eyes from his: they were green in the lamplight, with golden flecks and stars round the iris. Lightly his mouth touched hers. His lips were hot and smooth. His hands slid down from her shoulders and settled on her waist. Her arms hung at her sides like those of a rag doll. He drew her towards him, and she was unresisting. His lips opened on hers, and the taste and smell of him overwhelmed her. His tongue forced her lips apart, and she lifted her arms from her sides and wound them round his neck. He pulled her harder, almost roughly, against his body. She felt that massive hardness growing up again between their lower bodies. Her own wetness welled up like a spring from deep inside her, and she clenched her thighs and buttocks to stop it overflowing, but it flooded creamily down her thighs.

He swayed back, and she felt deprived as the contact between them was broken. She tried to follow his body with her own. He untied her belt and opened her gown. She tried half-heartedly to cover herself but he held her wrists, and studied her pale body with a rapt expression. 'You are lovely beyond the telling of it,' he murmured, and his tone was husky.

Her shyness evaporated in the warmth of his praise, and instinctively she pulled back her shoulders. Her breasts were pert and pointed. She saw by his eyes that he did not consider them too small. Her nipples felt pebble hard. She wanted desperately to feel his mouth on them again. She was possessed by utter wantonness. She reached up and took a double handful of the dense springing hair at the back of his head, twisted her fingers in his curls and drew his face down.

She gasped as his mouth closed on hers. She would never have believed the plethora of sensations that followed from such a simple act. His breath on her skin was alternately cool and warm as he inhaled and exhaled, his lips at first firm and dry, then soft and moist. His tongue squirmed like an eel, then lapped like a cat at a saucer of cream. He suckled on her, tugging and biting, and she felt the sensation repeated like an echo deep inside her.

When she reached the threshold of pain, he broke off suddenly, lifted her and carried her to her bed. He laid her on it as though she were something fragile and precious, then stepped back. He unbuttoned the front of his shirt, turned to the lamp on her dressing-table, cupped his hand behind the glass chimney and drew a breath to blow out the flame.

She sat up quickly. 'No!' she said sharply. 'Don't blow it out. You have seen me, and now I must see you.' She could not believe that she had spoken so brazenly. He came back and stood over her. Without haste he stripped off his shirt. His skin was ivory smooth and unblemished where it had been protected from the sun. The muscles of his chest were hard and flat, forged by swordplay and hard riding. He stood on one leg to pull off his boot, and his balance was rock steady. He laid the boot aside, careful not to drop it, and she was grateful for his consideration. He did the same with the second boot. Then he unbuckled his belt and stepped out of his breeches. She had seen him naked once before, and she had believed that the image would remain with her for ever. But she had not seen him like this. She bit her lip to prevent herself crying out with shock. He came on to her bed and knelt over her. 'Please don't hurt me,' she begged.

'I would die first,' he said. She whimpered as she felt him at the threshold of her being. She thought that something must tear or give way and she braced herself for the agony. She felt a wall of resistance within her.

This cannot be happening, she thought, but she was suddenly reckless of any consequences. She pushed up hard with her hips to meet him, and she felt him break through. The pain was sharp but transitory. He glided on and on into her, until he had filled her to her very depths. The pain fell away, and she was carried out over the void, terrified at first, then soaring upwards as though she scaled a mighty mountain range. When she reached the peak, the need to scream out her triumph was so powerful that she pressed her open mouth into the hollow of his neck to gag herself.

'Stay with me,' she pleaded, as, later, he rose to dress. 'Don't leave me so soon.'

'You know I cannot stay. It is late. Dawn is close, and the household will begin to stir.'

'When are you going away?'

He paused in the act of buttoning his shirt. 'Who told you that I am going away?' he demanded sharply. She shook her head. 'That is dangerous knowledge, Becky. If the enemy find out it could cost my life, and worse besides.'

'I will not tell another soul,' she said miserably. 'But I shall miss you.' She wanted his reassurance that he would return. Papa had said, 'Ships in the night, all of them, I'm afraid. One can not rely on them.' She did not want it to be like that.

He did not reply, but shrugged on his khaki tunic.

'Promise me you will come back,' she pleaded. He stooped over her bed and kissed her lips. 'Promise me,' she insisted.

'I never make promises I may not be able to keep,' he said, and then he was gone.

She felt tears close to the surface, but she forced them back. 'I will never be a whiner or a weeper,' she promised herself. Despite her bursting heart, sleep came down on her like a dark avalanche.

She woke to the sound of guns, but the shells were bursting near the harbour, where the attack had been beaten off. The Dervish were venting their spite. Her bedroom curtains were wide open, and sunlight streamed in.

Nazeera was fussing ostentatiously around the room. 'It is after eight, Jamal. The twins have been

340

gone two hours,' she said, as Rebecca raised her head sleepily from the pillow. 'I have filled two buckets of hot water, and laid out your blue skirt.'

Rebecca was still half asleep as she slipped out from under the sheet. Nazeera stared at her in astonishment, and she tried to brazen it out: 'Oh, Nazeera, you look as though you were frightened by a jinnee. How many times have you seen me naked?' She ran to the bathroom and poured one of the steaming buckets of water into the galvanized hip bath.

Nazeera gazed after her, then pursed her lips. She pulled back the bedclothes and started with alarm. There was a patch of dried blood on the undersheet. Nazeera knew at once that this was not menstrual issue: al-Jamal had seen her moon only twelve days before and it was too soon for it to rise again. This blood was bright and pure and virginal.

Oh, my baby, my little girl, you have made the crossing, and now you stand on a strange and dangerous new shore. She bent closer to the bed to scry the omen. The stain was no larger than her spread hand, but it was shaped like a bird in flight.

A vulture? That was an evil omen, the bird of death and suffering. No. She thrust away the thought. A gentle dove? A falcon, cruel and beautiful? A wise old owl? Only the future will tell us, she decided, and gathered up the sheet. She would wash it with her own hands, in secret. No other must be allowed to see this marking. Then she stopped, for she sensed that al-Jamal was watching her through the open bathroom door.

She dropped the bundled sheet on the floor and went through to her. She knelt beside the bath and picked up the loofah. There was no soap—they had

341

finished the last bar a week ago. Rebecca held her hair on top of her neck, and leant forward. Nazeera began the familiar ritual of scrubbing her back.

After a while she whispered her question: 'Which one was it, Jamal?'

'I don't understand what you are asking.' Rebecca would not look at her face.

'Who climbed the tamarind tree last night?' But Rebecca pretended she had water in her eyes, and covered them with both hands.

'It could not have been Abadan Riji, the pretty soldier. He has another woman,' Nazeera said.

Rebecca lowered her hands and stared at her. 'You are a liar,' she said softly, but with deadly ferocity. 'That is a cruel and hurtful lie.'

'So it was the soldier. I wish it had been the other, who might bring you happiness. The soldier never will.'

'I love him, Nazeera. Please understand that.'

'So does she. Her name is Bakhita.'

'No!' Rebecca covered her ears. 'I don't want to hear this.'

Nazeera was silent. She took Rebecca's arm and ran the loofah over it. When she came to her fingers she separated them and washed them one at a time.

'Bakhita is an Arabic name,' Rebecca blurted at last, but Nazeera remained silent. 'Answer me!' Rebecca insisted.

'You did not want to hear.'

'You are torturing me. Is she an Arab? Is she very beautiful? Does he love her?'

'She is of my people and my God,' Nazeera answered. 'I have never seen her, but men say she is very beautiful, and rich and clever. As to whether he loves her or not, that I do not know. Can a man like Abadan Riji ever love a woman in the same way that she loves him?'

'He is an Englishman and she is Arab.' Rebecca whispered. 'How can she love him?'

'He is a man and she is a woman before all else. That is how she can love him.'

'Nazeera, an hour ago I was happy. Now happiness has flown away.'

'Perhaps it is best that you are unhappy for today rather than unhappy for the rest of your life,' Nazeera said sadly. 'That is why I have told you these things.'

*   *   *

Two hours after the beginning of curfew the four men left the city. Penrod and Yakub wore turbans and Ansar *jibbas* for they would be riding north through the Dervish lines. Ryder and Bacheet wore simple *galabiyyas*, like common tribesmen, for they would return to the city.

Despite their outfits they were unchallenged as they crossed the canal behind Ryder Courtney's compound. The guard had been warned to let them pass. They were all heavily laden with weapons and woven sisal bags as they struck out into the desert. None spoke and they moved warily, keeping well separated but in sight of each other.

Bacheet led the way. He never slackened his pace even when the sand was ankle deep. They walked for two hours before they climbed a bank of shale that was frosty pale in the glimmer of the moon. One of the wadis that was carved out of the far side was filled with a dark amorphous mass of thorny scrub. There Bacheet paused and lowered his burden to the ground. He spoke a few quiet words to Ryder Courtney. Ryder handed him a leather bag of Maria Theresa dollars, and Bacheet went forward alone. The other three squatted to wait. In the distance they heard Bacheet utter the lonely haunted cry of a courser, the nocturnal plover of the desert. The call was answered from the wadi.

'So al-Mahtoum is here. He is a good man. I can rely on him,' Ryder said, with satisfaction.

'Let us go to join them.' Penrod Ballantyne stood up impatiently.

'Sit down,' Ryder ordered. 'Bacheet will come to fetch us. Al-Mahtoum will not allow a stranger to see his face. He lives a dangerous existence. When he has handed over the camels to Bacheet he will disappear back into the desert like a fox.'

An hour later the courser cried again, and Ryder stood up. 'Now,' he said, and led Penrod and Yakub forward. There were four camels couched among the scrub. Bacheet squatted beside them but al-Mahtoum was gone. Penrod and Yakub went to each of them to check their tack and their loads. There were dhurra loaves and dried dates in the food bags and one of the animals was loaded with camel fodder. The waterskins were less than a quarter filled.

Penrod remarked on this.

'Al-Mahtoum expects you to fill them at the river crossing. No sense in carrying more than you need. You should reach the Nile at Gutrahn before midnight tomorrow. Don't try to cross sooner. The Dervish are thick as tsetse flies this side of Gutrahn.'

Penrod replied tartly: 'Yakub and I have travelled this road before, but thank you for your excellent advice.' He went from one beast to the next, slapping their humps. They were plumped up with fat. Next he checked their limbs, running his hands down shoulder and haunch to the fetlock. 'Sound,' he said. 'They are in good condition.'

'They don't come any sounder,' Ryder said bitterly. 'These are *gimal*, the finest racing camels. They are worth fifty pounds each—stolen from me by your warlord Chinese Gordon.'

'I will treat them like my own children,' Penrod promised.

'I am sure you will,' Ryder said, 'although those who call you the Camel Killer, and they are legion, might have difficulty believing you.'

Penrod and Yakub mounted up, and Penrod gave Ryder an ironic salute with the goad. 'I shall give your respects to the ladies at the Long Bar in the Gheziera Club.' He knew that Ryder was not a member. It was another little burr in the rough texture of their relationship.

Yet Ryder was not particularly pleased to see him go. Penrod Ballantyne was never dull. He and Bacheet watched the little caravan meld with the night.

Bacheet grunted and spat. It was apparent that he did not share his master's feelings. 'The two of them ride together because they are both rogues and lechers, almost as quick with knife and gun as they are with their meat prods.'

Ryder laughed. 'You should rejoice that Yakub has gone. Perhaps you will now be able to enjoy a little more of Nazeera's company.' He swung the sling of his rifle over his shoulder.

'You should be equally grateful to see their backs,' Bacheet's tone was astringent, 'although the leopard has already been in the goat kraal, or so I have heard.'

Ryder stopped in his tracks and tried to fathom Bacheet's expression in the starlight. 'What leopard, and whose goats?'

'Yesterday morning Nazeera changed the linen in the palace bedrooms. She had to wash one set in cold water.' It was an oblique reference, but Ryder understood it. Hot water removes most stains, but not blood. For that, one used cold water.

They did not speak again until they had crossed the canal into the city. Ryder was still filled with disbelief and betrayal as he entered his compound and went to his private quarters. Of course he knew of Penrod Ballantyne's reputation as a lady-killer, but Rebecca Benbrook? Surely not. She was a young girl of excellent family and strict upbringing. His respect and affection for her had led him to expect certain standards of her, those a man might look for in his future wife.

Bacheet and Nazeera are notorious gossips—I do not believe it. Then, suddenly, he remembered an observation his elder brother, Waite, had once made: 'The colonel's lady and Katie O'Grady are both women under the skin. In certain circumstances both think with their organs of generation, instead of their brains.' Ryder had laughed at the time, but now it sickened him.

He did not feel better until he had shaved and drunk two large mugs of black coffee, almost the last of his hoarded supply. Even then when he sat down at his desk, he found it difficult to concentrate on his ledgers. The most lurid and disquieting images kept forming in his mind. It was with relief that he made the final entry in his journal, closed the heavy leatherbound book and went out to begin his morning rounds of the compound.

As he stepped into the animal enclosure, Saffron ran to meet him. She had Lucy the monkey on her shoulder. Unperturbed the remaining infant was clinging to Lucy's belly fluff with all four paws and suckling busily. Lucy had lost the other to a disease that not even Ali had been able to cure. Saffron skipped along beside him, blissfully relating every shred of information and gem of wisdom that Ali had shared with her that morning.

'Victoria is scouring,' she informed him.

'Are we discussing the female bongo, or the Queen of England and Empress of India?' Ryder asked.

'Oh, don't be silly! You know exactly who I mean.' Saffron laughed. 'Ali says that the acacia leaves do not agree with her. He and I are going to dose her as soon as he has brewed his medicine. It's what he uses for the horses.'

Ryder felt his dark mood lift a little. Saffron's company was always healing and distracting. 'Why aren't you helping Amber in the green-cake kitchens?' he asked, as they came to the last cages.

'My sister is a bore, so bossy and overbearing. She hasn't been here for weeks and today she appears and gives orders as though she was a duchess.'

They walked between the ranks of Sudanese women who were crushing the bundles of fresh greenery in the wooden stamp pots. Ryder greeted most by name and asked a question, which demonstrated his interest and concern for them. They giggled in gratification. Some of the younger girls were openly saucy and flirtatious for Ryder was a great favourite among them. He knew that the way to get the best out of his people was to make certain they liked him. Saffron took part in the banter with the women, for she shared their sense of fun and they enjoyed her sparkle. High spirits were rare in the city, where terror and starvation had turned the populace into wild animals. We have the green-cake to thank for that. It keeps all of us healthy and human, thought Ryder.

He tried not to show it but he was eager to get to the inner enclosure where the smoke was rising from the line of three-legged cauldrons. When they reached it they found Rebecca, Amber and five Arab girls weighing and packing the loaves of green-cake into woven baskets for distribution to those who needed it most. This was not easy to decide, for there was not nearly enough to go round. Rebecca was reading the scale and Amber was writing down the results as her elder sister called them out.

'This is our best day ever, Ryder. One hundred and thirty-eight pounds,' Amber announced with pride, as he came up.

'Excellent. You ladies have done wonderfully well.' Ryder turned to Rebecca. She wore long skirts and a wide-brimmed straw hat, for the sun was already high and hot.

'Miss Benbrook, I hope I find you well?' He could see that she had lost more weight. He was sure he would be able to encircle her waist with his hands. But the thought of touching her made him uneasy, and he shifted from one foot to the other.

She gave him the first direct smile since their indiscreet behaviour had been discovered, but it lacked her usual sparkle and verve. She seemed depressed and subdued. 'Thank you, Mr Courtney. For a while I was unwell but I am now fully recovered.' They exchanged a few more stilted pleasantries, while Saffron pouted because she had lost Ryder's attention.

'If you will excuse us we should get back to work.' Rebecca ended the conversation. 'Amber, we have finished with the scale and you may take it back to the shed. Saffron, you are killing Lucy and her baby with love. Go and put them back into their cage. We need your help here.'

Saffron pulled a face but went to do as she was told leaving Ryder and Rebecca alone.

'You are wearing Arab dress,' Rebecca remarked. 'That is unusual, is it not?'

'Not at all,' Ryder replied. 'I always wear it when I travel in the desert. It is cooler and more practical for riding and walking. Also, my people prefer me to do so. It makes me seem one of them, and less a stranger.'

'Oh? I thought it was because you and Bacheet went out to find camels for Captain Ballantyne and Yakub.'

'Who told you that?'

'For me to know and you to find out.'

'Nazeera's a chatterbox. You should not pay attention to everything she tells you.'

'You are jumping to conclusions, Mr Courtney. However, I have always found Nazeera's information highly reliable,' she replied.

If only you knew Nazeera's latest bulletin, he

thought, but she went on, 'Tell me, sir, did Captain Ballantyne get away safely?'

It was a direct question to which she obviously knew the answer. Ryder considered it carefully. It occurred to him that Penrod's departure had left the field clear for him, On the other hand did he really want the pretty soldier-boy's discarded toy?

'Well, did he?' Rebecca insisted on a reply. 'It is of no interest to me, but Nazeera will want to know about Yakub. He is her particular friend.'

Ryder grimaced at her delicate description of their relationship. Did Rebecca think of the soldier-boy as *her* particular friend, he wondered. 'I don't think that we should discuss military matters that relate to the safety of the city,' he said at last.

'Oh, la, Mr Courtney! I am not a spy for the Mahdi. If you don't tell me I shall simply ask my father. However, I thought you might save me the trouble.'

'Very well. I cannot see any pressing reason why you should not know. Captain Ballantyne left a little after midnight. He and Yakub are heading north, and in all probability will cross the Blue Nile tonight. They plan to join up with the Mahdist army that is moving north along the river towards Abu Hamed.'

Rebecca paled. 'They plan to travel in company with the Dervish? That is madness.'

'It is known as hiding in full view. They will conceal themselves among the host,' he assured her. 'You need not worry, Captain Ballantyne is adept at disguise. He can change like a veritable chameleon.' And he thought, She can take that as a warning, if she wishes.

'Oh, I am not worried, I assure you, Captain.'

The lie was transparent: she looked as though she might burst into tears.

There is no doubt now that Nazeera was telling the truth, and that Ballantyne has made her his doxy, but what of it? Ryder reflected. She was never mine, and I don't love her—at least, not now that she is spoilt fruit. Even in his own ears that did not ring true. He tried to be more honest with himself. Do I love her? But he did not want to face that question four square.

'I will leave you to your labours, Miss Benbrook,' he murmured, and turned towards the door of the shed. 'Amber!' he exclaimed. He and Rebecca had been so caught up in their own conversation that neither had noticed she had returned.

'How long have you been listening?' Rebecca demanded.

Instead of answering Amber asked, 'Are the Dervish going to catch Penrod?'

'Of course not. Don't be silly!' Rebecca turned on her. Both sisters were close to tears, 'Anyway you should not eavesdrop on other people, and you should not refer to Captain Ballantyne as Penrod. Now, come and help me to get the cauldrons filled again.'

Amber pushed past her and fled through the gates of the compound and back through the streets towards the consular palace.

Poor little thing, thought Ryder, but there are difficult days ahead for all of us.

*   *   *

Early each morning, the minute the bells of the old Catholic mission had tolled the end of curfew, the

351

women of the city streamed from the ruins, huts and hovels and scurried to the arsenal for the daily distribution of grain. By the time the gates opened several thousand were waiting in a line that stretched almost as far as the harbour. It was an agglomeration of misery. Starvation and disease, those dread horsemen, rode so rampantly through every quarter of the city that all cowered beneath their lash. Each of these poor ruined creatures, gaunt and ragged, some barely able to totter along, infants strapped to their backs or sucking vainly on their empty, withered dugs, clutched a battered dish and the tattered ration booklets issued by General Gordon's secretariat.

At the arsenal gates an Egyptian captain was in charge, with twenty men under his command. The dhurra sacks were dragged out one at a time from the granary. None of the citizens were allowed to enter the gates. Gordon did not want the populace to see for themselves how perilously low the stocks had fallen.

As each woman reached the head of the line, a sergeant examined her booklet to make sure it had not been forged. When he was satisfied he scribbled the date and his signature. The day's ration for her family was doled out into her dish with a wooden scoop. Two masters-at-arms, with clubs, stood ready on each side of the gates to discourage any argument or disturbance. This morning an additional twenty armed troopers were drawn up in a double rank on each side of the gates. Their bayonets were fixed, their expressions grim and businesslike. The women knew from bitter experience what this show of force presaged. They became restless and rowdy, bickering spitefully, jostling each other. The children sensed the tension and were fretful.

When General Gordon came striding down the street from the fort towards the gates, the women held up their children to show him their bruised, distorted features, the skeletal semi-paralysed limbs, and how their hair had turned to a sparse reddish fuzz, all sure signs of starvation, scurvy and beri-beri.

Gordon ignored these marks of affliction, the curses and supplications of the mothers, and took his place at the head of the squad. He nodded to the captain to proceed. The young officer unrolled the proclamation, which had been run off on the consulate printing press, and began to read it: 'I, General Charles George Gordon, by the authority vested in me by the Khedive of Egypt as Governor of the province of Kordofan and the city of Khartoum, do hereby proclaim that, with immediate effect, the daily ration of grain issued to each citizen of the city of Khartoum shall be reduced to the volume of thirty decilitres *per diem*—' The officer could get no further: his voice was drowned by jeers and screams of protest. The crowd pulsed and seethed like a black jellyfish, the women shaking their fists and waving their arms over their heads.

Gordon gave a sharp order. The troopers lowered their bayonets to present a bristling steel hedge to the advancing mob. The women spat, shrieked and hammered on the metal dishes they carried as though they were drums. The captain drew his sword: 'Back! Get back, all of you!'

This infuriated them further.

'You want us to starve! We will open the city

gates! If the Khedive and Gordon Pasha cannot feed our children, we will throw ourselves on the mercy of the Mahdi.'

The women in the front rank seized the blades of the bayonets, and held them in bloody hands, forcing the troopers back.

Gordon gave a quiet command to the young captain. There was a clash of breech-blocks as the troopers loaded their rifles. 'Company present arms, aim!' The troopers looked over the iron sights into the contorted faces of the mob. 'Fire!'

The rifles crashed out, aimed carefully over the women's heads. Black powder smoke enveloped them in a dense cloud and, stunned, they reeled back a few paces.

'Reload.' The crowd wavered before the menace of the levelled rifles, but then a new sound erupted. The women had begun the high-pitched ululation that goaded and inflamed the passions of the mob.

'Throw open the granary! Give us full ration!'

'Feed us!' they screamed, but the soldiers stood firm.

One woman picked up half a brick from a shell-damaged wall and hurled it at the front rank of riflemen. It did no damage, but provoked the rest to rush to the wall and grab bricks, stones and shards of pottery. The mob was transformed. It was no longer a gathering of human beings but a single monstrous organism, mindless amoeba of violence and destruction.

The stones and bricks flew into the thin ranks of troops. The young captain was struck full in the face. The red fez flew from his head, he dropped his sword and sank to his knees. He spat out a tooth and his mouth ran with blood. The women rushed forward, trying to reach the open grain sack, trampling the captain.

Gordon stepped into his place. The women saw his blazing blue eyes. 'Devil eyes!' shrieked those in front. 'Shaitan! Kill him!'

'Give us bread for the children! Give us food!'

The bricks clattered among the soldiers. Another man fell.

'Aim!' Gordon's voice carried, clear as a trumpet call. 'One round. Fire!'

The volley smashed into the mob at point-blank range, they went down before it and lay squealing like pigs in the abattoir. Those still on their feet wavered, and the ringleaders tried to rally them.

'Bayonets!' Gordon called. 'Forward!' They stepped out briskly, the bright blades levelled and the mob shrank back, then turned on itself and broke. They dropped their stones and bricks, threw aside their dishes and ran back into the alleys.

Gordon halted his men and marched them back into the arsenal. As the gates closed behind them, the survivors crept out from their hiding-places in the warren of slums. They came to find their dead, their wounded and their lost children. At first they were timid and terrified, but then one woman picked up a fist-sized stone and flung it against the barred gates of the arsenal. 'The soldiers are fat, their bellies stuffed full. When we beg for food they shoot us down like dogs.' She was a tall bony harridan, dressed all in black. She stood before the gates and raised both skinny arms towards the sky. 'I call on Allah to smite them with the pestilence and the cholera. Let them eat the flesh of toads and vultures, as we are forced to do!' Her voice was a high-pitched shriek.

The other women thronged to her. They began to ululate again, rolling their tongues so that their spittle flew as they emitted that terrible keening sound.

'The Franks also have food,' screeched the woman in black. 'They gorge like pashas in their palaces.'

'The compound of al-Sakhawi, the infidel, is filled with fat beasts. His storerooms are piled high with sacks of grain.'

'Give us food for our babies!'

'Shaitan is the ally of al-Sakhawi. He has taught him witchcraft. From grass and thorn he has taught him to make the Devil's manna. His people feast upon it.'

'Destroy the nest of Shaitan!'

'We are the children of Allah. Why should the infidel feast while our babies starve and die?'

The crowd wavered uncertainly, and the black-clad woman took charge. She ran to the head of the street that led to the hospital and beyond it to the compound of Ryder Courtney. 'Follow me! I will show you where to find food.' She broke into a shuffling dance, bobbing and ululating, and the crowd streamed after her, filling the narrow street from side to side with a dancing, keening flood of humanity.

The men heard the uproar and came out of their hiding-places among the ruins. The ululating of the women maddened them. Those who carried weapons brandished them. They joined the turbulent dancing procession, and burst into the war songs of the fighting tribes.

*   *   *

Ryder and Jock McCrump were in the main workshop. They had suffered many setbacks. This was the third time in as many months that they had been forced to remove the *Ibis*'s engine from the hull and painstakingly reweld the steam lines. Then they had discovered that the main drive-shaft bearings had also been damaged, and were knocking noisily at even moderate revolutions. Jock had made replacements: from a solid block of metal he had forged and filed the half-shells by hand. It was a monumental exhibition of skill and patience. At long last, after all these months of meticulous labour, the repairs were complete. Now they were putting it all together for a final check before they transported it to the harbour for installation in the steamer's engine room.

'Well, now, skipper, I think this time we've got it right.' Jock stood back with black grease to the elbows and his few remaining hairs plastered to his scalp with sweat. 'This time I think the old *Ibis* will be able to carry us out of this God-forsaken hellhole. There is a shebeen in Aswan run by a lass from Glasgow, a lady of my acquaintance. She sells genuine malt from the Isle of Islay. I would fain have the taste of it on my tongue again. It is the true nectar of the Almighty, and that's no blasphemy, mind.'

'I will buy the first round,' Ryder promised.

'And the rest,' Jock told him. 'You havenae paid me this year past.'

Ryder was about to protest the injustice of this accusation but he heard racing footsteps coming across the compound and Saffron's breathless squeaks: 'Ryder! Come quickly.'

Ryder stepped to the doorway. 'What is it, Saffron?'

She was holding her skirts high and her hat was hanging down her back on its ribbon. Her face was flushed scarlet. 'Something terrible is happening. Rebecca has sent me to call you. Hurry!' She grabbed his hand and pulled him with her. They ran towards the cauldron yard.

'Can you hear it?' Saffron stopped and held up her hand. 'Now, can you hear?' It was faint babble and murmur, like wind in trees or a distant waterfall.

'Yes, but what is it?'

'Our women say it's a huge crowd of the people. They are coming from the arsenal. Our women say that the grain rations have been cut again, and there is going to be terrible trouble. They are terrified, and they are running away.'

'Saffron, go and fetch Rebecca and Amber.'

'Amber is not here. She is sulking in the palace. She has not come back since she heard that Captain Ballantyne had gone away.'

'Good. She will be safe there. Let the women go if they want to. Bring Rebecca, Nazeera and any others who want to stay to the blockhouse. You know how to shutter the windows and bar the doors. You also know where the rifles are kept. You and Rebecca arm yourselves. Wait for me there.'

'Where are you going?'

'To call the men. That's enough questions. Now, run!'

It was for just this sort of trouble that Ryder had fortified the compound. The walls were high and solid and the tops were lined with shards of broken glass. He had designed the interior of the

358

compound as a series of courtyards, each of which could be defended, but when one was overrun they could fall back into the next. In the centre, the blockhouse comprised his private quarters, treasury and arsenal. All the windows and doors could be covered with heavy shuttering. The walls were pierced with loopholes for rifle fire and the reed roof was heavily plastered with river clay to render it fireproof.

The first line of defence was the outer wall with its heavy gates at front and rear. He sent Jock with three men to barricade the rear gates, and stand guard there. Then Ryder took Bacheet and five of his most reliable men to the front gates, which opened on to the narrow street. They were all armed with long wooden staves. Ryder made certain the gates were bolted and the heavy timber bars were in their slots. It would take a battering-ram to break them down. There was a low wicket gate in the wall to one side, wide enough to admit one man at a time. Ryder stepped through it. The city street was empty, except for a few of the women from the green-cake kitchens. They were scurrying away like frightened chickens, and within seconds the last had disappeared.

Ryder waited. He was deliberately carrying nothing more provocative than the wooden staff. A rifle was worse than useless against a mob. A single shot might drop one person, but would merely infuriate the rest, and they would be on him before he could reload. A certain way to get yourself torn to pieces, he thought, and leant casually on the staff, assuming a calm, relaxed pose. The noise of the crowd was nearer now, becoming louder as he listened. He knew what that keening chorus of

359

women's voices meant. They were whipping themselves and their menfolk into a frenzy.

He stood alone in front of the gates, and the sound built up into a muted roar, coming down on him like the wild waters of a river in flash flood. Suddenly the front rank of the mob burst into view two hundred paces down the narrow street from where he stood. They saw him and faltered. The hubbub subsided gradually, and a strange hush fell over them. They knew him well and his reputation was formidable.

Damn me, if I don't do a Gordon on them. Ryder smiled inwardly. Chinese Gordon was famous for the hypnotic power he could wield over a tribe of hostile savages. It was said he could calm and control them by the sheer power of his personality and the gaze of his steely blue eyes.

Ryder straightened until he stood tall, and glowered at them with all the ferocity he could command. He knew that they looked upon green or blue eyes as those of the Devil. The hush became silence. For the moment it was a standoff. It needed but a small push to topple it one way or the other.

He started to walk towards them. Now he held the stave threateningly, and paced with calculated menace. They backed off slowly before his approach. One looked back over his shoulder. They were on the point of breaking.

Suddenly a tall, gangling female figure bounded into the alley. Her features were withered with starvation. Her lips had shrunk back to expose bone-white teeth, too large for her pale pink gums, which were studded with open ulcers. She was the harpy of mythology, swathed in black cloth. As she

360

danced towards him, her shanks beneath the black skirts were thin as the legs of a heron, and her enormous feet flapped like the carcasses of stranded black catfish. She threw back her head and emitted the cry of a banshee. The mob behind her roared and poured after her, filling the alley.

Ryder held up his right hand in a placatory gesture. 'I will give you whatever you want,' he shouted. 'Stop.'

His voice was drowned by the wild shrieks of the harpy: 'We have come to take what we want, and we will kill all who stand in our way!'

Slowly Ryder lifted his left hand and made the sign of the evil eye. He pointed at the woman's face, and saw her eyelids flutter as she recognized the sign. She stumbled and checked, but then she gathered herself and leapt forward again. He saw the madness in her gaze and knew she was too far gone to respond even to the most dire witchcraft.

Still he stood his ground until she was almost upon him. Then he stepped forward to meet her and drove the point of his staff into her midriff just below the ribcage. The spleens of most river-dwellers were swollen with malaria. A blow like that could burst the organ and kill or maim. The harpy dropped like a bundle of black rags, but the leading ranks of the mob leapt over her body. The man in the forefront swung a broadsword at Ryder's head. He ducked and darted back through the wicket gate. Bacheet slammed and bolted it behind him. They heard and felt the impact as the mob crashed into it on the far side.

'We will let them through the gate one at a time, and we can crack their skulls as they come through,' Bacheet suggested.

'Too many.' Ryder shook his head. 'I will climb to the top of the gate and try to reason with them.'

'You cannot reason with a pack of rabid dogs.'

Somebody was tugging insistently at his coattails and Ryder tried to pull away. Then he looked back. 'I thought I told you to stay in the blockhouse,' he exclaimed angrily.

'I brought you this.' Saffron held up his gunbelt with the holstered revolver dangling from it and the rows of brass cartridges in their loops.

'Good girl!' He strapped it on. 'But now get back to the blockhouse and stay there.' He did not watch her to make sure she had gone but turned back to Bacheet. 'Fetch the long ladder from the workshop.'

They placed it against the wall. Hand over hand Ryder shot to the top and looked down into the street. The length and breadth of it was filled with humanity. He picked out the harpy he had felled: she was on her feet again, doubled over and hobbling with pain, but her voice was as shrill and strident as before. She was directing the crowd to gather anything that would burn from the buildings that lined the street. They were dragging out baulks of timber, dried palm fronds, old furniture, rubbish, and piling it against the outside of the compound gates.

'Hear me, citizens of Khartoum,' Ryder shouted in Arabic. 'Let the peace and wisdom of God guide you. There is nothing within these walls that I will not give you gladly.'

They looked up him uncertainly as he balanced at the top of the ladder.

'There is the disciple of Shaitan!' the harpy screamed. 'The infidel! Look at him, the pork-eater! The brewer of the green manna from hell!' She shuffled into a painful dance, and behind her the crowd growled. They threw stones and sticks at him, but the wall was high and the range was long. The missiles hit the wall and bounced back, clattering in the dusty street.

'What you call the Devil's manna, is cooked grass and reeds. If you will feed them with it, your children will thrive and regain their health.'

'He lies! These are the falsehoods that the Devil has placed in his mouth. We know you are eating bread and meat, not grass. Within these walls you have dhurra and meat. Give it to us. Give us your animals. Give us the dhurra you have in your warehouse.'

'I have no dhurra.'

'He lies!' screeched the harpy. 'Bring fire! We will burn him out of this nest of evil and sacrilege.'

'Wait!' Ryder shouted. 'Hear me!'

But the roar of the crowd drowned his voice. One of the women ran up the crowded street. She was carrying a lighted torch, a bundle of rags soaked in pitch tied to a broomstick. A thick black tarry smoke billowed from the flames. She handed the torch to one of the men, who ran with it to the gate. Ryder glanced down in alarm as he realized how high the rubbish had been piled against the main gates. The man threw the smoking torch on top of the bonfire. It rolled half-way down, then stuck. In the dry desert air the flames caught at once and licked upwards. The gates had stood in the sun for many years. Even though Ryder had his people paint them regularly, the wood dried out and cracked faster than they could repair it, and now the dried paint flared, and the flames shot high. They were almost colourless in the bright sunlight. Ryder considered ordering Bacheet and his men to form a bucket chain to douse the flames before they could burn through the gates, then realized that there were neither enough men nor buckets, that the river and the well were too far, and the flames were already leaping higher than the top of the wall. The heat was intense and drove him off the ladder.

'Bacheet, we could fight them here, but I don't want any shooting. I don't want to kill anybody.'

'It is me that I am worried about, Effendi. I don't want to be killed either,' Bacheet replied. 'These are animals, mad animals.'

'They are starving and they have been driven to this.'

'Should I send one of the men with a message to Gordon to bring the soldiers to drive them away?' Bacheet asked hopefully.

Ryder smiled grimly. 'Gordon Pasha is not our friend. He values us only for our dhurra and our camels. If you send one of our men out there the mob will tear him to pieces. I think we will be forced to save ourselves without the help of Gordon Pasha.'

'How will we do that?' Bacheet asked simply.

'We must fall back to the main compound. They will not be able to burn that gate. The fire hose will reach it.' He had to raise his voice above the howls and shouts of the crowd in the street outside and the crackle of the flames. 'Come! Follow me!' The paint on the inside of the gate was already charring.

He ran back to the inner gate, and gave orders to have the water pump and fire hose rigged. There was a firing platform along the top of the inner wall, and reluctantly Ryder issued Martini-Henry rifles to those who could handle them. Apart from Rebecca and Jock, he had trained only five of his men, including Bacheet. The Arabs took little interest in musketry and showed even less aptitude for it. Rebecca could outshoot most of them. He left the women and Jock in the blockhouse, guarding the loopholes.

From the firing parapet he watched the main gates sag slowly inwards, then crash to the dusty earth in a final burst of sparks and burning fragments. The mob poured through, leaping and pushing each other over the still flaming remnants of the gates. One of the older women lost her footing and fell into the flames. They caught at once in her voluminous robe. The rest of the crowd ignored her agonized shriek, and within seconds she lay still. The smell of her roasting flesh floated sickeningly to where Ryder stood on the parapet of the inner wall.

Once the leaders were inside, they came up short. They were in unfamiliar territory and they looked about curiously. Then they caught sight of the row of heads above the parapet of the inner wall, and the hunting chorus went up again. They charged straight at the inner gate like a pack of savage hounds. Ryder let them get half-way across, then fired into the hard-packed clay in front of the leaders. The bullet kicked up a spray of dust and gravel, then ricocheted away over their heads. It stopped them short, and they milled indecisively.

'Don't come closer!' he shouted. 'I will kill the next one who comes.' Some turned, and started to creep away. Then the harpy hobbled through to the front. She broke once more into her grotesque dance. From somewhere she had armed herself with a cowtail fly switch. She brandished this as she screeched her threats and curses at the men on the parapet.

'You foul and stupid old woman,' Ryder muttered, in frustration and despair, 'don't force me to kill you.' He fired at her feet, and when the bullet kicked up dirt under her, she leapt into the air, flapping the black wings of her robe like an ancient crow taking flight. The crowd howled again. She hit the ground and came straight on towards the inner wall. Ryder levered another round into the breech and fired. Again she jumped high, and the men behind her imitated her, laughing. The sound had a deranged, obscene quality that was as menacing as the shouts of rage had been.

'Stop!' Ryder muttered. 'Please stop, you old bitch.' He shot again, but now the mob had realized he would not shoot to kill and lost all fear. They came on after the prancing figure in a swarm. They reached the gate and beat against it with the weapons they carried and their bare hands.

'Wood!' shouted the harpy. 'Bring more wood!' They ran to fetch it, and came back to pile it against the gate as they had before.

'Get the pump started!' Ryder shouted, and two men seized the handles and swung them up and down. The empty canvas hose, laid out across the yard, swelled and hardened as the pressure built up and a powerful stream of river water spurted from the nozzle. Two men on the parapet pointed it down on to the kindling below. It struck with such force that the pile tumbled over.

'Aim at her.' Ryder pointed out the harpy. The

366

stream hit her full in the chest and knocked her backwards. She struck the ground on her shoulder-blades and rolled. The hose stream followed her. Every time she regained her feet, it knocked her down again. At last she crawled out of range on hands and knees. Ryder turned the hose on the men in the front of the crowd and they scattered. Then they spread out to search the other buildings of the compound, which lay outside the inner fortifications. Within minutes Ryder heard hammering and banging coming from the direction of his warehouses.

'They are smashing down the doors of the ivory storeroom,' Bacheet shouted. 'We must stop them.'

'A thousand of them, and ten of us?' Ryder did not have to say more.

'But the ivory and skins?' Bacheet was entitled to a small share of Ryder's profits, and now at the thought of his losses his face was a pattern of dismay.

'They can have the elephant teeth and the animal skins, rather than my own teeth and skin,' Ryder said. 'Anyway, they cannot eat ivory. Perhaps when they find no dhurra in the stores they will lose interest.'

It was a vain hope, and he knew it. It was not long before the men were streaming back, egged on by the wild ululations of the women. They were carrying some of the largest elephant tusks and bundles of sun-dried animal hides. They piled these at the foot of the wall. Their intention was clear. They were building a ramp to scale the wall. Immediately Ryder ordered the men on the hose to direct the stream on to the pile. The tusks and the heavy bales were much more solid than the rubbish

367

they had used in their first attempt and the hose stream made no impression upon them. Then they tried to drive off the men, but although the hose beat down on them most stayed on their feet and placed more tusks on the growing ramp. When one was knocked down, three others rushed forward to take his place. They kept piling up the heavy material until it reached just below the top of the wall. Then they reassembled in the outer courtyard out of range of the fire hose. The black harpy pranced among them.

'You should have hit her harder,' Bacheet muttered darkly, 'or, better still, you should have put a bullet through that ugly head. It's still not too late.' He lifted the Martini-Henry and aimed it over the top of the parapet.

'She is in no danger, with you doing the shooting,' Ryder remarked. Despite the hours of instruction he had lavished on Bacheet he was a long way from mastering the art of musketry. Bacheet looked pained at the insult, but he lowered the rifle. 'See? The old witch is picking out the best men to climb the walls.'

Bacheet was right. Somehow she had kept hold of the switch even when the hose had hit her squarely. It was secured round her wrist by a loop of rawhide. She was moving among the crowd and marking the ones she chose by slapping them in the face with it. Quickly she picked out thirty or forty of the youngest and strongest. Many were armed with broadswords or axes.

Encouraged by the harpy the women started that dreadful cacophony again. The assault troop brandished their weapons and rushed at the wall. The jet of water from the hose struck the leaders but they linked arms to support each other.

'Let us shoot, Effendi,' Bacheet pleaded. 'They are so close even I cannot miss.'

'I would not give odds on that,' Ryder grunted, 'But hold your fire. If we kill just one they will go berserk and start a massacre.' He was thinking of the women in the blockhouse. Little else mattered.

Even with the hose playing over them the attackers climbed swiftly to the parapet. Ryder and his men checked them there, swinging at their heads with clubs and staves. They had the advantage of height. At a range of only a few feet the fire hose was almost irresistible, and the long staves kept the attackers from getting close enough to use their swords. But when some lost heart and retreated down the ramp of bales and tusks the harpy was at the bottom to meet them, lashing their faces with the switch and screaming abuse. Three times they fell back and each time she sent them up again.

'They are giving up,' Bacheet panted. 'They are losing heart.'

'I hope Allah is listening to you,' Ryder said, and plied his staff, cracking it across the temple of the man in front of him. He rolled down the ramp and lay still at the bottom. Even the harpy's stinging blows with the switch could not rouse him.

Then a man pushed through the throngs of ululating women. He walked with the rolling long-armed gait of a silver-backed gorilla bull. His head was round, shaven and shiny as a cannonball. His skin was the colour of anthracite and his features were Nubian, with thick lips and a wide, flattened nose. He had stripped to his loincloth and the muscles of his chest bulged under the oiled skin,

369

and writhed like a black silk bag of pythons. 'I know this one,' Bacheet croaked huskily. 'He is a famous wrestler from Dongola. They call him the Bone Cruncher. He is dangerous.'

The Nubian climbed the ramp with astonishing agility. Ryder ran down the platform to confront him, but he was already at the parapet. He raised himself to his full height, balanced like an ebony colossus.

Ryder placed the butt of the long stave under his arm, like a lance, and ran at him. The sharpened point caught the Nubian in the centre of his chest and snagged in his flesh. Ryder threw his weight behind it, and the Nubian hovered at the point of balance, his arms windmilling, body arched backwards.

Bacheet sprang to Ryder's side and the two threw their combined weight on the staff. The Nubian went over like an avalanche of black rock. He tumbled into five men behind him, and they tumbled down the steep incline of the ramp in a confused jumble of arms and legs.

The Nubian hit the sun-baked earth on the back of his shaven head and the impact reverberated like the fall of a lightning-blasted mahogany tree. He lay quiescent, mouth agape and thunderous snores echoing up his throat. The harpy jumped on to his chest and lashed at his face.

The Nubian opened his eyes and sat up. He swatted her away with the back of one hand and shook his head groggily. Then he saw Ryder and Bacheet grinning down at him. He threw back his head, bellowed like a bull buffalo in a pitfall, then groped for his sword, lurched to his feet and charged straight back up the ramp.

'Sweet Mother of God,' said Ryder. 'Just look at him come.' He raised the staff again, and as the Nubian reached the top he thrust at him viciously. With a flick of the blade the Nubian lopped two feet off the end. Ryder stabbed at him again with the butt. The Nubian cut again back-handed and left Ryder with a stump no longer than his arm. Ryder hurled it at him. It struck the Nubian in the centre of his sloping forehead. He blinked and roared again, then came over the top of the parapet, hacking wildly.

'Back to the blockhouse!' Ryder yelled, as he ducked under the blade.

Suddenly he realized he was alone on the parapet. The others had anticipated his order and taken themselves off at top speed. He dived down the rickety ladder into the yard and raced for the door. He could hear the Nubian close behind him, and the swish of his sword fanned the short sweaty hairs on the back of his neck.

'Run, Ryder! He's right behind you,' Saffron shrilled from one of the loopholes. 'Shoot him—I gave you your gun! Why don't you shoot?' In theory it was good advice, but if he lost even a second in loosening the flap of his holster the Nubian would take his head off at the shoulders. He found an extra turn of speed and began to catch up with Bacheet and the other Arabs.

'Faster, Ryder, faster!' Saffron yelped. Close behind him he could hear the hoarse breathing. Ahead, the others burst through the blockhouse door.

Rebecca was holding it open for him. Now she levelled the rifle and seemed to aim straight at his head. 'I can't shoot without hitting you,' she cried,

371

and lowered the barrel. 'Come on, Ryder, please, come on.' Even in the desperate circumstances, her use of his first name gave him a sweet thrill and added wings to his feet. He flew through the doorway and Rebecca and Saffron slammed it behind him. On the far side the Nubian crashed into it with a force that shivered the frame.

'He's going to smash it off its hinges.' Rebecca gasped. They heard the Nubian hacking and kicking at it.

'Steel door, steel frame,' Ryder reassured her, and grabbed the rifle Saffron handed him. He opened the breech and checked the load. 'We'll be safe in here.'

He stepped up to the loophole and Rebecca stood close beside him. Through the narrow opening they had a view across the yard to the door of the workshop and in the other direction to the inner gate of the menagerie. The broad sweat-gleaming back of the Nubian appeared in their field of vision. He had abandoned his assault on the blockhouse door. Now he was striding across the yard to the barred inner gates. When he reached them Ryder watched him lift the heavy teak locking bars and toss them aside. Then he stood back and kicked the brass lock off its hinges. As the gates swung open the harpy was first into the yard. The horde poured in behind her.

She headed straight for the blockhouse, and the rest followed her closely. It was a horrific spectacle, as though the gates of hell had burst open and spewed out the legions of the damned and long-dead. Their faces were ravaged by disease and hunger, their eyes too large for their wizened, emaciated heads, their lips and eyelids swollen and inflamed with running ulcers and carbuncles. Starvation and disease emit their own odour as the body devours itself and the skin releases the fluids of decay and dissolution: as they crowded to the loopholes the stench oozed through into the hot, airless interior and filled it with the reek of open sepulchres. It was a miasma that was difficult to breathe. The ruined faces leered and grimaced through the openings. 'Food! Where is the food?' They thrust their arms through. Their limbs were thin and gnarled as dead branches. The palms of their hands were as pale as the bellies of dead fish.

'Oh, Jesus, have mercy on us,' Rebecca gasped, and shrank against Ryder, instinctively seeking his protection. He placed one arm round her shoulders. This time she made no effort to pull away from him. 'What will happen to us now?'

'Whatever happens, I will stay with you,' he said, and she pressed closer to him.

The harpy was shrieking orders to the mob. 'Search all the buildings! We must find where they have hidden the dhurra! Then we will smash the pots in which they have brewed the Devil's manna. It is evil and an offence in the sight of God. It is this that has brought misfortune upon the city, and visited us with pestilence and disaster. Find where they have hidden the animals. You shall feast on sweet meat this day.' Her shrill voice reached to the depths of their starved bodies. They responded to her with a kind of blind, hypnotic obedience and rushed away from the rifle slits so that Ryder could see out again. He and Rebecca pressed their faces to the same opening, breathing the cleaner air and watching the hordes streaming towards the gates of the menagerie, led by the colossal Nubian and the harpy.

'Well, them bongos of yours ain't going to be shitting on the decks of my ship again, skipper,' said Jock McCrump lugubriously. Suddenly he remembered his manners and touched the brim of his cap to Rebecca. 'If you'll forgive my French, ladies.'

'What are they going to do with them, Jock?' Saffron's voice was fearful.

'It's the cooking pot for all of them beasties, d'ye ken, Miss Saffy?'

Saffron flew at the door and tried to tear open the locking bars. 'Lucy! I have to save Lucy and her baby!'

Ryder took her arm gently but firmly, and drew her to his side. 'Saffron,' he whispered huskily, 'there is nothing we can do for Lucy now.'

'Can't you stop them? Please! Won't you stop them, Ryder?'

There was no reply he could give her. He held the two girls tightly, Saffron on one side and Rebecca on the other. They clung to him and watched some of the mob crowd the gate that led to the menagerie and try to break in, but it was stout and resisted their efforts. Then the Nubian shouldered them aside. He braced himself against the gate and shook it until it rattled in its frame, but it did not give way. He stepped back, charged and crashed into it with one massive shoulder. The hinges were torn from the frame and the door flew open.

Ali, the old keeper, stood in the open doorway with a rusty sword in his hands.

'Ali, you old fool.' Ryder groaned and tried to turn the girls away so that they would not see what was about to happen. But they resisted and stared ashen-faced through the loophole.

Ali raised the sword above his head. 'Begone, all of you! You will not enter here.' His voice was high-pitched and quavering. 'I will not allow you to touch my darlings.' He hobbled towards the giant, threatening him with the dented weapon. The Bone Cruncher shot out one thick arm and seized the old man's sword wrist. He shook it as a terrier shakes a rat, and they heard the bone of the old man's forearm crack. The rusty sword dropped into the dust at his feet. Using the broken arm as a handle the Bone Cruncher lifted Ali's wriggling body above his head and slammed him into the jamb of the gate with such force that his ribs snapped like dry kindling. He dropped the broken body, and stepped over it. The crowd rushed after him into the menagerie, but as they passed they hacked at Ali's head with club or sword.

A great roar of greed and hunger went up from within the menagerie as the mob saw the rows of cages and the terrified animals they contained.

'Food! Meat!' screamed the Harpy. 'I promised you a feast of fresh red meat. It is here for you.' She rushed at the nearest cage and tore open the door. It was filled with scarlet and grey parrots, a swirling screeching cloud of wings. She leapt in and slashed at them with the whisk, knocking them to the floor of the cage and stamping on them with both horny feet.

The crowd followed her example, breaking open the monkey cages and clubbing the terrified occupants as they bounded around. Then they attacked the stockades and pens of the antelope.

In the blockhouse they could hear what was

happening. Above the crash of breaking cages and the uproar of the mob, Saffron was able to identify the terrified voices of her favourite creatures: the shrieks of the parrots and the howls of the monkeys.

'That's Lucy, my poor darling Lucy,' she sobbed. 'They can't eat her. Tell me they won't eat Lucy.' Ryder hugged her but could find no words of comfort.

Then there came wild bleating and bellows of pain from the larger animals.

'That's Victoria, my bongo!' Saffron struggled again. 'Let me go! Please, I have to save her.'

The female bongo bounded out through the gates of the menagerie where old Ali's corpse still lay in the bloody dust. She must have escaped from her pen as the mob tore it down and seemed unhurt.

'Run, Victoria!' Saffron screamed. 'Run, my baby.'

A dozen men and women ran after her with spears and swords. The large, strikingly coloured animal saw the open gate ahead of her and swerved towards it, her sleek hide glistening dark chestnut with creamy white stripes, ears pricked forward, eyes filled with terror, huge and dark in her lovely head. She had almost reached the open gate when one of the spearmen checked and swivelled his shoulders, his left hand pointing straight at her, the right cocked back and holding the spear. He swung his weight forward and the spear flew in a high arc, then dropped towards the animal. It struck her just forward of the croup and the spearhead buried itself. The point must have struck the spine, for her paralysed hindquarters dropped, and she stood still on her front legs.

A triumphant howl went up from the hunters and they crowded round the maimed animal. They made no effort to put her out of her misery, but hacked off lumps of her living flesh. The Nubian rushed up and, with a sweep of his sword, opened her belly as if it were a purse. The pale bag of her stomach and the entwined ropes of entrails bulged out through the gash. These were delicacies, and the mob dragged them out of her, and devoured them voraciously. The yellow contents of the uncleaned guts mingled with the blood, and dribbled from their lips and jowls as they chewed.

Rebecca gagged at the sight and turned away her face, but Saffron watched until at last the bongo collapsed and the crowd swarmed over her carcass like a flock of vultures hiding it from view. From the gates of the menagerie others ran out carrying bleeding lumps of meat and the battered carcasses of the birds and monkeys. They tried to escape before the latecomers from the city streets joined in. They were too late, and all across the compound vicious squabbles and fighting broke out. Saffron saw one of the children pounce upon a scrap. He stuffed it into his mouth and tried to swallow it. But the woman who had dropped it set upon him, beating him and pummelled him until he was forced to spit it out. Before she could pick it out of the dust, someone else snatched it and ran out of the gates with the woman chasing after her.

Another group broke down the door of the shed that contained the day's cooking of green-cake. They gathered up slabs in their shirts, but before they could make off with it the harpy fell upon them. She seemed to have risen above the simple need to find food and ran among them, striking at random with her whisk, screaming, 'That is the poison of Shaitan! Throw it on the fire. Throw it into the latrines where it belongs.' Although a few ran off with their booty, the harpy forced most to fling their share into the cooking fires or down the latrine pits.

'She has destroyed it all. What a shameful waste,' Rebecca cried in anguish. 'And she is making them smash our cauldrons. Now we shall all starve.'

Ryder watched the harpy helplessly. He saw how dangerous this raving demagogue was, that at any moment she might trigger another explosion of murderous passion and insanity. However, most of the mob had disappeared, and it seemed that the riot must soon die of its own accord.

Even though the damage they had wreaked was punishing, Ryder sought some small comfort in the fact that they were making no effort to take the ivory. It was clearly too heavy to carry far. Most of his other valuable possessions were locked in the strongroom in the blockhouse. Just as soon as the *Intrepid Ibis* was seaworthy again, he would load what was left of them and be ready for instant flight.

But the harpy was still prowling round the yard, stopping every few minutes to shake her whisk at the blockhouse and scream curses and insults at the white faces she could see watching her from the loopholes. When she paused at the door of the workshop, Ryder was not seriously alarmed. Some of the other looters had gone in there but had soon come out again. There was nothing in there for them to eat, nothing of obvious value for them to carry away. However, the harpy was in the workshop for only a minute, before she rushed out and screamed across the yard for the Nubian wrestler. Like a tame gorilla responding to its trainer, he crossed the yard with his massive rolling gait. She led him into the workshop. When the Nubian came out again he was carrying such a heavy burden that his legs were bowed under its weight.

'Look!' shouted Jock, in consternation. It was a burden that would have taken the strength of five ordinary men, but the Nubian was carrying the main steam pipe from the *Intrepid Ibis*. Jock had laboured over this piece of machinery for months and now it was ready to reinstall in the steamer.

The harpy screeched towards the blockhouse, 'You think to escape the wrath of the Mahdi? You think to run away in your little steamer? We are going to throw this thing into the Nile. When the Mahdi comes, your white and leprous corpses will rot in the streets of Khartoum. Even vultures will not eat them.' She drove the giant Nubian like an ox towards the gates.

'Even he can never carry it to the river!' Ryder exclaimed. But the harpy was now shouting for others to help him. A number were hurrying to his aid.

'I give you my solemn oath that he is taking my steam pipe nowhere,' Jock growled. He swung up the Martini-Henry, and the crash of the shot in the narrow confines of the room numbed their ears. The rifle kicked back, and the sweet stink of black powder smoke stung their nostrils.

The Nubian had reached the gates. He was less than sixty yards from the rifle slit. The heavy lead bullet caught him just behind the ear and angled forward through his brain. In a pink cloud of wet tissue, it burst out through his right eye socket. He collapsed, with the weight of the steam-pipe chest pinning his corpse to the sunbaked clay.

'You killed him,' Ryder exclaimed in disbelief.

'I aimed at him, didn't I?' Jock said brusquely. 'Of course I damn well killed him.' With his calloused thumb he pushed another cartridge into the breech of the rifle. 'And I'm going to kill anybody else who touches my engine.'

In the yard there was an abrupt and breathless silence. The rioters had almost forgotten the presence of the white prisoners in the blockhouse. They stared at the huge half-naked corpse in awe.

The harpy was the only one not bereft of the power of movement. She snatched an axe out of the hands of the man nearest to her and rushed at the length of pipe. One of the many duties of a Sudanese woman is to cut the firewood for her household. As the first stroke of the axe clanged against his steam pipe, Jock knew she was an expert. She swung the axe again, and hit exactly the same spot. Jock could see that she was aiming at one of his welds. The metal there would be annealed by the heat of his torch. Already it was buckling. Two or three blows like that and she would puncture and distort it. It might take days to repair the damage she had already done. If he didn't do something to stop her she might inflict damage beyond repair.

'We will have no more of that nonsense,' he muttered.

Ryder saw him lift the rifle again. 'Don't shoot!' he shouted. 'Jock, *don't shoot her.*'

'Too late!' said Jock, without the least note of contrition in his voice, and again the Martini-Henry bucked and bellowed in his hands.

The bullet caught the harpy full in the chest. It picked her off her feet and threw her against the wall. She hung there, her mouth wide open, but the scream was trapped for ever in her throat. Then she slid down the wall, leaving a long bright smear on the whitewash.

The remaining rioters stared in consternation at the bodies of the two ringleaders. Retribution had come swiftly and unexpectedly. When would the next shot crash out, and who would fall? A wail of alarm went up, and they rushed for the gates.

'Keep them on the run!' Ryder had resigned himself to making the most of Jock's precipitate action. He snatched up his own rifle and fired over the heads of the rioters. Within minutes the yard was empty, except for the harpy and her Nubian.

Ryder opened the blockhouse door cautiously and called to Rebecca, 'Keep Saffron in here with you until we know it's safe for you to come out.' With rifles loaded and held at high port, ready to get off a quick shot, the men swept the compound to make certain no danger still lurked. Jock hurried directly to his steam pipe and knelt beside it. He peered anxiously at the axe marks on the metal, removed the greasy and battered cap from his head and polished the marred surface tenderly, then he replaced his cap and studied the marks again. He sighed with relief. 'Ain't too much damage done.' He picked up the whole pipe as easily as the Nubian had, and carried it lovingly back into his workshop.

Ryder walked over to the two corpses. The harpy

was sitting with her back against the wall. Her eyes and her mouth were open and her expression was faintly quizzical. He prodded her with the toe of his boot. She flopped on to her face and lay still. He could have fitted his clenched fist into the deep dark bullet-hole between her shoulder-blades. He did not need to examine the Nubian. His head lay in a puddle of his own brains.

'I don't approve, but that was not bad shooting, Jock,' he muttered, then called to Bacheet, 'Dump them in the river. The crocodiles will take care of them. No need to report this. Gordon Pasha is a busy man. We don't want to give him more to worry about than he already has.' He waited until Bacheet and his Arabs had dragged the bodies out of the yard and through the gates that led to the canal. Then he went back to the blockhouse and opened the door. 'All is safe. You may come out.'

Saffron rushed past him and darted to the menagerie gates. Old Ali lay curled beside the gatepost. He had been her friend. He had loved the animals as much as she did, and he had taught her how to care for them. She knelt beside his body. In the months since the beginning of the siege she had been exposed to death in many of its most hideous forms, but now she gagged as she looked at her friend's body. The rioters had battered his head until it was shapeless, no longer recognizable as human.

'Poor Ali,' she whispered. 'You died for your animals. God will love you for that.' She found his bloodsoaked turban and covered his face. 'Go in peace,' she said in Arabic.

She left him and went on into the menagerie. There she stopped again. She gazed around at the devastation and her knees went weak under her. Every cage had been smashed open and every one of the animals was gone. Clouds of blue flies hummed over puddles of their blood that were drying and caking in the desert sun. With an effort, Saffron steeled herself and went on down the rows of empty cages.

'Lucy!' She called as she went, and she imitated the chittering sound that was the monkey's special recognition call. 'Billy! Billy, baby, where are you?' She reached Lucy's cage. The door had been torn off, and the cage was deserted. She stood before it, grieving. She had been so young when her mother died that she could barely remember it but she knew she had not felt as bereaved as she did now.

'They couldn't have done this. It's so cruel.' She knew that if she stood there longer she would start to blubber and her father would be ashamed of her. There was only one other place in the menagerie to search. She went to the feed shed at the far end of the enclosure.

'Lucy!' she called. 'Billy, where are you, my baby?' She peered into the gloom.

'Billy!' She made the chittering monkey sound, and a tiny dark shape shot out from behind a pile of straw. With a single bound it landed on her hip, climbed on to her shoulder and chittered softly in reply to her call.

'Billy!' whispered Saffron. 'You're safe!' She sank to the floor and hugged the small furry body to her chest. Despite everything her father had told her, she began to cry and could not stop.

*   *   *

Before sunrise the next morning, just after the mission bells had sounded the end of curfew, Ryder heard feminine voices in the yard, followed by the slamming of the door to the green-cake shed. He wiped the lather from the blade of his razor on to his wash-rag, and made one last pass from the bulge of his Adam's apple to the point of his jaw. He examined his cleanshaven image in the hand mirror, and grunted with resignation. Despite the kiss of the razor, his jaw was still blue. Not everybody can have whiskers like the pretty soldier-boy. He folded his razor, laid it carefully in the velvet slot in its fitted leather case and closed the lid. Then he left his private quarters in the blockhouse, and went out into the yard.

He glanced at the gate to the menagerie, and felt the surge of fresh anger and grief for the wanton slaughter of his animals. He could not yet bring himself to go into the enclosure. At least Bacheet had removed old Ali's body and buried it before yesterday's sunset, in accordance with the law of Islam.

Now Bacheet and his men were collecting tusks from where they were piled against the inner wall, and carrying them back to the warehouse. Ryder called Bacheet to him, and they went to inspect the main gates. There was nothing left of them but a few charred planks. 'We will have to abandon everything in the outer stockade,' Ryder decided. 'We will move into the inner fortifications. The gates are solid and strong. We can defend them.' He left Bacheet to carry out those orders.

For the last half an hour he had heard the hammering of metal on the anvil coming from Jock's workshop, but now there was silence. He crossed to the workshop and looked in at the door. Jock McCrump had just lit the blue acetylene flame of his welding torch and was lowering the smoked-glass goggles over his eyes. He looked up at Ryder. 'Old vixen could swing an axe like a lumberjack, and she packed a punch like John L. Sullivan hisself. It's going to take couple or three days to fix this. Now make yourself scarce.' He bent over the damaged pipe and played the flame on to the gash in the metal.

'In one of our bloody moods today, are we?'

'Ain't nothing to laugh and dance about. You should have let me shoot her before she did this.'

Ryder chuckled. They had been together a long time and knew each other's foibles. He left Jock to get on with it and went to the green-cake shed. Nazeera and all three Benbrook sisters were there. They were wearing the working aprons and gloves they had made for themselves, and they were trying to restore order to the devastated kitchen.

'Good morning, Ryder.' Rebecca smiled at him. Ryder was taken aback by the warmth of her greeting and because she was still using his first name.

'Good morning, Miss Benbrook.'

'I would be obliged if in future you would address me by my Christian name. After the way you protected my sister and me yesterday, we need no longer stand on ceremony.'

'What little I could do for you was only my duty.'

'I was particularly pleased that you were so restrained in your use of force. A lesser man might have turned the riot into a massacre. You have the humanity to realize that those poor people had been driven to excess by the terrible dilemma in which they are caught up. However, I would like to express my sympathy for the grievous losses you have suffered.'

Saffron had been listening to her elder sister impatiently. She was not pleased by this new warmth between Rebecca and Ryder. She told me she despised him, but now she's cooing at him like a dove, she thought. 'You should have shot all of them, not just two,' she said sourly. 'Then we might have saved Lucy.'

'At least Billy seems none the worse.' Saffron's severe expression softened and Ryder took immediate advantage. 'How are you going to feed him? He isn't weaned yet,' he enquired solicitously.

'Nazeera has found a woman who lost her new baby from cholera. We're paying her to feed Billy and he guzzles her milk like a little pig,' Saffron replied.

Rebecca blushed. 'I am sure Ryder does not want to hear all the gruesome details,' she told her little sister primly.

'Then he should not have asked,' Saffron replied reasonably. 'Anyway, everybody knows how babies are fed, so why are you turning red, Becky?'

Ryder looked around for an avenue of escape, and found one. 'Good morning, Amber. You missed all the excitement yesterday.'

But Saffron did not want to relinquish Ryder's attention to yet another sister. 'Don't mind her,' she said. 'She has been grumpy since Captain Ballantyne went away.' Before Amber could protest she went on blithely, 'All the Sudanese women have run away. They won't come back to work here. They have been threatened by bad men in the town who say that we are doing the Devil's

386

work by making green-cake.'

Ryder looked at Rebecca with concern. 'Is this true?'

'I am afraid it is. They were too terrified to come to tell us themselves. But one went to Nazeera. Even then she was taking a grave risk. She says that the Dervish sympathizers in the city have discovered how valuable the green-cake is to our survival, and they are trying to stop us making it. That female creature and the Nubian wrestler who led the riot against you were Mahdists.'

'That explains a great deal.' Ryder nodded. 'But what do you plan to do?'

'We will go on alone,' Rebecca replied simply.

'Just the three of you?'

'Four, with Nazeera. She is not afraid. We Benbrooks don't give up that easily. We have found two cauldrons that were not smashed and our first batch of green-cake will be ready by this evening.'

'Pulping the vegetation is hard work,' he protested.

'In which case you should let us get on with it, Ryder,' Rebecca told him. 'Why don't you go and help Mr McCrump?'

'A man knows when he is not wanted in the kitchen.' Ryder tipped the brim of his hat and hurried back to the workshop.

A little after noon Jock pushed the welding goggles to the top of his head and smiled for the first time that day. 'Well, skipper, that's about the best I can do. Maybe she'll hold up without blowing out under pressure and giving us another steam bath. We can only pray to the Almighty.'

They loaded the drive shaft and steam pipe into a Scotch cart and covered them with a tarpaulin to hide them from the eyes of Dervish agents while they moved them through the streets. No draught animals remained in the city. They had all died of starvation or been eaten. Ryder joined Jock, Bacheet and the Arabs in the shafts of the cart and they trundled it down to where the *Intrepid Ibis* lay at the wharf. By lantern light they worked on in the engine room long after dark. When even Jock was overtaken by exhaustion they stretched out on the *Ibis*'s steel deck plates and snatched a few hours' sleep.

They woke again at dawn. The food bag was almost empty, but Ryder ordered Bacheet to dole out a few dates and scraps of smoked fish for breakfast. Then they went back to work in the engine room. In the middle of the morning Saffron and Amber came down to the harbour. They had two small loaves of freshly made green-cake hidden in Saffron's paintbox.

'We put them there because we did not want anyone to know what we were doing. This is our first batch,' Saffron announced, with pride. She held up her hands, 'Look!' Amber followed her example.

Ryder saw the blisters in their palms. 'My two heroines.'

There were only a few mouthfuls for each of the men, but it was enough to boost their flagging energy. Saffron and Amber sat with Ryder on the edge of the deck, their legs hanging over the side, and watched him eat. He was touched by the womanly satisfaction that they showed, even at their age, to be feeding a man. They watched each piece go into his mouth just as his mother had so many years ago.

'I am sorry, but that's all,' Saffron said, as he finished. 'We'll make some more tomorrow.'

'It was delicious,' he replied. 'The best batch yet.'

Saffron looked pleased. She pulled her knees up to her chin, and sat hugging her long skinny legs. 'It makes me sick to think of all those horrible Dervish eating their heads off over there.' She stood up reluctantly and brushed down her skirts. 'Come on, Amber. We must get back or Becky will give us the sharp edge of her tongue.'

Long after the twins had gone, and the men were struggling to manoeuvre the long drive shaft into its chocks in the confines of the engine room, Ryder pondered Saffron's casual remark.

It was mid-afternoon when Jock announced at last that he was cautiously optimistic that this time the engine might perform as God and its makers had intended. He and his crew fired up the boiler, and while they were waiting for a head of steam to build up, Ryder shared one of his last remaining cigars with the Scotsman. They leant together on the bridge rail, both tired and subdued.

Ryder took a long deep draw on the cigar and passed it to Jock. 'The Mahdi has a hundred thousand men camped on the other side of the river. Tell me, Jock, how do you suppose he is feeding them?' he asked.

Jock held the smoke in his lungs until his face turned puce. At last he exhaled explosively. 'Well, first off they have thousands of head of stock that they've plundered,' he said. 'But I reckon he must be bringing dhurra downriver from Abyssinia.'

'In dhows?'

'Of course. How else?'

389

'At night?' Ryder persisted.

'Of course. On a moonlit night you can see the sails. Lot of traffic on the river at night.'

'Jock McCrump, I want you to get this old tub of ours working under a full head of steam by tomorrow evening at the latest. Earlier than that, if you like.'

Jock stared at him suspiciously, and then he grinned. His teeth were as ragged and uneven as those of an ancient tiger shark. 'If I didn't know you better, skipper, I'd think you were up to something.'

*   *   *

There were no clouds in the desert sky to provide a canvas on which the setting sun could paint its setting. The great red orb dropped like a stone below the horizon and almost immediately the night came down upon the heat-drugged land. Ryder waited until he could no longer make out the opposite bank of the river, then gave orders to Bacheet to cast off.

With his engine telegraph at 'dead slow ahead', he eased the *Intrepid Ibis* out through the harbour entrance and into the main stream of the river. As soon as he felt the tug of the current he turned the bows into it and rang down to Jock for 'half ahead'. They pushed up against the flow of the river and Ryder listened anxiously to the beat of the engine. He could feel the hull quivering under his feet, but there were no rough vibrations. He held her at that speed until they had rounded the first bend of the Blue Nile and a long deep glide of the river lay ahead.

He took a deep breath and rang down for 'three-quarters ahead'. The *Ibis* responded with the panache of a toreador parading into the bullring. Ryder let out a long sigh of relief. 'Take the wheel, Bacheet. I am going below.'

He slid down the engine-room companionway. Jock was shining the beam of his bullseye lantern on to the shaft, and Ryder went to stand beside him. They watched it turning in its new bearings. Jock lowered the lantern and in its golden light they studied the outline of the silver column minutely, looking for the tiniest flutter or tremble of distortion. Like a gyroscope, it was spinning so evenly that it seemed to be standing still.

Jock cocked his head. 'Listen to her sing, Skipper.' He raised his voice above the hiss and slide of the cylinders. 'Sweeter than Lily McTavish!'

'Who in creation is Lily McTavish?'

'Barmaid at the Bull and Bush.'

Ryder let out a roar of laughter. 'I never realized what a connoisseur of opera you are, Jock.'

'Can't really say I know much about it, skipper, but I do know a fine pair of tits when I see 'em.'

'Can I push the *Ibis* up to full revolutions?'

'Just like Lily McTavish, I reckon she's game for anything.'

'I'd like to meet this Lily.'

'Get in the queue behind me, skipper.'

Still laughing Ryder went back to his bridge and took the wheel from Bacheet. When he pushed the telegraph to 'full ahead', the *Ibis* surged forward against the current.

'Twelve knots!' Ryder shouted gleefully. He felt a great weight slip from his shoulders. He was no longer a prisoner in the fever city of Khartoum. Once more all three thousand miles of the Nile belonged to him, his high road to freedom and fortune.

He pulled back the lever of the engine telegraph to 'half ahead' and kept on up the river; before he reached the next wide bend he had counted five head of sail, all heavily laden trading dhows coming down from the Abyssinian highlands to Omdurman. He turned across the flow, and ran swiftly back downstream. Then he shouted down the voice tube to the engine room: 'Jock, come up here where we can talk.'

They leant on the bridge rail together. 'After what happened at the compound yesterday, I am not taking any more chances. The mood of the people is ugly and dangerous. The city is crawling with agents and sympathizers of the Mahdi. They will know by morning that the *Ibis* is seaworthy again. We must expect an attempt at sabotage. From here on, we must keep an armed guard on board twenty-four hours a day.'

'I was going to do that anyhow.' Jock nodded. 'I've already moved my bed and duffel back on board, and I'll be sleeping with a pistol under me mattress. My stokers will be taking turns at guard duties.'

'Excellent, Jock. But apart from that, as soon as it's light enough I want you to move her from the harbour into the canal and tie her up at the jetty at the back gate of the compound. She'll be much safer there, and easier to load.'

'You thinking about your ivory?' Jock asked.

'What else?' Ryder smiled. 'But also I want to be able to make a run for it if things go wrong again.

I'll be waiting for you to bring the *Ibis* up the canal at first light.'

*   *   *

'What's all that din?' Ryder had been woken by Bacheet hammering on the blockhouse door.

'One of the Egyptian officers is here with a message from Gordon Pasha,' Bacheet shouted back.

Ryder's heart sank. No news from Chinese Gordon was ever good. He reached for his trousers and boots and pulled them on.

The Egyptian had two black eyes and a scabbed, swollen lower lip.

'What happened to you, Captain?' Ryder asked.

'There was a food riot at the arsenal when the general reduced the ration. I was hit in the face by a stone.'

'I'd heard that your troops shot twenty of the rioters.'

'That is not correct,' the officer said hotly. 'To restore order, the general was forced to shoot only twelve.'

'How abstemious of him,' Ryder murmured.

'You also had trouble with the rioters, and were forced to shoot,' the captain added.

'Only two, but they killed one of my men first.' Ryder was relieved to have confirmation of the shooting at the arsenal: Gordon was no longer in a position to point the finger at him. 'I understand that you have a message for me from Gordon Pasha.'

'The general wishes to see you at Mukran Fort as soon as possible. I am to escort you there. Will you please make ready to leave at once?'

Schoolboy being called to the headmaster's study, Ryder thought wryly. He took his hat down from the peg on the wall. 'Very well. I am ready.'

*　　　*　　　*

Gordon was at his usual station on the battlements of the fort. He was standing behind his telescope, peering downriver towards the Shabluka Gorge. Two brilliant coloured flags flew from the flagstaff of the watchtower. The red, white and black of Egypt was surmounted by the red, white and blue of the Union Flag of Great Britain.

Gordon straightened up and saw Ryder's upturned face. 'Those flags will be the first thing that the relief force sees when they come up the river. Then they will know that the city is still in our hands, and that we have withstood all the forces of evil and darkness.'

'And all the world will learn, General, what one Englishman alone and almost unaided has been able to achieve. It is a story that will be written large in the annals of Empire.' Ryder had meant it to be ironic, but somehow it did not come out that way. He was forced to admit, however reluctantly, that he admired this terrible little man. He could never feel the slightest affection for him, but he stood in awe of him.

Gordon raised a silver-grey eyebrow beneath which a cold blue eye glinted, acknowledging the barbed compliment from an adversary. 'I am informed that you took your steamer out on trial last night, and that it was successful,' he stated crisply.

394

Ryder nodded cautiously. The old devil misses nothing, he thought. Now he found himself hating the man as strongly as ever.

'I hope that does not mean you are planning to sail away in her before the relief arrives?' Gordon asked.

'The thought had crossed my mind.'

'Mr Courtney, despite your mercenary instincts you have made, perhaps unwittingly, a significant contribution to the defence of my city. Your production of the foul-tasting but nutritious green-cake in itself has been of great assistance. You have other resources at your disposal that might save lives.' Gordon stared at him.

Ryder stared back into the sapphire eyes and replied, 'Indeed, General, and I feel I have done as much as I can. However, I have a premonition that you will try to convince me otherwise.'

'I need you to remain in the city. I do not want to be forced to impound your vessel, but I shall not hesitate to do so if you defy me.'

'Ah!' Ryder nodded. 'That is a compelling argument. May I suggest a compromise, General?'

'I am a reasonable man,' Gordon inclined his head, 'and I am always ready to listen to good sense.'

That is not a widely held opinion, Ryder thought, but he replied evenly, 'If I am able to deliver equal value, will you allow me to sail from Khartoum whenever I wish, with the cargo and passengers of my own choice without restriction?'

'Ah, yes. I believe you have become friendly with David Benbrook's daughters,' Gordon smiled bleakly, 'and that you have several tons of ivory in your warehouse. Those would be your passengers and cargo, would they not?'

'David Benbrook and the three young ladies will be among those I shall invite to sail with me. I am certain that this would not be in conflict with your sense of chivalry.'

'What do you offer, sir, as your part of the bargain?'

'A minimum of ten tons of dhurra grain—enough to feed the populace until the arrival of the relief force and forestall any further rioting. You will pay me twelve shillings a sack, in cash.'

Gordon's face darkened. 'I have always suspected that you had a hidden hoard of grain.'

'I have no secret hoard, but I will risk my ship and my life to obtain it for you. In return I want your word of honour as a gentleman and an officer of the Queen that on delivery to you of ten tons of dhurra you will pay me the agreed price and allow me to sail from Khartoum. I suggest that this is fair, and that you have nothing to lose by agreeing to it.'

*   *   *

Ryder had spread a black tarpaulin over the *Ibis*'s white superstructure, and coated her hull above the waterline with black river mud. Using long bamboo poles they punted her quietly down the shallow canal to the open river. Under her camouflage she blended so well into the darkness, that even in the brilliant starlight she was almost invisible from any distance over a hundred yards. As she slid into the main current of the river and the long poles could no longer find the bottom, Ryder rang down to Jock in the engine room for 'half ahead'. He turned upriver and cruised eastwards along the Blue Nile.

He was deliberately avoiding the main branch of the White Nile, because the Dervish artillery batteries were all concentrated on the northern approaches. It was plain that by this time they were expecting the arrival of the British gunboats from that direction. However, in making these dispositions they had left the other branches of the river to the east and south unguarded. Until the Dervish realized this mistake the *Intrepid Ibis* had the run of thousands of miles of river.

All the dhows coming down the Blue Nile would be Abyssinians. Like Ryder, they were just honest, hard-working traders, selling their grain to the highest bidders. Of course, it was to be regretted that their main customer was the Mahdi.

Ryder angled the darkened *Ibis* across the river. For all the obvious reasons, the captains of the grain dhows were keeping closely to the bank furthest from Khartoum. Ryder and Bacheet stared ahead, watching for the first flash of canvas or the shine of starlight on one of the reed-matting lateen sails. Ryder's lungs ached with the craving for a good cigar, but his stock was dwindling. Abstinence makes the heart grow fonder, he thought sadly. I might end up smoking black Turkish tobacco in a hookah. How have the mighty descended in the world.

Bacheet touched his arm. 'The first little fish swims into our net,' he murmured.

Ryder watched the other vessel materializing on the dark waters, and muttered regretfully, 'Small fishing-boat. Riding high in the water. No cargo on board. We will let her go.' He spun the wheel and sheered away from her.

There was a faint hail from the smaller vessel:

'In God's name, what ship are you?'

Bacheet called back: 'Go in peace, with blessings of Allah upon you.'

They cruised on. As they rounded the first wide bend of the river, two miles above the city, another hull seemed to spring miraculously out of the night. They were closing so rapidly that Ryder had only seconds to make his decision. It was large dhow, broad-beamed and low in the water. She had only a foot of freeboard. Her bow wave creamed back in the starlight, almost slopping over her bulwarks.

'Heavy with cargo,' Ryder said, with quiet satisfaction. 'This one is for us.' He swung in sharply towards the prize, and as they closed there was a cry of alarm from the man at her helm. As the steel hull made heavy contact with the dhow's timber side, the three heavy grappling hooks shot from the *Ibis* and clattered on to her deck. They bit and held in the dhow's bulwarks, locking the two vessels together. With a burst of power and hard left rudder Ryder forced the dhow's bows to slew across the current, spilling the wind out of her sail so that she wallowed helplessly. Then his men swarmed over the rail.

Before they realized what was happening the crew of the dhow were trussed up securely. Ryder jumped down on to the deck, just as the captain came up from his stern cabin. Ryder recognized him immediately. 'Ras Hailu!' he exclaimed, then greeted him in Amharic: 'I see you are in good health.'

The Abyssinian started with shock, then recognized Ryder. 'Al-Sakhawi! So you have turned pirate.'

'I am no pirate, but you have been dealing with

one such. I hear the Mahdi is gouging you on the price of your dhurra.' He took Ras Hailu's arm. 'Come aboard my steamer. Let us drink a little coffee and talk business.'

Jock held the two vessels in mid-stream while they settled down in the *Ibis*'s cabin. After a decent exchange of pleasantries Ryder broached the matter in hand. 'How is it that you, a devout Christian and a prince of the house of Menelik, can deal with a fanatic who is conducting a *jihad* against your Church and your countrymen?'

'I am covered with shame,' Ras Hailu confessed, 'but, Christian or Muslim, money is still money and a profit is still a profit.'

'What price is the wicked Mahdi paying you?'

Ras Hailu looked pained, but his eyes were shrewd in the lamplight. 'Eight shillings a sack, delivered at Omdurman.'

'Christian to Christian, and friend to old friend, what would you charge me if I paid in silver Maria Theresas?'

They both enjoyed the trading for it was in their blood, but time was too short to savour it. Dawn was only hours away. They struck a bargain at nine shillings, which left both men pleased. Jock towed the dhow into a quiet bay off the main river, known as the Lagoon of the Little Fish. Screened by the papyrus reeds, all hands turned out to tranship the cargo of dhurra to the steamer. It took all day, for the dhow was fully laden.

As darkness fell Ryder and Ras Hailu embraced warmly and took leave of each other. The dhow caught the evening breeze and ran up the Blue Nile towards the Abyssinian border. Ryder took the *Ibis* downriver to Khartoum. She was so deeply laden that they had to tow her from the bank of the canal to her mooring at the rear of the compound.

As soon as curfew ended, Ryder sent Bacheet with a message to General Gordon. Within the hour the general had arrived on the canal bank. He was accompanied by a hundred Egyptian troops, and quickly set up a chain of men to unload the sacks of dhurra. The work went swiftly, and Ryder stood by, counting each one and making notations in his little red book. 'By my calculations, General, this is considerably more than the contracted amount.' He cast an eye over the column of figures with the rapidity of a bookkeeper. 'Even allowing for ten per cent underweight in the sacks, it's more in the region of twelve tons than ten.'

Gordon laughed—a rare sound, for Chinese Gordon was not given to frivolity, 'Surely, Mr Courtney, you are not suggesting that I should return the excess to the Mahdi, are you?'

'No, sir. I am suggesting that I am entitled to recompense for the overflow,' Ryder replied.

Gordon stopped laughing. 'There must be some limit to your avarice, sir.'

'I have rendered unto Caesar,' Gordon frowned at the biblical reference, but Ryder went on unperturbed, 'and now I would like to keep a ton of the dhurra for my own use. My compound was pillaged by the rioters. My own people are as close to starvation as any in the city. I have a duty to provide for them, as if they were my family. That does not add up to avarice in my book.'

They bargained shrewdly. At last Gordon threw up his hands. 'Very well, then. Keep two hundred sacks for yourself and be thankful for my generosity. You can come up to the fort to collect

400

your Judas shekels.' He stamped away towards the arsenal. He wanted to see his precious grain safely behind the walls. But there was another consideration behind his abrupt departure: he did not want Ryder Courtney to see the softening of his expression or the shadow of a smile in his eyes. What a pity to lose a young rascal like that. We should have had him in the army. I could have made him into a first-rate officer, but it's too late now. He is spoilt by the lure of Mammon.

The train of his thoughts led him on, and he thought of another likely lad. As he reached the gates of the arsenal he paused and looked towards the north.

Ballantyne has been gone fifteen days already. Surely by this time he must have reached Stewart's encampment at the Wells of Gakdul and given him my message. I know in my heart that God will not allow all my efforts to come to naught. Dear Lord, grant me the strength to hold out just a little longer.

But he was tired to the marrow of his bones.

GLOSSARY

Arab names will not go into English, exactly, for their consonants are not the same as ours, and their vowels, like ours, vary from district to district. There are scientific systems of transliteration, helpful to people who know enough Arabic not to need helping, but a wash out for the world. I spell my names anyhow, to show what rot the systems are.

T. E. Lawrence, *The Seven Pillars of Wisdom*

Abadan Riji—'One who never turns back'. Penrod Ballantyne's Arabic name

abd—slave

aggagiers—élite warriors of the Beja tribe of desert Arabs

Ammi—aunt

angareb—a native bed with leather thong lacing

Ansars—'The Helpers', warriors of the Mahdi

ardeb—Oriental measure of volume. Five *ardeb*s equal one cubic metre

asida—porridge of dhurra (*G.V.*) flavoured with chili

Bahr El Abiad—the White Nile

Bahr El Azrek—the Blue Nile

bombom—bullets or cannon shells

Beia—oath of allegiance required by the Mahdi from his Ansars

Beit el Mal—the treasury of the Mahdi

Buq, al-—War Trumpet, Osman Atalan's charger

403

cantar—Oriental measure of weight: one cantar equals a hundredweight
djinni *see* Jinnee
dhurra—*Sorghum vulgare*; staple grain food of men and domestic animals
Effendi—lord, a title of respect
falja—a gap between the front top teeth; a mark of distinction, much admired in the Sudan and many Arabic countries
fellah (pl. *fellahin*)—Egyptian peasant
ferenghi—foreigner
Filfil—pepper, Saffron Benbrook's Arabic name
Franks—Europeans
galabiyya—traditional long Arabic robe
Hulu Mayya—Sweet Water, one of Osman Atalan's steeds
Jamal, al-—'the Beautiful One'; Rebecca Benbrook's Arabic name
jibba—the uniform of the Mahdists; long tunic decorated with multi-coloured patches
jihad—holy war
jinnee (pl. jinn)—a spirit from Muslim mythology, able to assume animal or human form and influence mankind, with supernatural powers
jiz—scarab or dung beetle
kufi—Muslim traditional skull cap
Karim, al-—'Kind and Generous'; variation of Ryder Courtney's Arabic name
kittar—bush with wicked hooked thorns
Kurban Bairam—Islamic festival of sacrifice, commemorating the sacrifice of the ram by Abraham in place of his son Isaac; one of the most important holidays in Islam
kurbash—whip made from hippo hide

khalifa—deputy of the Mahdi

khalifat—the senior and most powerful *khalifa*

khedive—the ruler of Egypt

mulazemin—the servants and retainers of an eminent Arab

Mahdi—'the Expected One', the successor to the Prophet Muhammad

Mahdist—follower of the Mahdi

Mahdiya—the rule of the Mahdi

nullah—dry or water-filled streambed

ombeya—war trumpet carved from a single elephant tusk

souk—bazaar

sitt—title of respect, equivalent to 'my lady' in English

Sakhawi, al-—'Generosity', Ryder Courtney's Arabic name

sirdar—the title of the commander-in-chief of the Egyptian Army

shufta—bandit

Tej—strong beer made from dhurra

Turk—derogatory term for Egyptian

Tirbi Kebir—the great graveyard, large salt pan in the Bight of the Nile

wadi—Gully or dried watercourse

Yom il Guma—Friday, the Muslim Sabbath

Zahra, al-—'The Flower', Amber Benbrook's Arabic name

zareba—fortified stockade of stones or thorn bush

zenana—women's quarters in an Arabic household

Selbourne Court 11|13

Eventide